Choice, Set Free
Book 6

by Dr Joseph Ireland, PhD. "Dr Joe"

National Archives of Australia Cataloguing-in-Publication entry

Author:	Ireland, Dr Joe.
Title:	The Tae'anaryn and the Khozmoh Djinn
Series:	Choice, set free. Book 6
Imprint:	Dr Joe (manager at Creating Science)
ISBN:	9780648494157
Date:	25 October 2019
Pages:	372
Size:	140mm x 216 mm (5.5 x 8.5 in)
Spine Width:	1.011 inches = 25.679 mm
Weight:	1.279 lb = 580.134 gm
Target Audience:	Primary school age. "Middle fiction".
Subjects:	Individuality--Juvenile fiction.
BISAC:	YAF000000 Young adult fiction
Dewey Number:	A823.4 F IRE
Lexile Number:	750

By Dr Joe Ireland

Elder Gods

By Aimhirghin Muirín, gnome historian of Fae'merel

Serros – God of the sun, keeper of laws. A strict lawgiver and impartial judge, he is visibly apparent as he is the sun. Sworn enemy to the darkness that is Pumos. His servants are the angels, and he manifests as every sunbeam, or in avatar state as fiery pillar of yellow light.

Lumos – Goddess of the moon, keeper of times. Sister to Serros and a strict timekeeper, her watch over the world never ceases as she is the moon. Famous for her patience she is visible in the sky at all times, but is brightest in the hours before dawn begins. Her servants are the stars, and she manifests as the light blue moonbeams or burning falling stars.

Waglah – Goddess of the waters, keeper of knowledge. Less sociable than other deity, she is visibly apparent as the waters upon any world; rivers and lakes and such. Her servants are the leviathan, and she manifests as the deep blue of the oceans or, in her battles with Serros, as the storm.

Planas – God of plants, keeper of health and wealth. A soft-spoken being, Planas is visibly apparent as the life of every living plant in the world. His star is the brightest in the sky, taking light from Serros. His servants are the fey, and his twin sister is Annas.

Annas – Goddess of animals, keeper of both love and war. Twin sister to Planas, she is manifested as the breath of every being or in the orange banners of both fire and war. She is known for her temper and passion, and her first servants are the dragons.

Pumos – God of darkness, keeper of the dead. Sworn enemy to Serros, Pumos guides the souls of the dead to their resting place in judgement. Known as a harsh, unforgiving soul, few risk his wrath by either lying, or not invoking his name at every funeral. He is sometimes reported to manifest as a deep purple, almost black mist. His servants are the shadows.

Mya – Goddess of the earth, keeper of life. Youngest of the Elder gods and the only self-manifested one. Mortals walk upon her form each day, as she is the world. Her life is in the red blood of most humans and animals. Her servants are the giants.

The Sanctum Brumae

By Piex, winter, 313CY

Approximate room location as instructed by Kialessa, thus note such are only approximations. Countless corridors and stairways, many leading back on themselves or to nowhere, make navigating the fortress of the "Winter Sanctuary" extremely hazardous. The full extent of the Forests of Shadows, and the Dark Trap, are not shown. The battle arena, central area, was not labelled. The art is my own, though the text is Patsi De Vere's.

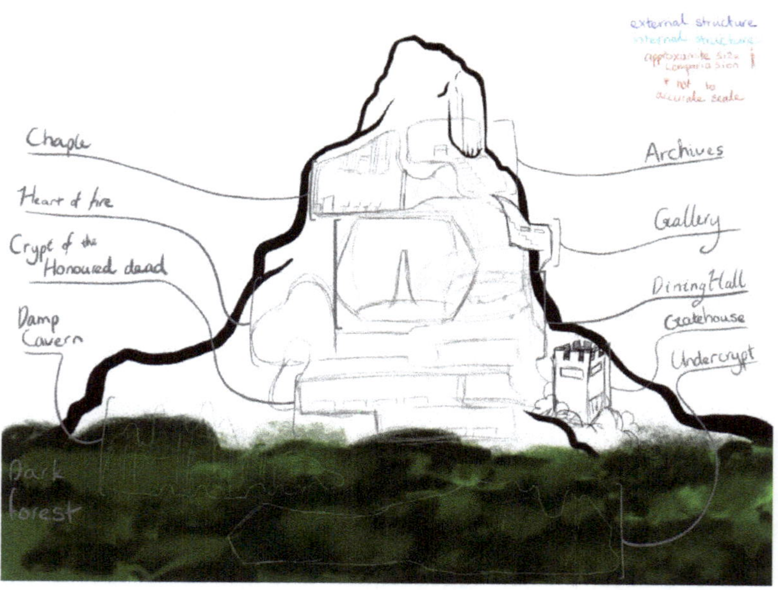

By Dr Joe Ireland

More wonderful titles by Dr Joe & Creating Science:

Delightful high fantasy for the thoughtful young reader
Choice, set free;
1: The Quest of the Tae'anaryn
2: The Tae'anaryn and the Wizard's Apprentice
3: The Tae'anaryn and the Paladin's Squire
4: The Tae'anaryn and the Enchantress's Chrysalis
5: The Tae'anaryn and the Spear of the Troll Prince
6: The Tae'anaryn and the *Khozmoh Djinn*

An engaging science fiction adventure that introduces real science concepts to readers.
Space Chase 1: Arrendrallendriania
Space Chase 2: Elizabeth
Space Chase 3: Daniel
Space Chase 4: The Mechanizer
Space Chase 5: Moiya
Space Chase 6: Pancake

Thrilling young adult science fantasy adventure.
The Dragon Riders of Pearl
The Dragon Riders of Pearl 2: Seven Worlds
The Dragon Riders of Pearl 3: Return of the Plague
The Dragon Riders of Pearl 4: Rage of the Dragonmen
The Dragon Riders of Peart 5: Twilight of the Giants

And for the budding scientist:
<u>Creating Science – Dr Joe's book of science
experiments and activities</u>

Dedicated to:

For the angels within us.

And

*To all those questions science can **inform**, but **cannot** answer.*

And my beloved Samantha whom I belove

20,91,1 50,2 100,5,50 9,91,1,99,61,8 91,5,32,32,6,99 9,2 61,2,2,50 32,6,2,32,26,6,18

          By Dr Joe Ireland

Contents

By Dr Joe Ireland

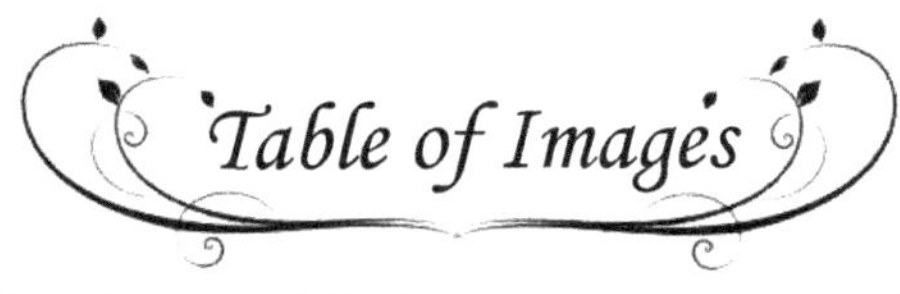

Table of Images

Characters

Kialessa – the hero of the story. She is a tae'anaryn; a race with a demon as one parent. She has red skin, small horns, and a tail. Few like her, and fewer trust her even if she *did* save the king's life once.

Allies

Mak – Kialessa's half-brother. Mak has supernatural physical strength and endurance, and huge set of wings that allow for powered flight. He has been living alone for many years since his mother went to jail for theft.

The Child – A six-year-old girl with a poorly formed body, twisted horns, and hooves for hands that make it hard for her to hold things. Most people ignore her, and she has to beg for food.

Raynah – A skilled wizard of about fifteen, she struggles with issues of self-worth and self-harm. She has a pet owl.

Lossel – Daughter of a Nomerellian noble, Lossel is able to pass as entirely human apart from her supernatural physical strength and skill. Ambitious and aspiring to knightly ideals, Lossel is willing to fight for the underdog in a tough spot, though she can also be a bit of a bully at times.

Amber – A rare fey tae'anaryn, Amber just wants to go home, and has not spent much time developing her formidable natural powers.

Arpil – A terranoid tae'anaryn, Arpil has a hard time accepting her father and tries to kill him on sight, straining their relationship somewhat. She has a murderous hatred for her half-brother, the stone giant Ka.

Charl 'the prophet' – A rare chosen of the Eternal, Charl has never heard the teachings of the god he innately worships. He is a caprivald tae'anaryn with ram horns, almost no tail, and is almost entirely blind.

Daygon – the oldest living son of Tyran Noblax, apparently. He tries to organise the other children in the fortress with a semblance of dignity and order, though he looks old enough to be the merchant's dad. He has goat horns and irises.

By Dr Joe Ireland

Antagonists

Tyran Noblax – Arguably the most powerful merchant prince of the last 100 years, he is noted for his impressive knowledge and massive personal wealth.

Shadowmonger – One of the oldest students at the Sanctum Brumae, Shadowmonger is an unparalleled student of the shadow realm, though he shares his knowledge with no one. His wings are augmented with shadow weave, and his powerful swords drawn entirely from the shadow realm.

Ka – A half stone giant tae'anaryn, Ka possesses unsurpassed knowledge of stone and earthquakes, and has unmatched physical strength. Stone appears to weigh a quarter as much at his touch, and he can burrow through the stone and earth at will. He speaks little, and acts like a child at times, but obeys the will of the Khozmoh Djinn without question.

1 Flameheart and Shadowmonger

Flameheart – A powerful elf tae'anaryn with a snake body from the waist down and coal wings that burst into flame when she wants to fly. She is not a child of the Djinn; her elven father remains unknown. Flameheart shares Kialessa's immunity to fire, but surpasses her when it comes to summoning, controlling and manipulating the element. The true extent of her abilities is unknown, but she wields twin flaming whips of barbed fire that few risk confronting. The past year has seen her becoming increasingly moody and withdrawn, and now she refuses to speak to almost anyone but her peers.

2 Ka and Rawhawk

          By Dr Joe Ireland

Rawhawk – A human tae'anaryn with birdlike wings and powerful air manipulation powers, Rawhawk used to flee most danger as soon as it presented. The past year, his growing alliance with Shadowmonger, Ka, and Flameheart has seen him becoming bolder, even belligerent. His shifting blade is composed of dream weave.

The Khozmoh Djinn – a legend, one would hope, of a soldier turned traitor who became a powerful demon and steals the lives of children who run away from home.

Lesser tae'anaryn

Arbour – a third-year student who gets into tussles a lot

Beomith– a fourth-year student who is a dream tainted tae'anaryn

Broose – a second-year student who tries to hoard all the blankets

Drake – a fourth-year student and capable dream weaver

Ghap – a sixth-year student who likes to pick on the kitchen imps

Pachah – a fifth year who holds a jade blade effective against ghosts

Perigaul – a seventh-year student who studies many weapon styles

Plough – a male eight-year student and part bear tae'anaryn

Tetrarch – a female fourth year who works with Drake and Beomith

Djinn – a specific kind of desert spirit from the blithling lands. Not always evil, and not always born demonic, these creatures are recorded in stories to do everything from grant wishes, to steal lost children. While they can manifest legs they are usually depicted with tapering winds from the hips down, which allow them to fly with great skill through the desert landscape that is their home.

-    *Piex, Ruminations of the Lost Wizard p604*

Glossary

Adept – with great skill and capacity

Affectations – pleasant words designed to trick someone

Affixed – stuck on to

Alabaster – a kind of soft, white stone easily carved into things

Algorithms – programmed instructions, a list of rules to make things happen

Ameliorable – to improve, make better, be more agreeable

Amorphous – a body that can easily change shape, i.e., play dough

Appreciable – easily noticeable

Avatar – a physical manifestation of a deity in bodily form

Barbican – the outer defence of a castle, the tower above a drawbridge

Behove – necessary, or advantageous

Belligerent – constant rebelliousness

Benevolent – generous or kindly

Billet – a place where soldiers stay, usually a normal person's home

Blithling – a race of people to the far northeast who live in a sandy desert

Buoyed – lifted or carried up

Cache – collection or treasure hoard

Caldera – the bowl of a volcano

Camaraderie –friendship among friends

Cathartic – purging deep emotions

Channelling – flowing through, such as water or power

Chaos – unworkable confusion & mess

Commiserate – to share sorrows with

Compromised – while claiming loyalty, cannot provide it

Coterminous – ending in the same place, often, being in the same space

Cowered – to cringe due to great fear

Crooned – to hum or sing softly, even pleasantly

Decanter – a bottle, specifically, a jug

Decorum – good behaviour and proper etiquette

Deluded – to attempt to believe something that is not true

Demotion – to lose position or power

Denizen – a creature that is found in a particular place

Depravity – sinister, wickedness

Desecration – to make the holy unholy or profane

Discretion – with politeness, keeping important things secret

Disdain – hatred or disgust

Dissonance – clashing sounds, the opposite of consonance

Divining – using divine powers to reveal information

Divisive – prone to causing arguments

Dominant male – among animals, the most powerful male. Usually this individual takes care of and may claim breeding rights from all the females

Dossier – a collection of documents

By Dr Joe Ireland

about a person or event

Eclectic – made up from many different sources

Empathetic – able to understand, or often, to feel the feelings of others

Enchantments – a kind of native or innate magic in this world. Often contrasted with wizardry, which is studious or scientific

Epithet – a label or a title

Exorcised – to cast out a demon or unclean spirit from a person or place

Exquisite – extreme, such as powerful feelings or masterwork jewellery

Exultation – a feeling of jubilation or triumph, often religious

Feuerdrache – a mountain range to the Northwest of Lenmer'el, populated almost exclusively by the dwarves. It divides the Great Kingdom from the troll lands to the southwest, and borders the Great Maelstrom sea to the northwest

Glaives – a long, broad sword, often on a long pole

Havoc – chaos, widespread destruction

Hessian – a rough kind of cloth made from plants

Impending – approaching soon

Impenetrable – impossible to enter or traverse

Inadequate – lacking, insufficient for a purpose

Inaudibly – so quiet it cannot be heard

Incarnate – in a body, or rather, made

real

Incensed – angry, enraged

Incomparable – unable to be compared, superior in all respects

Inconvenience – unhelpful

Incorporeal – without a physical body

Incredulous – unbelieving, unwilling to agree

Indignation – anger or annoyance at a perceived injustice

Indistinguishable – unable to be told apart from something similar

Inevitable – unavoidable or certain

Initiation – often a ritual to symbolise a person's joining a club or group

Insatiable – a desire unable to be quenched or satisfied

Interjected – interrupted with a statement

Intimidating – scary and bossy

Intone – to say or recite with little variation in tone and pitch

Intoxicating flux – symbolising a flow of enormous, irresponsible power

Iridescent – glowing light that changes colour when seen from different angles

Irreplaceable – one of a kind

Jubilant – joyful and triumphant

Labyrinth – a maze

Languished – to grow weak, forced to stay somewhere unwanted

Lingering – waiting around

Magnanimous – generous or gracious

Meagre – small, insufficient

Menacing – threatening and dangerous

Midst – in the middle

Nemesis – a sworn enemy, or an inescapable cause of a downfall

Nexus – a connection between points, usually the centre or focal point

Obeisance – a show of special respect, such as a bow or salute

Obnoxiously – really, really annoyingly

Obstinacy – stubborn, really stubborn

Pearlesque – like a pearl in colour

Perverse – polluted, sick, disgusting

Precarious – teetering, unsecured, frail

Preeminent – the first among many

Prescient – wise, precognitive, prophetic

Quarter, gave no – not allowing rest

Quartzian – like quartz in appearance

Quasi – almost, partly, sort of

Realm – another dimension, a world or universe where creatures live and things can happen

Reminiscent – reminding one of

Remuneration – repayment, often money

Repercussions – consequences, or results of one's actions

Resilient – able to recover quickly from damage or insult

Resolute – determined, with conviction

Sanctum – Dragon speech for 'sanctuary'

Saphirum – fantasy metal with angelic, celestial qualities

Scandalised – to shock or horrify someone with a real or imagined transgression of manners or morality

Sentiment – feeling or emotion

Strewn – thrown about everywhere

Substantiated – proven or having strong evidence for

Subtle nuance – a small point that makes a big difference (a tautology)

Supernatural – above or beyond the natural, such as angels or spirits

Syllables – units of pronunciation, having at least one vowel sound.

Tendrils – slender, threadlike appendages, like tentacles of smoke

Tentative – cautiously, or not certain

Theatrically – like a theatre performance

Transgress – to break a law or rule

Twingle – a portmanteau of tingle and twinkle, to represent the physical sensation of magic in this world

Unpronounceable – cannot be speacht, speeeched. *Said*. Cannot be said.

Unsympathetic – without pity or sympathy

Vendetta – seeking revenge, usually a death for a death

Veritable – truthful

Vulnerability – a weakness, being exposed to potential harm

Wanton – wilful, rebellious

Witless – stupid, without thought

Wreaking – to cause a lot of damage

By Dr Joe Ireland

The Storyteller

*Very well, very well! I will tell you a story, if you consider hearing, about honest men deceived, and of cruel, unholy **murder**.*
The Storyteller, Recollections of the Tae'anaryl.

Kialessa laughed as the old man told his stories. She was five, and he at least seventy-something. He came to the inn every year around the dark days of the winter eclipses, just before midwinter. He told the funniest tales, and his visit was just about the only time her mother allowed her away from her chores for an afternoon to hear him.

Kialessa loved the old man's stories. There were stories about mighty kings of faraway lands, and princesses who wrought weapons out of dreams. There were stories about powerful unicorns that the mightiest of hunters could not catch, and gods who stole dinners from other, meaner deities.

She sat now with another, older human girl, and a gnome child, both children of the patrons who just happened to be staying there at the inn. They listened to his stories, focused on nothing else, except, perhaps, being careful not to touch her. For through no fault of her own Kialessa was a tae'anaryn; a half demon, 'half-souled', though the full realisation of what that meant was still many years away to her.

'Go on,' the human girl plead. 'Tell us another one. Tell us about … demons!'

'Demons?' The storyteller feigned choking on his own breath. 'Those stories are the most dangerous! To speak of the worst kinds of evil… well… are you sure you want to hear *those* kinds of stories?'

Kialessa didn't really believe there was any danger in a story, even though the world was full of magic. At least, there was no danger to her, safe in her parents' inn, warmed by their fire, listening to the old stories of a funny old man. It hadn't even entered her thoughts that she looked like one of the monsters from those stories, at least, not for another year or two. But with dusk red skin that did not burn, and two horns that poked from her forehead, it was only a matter of time.

The old man smiled, and seemed to be wrestling with his own thoughts while they begged him a few moments more. It was customary to pay a storyteller, but he seemed to consider their gratitude and a drink at the bar payment enough each winter. 'Very well, very well!' he said, 'I will tell you a story, if you consider hearing, about honest men deceived, and of cruel, unholy *murder*.'

'Ooh,' they chimed.

'I will tell you,' he said, leaning closer, his voice little more than a whisper, 'about the *Khozmoh Djinn*.'

The others oohed once more, but Kialessa didn't feel like speaking. Her skin felt like it was pricked all over by fairy needles. There was something about that name that made her feel very, very strange.

She was glad her father was there that night, out back, sampling the mead. Her mother was away on business. She was safe, there was nothing a

     By Dr Joe Ireland

story could do to harm her…

'Oh, quick!' the storyteller hastened, 'circle your hearts, circle your hearts! Ward against the evil, now, now, now!' And he made such a fuss about it they couldn't help but giggle.

'There!' he proclaimed once they were done. 'To speak the name of a demon is a **terrible** thing, and one that must be done with utmost **caution**. So I will not utter that name again, and let us hope you never have cause to hear it either! I will say, instead, **the demon**. You'll know what I mean.'

She nodded along with the others, ready to begin an amazing journey into her imagination, where angels often trod, and goodness always won.

3 Three avid listeners

'This was long ago. One hundred and eighty-five years ago, to be precise. Can you remember what happened then?' he asked.

'Oh!' The gnome patted her legs in excitement. 'I know! The second demon war.'

'That's right!' the storyteller proclaimed. 'The **demon** wars. The worst of them. All the land was turned upside down, brother fighting brother, kingdoms fell. Monsters roamed the land unchecked by brave heroes such as yourselves. It was a terrible time. A terrible time for everyone. Mistakes were made, mistakes by **good people!** And I will tell you about one of those people.'

He leaned closer, allowing them to sit on the edges of his long, woollen cloak. It was soft, and comfortable. 'His name I no longer recall, but he was a soldier for Emerel. Not a great soldier, but not a poor one either. He held the bridge at Farroswell single handed to allow his companions to flee. They expected him to die, but he cut down every demon that came his way, slicing and hewing like this and that! They returned to find him standing, the bridge destroyed and a score of demons slain. He was promoted to captain. Everyone said he'd have such a promising career then…'

The storyteller's face drew grim then, much less as if telling a sad story, but as if remembering one. 'But later that spring, the King of Emerel, who was under a demon curse at the time, commanded his armies to halt a demon horde that was wreaking terrible havoc at the Blithling lands. Our soldier knew it was folly; but he was a good soldier, so he went anyway. Day after day they were hounded, hunted by slavering monsters that gave no quarter. It is one of the most tragic stories of the war! Most soldiers were slain; some lost heart and simply lay down and died in the desert. They even say some went mad, slaying their own comrades.'

'No,' the gnome child said.

He nodded, 'Eventually, our soldier could stand it no more. He broke his sacred oath, and volunteering for sentry duty that night, *abandoned* his

By Dr Joe Ireland

post. For days he wandered in the blithling desert. Days without water, without hope. Then, one dark evening as he felt his life finally begin to leave him, he found a dark pool of water. An oasis in the thirsty desert.'

Kialessa leaned forward, holding her breath to catch every word.

'But it was no normal oasis. Within the moonlit reflection of that pool he saw a beautiful woman standing beside him, and he knew it was an enchanted pool. Almost too weak to move, he knelt there, waiting.

' "Drink",' she told him, ' "aren't you thirsty?"

' "This pool, is it enchanted?" he asked.

' "Of course!"

' "Will it harm me?"

' "No," she told him, "as a matter of fact, it will only make you stronger. Any who drink at this pool will have perfect health, immortal life, and riches beyond their imaginings! Go on… I know you're thirsty… take a drink."

'He looked at the cool, thirst-quenching waters. His mouth burned for water! But inside his heart he knew … it was all too good to be true.

' "Who are you?" he asked her.

' "Just a friend…" she replied.

' "Are you a demon?"

'She smiled sweetly, "You already know I am."

'He was too tired to even get up. "I don't want what you are promising me. I just want to go home."

'She laughed, "Look, you are dying of thirst. You can't even stand up! You will never go home unless you drink at my oasis."

'The soldier was so weak; he needed a drink! So, he had a clever idea. He knew demons had to keep their promises, so he said, "I will drink, but only to stay alive. I want none of your powers of immortal life and power. I only want to drink. So, if you promise this water will not harm me in any way, I will drink."

'She looked displeased, "Very well then, drink away. I promise this water will not harm you, not in any way." And she turned away as though disappointed.

'So he drank, and the moment his lips touched the water he felt every kind and generous desire die in his heart. His limbs felt strong again, but his soul as cold as stone. In that moment he knew he had become a demon as well.

' "You lied to me!" he cried out.

'She turned back, a cruel smile on her lips. "I promised the waters wouldn't harm you, and they have not. But I didn't promise that they wouldn't change you forever!" Laughing, the demoness slipped away, never to be seen again.

'So the dishonourable soldier lived, becoming extremely wealthy and deviously cunning. Some say he is immortal, and cannot be slain. Some even say that he is alive today, and goes about tempting soldiers to abandon their duty as he once did. But I have met him, and I can tell you that he is a lost soul. A shallow and tortured being, a man who lives like a slave to his thirst for life and power. A slave, because cannot forgive himself.'

'Sounds like he got a good deal to me,' the human girl grinned.

'Does it?' the storyteller looked surprised, 'or is that because I'm not telling you the full story? Some say he even hunts lost children, and takes them away to his desert home. No one knows what happens to those poor children, but one thing is certain… they are never heard from again!'

Kialessa was as silent as the others.

'That is a bad story,' the gnome said, tears in her eyes.

'What are you doing, storyteller?' a gruff man shouted from the door, it was her father. His voice seemed to chase away the fear. 'You givin' the children bad dreams with all yer made up nonshensh!'

'Nonsense?' The storyteller smiled, perhaps it really was just a made-up story after all. 'Perhaps, perhaps it is. But of one thing I am certain. It is important for children, especially young children, to stay at home with their family, till they are full grown. Or else the dishonoured soldier might find them, and snatch them far, far away!'

'Yeah right!' the human girl shouted.

'Not me! I'm staying with my family!' the gnome shouted, hitting the storyteller on his knees. He waved his hands in the air as though it might protect him.

'Yeah, me too!' Kialessa shouted.

The other girls nodded, agreeing with each other, no longer bothered by the haunting tale.

Then the storyteller took the instant to look down at her, patting her on the head, 'We will hold you to that, little Kialessa,' he whispered.

The Question

I turned the burning coal in my hands, letting it die from the lack of heat between my fingers. The crowded tavern was silent now, two dozen tough and crude patrons brought to silence by the sight of a little girl holding a fire. I hated these moments, being entertainment at my mother's inn, but I held my head up high. I did not like to let others see me cry.

Kialessa the Tae'anaryn, from Recollections of the Tae'anaryl, CY 317.

The years flew by for Kialessa, till the day the soldiers came.

There was no way she could have anticipated it. She was a servant; a slave. Working from before sunup till after sunset at her uncaring mother's inn, her pleas were long ago silenced by her drunken father's wilful ignorance of the situation. What little kindness existed in her world was often crushed by the cruelty of her mother's customers. They mocked her, the little girl with red skin, grabbing her horns and pushing her to the floor. They liked to see how she was immune to fire, and in their more polite moments simply stood to watch her holding the coals in her bare hands. But there was a time one man had held her upside down in front of a laughing room just so they could see her long, twisting tail, and mock.

Life was hard at the inn, but at least her parents kept her inside at night, and kept back the worst of the customer's insults. And there was her almost adopted brother Kiel, whom her mother had purchased off a strange traveller six years ago. Kiel and Kialessa looked out for each other, for few kind words were spoken at the inn.

But then the day came that the king's guard arrived. They promised to take her from her wretched life and make her a student at the king's

By Dr Joe Ireland

privileged college. There she could make new friends, and learn from the best tutors in all the land. She'd learn how to fight and defend herself. She'd learnt how to read.

But that was almost a year ago, and since then so very much had changed!

But there was one sight that worried Kialessa as she rode away from her old life. It was the little boy watching out from behind the barrel of water, his washing apron wrapped around his waist. Kiel put his face in his hands and cried as hard as she'd ever seen him cry, pressing his small human body against the cold, uncaring stones of her parents' inn – and she would find herself wondering in later years; it was she that had been given this opportunity, not him. Now he had to face that home and what it meant without her to protect, or to protect him. Why? He'd done nothing wrong, but she was being taken away from him; his only sister and probably his best friend. What was he going to do?

He was a good kid, and once again life had dealt him a crushing blow. And she would sometimes wonder; Why **did** bad things have to happen, even to **good** people?

The Festival at Winter's Dawn

Keep your friends close, and your enemies even closer.
High King Malkom.

One year later, the merchant sat at the king's left hand. He had the noble bearing of a prince, which in some ways he was, being the richest visiting merchant by far in all the lands of Lenmer'el today. He wore a loose-fitting tunic in prominent red and black, cured leather about his muscular chest. His short yet full beard was all the more intimidating under his imperious glare. A gold gilded sword hung at his waist, and he looked fifty human years old, about as old as her king. And despite having a dozen personal guards, including two wizards, an almost tangible aura of power surrounded him. It was difficult to stand near him without being afraid; awed by his lordly presence.

A presence Kialessa had felt, and loathed, ever since she'd heard he was coming to sort out his trading ventures at the end of year celebration for the college. The room was filled with the best entertainment the kingdom had to offer. This man's riches were vast, his knowledge of how to obtain rare and valuable items apparently unsurpassed.

She watched him from the lintel of the doorway, clinging to it as though it might protect her from his gaze. Thankfully, he seemed more engaged by the dancers in the centre of the room, more caught up by the polite conversation of King Dunnkan of Lenmer'el.

By Dr Joe Ireland

It was supposed to be a happy time, celebrating the end of her first year at the college, and what an eventful year it had been!

'Kialessa!' a voice broke her out of her musing. It was her good friend, the newest enchantress of the kingdom – Allastassia. She broke around the corner, her hair already taking on the snow-white highlights of winter. She wrapped a hand of friendship around Kialessa's arm. 'Whatever are you doing hiding by the door?'

Kialessa looked at her friend, who was never afraid of meeting someone new, or of meeting anyone's gaze. She didn't know what to tell her.

'Come,' Allastassia offered, trying to pull her from the doorway. 'You've spent the entire year being shy. It's time to change now! How can you be like this? You saved my life, you stopped a war. You even saved the king's life! What makes you dally by a doorway?' Her face melted into a wintry kindness. It made Kialessa glad to know winter wasn't a cold time for the powerful enchantress.

But still she didn't know what to say.

With the understanding of a true friend, Allastassia said no more, nor tried to force her into the room. She simply danced ahead, and showed her how to have fun. Sparkles of light trailing from her fingertips, Allastassia joined the dancers on the floor, matching them perfectly in unrehearsed beauty. Most people stopped to watch, and even the servants had to be hurried back to work. That was what it was like to be Allastassia.

'It's Tyran Noblax, a merchant prince, and some would say sage of Emerel,' a small boy's voice spoke next to her.

Kialessa didn't need to turn around to know who it was. Piex, the wizard's apprentice: and her first, and possibly best, friend. He was part dragon, and without a doubt the smartest boy she'd ever met, perhaps the greatest young mind in the entire kingdom. Together they'd resisted the will of his evil uncle archmage Tobiuus, and refused the power of evil. Together they trained in illusionary battlegrounds in preparation for plundering the dungeons of faraway lands. Together they'd even managed to bring his talent to the attention of the Loremaster, greatest wizard in their country of Lenmer'el. He studied privately under the tutelage of this great master, the first ever to do so.

Kialessa turned to face him, still unwilling to speak.

'But I guess you'd already know that,' he said, unsure of what to say next. He always had some free information on one topic or another, but grew strangely silent when emotions were around. It was the irony of being Piex; most promising scholar of the kingdom, apparent fool in matters of the heart.

So he stood there, waiting in silence. She was glad, for this was not the kind of problem he knew how to deal with. He couldn't tell how her dreams had been troubling ever since she'd heard the merchant was coming. He didn't know what to say about the terrible feeling she had just being in this man's presence. It just wasn't the sort of thing he knew about.

So without a word of apology or explanation, he just walked off when something else grabbed his attention. There seemed to be some other wizard students at a table, and perhaps they had questions for him, though they were all his senior. That was what it was like to be Piex. Wise beyond compare, yet distant at times, uncertain, and young. But already the most feared wizarding student at the entire collage.

The next thing she knew Kialessa was squished against the door with the sudden and unannounced arrival of another of her good friends. Posk, not watching where he was going in his race to arrive at the dinner tables. He stopped as soon as he noticed her, three paces away already, his steel gauntlets helping him skid to a halt.

It made her smile.

He rushed back to her, greeting her with his unbridled enthusiasm, patting her on the shoulder and head.

'Tauira!' he called her by his favourite phrase of respect, mustering his most sincere grin, 'Master.' The headband of wizardry was firmly affixed to his head, as it always was now. It meant his natural mental disabilities were overcome, for the most part, and he could function in the college as well as any other student. But he still could not read and, try as they might; he never really showed any interest in learning how. But he looked very fashionable, in a troll sort of way, in his new vest made of almost indestructible dragon skin, donated by a mutual friend, to help him resist cold and acids.

Yet his brow furrowed as he saw the expression on her face. He cradled her jaw in his massive hand. She was impressed, again, at the almost mystical gentleness he could display, since he was, without argument, the strongest and yet the youngest student at the college. He was half troll, with green skin and tusks, at least until he'd had the last one knocked out by a troll warlord bent on rekindling a three-hundred-year-old war with Emerel. A war she was credited with, singlehandedly, preventing among the five massive troll nations that lay just to the west of the Great Kingdom. A war which, were one to ask any within the Great Kingdom, she was not even present at, and was stopped by just about anything other than an eleven-year-old girl.

Posk looked at her, then leaping back punched his fists into the ground. What he was trying to say was not made of words, but she knew he didn't need them to get his message across. He wanted her to shake off her fear, and to join him in the celebration.

So she simply smiled, and shook her head.

Posk sighed. Then shrugged. Then, with a grin, he ran away towards where the food was kept. Posk was powerful, and such power had to be fed. He never let things keep him down for long, and was staunchly loyal to his companions. That was what it was like to be Posk.

And is **this** *what it means to be Kialessa?* she wondered as she clutched to doorframe. She watched the merchant with fearful eyes. What was it about him that made her so afraid? No one else appeared bothered, least of all her greatest friend and protector, the King.

Worse yet, why could she not turn away?

Perhaps it was because at least, here, she knew where the merchant was.

But she could not bear her fears anymore. There was happiness to be found in celebrating the end of her first year at the college, and Kialessa knew that anywhere the mysterious merchant was would not be that place. She had to be somewhere else to find peace. Somewhere hidden, where she could wrap the shadows around herself and conceal herself with darkness. Somewhere that felt safe.

She turned, and gasped. There, apparently waiting with her this whole time, was the young squire of the most famous paladin in the entire Great Kingdom: Darrix. She found his presence deeply comforting, but she didn't dare touch him. No one in Lenmer'el liked her to touch them. She was tae'anaryn, after all, cursed all her life to look like a demon. It was a curse she bore since one of her ancestors was wounded in the second demon war, but she'd learned this year how to make of her strange and different body an opportunity. Still, no one trusted her at first glance.

No one, that was, except Darrix. He was the first, and still, perhaps, the only one who could see her for what she truly was, and what she *chose* to be. His friendship alone protected her from almost every unkindness or bully that could be found in the college. He chose to stand with her in every combat practice and, the more she got to know him, the more she wanted to choose him for everything she would experience as well.

It wasn't just his tall stature, or the fact that his father, seated to the far left of Tyran Noblax, was a rich gem merchant. Darrix was devout. Deeply religious. Powerfully prayerful, and that was an amazing thing in a world full of magic. Darrix could heal sicknesses and minor injuries with all the skill and faith of any of the young priests of the Old Pantheon. Just this year he'd exorcised a wisp demon that was trying to oppress the entire Great Kingdom. And his integrity was such that even the high priestess trusted the thirteen-year-old boy with the most sacred of shrine funds. He was the only one who had had the courage to help her come to accept a relationship with the divine in her own life, and he sat by her in church when none others dared. He was fearless, not only of battle, but of anything that came at him. That was what it was like to be Darrix.

'That man,' he said, his tone unusually serious, 'has the darkest cloud of light I have ever seen around a man before.'

And he could see the souls of other people, apparently.

Kialessa turned, and watched the merchant again.

'I don't know why the king allows him to sit at his table.' Darrix continued. 'Perhaps it is to redeem him? But I think it may have more to do with drawing him out, you know, keeping your enemies closer. I don't know.'

Kialessa still said nothing.

'I have prayed for you,' Darrix told her. 'And I believe no harm will come to you this night.'

He smiled, and she felt more confident in his words. She, too, could pray to know, but Darrix was *especially* prayerful.

It gave her hope. It was just what she needed to hear right now.

Just enough hope to not run for her life when in the next instant King Dunnkan, keeper of the people of Lenmer'el, turned and saw her. With his friendly grin and an enthusiastic wave of his hand, he called her over.

She stopped smiling.

Kialessa was torn. She could not face that merchant. She did not want to come under his stare.

But she could not disobey her king. Not only was it a law, she could not bear to disappoint her deepest friend. He had personally called for her, and welcomed her to his college. He had ordered the students to respect her, and published it to everyone once she'd saved his life. Each week he made time to talk to her, and they would walk around the gardens and she would share what she was learning. She had no family here, and no family who would be interested in what she was learning at home. The more they talked the more she grew to love him, as the kind grandfather she had never known. She loved him more than anyone in Lenmer'el. More, perhaps, than anyone in the whole world.

But her skin paled as she clutched the lintel of the doorway, her dark fingernails pressing into the hard wood with bone white fear she could not express. All the love in the world could not make her face her fear today.

Then she felt a hand on her shoulder. It was Darrix, she knew. He would be praying for her.

She was praying for herself.

With shallow steps, and a heart full of misgivings, Kialessa walked over to meet her king.

He smiled kindly to her from over the rim of his half-emptied crystal wine goblet, seeming to respect her misgivings. She carefully glanced at the merchant; he still didn't seem to have noticed her. Beside him sat a woman of exotic beauty, her silk dress threaded with glass beads that reflected the blithling culture. It seemed she might be familiar to Kialessa, but she did not dwell on it. Behind him, arms folded and surveying the entire area with a glower of distaste, stood the merchant's man at arms. He was muscular and tall, to rival even the king's general, and twin scimitars waited at both his back and hips. Further to his left sat another merchant, older, with a dark look and cunning eyes. And deep in the shadows of the hall, not three paces from his master, stood another servant. He checked over everything, and everyone, that approached with eyes that were scarcely seen from the folds of his hooded cloak. In spite of the hideous disrespect at doing so in the presence of the king, he was cleaning the dirt from his fingernails with a curved, stencil thin knife.

And then the merchant saw her. She tried not to meet his gaze. He had a thick jaw, like a warrior, and the piecing gaze of a priest. His posture was regal, and his reputation for knowledge was vast. He was Tyran Noblax, merchant prince of Emerel.

        By Dr Joe Ireland

And he was looking right at her.

'And may I present to you Kialessa, the tae'anaryn,' King Dunnkan said.

'Ahh, yes! So this is the little tae'anaryn I have heard so much about!'

The merchant's voice was deep, and powerful. She knew she didn't want to hear him raise that voice, ever.

As duty bade her she curtsied. She stole a glance at her king. She could see him sympathising with her obvious discomfort. But he was never one to deny her the opportunity to challenge herself, whether she thought she was ready or not. Being fearless had helped save his life.

'Indeed,' King Dunnkan said, 'and future hero of the Great Kingdom, I can assure you. Aside from the episode with the fire dog, she has also this year helped to bring down archmage Tobiuus, expose the demon threat to the Pantheon and Kingdom, prevented great devastation due to a baleful chrysalis – '

Incredibly, the merchant interrupted, 'And, if my sources are correct, single handedly slew the troll warlord that coveted war upon our fair cities?'

The king was silent a moment, 'Few know this, and of those that do, fewer seem willing to believe it.'

The merchant smiled at her, his perfect rows of teeth and disarming grin doing nothing to comfort her fear, 'Oh, I think I could believe it.'

'You can?' asked the king. 'Then you are a good judge of character.'

He nodded, 'Thank you, your eminence. So, what is her family name?'

Kialessa did not reply. She came from a family with no name. Her parents kept a tavern, and a little boy they pretended was their son and not a slave. To the locals, they were the Tavernskeep, but it was not a proper name.

'Her parents keep a tavern, a day between here and the docks,' the King replied.

'I know the place,' the man smiled, hidden secrets edged in that heartless smirk. 'Still, it is an honour to meet such a fine young dame of such humble lineage. Dame Kialessa Tavernskeep, the Tae'anaryn.'

He inclined his head as if in a respectful bow, and for just a moment she thought she might, perhaps, learn how to be able to get along with this man, even if she might never learn to trust him. She tried to curtsey with respect, and hoped their conversation would be over soon. Meeting famous people she did not like, Kialessa was beginning to realise, was one of the things she just going to have to learn how to do.

But then he spoke again, to the king. 'Perhaps, if it isn't a step away from your will good king, you might allow your little tae'anaryn here to show us some of her, what's the word I'm looking for, tricks?'

He probably hadn't meant to, but his final words set her on rage. Kialessa glared at him, but he was too busy watching for the king's reaction. All her life, all her existence before the king had rescued her from her life and taken her to this college which she loved, and which held her only friends. All her life, all she had ever been was a mere curiosity, an entertainment, for the guests at her mother's inn. It was a year ago, but it may have been a lifetime. Here, while she was still feared for who she looked like, she had at least gained a lot of respect. She had done great things, and was worthy of the title 'dame' that the king had given her. At home, she was nothing more than a slave, a curiosity to entertain the rude and smelly guests at her mother's inn with her "tricks" – her skin which did not burn, her eyes which could glow. Her tail.

But the king wasn't thinking of that. He was probably just looking for another way to impress his important guests, or at best, to honour his college and demonstrate his favourite student's skills. 'Yes, yes, what a good idea! Clear the stage, make room. Kialessa, show him that trick with the whip and fire! And the shadow, oh that is a very clever thing!' Instantly the music stopped, and the dancers fled to the edges of the room.

Kialessa's heart ached. What was she now? A show thing? An entertainment? Had all she'd done, to save his life and the entire kingdom, lead to her being nothing more than entertainment for powerful people while they had too much to drink?

The pretty woman saw her, and covering her mouth allowed her face to show her pity.

Kialessa's eyes stung with tears, her hands trembling in rage.

King Dunnkan looked chagrined, 'Was it something I said?'

She spun around and ran out of the room, covering herself in a thick darkness that seemed to echo in the silence.

***

Darrix found her, sobbing in the girl's dormitory. He would not enter without permission, but instead went around to the window, and tapped.

She opened it, and clutching his hand, continued to cry.

'It was a boring party anyway,' he said, and waited in silence with her until time stilled her tears, and the evening bell rang and announced it was time for the students to go to bed.

Home.

Where we love is home; our feet may leave, but not our hearts.
Pardgalia, 2nd Sage of Lumos, keeper of times.

A week later she stood, alone, in front of her parent's inn. She saw it now, for the first time in almost a year, and with eyes that had seen more than she'd ever seen in the eleven years she'd spent here. The building was a mess; dilapidated, unworked, and crumbling under the weight of decades of neglect. One window was boarded up clumsily; probably broken in a tavern brawl sometime in the last year, yet who could afford glass? There was the old shed to the left, but Kialessa knew it contained little more than the reinforcement struts her father and others had placed there to try and convince the building to stop tilting, and to stay upright just a little longer. She saw the well to the right, one of the few reliable sources of water in the community, its winch and cover now gone, requiring all effort be done by hand. The place was tired, and the stonework crumbled. But it was home.

For a long moment Kialessa just stood there, wondering if she really wanted to be here. The city guards that had brought her here had already left. She knew the moment she opened the door her parents would see her. She knew once they did her father would embrace her through his tears; if he wasn't too drunk to stand. Her mother would nod, then send her into the kitchen to clean up dishes or start the dinners early. Would they even ask her about everything she'd learnt this year? Would they even care? Kialessa's heart began to shrink, and she wondered why she was here at all.

'Kia!' a young boy's voice shouted. It was Kiel, her almost half-brother, her mother's other "slave". They weren't allowed to tell anyone that; slavery

By Dr Joe Ireland

was very illegal. But little Kiel had nowhere else to go, and his family, they were told, were all slain in some tragedy years ago. So their mother had purchased Kiel off a traveller for a night's stay and some ale several years ago. So here he stayed, calling them his parents, and calling Kialessa his sister, all for appearances.

He dropped the bucket, water splashing everywhere, and ran to throw his arms around her. She hugged him back, and let his affection warm her heart once more. He was still smaller than her, freckled, and shy. His ears still stuck out, his clothes a mess. As he stood back, she noticed him push away the tears from his eyes.

'Kiel, I'm so happy to see you again!'

'Me too! Mother, mother!' he called, 'Kialessa is back, my sister! She's back!' His grin was wide and unafraid.

Then she heard footsteps from inside. She had wanted, so much right then, to ask Kiel about his year. About what he had experienced, and remembered. At least half a dozen times he had appeared in her dreams to help her. She really needed to know if that was all her own imagination, or if it was real, and if Kiel actually did possess the rare talent of the Dreamwalkers.

But now was not that time.

The door flung open. It was her father.

'Kia-lesha!' he shouted, and laughing, reached down to grab her up. She couldn't help but laugh in his arms as he swung her about like a child still. She looked in his kind face, the kindest she had known, and saw in his weathered features the memory of her king. But this man's eyes were dim, unfocused. His nose large and red, and his breath smelt like ale even though it was only midday.

'My prinshess,' he shouted, stumbling backwards as Kiel tried to stop him from falling over altogether. 'It'sh good that yer home!'

She laughed, and flung herself away from him. Then she curtsied, and laughed again.

He seemed to sober up, for a moment. 'Look at you, all gentle like. You're almosht a woman…'

She smiled, and Kiel held her hand.

'Oh!' her father said, 'in, inshide now. Oh Jewel,' he called out to her mother, 'yer daughters' home!'

Laughing and smiling, they pushed her inside. Every sight and smell reminded her of the world she had grown up in. The unvarnished wood, the unwashed tables. Ale mixed with vomit. Yes, Kialessa was home.

She looked around, and soon found her mother standing, in shadow, on the stairs. Behind her a girl in her late teenage years stood, her clothes unnecessarily tight and poorly fitting.

'Well?' her father asked.

'What's she doin' 'ere?' her mother protested. Her uneducated voice was flat and unkind, her demeanour unwelcoming.

Kialessa's smile died, and the fleeting hope she'd find happiness here evaporated.

'She's yer daughter,' her father pled, holding her by the shoulders. Protecting her.

Her mother tutted, and marched down the stairs. She walked over and looked at Kialessa up and down, her face a barely concealed snarl. 'Well, I suppose we can make the best of it. Horns, get into tha' kitchen and start making dinner for the guests.'

Kialessa couldn't believe it. She had expected at least a greeting, at the very least a nod. But it was as if her mother was *annoyed* at her for leaving home and getting an education. It was as if… her mother was annoyed that her favourite kitchen slave had escaped, and then had the audacity to return again.

Her blood boiled, her eyes filled with unwelcome tears. But Kialessa also knew whom she had become. She was not the frightened little slave her

By Dr Joe Ireland

mother had shed false tears over losing one year ago, neither was she the obedient minion her mother seemed to want now. She was a trained young warrior in the greatest college in Lenmer'el. She had watched the teachings of some of the greatest wizards in all the land. She had helped stop a demon war, she had helped stop a troll invasion. She was Kialessa, and she was a friend to a king.

'No,' she said.

'Wha' did you say, horns?' Her mother openly scowled this time.

Kialessa drew a shuddering breath. This was taking more courage than comforting a wounded dragon. 'I said no, mother. I am not your slave here anymore. I am going to pay for my stay this winter, and I am going to stay in one of the guest rooms. I'm not the little child you sold away a year ago.'

Her mother's features grew angry; the air around her filling with a rage similar to what Kialessa had felt in the presence of a demon. The older woman stuttered, and looked up at her husband. Kialessa knew she would find no support there.

'Fine. Nine silvers for your stay.'

Kialessa knew it was an exorbitant price. Only the greatest inns in the land dared charge a silver a week for someone's stay.

But Kialessa was not to be outdone, 'Nine?' she asked.

'Come, love-' her father began.

'Don't you dare!' her mother shouted.

He backed down immediately. He almost always did.

'Is that all?' Kialessa said.

She heard everyone gasp.

'Fine…' her mother seemed to be pondering. 'Ten then.'

Kialessa laughed, and using a trick she'd learned recently she reached into the shadows of the edge of the doorway. Covering her hands with the mysterious wafting threads of the shadow realm she reached into the alternate place. Stretching out an impossible distance in a moment she reached her way back to the castle, to the chest that was still placed at the end of her bed in the girl's dormitory. There inside she easily grabbed the small pouch of leather, containing what remained of the treasure she'd earned this year making a difference in the world. She removed it, and it came with her hand back into the shadows by the doorway of the inn.

Everyone looked very impressed, and slightly worried.

Then Kialessa took out a gold coin, and threw it on the ground.

As expected, her mother lost no dignity to scurry over and fall on her knees to catch it before anyone else could. She looked up at Kialessa, eyes full of greed.

Was she really this kind of woman a year ago? Kialessa wondered.

Her mother pocketed the coin, then spoke, her voice subdued, 'Well, I suppose then ye can stay in the attic, with Kiel.'

'The attic!' Kialessa said, momentarily surprised to hear Kiel wasn't sleeping by the stove anymore.

'Wa, ye think I don't 'ave any more guests? That college 'as spoilt ya! An' don't think I won't 'ave ya doing yer chores around here missy!'

'Oh, I'll do my chores, but only so I have something to do! And so that you don't boss Kiel around just because I'm here!'

'Fine. Get up ta yer room!' Her mother scowled, 'And you, boy, where's that water! Git up, look lively! And what are you stand'n around for old man!'

Kialessa didn't look back, but stormed up the stairs to head towards her room. She was angry; angry at her mother. Angry at her father for never standing up for her. Angry at the world for making a place as horrible as this and then making her call it home.

She shoved past the new girl, taking only a moment to register her unwashed apron and unclean fingernails, when her father called out after her. 'Kialessha. Welcome home, luv.'

She turned, and looked at him.

                    By Dr Joe Ireland

He nodded, and she smiled. Then she left so that she couldn't hear them argue and shout at each other once more. She pulled down the stairs to the attic and kicked them into place. She stormed up, but didn't bother pulling them up again. As the light streamed in through the cracks in the roof, making the dust glow, she threw herself onto whatever pile of blankets she could find and buried her face, stifling her tears and screams in the pillows. She hit them again and again, at least until she felt tired.

She threw herself on her back, and watched the dust dancing in the sunlight, wondering what unseen magic there would be amongst them. Wondering what unseen eyes might see her now, and feel for sorry for her life.

She took out her little leather circle then, the one Darrix had made for her at the start of the year. She held it in her hands, and prayed for the strength and wisdom to go on.

Then she remembered that, in every trial she'd faced in the last year, it had been her goal to make the most of it. To find the opportunity in every situation. The room she was in was almost too small to stand, but it was not a prison. The people here were her friends, and her family, which was more than some could say. She wasn't hurt in any way, except for inside.

With a sigh she realised; she would survive. This wasn't the worst thing that had happened to her. She still had a place to stay. She could see her father, and her little brother. She could run through the fields that would soon be covered with a soft blanket of snow. And she wasn't sleeping by a stove anymore.

She made her bed, taking nothing from what Kiel probably used. She dried her tears, and took a deep breath. But she would rather spend time doing something than nothing. Knowing Kiel would be working double time with her mother's mood she rolled up her sleeves and went downstairs to help with the dishes.

***

Kialessa laughed. She and her brother were out picking the late autumnfruits, the few that remained in the cool weather, by the old fence where dogs had once tried to kill her. Dark storms rolled down each evening from the dwarven lands at the Feuerdrache, and even though those were far away, they always brought rain. And each day that rain got colder and colder as winter approached. Travellers hurried to the inn more often to escape the biting winds, hoping to warm themselves in the open fires or with a ladle of potato soup. It would be a profitable time for the inn; profitable, and busy.

Kialessa looked at her brother. Kiel was recounting a story of when he and another boy in town had taken a shortcut through Farmer Barley's paddock and ended up getting chased by the dominant male posk, almost getting crushed in the process. It sounded like quite an adventure.

'I'm glad you got away!' Kialessa said, climbing down the rickety stepladder in order to unload a new armful of fruits into the wheelbarrow.

'Still, nothing like you've been through. Did you see the king? What adventures have you been on?' he said with a smile.

It made her pause; it looked like now was the time to ask. 'You mean you don't already know?'

He froze, his hand halfway reaching up to grab another autumnfruit. When he turned, he looked shy.

He knew.

'I thought so,' she told him.

He tried to continue as if nothing had happened, 'What, I don't know what you're talking about.'

He was a terrible liar. His lip quivered and his hands shook.

'You're a dreamwalker, aren't you?'

'No, not at all!' he insisted.

By Dr Joe Ireland

She waited.

'I don't know what you mean,' he repeated, climbing from the ladder tried to put some distance between them.

'You don't remember helping me when the archmage captured us? You don't remember battling the enchantress in the dreamworld, and *winning*? None of this?'

He stumbled, and drew a shuddering breath that made it look like he was going to burst into tears. He dropped his bundle and knelt on the ground, almost crying. 'No… no… it's all just dreams. It doesn't mean anything… it never **really** happens!'

She didn't know what to say, so she just knelt beside him, and patted his back. So… he knew, but … he didn't know.

'How… how long has this been going on?' she asked.

He pushed the fallen fruit around as though he might gather it up again, 'My whole life, ever since I came here, which is as long as I can remember. Oh!'

'Kiel,' she said, 'don't be so sad, this is a good thing! A rare talent, you can use it to help people! You already do!'

'No. No I don't, not all the time. Sometimes it's like I'm someone else. Sometimes I hurt people. But then I wake up and tell myself it's just a dream. Now you're here. Now you're telling me it's not!? Kialessa, you don't know what that means… I see people, and I go places. I can't tell the present from the future… If even half the things I see are real than that means-'

He sat down beside an old Winterwillow, the only tree that bloomed in winter, always just a degree or two warmer than every other tree. The Winterwillows covered the valley all over, and always had. He was in a panic of tears, trembling and pale. She knew she had to help him, to help him bring his dream world into the waking reality, in just the way he'd protected her in the dream world more times than she probably knew. 'Hey, it's all right, it's going to be all right Kiel. You know, this year, I met an enchantress?'

'… the dryad?' he said. 'The one that hit you with a religion symbol on your face, and then became your best friend?'

'Yeah, that's the one.' It was as if he was trying to narrate her life for her. 'Well, she's an enchantress, and she taught me how to do enchanting, and that dreamwalkers are a form of enchanter, you know. It's not hard; you just have to take some time out each day to really vividly imagine the things you want to happen. To really feel them. You can do this, you already do.'

'But what if I, you know, use these powers for evil, Kia? I'm not like me in there… but… it's…'

'Better than being out here?' Kialessa finished for him.

He nodded, 'For me. It really is. Bad things happen, and I get very close to them in the … dream… world.'

She smiled, 'Here; here's how to protect yourself if you're ever afraid… a wise boy once told me to stop imagining evil, to imagine safety, to focus on the good things that protect us, and it will help chase away all the evil in the world. That's all we need to do.'

He looked so afraid, but then her words seemed to comfort him. Perhaps he'd just remembered that those were the words he had spoken to her, once, when they were trapped inside a dream. 'I -'

His voice was cut off by their mother's screeching, 'Horns, get in here now!'

'It's all right,' Kialessa told him, 'We'll talk about it later.'

'Yeah, that'd be good,' he told her, looking for all the world like it was the last thing he ever wanted to talk about again.

Inside, for once, there was a pleasant surprise waiting for her. The old storyteller had stopped by for his annual visit. He was a doting old man, friendly, yet absent minded. It seemed he enjoyed the company of others, and especially enjoyed telling stories to the children. It was the early afternoon, so four or five families from the local community seemed to have found the courage to bring their young children along. It was how he paid for his stay at the inn before wandering off into the valley below, where it appeared he would weather the winter in a cottage he had built somewhere. His stories were almost magical, and he could hold the attention of the entire inn with ease. He was most fond of historical tales, and would always tell them like he had really been there. Mother was always very polite when he came, as he gathered a well-paying audience for his visit.

As usual, he was quick to pat Kialessa's head when she arrived. 'Little one; it warms my heart to see you once again. I hear you've made quite the story this year.'

'You heard? Of course you heard. You're a storyteller.'

'And I've many a new story to share with you this year. But first we must attend to the children! You're a big girl now, so I'll forgive you for not listening to my repeated rendition of "The Little Fox" once more.'

Kialessa smiled, it was his best and most often told story, and the children already gathered around his knees. Reluctantly she walked off to wash the mugs at one of the small sinks behind the front counter. As she did she noticed a strange bottle of wine that she'd never noticed before, behind a locked glass cabinet. The tiny runes etched in the base indicated the presence of magic was in that bottle, probably enspelled to hold its bubble and flavour for longer.

Her father noticed her noticing, 'Well, that! Ahem, is what we decided to spend your small fortune on that the king sent for saving his life.'

'So you bought wine? That was a hundred gold coins, Dad. Why didn't you get the window fixed? Or the awnings?'

He seemed embarrassed. 'Well, the idea at the time was to improve the reputation of the inn with some high-class elven wine from before the Great Kingdom was formed. Maybe… not the wisest thing I've done. Seems a little out of our customers' financial reach. Tastes amazing though.'

'You drank it yourself?' Kialessa said in disbelief.

'There's still half a bottle in there!' he protested with a disarming grin.

It was hard to be mad at him, but a part of her still was. A lifetime supply of gold and he spends it on wine he drinks himself!? That was her dad though. He tended to do things like that.

The evening wore on with pleasant stories as a kind spirit seemed to settle at the inn. The storyteller stayed late that night, paying for a small glass of the elven wine to share with her father with some herbs he claimed were extremely exotic and rare.

Kialessa noticed that the people didn't seem to mind her being at the inn so much this winter. Perhaps her reputation for saving the king had preceded her, if nothing else. At least they didn't bring any dogs with them this time – they kept them well away from the inn nowadays. But it was the dog attack that had motivated the king to protect her in his college in the first place.

And as the evening wore on and her eyes grew tired, the storyteller suggested she put herself to bed. So she did.

Father

What is it that makes a man our father? Is it by birth? It is by accepting his teachings? Is it simply a title we bestow upon some man? For whom we may grant such a title in honour, or discipleship, or by birth – who in our lives can we truly say has earned such a noble appellation?

Theglios, archpriest of the god Serros.

The next dawn, Kialessa awoke with a fright.

Something was terribly wrong; she could feel it in her heart. Not dangerous, just very, very wrong.

Using the magical sash the king had given her, she swapped out her night clothes for her day clothes. She stood up, wrapping her magical whip her father had given her around her waist, then hid all her other possessions via the shadowrealm in the safety of her magical treasure chest far away at the castle. Only then did she notice the silence of the morning birds. It was a poor omen that resonated with the misgivings in her heart.

There was a man's voice downstairs. It was deep, and echoed in the tavern. It made her both afraid, and angry, but she couldn't place the voice.

Leaving Kiel where he slept she opened out the steps and crept out to explore the source of her unnamed fear.

She heard her mother speaking as she approached. Her voice was clear and direct, businesslike. It was a tone she'd never heard her use before.

Kialessa rounded the top of the stairs and saw the new guest, a raging fear and terror sweeping through her.

It was Tyran Noblax, the merchant prince.

And he was here, it would seem, alone.

He held up his hand, and her mother immediately stopped speaking. 'I see she's here,' he told her, indicating in Kialessa's direction.

She could not have ducked away if she'd wanted too.

Then her mother looked up at her. Her face was a strange expression, one she wasn't sure she'd ever seen before; it was pity, mixed with… resignation.

The kind of expression she had when beheading the chickens for dinner.

'Yer'd betta get down here, girl.'

It was even a name she rarely used to refer to her only daughter.

Kialessa did not move, at first, but her fear was replaced with anger. Why was this man here? What trouble did he wish on this little family, and their small home? Why was *he* here?

He watched her with an amused look on his face as she glared at him, following her mother's instructions to join them. But she stopped at the last foot of the stairs, perhaps hoping that not touching the floor he was on would keep his evil away from her. He looked dark in the shadows, but seemed to belong there.

'Congratulations, dame Kialessa,' the merchant prince grinned at her. 'Today, you graduate from innocence to learn the true meaning of the world, and of your place in it.'

Without explanation, Kialessa felt a new wave of rage wash over her. Who was he, thinking he could tell her, her place in the world?

'Pack yer things, Horns. Yer leav'n,' her mother informed her.

'What?!' Kialessa could not believe what she was hearing. She heard the rustle of footprints from the stairs above – Kiel had arrived.

'You 'eard me!' her mother shouted, her voice harsh and cruel.

The merchant held up his hand and the old woman fell silent, as though he owned her as well. 'You have every right to know, young Kialessa. Your mother should have told you a long time ago, she should have told you as soon as you were old enough to know. Did you really think your gifts and talents were from some ancestor wounded in a distant war? That your horns and tail are a curse of some kind? No. They are not. It is a blessing from your parents, well, from one of them at least...'

And with that, he waved his hand in front of his face. Kialessa felt the familiar twingle of magic that she'd learned to recognise when one unweaves an enchantment; infornium or the illusion hall this time, if she was correct. And in its wake it altered the merchant's face, revealing a grotesque image. His dark goatee lengthened, and his ears elongated in a jagged pattern. His hair grew wild. Dark leathery wings unfurled from the form that was his cloak. And two massive, axe-like horns curved from the front of his forehead to stretch behind his skull.

Horns. She had horns too.

Her mother stumbled, and fell on a chair. She trembled, but refused to look up at the merchant now.

Kiel peeped like a mouse, and hid at the top of the stairs.

Kialessa's heart filled with a blood burning rage. 'No...' she gasped. 'No!' she screamed, so loudly the humans covered their ears, and a glass in the window split in two.

The merchant prince just laughed. 'They're always a little like this, aren't they, Jewel? Come, Kialessa, compose yourself. You've always known this truth, haven't you?'

'You...' she stumbled for words, even as she stumbled angrily into the room to confront the man. Without thinking, her armour folded around her, the acid dagger that was a gift from a dwarven queen found its way into her hand. 'You are not-'

The old merchant shouted, but she did not flinch. His voice was every bit as commanding and terrifying as she had feared. 'Oh, and I suppose you know who is? This man?' he shouted, and pointing into a darkened corner. Kialessa turned to find her father, his bloodshot eyes barely focussed over the empty bottle of elven wine in his hand.

'Father!' Kialessa was shocked. This was not the time to be blind drunk. But he was, again.

The merchant laughed.

Kialessa ran over to him. 'Father, what are you doing? Father, I need you...'

She heard the merchant approach, and towered over the quivering man. 'This... man? You think to call *him* your father? Look at him!'

Her father could barely keep his eyes straight.

Then the merchant grew serious again, 'When I found this family, Kialessa, it was already in tatters. Falling apart. I gave them a gift; I gave your mother a precious gift. I gave them you. But it was always with a promise, an understanding. She would have you until the year you turn twelve. Then you would live out the rest of your life with me. You are turning twelve in a few weeks, Kialessa. It is time for you to learn the truth about-'

'I will never leave with you!' Kialessa spat. 'You are not my father, and you have no say-'

'Actually,' her hateful mother interjected, twirling the hem of her apron while not looking at anyone in particular, 'tha' was ... the agreement.'

'What?' Kialessa almost begged. She could not believe this was happening. What were her parents about to do, sell her out?

The merchant demon smiled, his visage calm and accepting. But Kialessa hated it. She hated that face every bit as much as any had hated her, and she must have looked it. The horns... they curved right from the sides of his forehead. Just like hers.

She tried to calm down, but her voice still cracked and splintered as it raised to a shriek. 'No. I belong here, with my family. I'm staying inside the circle with my family!!'

He smiled till the echoes of her scream died in the room. 'You are coming with me, and it does not matter what you think about it. Your parents have *lied* to you. They have lied and they have hidden the truth that

     By Dr Joe Ireland

you deserved to know! They let you believe that you were the half-caste slave of this… gentleman, here. Do you really think that a young woman of your power, and intelligence, could be the natural daughter of *this* man? This worthless, pitiful, drunkard! Look at him!'

Her father said nothing, but grinned as he stared out, out beyond the windows to the mountains far away. Grinned, as though he heard nothing of what this demon had accused him of. Grinned, as though he didn't care at all.

'Father?' Kialessa begged, her tears falling freely.

He glanced in her direction, but spoke to the window, 'I guess… it's probably for the best,' he muttered.

'What?!'

He looked like he tried to glance at her as he spoke, his voice oddly clear, his eyes a brighter shade of blue than they were normally. 'You'll see; it's probably for the best. It'll all work out in the end. You'll be fine. Sometimes bad things… you gotta do hard things, like dig a well if you want some water. Things look bad at the time, but it all works out. Everything will be fine; it'll all work out in the end.'

It broke her heart. He had said nothing… he had done… nothing. He was failing to listen to her, or care for her, or protect her – again. But she still could not feel angry at him.

She was angry at someone else, at someone convinced he could destroy the illusion of her life, and force her to follow him just because he was rich, or powerful, or….

'Kialessa, I am your father,' the merchant proclaimed.

With a cry of betrayal and hatred she scratched out at him, trying to gouge out his right eye. He caught her hand without effort, and with a flick of her dagger so quick she hadn't even though about it, she tried to stab him in the hand. He moved so fast she missed, and almost fell over.

'I am your father, Kialessa, and now you need to come with me.'

She felt the imposition of magic in his words, and screamed against them. The enchantment shattered at her voice.

He pulled her up, clutching her armed hand with his other hand, enormous wings steadying him as they scattered chairs and tables.

'You are NOT my father, and I am NOT going with you!' she screamed.

He looked at her, an almost supernatural calm in his eyes. His dispassionate, unsympathetic eyes. With terrible certainty she realised this was not first time he had taken children from their homes, and a dread fear settled on her.

She saw him begin to move, planning to drag her out the door. It was at that precious moment that Kialessa had an idea she had never had before. If it was possible for her to move her hand into the shadow realm to hold her dagger, it should be possible to move her whole arm.

Pulling away from the massive demon before her, she poured all her will into moving her arm, not away, but into the shadow realm.

It worked.

His hand clenched around empty air.

And Kialessa fled.

With all her might she ran through the inn, leaping under table and over chair to escape the demon. She had no thought of where she was going, or where she could hide. She just ran.

She only ever made it to the foot the stairs. She heard the crash of tables and chairs as he raced after her, and then a powerful thud as he beat down his wings. There was an odd, almost surreal silence, and then she felt his clawed hand wrap around the back of her neck. Without sympathy or compassion, he dragged her to the exit.

It hurt so much she could not breathe. Desperately she clutched at his fingers, but they were harder than steel. She struggled for her whip, but found she needed both hands just to keep from choking. 'Mum, Dad, help me,' she pled.

                    By Dr Joe Ireland

They dared not move.

Dangling helplessly from his fist he carried her to the front door, and he opened it with surprisingly great care. 'Thank you, gentles, for taking care of my daughter, but your desperately inadequate services are no longer required,' he stated.

And as he carried her effortlessly out of the room, Kialessa stole one last look at the shattered remains of her family. Her father was on the floor, weeping. Her mother cowered by the bar. And Kiel still stood at the top of the balcony, his knuckles white as they clutched the unheeding railing in complete, utter, helplessness, chairs and tables scatted about like the shattered remains of her broken heart.

Brother

Brothers will fight, they always do. But they have the power to make up too! You might never have a better relationship than the one you have with your brother. It's not always what you want. It's not always what you expect. It's not always what you imagined or hoped. But it's one of the most important things in the world.

Humdug, dwarf scholar.

No one was listening to her pleas, and no one had fed her all day. Again and again she kicked the door, knowing no one would open it. She screamed with all her might, knowing while *he* heard, there was no friendly face to free her.

And Kialessa wondered how it possibly could have all come down to this…

She was in some kind of iron caged wagon. It was rickety and old, and rode the ground poorly as though they hated each other. She was cold against the iron, but no one spoke to her. There were at least four other men, mercenaries or thugs by the look of them, and the cart was driven by black furred posks.

They were heading out towards the troll lands, through narrow trails Kialessa never knew existed. Yet as the day wore on the mountains seemed to move past much faster than should have been possible. Clearly, this was some kind of enchanted path, or magical carriage that the merchant demon drove.

He had tried to be… "polite". He had taken on his human form and tried

By Dr Joe Ireland

to speak to her. 'I know this is hard for you, young Kialessa. But it will all be worthwhile in the end. Come, stop your quarrels. Sit with me at the head of this caravan, and let me tell you the truth about who you are, and what you are capable of.'

So she'd tried to bite him, and he'd thrown her back in here.

That evening they stopped by a river that led to a wide lake. Kialessa noticed how he, and all his men, avoided the open sky as though they feared it watched them. Finally, one of his men pushed a small metal bowl into her cage, filled with water from the lake. It was the kind of metal bowl they were also using to water the dogs.

She was too thirsty to care this time, and lifting it to her lips she drank it all. The water was fresh, and cool, coming down from the dwarven Feuerdrache mountains, no doubt it was melted snow this time of year.

It was clear they were not trying to kill her. At least, not today.

'Where are you taking me?' she asked the guard.

He did not answer right away. 'To the master's winter fortress, though we never enter there ourselves, just the children, and his most trusted.'

It was a lot of information. The guard looked young. Human. Of Emerel if she wasn't mistaken. She decided she needed a friend, and hoped for more information. 'Why have we stopped here then?'

'We're never told that kind of thing,' he answered as if that ended the entire conversation.

Kialessa heard the running of wheels approaching from the north. Soon, six or so caravans came into view. They were very different, three of them painted in red or gold, embellished with what looked like blithling artwork.

And riding at the head carriage, driven by two black posks, was the very beautiful woman. Again she looked familiar to Kialessa's eyes, but she could not quite place where she'd seen her before.

The merchant stood in her presence, and raising his hand helped her from the carriage. She stood down with much grace, almost inhuman. They acted like they were a couple, though they barely touched. He seemed very pleased to be in her presence, and she was glowing with confidence in his.

They were talking, and Kialessa began to strain to hear what they were saying.

'I trust your journey was pleasant?' he asked her, the picture of good manners.

'Darling, every hour on the road flew by knowing I was an hour closer to basking in your smile.'

He laughed and smiled, holding both her hands in his. He said something Kialessa couldn't hear, and the woman laughed like a child.

For some reason his happiness tore at her heart. It made her even angrier, and if she had any voice left, she would have spent it all just to swear at him.

He seemed to be waiting.

'Oh, how careless of me!' she waved her hand with a false apology. 'Tyran Noblax, may I present to you; your son – Mak, scourge of Nomer'el!'

Then, from the carriage the woman was riding, a young man leapt up to the roof.

A young man unlike any Kialessa had ever seen before. The first thing she noticed were the massive, black, batlike wings that spread from his back. He clearly could fly with them. He had a thick, spear-like tail, and pure, flawless skin. He stood, glaring at everyone, arms folded against his chest. The human guards cowered at his appearance. Despite all this, he looked about her age.

Exactly her age.

'My woman does not exaggerate!' the merchant prince boasted with a dignified bow, 'You are a *terror* to behold.'

By Dr Joe Ireland

4 Mak, the broad winged battle taint

The young man nodded; pleased to see the effect he'd had on the others. He was wearing a thin shirt and some dirty leggings held on by a cloth sash. He looked like a boy who had been raised on the streets – with bat wings and a thick tail. Then he kneeled on the carriage roof, and said, 'So, they tell me, you are my father.'

'Yes, indeed I am,' Tyran said with dignity and pride.

The boy flew down to stand on the ground. He was not as tall as the merchant, but he looked unafraid. 'I guess that does explain some things.'

The merchant reached out, and put his hand on the young tae'anaryn's shoulder. 'Son, if you'll allow me, there's a lot more I'd like to explain to you. If you don't mind?'

'Sure, sounds good… dad.'

The older man smiled and shook the young boy's shoulder, and they both grinned. A moment later Tyran Noblax flung his arm over his "son's" shoulder and they walked off, laughing happily.

Kialessa wasn't sure what to say. The demon Tyran could clearly be very charming when he wanted to. But he'd taken her by force from her parent's home. Perhaps this boy did not have any home to go back to?

Suddenly there was a fuss at the door to Kialessa's cage. The woman was speaking, 'Oh, no! Not like this!' She sounded so flustered. A moment later a key struck the lock of the carriage and the door flew open.

The beautiful woman was standing there, looking in with deep sympathy at Kialessa. She looked so familiar!

'Darling,' the woman muttered, her words soft and kind. 'My mate does have a brutish side, does he not! I'm so sorry; you should not be travelling in this prison.' She held out her hand.

Kialessa did not trust her. She was too sweet, too… clean. Her body looked fit, like an athlete or performer. And she was trying to be nice to someone who was not supposed to be here.

She was just the kind face of a kidnapping. Therefore, just as dangerous, and just as guilty.

The woman was looking at her. 'I like you.'

Kialessa scowled back.

'Will you not have some bread?' The woman offered. 'It will not do to be starving when you meet all your brothers and sisters.'

That thought struck her. Others? How many?

The woman laughed. 'You have a future with us, Kialessa Tavernskeep. You are a tae'anaryn, and you are going to be safe with us. You belong with us. We will show you the one place where you truly belong.'

Her heart twisted in bitter anger. Belong? Hadn't she learnt in the entire past year where she belonged? And what was the point of talking? They

                    By Dr Joe Ireland

were going to take her away from her family anyway. How she'd prayed her king might hear her pleas, but there was a strange silence in the heavens

The woman sighed, sitting on the carriage edge. 'Well, it's … a lively venue, I'll give the tae'anaryl that.'

'Who is he, really?' Kialessa asked after a pause.

'Tyran Noblax?' the woman answered. 'Just… another man who's had to learn to be strong protecting himself from a cruel and indifferent world.'

Kialessa sank. Her family was broken, but her world was not all cruel. She'd made friends at her college, she'd found some acceptance in her world. Why did they think they had the right to take that away?

'Hey, what's up Jasmin?' a boy's voice asked. It was the young tae'anaryn.

'Kialessa,' the woman said, 'meet your brother, Mak.'

He stuck his head right into the prison wagon. He stared at her.

She stared back. His face was young – still innocent. But his brow was knit as though he spent all his time worrying for his life. His nails were clawed; black like her own. And deep inside her heart, she felt a twinge of sympathy and maybe love. Was this boy really her half-brother?

'Why is her skin red?' he asked Jasmin.

'Mak, don't be rude,' Jasmin protested, slapping his shoulder very playfully. 'She is right here, ask her yourself.'

'Yeah,' he admitted. He stared for a moment, then he ran away without asking anything.

Jasmin shook her head. A moment later she sat up straight.

Tyran Noblax appeared at the edge of the carriage.

Kialessa felt her dark hatred rise at the man.

'We will be travelling through the next six hours,' he said to Kialessa. 'Again, you can ride with me in the front, if you are willing to listen.'

Jasmin gasped, 'Six hours with the merchant sage prince Tyran Noblax? Nobles in Emerel pay a thousand gold coins for that privilege!'

He smiled at his woman, then looked at Kialessa.

She did not move. Was denying him the only freedom she had left? Or did she fear he knew only knew things that she did not want to learn?

Least of all the dreaded wisdom – was he telling her the truth?

She did not speak.

'Suit yourself,' he said, and gently closed the prison door.

Jasmin was protesting, pouting like a child, but putting little effort into it. She seemed very determined to please that man.

Kialessa pressed her face up to the far window, where she could see the boy Max spreading out his wings for the admiration of the caravan guards. They looked impressed, as though they'd seen many tae'anaryl wings before but never any so large.

He looked… like no one had ever appreciated his wings before. In his whole entire life. He showed them how he could jump right up to the trees, and dodge among them. He would be an impossible catch in a crowded city to the average human.

Mak seemed happy.

***

Kialessa marvelled as the mountains sped by. For the first time in her life, she was going to the very edge of the Dwarvenspine Mountains, just south of the elven kingdom. Technically, the land belonged to her kingdom of Lenmer'el, but none had the strength to claim it from the wild things that lived here.

Like, for example, a demon pretending to be a merchant prince.

Her carriage suddenly rocked as something heavy landed on it. Then there was the thud of wings.

It would be Mak.

He started talking immediately, with all the unbridled enthusiasm of Posk, but with a dark undertone all of his own. 'Yo, sis!' he said in a strange greeting she'd never heard before. 'You all right in there?'

She paused, after a moment answered sincerely; 'No'.

'I hear we're going to the *Sanctum Brumae.* That's his "winter fortress", so I hear. They say dad's got heaps of kids and he's just going to take us there. Sounds pretty cool, eh?'

To Kialessa, it did not sound… "cool". It sounded like jail. She wondered if Mak knew he was probably being kidnapped too. 'What about your home?'

He scoffed. 'This time last week, I was fighting for my life on the streets of Hamelthorpe. That's in Nomer'el. Mum moved us there about four years ago… then she got herself arrested.' He sounded sad, but cheered quickly. 'I've been surviving on my own since then! Crazy town. Lots of spare coins lying around. I found a guy that'll sell me bread – but only because he's half blind and I go at night. If you ask me, this fortress sounds better than any place I've holed up in the past eleven years.'

Kialessa had to think about that. Not everyone had the, well, grew up in the family she had.

Mak kept talking. 'Mum tried to hide me once she saw me. Tells me the midwife tried to drown me that night. They got away before my grandfather got home… he came after mum with an axe, she's still got the cut to prove it! Ha, ha! Tough girl, my mum.' He paused. 'We were living in an old basement no one used that backed on to the sewers. Till they started using it again and we had to leave. That's how we got found. I almost didn't get away. But I did. Win!' and he pumped his fist.

Kialessa was astounded. He was certainly … resilient. But his life had been tough. No wonder he wasn't so upset when his "dad" turned up to get him. 'Why do you think … the merchant waited till now to find you?'

Mak was quiet a moment. 'Yeah. Took his time,' he agreed.

It gave her confidence, 'Mak, he is a very, very bad man. You have to escape.'

Mak just sat there. 'Jasmin made it sound nice.'

'Mak, I'm in a cage.'

He thought for a moment. 'Yeah, but you don't have to. You can ask to be let out any time. He says it's just so that you don't try to run away.'

She was confused by that. Running away was the point. Running away was what Mak should be doing **right now**. But he wasn't. Had his life been really so terrible that becoming a prisoner was preferable?

'He says we got stuff to learn, Kialessa,' Mak told her. 'Jasmin says we're going to a college that's only for tae'anaryl. It's where we can learn to use our powers to their full. And I, for one, am very curious to know what a college full of tae'anaryl can teach me. I have never been to a college before.'

She pondered before replying. 'We're in trouble, Mak,' she told him.

Dark carriage wheels squeaked along underneath them, following solemn ruts dug deep by repeated use. They turned in neither direction, but led directly on towards the winter fortress of a demon prince.

'Yeah,' he agreed. 'I know.'

Sanctum Brumae

You may choose your friends; you may not choose your family.
Elven Queensage – Sagesse L'aimé, 316CY.

The first time Kialessa saw the *Sanctum Brumae*, she wasn't sure whether she was looking at a fortress or a mountain, it looked like a little of both. It was intimidating, and obviously well defended. Surrounded on all sides by foreboding thornbrush, the sides of the *Sanctum* rose high and steep from the landscape like the sides of a volcanic core, or the stones of an unworked fortress. Small windows and ledges were visible in its rough surface, with pale flickering lights within that gave the impression of the entire structure being more a prison than a fortress. Enormous trees and shrubs were visible in the moonlight, clinging with unnatural determination to the walls of the fortress. And the vaulted heights of the mountain ended in cragged structures like naturally formed crenulations, making the perfect vantage point for a dragon to survey the surrounding territory. To Kialessa it reeked of despair, imprisonment, and isolation.

She said little now, her face pressed to the small, cold bars of her iron cage. The path before was blocked by thorns and briers, but the demon merchant stood, and with an imperious wave of his arm, shrubs and trees scurried to get out of their way, leaving a smooth and cobbled pathway before them. The prison carriage bumped down the foreboding trail with the rest of the caravan.

They were taken to the edge of a crevasse, separating the woodlands from the fortress itself. Deep purple and black shadows rose up from the invisible depths of the moat, radiating terror and death to any who would assault, or consider leaving it apparently. The ground thundered gently as the caravan approached. Again the demon merchant stood, and uttered words of power of such horror and profanity she had to cover her ears. A deep groaning sounded from within the earth, and moments later a stone bridge appeared to grow up from the crevasse itself. He did not pause, but rode straight out over the dark stones towards the mountain.

A strange feeling settled on Kialessa as they rode over the moat, as if, for a moment, her connection to the shadowrealm disappeared, and when it reformed it felt different somehow – more powerful, but it no longer obeyed her will like it used to. Here, the shadowrealm belonged to someone else.

Soon they were at the foot of the mountain. There was a large ornate entrance, the inner stone doors protected by a double barbican; two massive iron grates separated by a chilling gatehouse. The unworked stone below was frosted with ice, and she felt her bones chill as they passed through.

Then they entered the mountain. They rode though a pitch dark corridor, lit by nothing and yet everyone acted as though they could, like herself, see perfectly well in darkness.

Soon orange light lit up a wide cavern. The air became warmer, smelling more like the fortress servant's quarters, and there were voice from within. A trumpet sounded their arrival, and then the shouting started.

Then there were dozens of them. Scores. Tae'anaryl of all shapes and sizes. Ram horns and deer antlers, bat and fire winged, red skinned and black. They bore an assortment of magical arms and armour – they looked like a very small, very elite army.

But they were all young. None looked a day more than twenty.

That was when a dark fear settled on Kialessa's heart. A frightening story she'd once heard, about a traitorous solider who became a demon and stole children no one ever hears from again. And she had a very, very bad feeling that she was about to become the next victim of that story.

Tears filled her eyes. Who were these children? These youths? None looked younger than twelve, except for one young tae'anaryn girl with blond hair and goat hooves for hands and feet. Another was huge, a moving stone monolith, a stone giant tae'anaryn – Kialessa didn't even know it was possible for them to exist.

There were about fifty youth in total, and they set about unloading the wagons. More than half of them flew, so the work progressed very quickly.

'Daygon!' she heard the merchant prince shout with joy.

Kialessa adjusted her view to see what the news was. There was an old man approaching, well, older than the merchant. He was a human tae'anaryn, well fed and a little overweight, with small horns and a tail much like her own. But his skin was deep brown. Of Sanmer'el perhaps? He had a cheery smile and warm lips. He rushed up to greet Tyran the demon merchant with a large, affectionate hug.

'It's good to see you again, son!' Tyran shouted, slapping the older man on his shoulders.

'And it's good to see you too, father,' Daygon replied. 'All present and accounted for!'

They hugged again. For whatever reason, the kidnapping merchant who claimed he was Kialessa's father seemed rather fond of this one old man, who might possibly be Kialessa's half-brother somehow.

Kialessa watched them talk briefly, and then the merchant indicated towards her prison carriage.

She pulled back.

In the next moment the doors flung open. Apparently they were unlocked. The merchant demon and his older son stood looking in at her.

'Oh, you poor, poor, child,' the son Daygon said with such empathy in his voice that Kialessa's rage melted, and all her trembling vulnerability flew forth. 'You have every right to be upset tonight. But you will find this place here is a wonderful opportunity. You are going to learn things you never knew you never knew! It's all right now, you will be all right.'

The next thing she knew, she was bursting into tears and clutched in desperation at the old man's hand. His skin was soft and his embrace gentle.

Even the demon seemed wise enough to give her space.

'Come,' Daygon seemed to plead. 'Let us take care of you.'

Kialessa let herself be led out of the carriage, clutching onto the gentle old man's hand. The room was rowdy, everyone shouting. And everyone looked at least a year older than her, except Mak and the other little one.

The next moment a pretty, blond haired girl stood in front of them. She looked about sixteen or seventeen, and was the most human-like girl Kialessa had seen here. If she'd seen her anywhere else, she would have mistaken her for being entirely human – no horns, no wings. Her blue eyes and pale skin were no different to any other human of Nomer'el that Kialessa had ever seen.

Daygon hid Kialessa behind him, but she peeked out.

'Father,' the young woman began in a business-like manner. 'Only two? The harvest is poor this year.'

'Lossel!' Tyran Noblax chided her, 'Loosing even one of your siblings is a tragedy I cannot bear. Yes, we have few to add to our numbers this year, but once you get to know these two I am sure you will find them worth three times their value, you will see.'

The young woman named Lossel nodded, Kialessa thought, like a soldier. 'I will secure the provisions, father.'

'I have no doubt, honoured daughter. But look,' he pointed up at a wagon being unloaded. 'Extra pork for the winter festival!'

'We will feast this season!' a half bear boy shouted, and the tae'anaryl in the cavern cheered.

Tyran Noblax laughed as though pleased with himself.

Lossel looked worried, 'They won't all fit in the icebox, you realise?'

Tyran shrugged. 'Get your stone giant brother Ka to dig it out.'

'We need more ice,' Lossel demanded, almost threatened. There was

　　　　　By Dr Joe Ireland

some kind of issue there.

Again Tyran looked unflustered. 'Have that bitter sister of yours, what's her name? Niarch, or something.' Tyran laughed, and while he looked to Daygon to join in, he did not.

'Raynah?' Lossel pondered.

'Is that what she's calling herself now?' He smiled to himself. 'Fine, yes, her. Have her ice it up for us.'

'She will not do so willingly.'

'Then *make* her,' Tyran whispered with a threat.

More cheering echoed about the cavern as the young tae'anaryl uncovered more treasures. In their noise Kialessa's mind seemed to snap back into her own body. Why was she holding this man's hand again? She pulled away, and looked out at the room with clear eyes. Tae'anaryl. Her brothers and sisters, most likely. More tae'anaryl than she thought could exist in the entire Great Kingdom, and now they filled a room together. It was inspiring and terrifying all at once. But why were they all here? And did they all call this man "father"? And just how literal was that title? The thoughts rushed inside her mind like the chaos about her.

'Tyran!' A black skinned tae'anaryn with black feathered wings shouted. He was sitting high in the rafters, as though he'd done nothing to help so far.

The demon merchant scowled at him. That was clearly a name that boy should not be using. The room fell silent.

The boy leant forward, 'So, are we feasting with the horn tonight?'

All eyes turned to the merchant for his answer; everyone seemed to be holding their breath. 'Very well!' Tyran Noblax shouted, and the tae'anaryl in the room cheered. 'Tonight we feast by the horn of plenty!'

The cheering increased.

Kialessa was jostled to and fro in the chaos as they were rushed through another tunnel and into a large feast hall. The youth set about preparing a feast. She was almost stepped on multiple times, till Lossel pulled her over to one corner. 'Sit there,' the young woman ordered.

Kialessa did not sit; it seemed safer just to stand there.

Within moments a great feast was prepared. Four pigs roasted on giant spits, where red skinned tae'anaryl turned them in the fire by hand, though one used a complex system of pulleys and simply peddled theirs. It was quite ingenious. Magic was everywhere – from the pots that boiled at a command, to the dancing cutlery that set itself as if by some enchantress's whim.

Her siblings, if that's what they really were, ignored her for the most part. Some few mocked her, smiling as if teasing was the only greeting they knew. Some stole dangerous glances in her direction as if she was some kind of growing threat. Most ignored her. Mak seemed to fit right in.

So lost in the din was she that Kialessa was startled when someone struck a large gong. Within an instant all the tae'anaryl where seated, silent, and looking at the far door.

In walked Tyran Noblax, his woman Jasmin at his arm. Behind him the giant stone tae'anaryn grunted as he carried some kind of stone obelisk that would have weighed several tonnes. He set the stone up on the cavern floor with a thunderous crash.

Nobody moved. While all plates were empty, the table was well set, stocked with enough food to feed a king. It was an ambitious feast.

They waited until Tyran seated his lady, then he sat down himself.

Everyone waited.

Finally the demon merchant spoke, 'My children. Tonight, we mourn those who cannot be here with us at this feast, who never came to this sacred sanctuary, and those who have moved beyond, and left us here.'

Everyone bowed their heads in great respect. A moment of silence passed. Mak stole a cheeky look in her direction but did not make a sound.

Tyran spoke again, 'But we rejoice, for this year we are joined. It is my

     By Dr Joe Ireland

deepest honour and warmest joy to present to you another of your two siblings. May I present to you Mak -'

Here the young man stood as if in honour, spreading his massive wings wide. They were quite possibly the widest here.

Tyran continued as her … siblings… marvelled. 'Scourge of Hamelthorpe, Mak has survived the past four years alone!'

'Good on you!' a tae'anaryn cried.

'Yup, just like the rest of us,' someone else muttered.

'With wings of steel,' Tyran continued his praise. 'Mak has evaded capture by the city watch, by priests of Serros and of Pumos, and has even crossed blades with a sanctum squire of the Paladin Tomin himself!'

Kialessa's ears pricked up at the paladin's name. She knew Tomin. He was a good man – but he did not like tae'anaryl. But she also knew one of his other squires, and he was one of her best friends.

And a sanctum was another race, like tae'anaryl. Only they were descended from the angels of Serros rather than demons like… like some of these kids were.

Everyone clapped for Mak, some slapping the palms of their hands against his hand in some odd gesture she did not know.

The merchant waved his hand, and a new name wrote itself at the bottom of the long list of names. It looked like *Mak, Scourge of Hamelthorpe.*

Then Tyran Noblax raised his glass in her direction. 'And I give you Kialessa Tavernskeep – demonbane and stayer of the western troll hoards, friend to the enchantress and solver of the archmage's riddle – '

She did not like this. He knew too much. Most people didn't even believe what they'd heard about her. But he did. And he knew.

He continued, 'AND, the very hand that slew an elemental flame hound and saved the life of the king of our fair nation Lenmer'el.'

No one clapped, until a younger tae'anaryn almost shouted, 'What, HER!'

Everyone laughed.

'I could snap her bones with my little finger,' someone boasted.

'She sits in the corner weeping,' one girl muttered.

All Tyran Noblax had to do was sit up, just a little straighter, and maybe crease his brow a little. It was clear that he was annoyed at this reaction.

The room fell dead silent in an instant.

'Yes. She did,' he informed them.

The young tae'anaryn that had started the teasing sunk so low in his chair he looked like he might vanish altogether.

People looked at her with a touch more respect from that moment on. Respect, and envy… or was it loathing…

The demon father spoke with a soft dignity that held a gentle threat, 'It has come to my attention that some of you may not be treating students new to this hallowed ground with the same dignity and camaraderie as your older friends. It would give my lady, and myself, great comfort to know you are helping each other to feel welcomed and safe here, and that you are treating all students, regardless of upbringing, tradition or race, with the kindness we show each of you every day.'

Kialessa almost gagged. He had just recited something her king had written, to protect her from the bullying at the start of the year. How could he know that, seasons ago in a castle that was days and days away?

The merchant looked at her, clearly noticing his vast knowledge was not lost on Kialessa. He nodded at her, but she said nothing in reply, nor did she stand. She had not been fleeing the city guard and rescued by a rich merchant prince claiming to be her father. She had been violently taken from her home by a disguised demon, and forced to confront a reality no child should ever have to face, and that in the worst possible way.

With a wave of his hand her name was written on the stone, in golden engraving. *Dame Kialessa Tavernskeep.*

He looked bothered by that, but said nothing. Then he grinned at his

By Dr Joe Ireland

fellow tae'anaryl, and they began to cheer.

He waved to his woman, and from her low cut blouse she drew a small, gilded horn of exquisite ivory. It was inlaid with expensive pearls and glittering sapphires. Everyone cheered. They presented her with a large decanter of what must have been gravy. The room fell silent as she help up the horn, and to the rousing cheer of the tae'anaryl placed a single drop of oil from the horn into the decanter. Then she returned the horn into its place.

The tae'anaryl cheered as the vessel was stirred thoroughly, Lossel somehow having the honour. She then began to pour the gravy over the meals and a little onto every plate.

Then, with a grin and a nod, the merchant prince and his lady stood and departed.

Decorum failed almost as soon as the door was shut. Everyone pounced on their food like it was their last meal on earth. Some even reached over to their neighbour's plate and snatched what gravy they could.

It made her feel sick.

One boy, with green skin and horns twisted in random directions, looked over and pointed at her plate, begging perhaps to eat the food she was ignoring.

She nodded.

Before she'd even finished he was licking the plate clean, cooing to himself in content.

Then they started on the other food. Many ate with their hands. A few had some sort of dignity; in particular a group of about four of them, the oldest students. They did not rush, indeed, the food seemed a little unpalatable to them. But none ignored their magically enhanced gravy.

There was a loud thump as someone crouched on the table to get a better go at the buttered chicken, and the little tae'anaryn with hooves for hands was pushed to the floor near Kialessa. It looked like it must have hurt, but she didn't complain. She just pressed her hand-hooves together and made a soft, hooting noise.

She was begging. Begging her brothers and sisters for food.

It was disgusting to Kialessa. She looked around, and noticed that the chandeliers of food were mostly untouched. They may not have had much gravy, probably none. Every now and then a flying tae'anaryn would flap up there to grab some morsel.

Kialessa could not fly, but she knew how she could get up there.

She unwrapped her father's whip, the one he'd once used to break up bar fights, the one he'd given her to keep her safe at college, the one a wizard friend had enspelled so that she could set it on fire and it would not burn. She lashed it out around a hanging rod of the chandelier and it gave an unexpected crack. The entire room stopped dead to watch. Without waiting to check their reactions she climbed up, catching the whip on her tail just like in combat training so that it didn't dangle behind her. Once there, she began placing some small morsels of food into a napkin. Then dangling from her tail like a rope, she leant down and placed it on a plate on the table.

People shrugged and kept on eating, and the noise resumed. With trained circus grace she twisted down and took her seat.

The little girl's eyes brightened up intensely as she saw the food. Then she looked visibly disappointed when she saw there was no gravy. For a moment she looked longingly at the table, then she must have decided she was just too hungry to care and so she popped open her mouth so that Kialessa could feed her.

Again, Kialessa felt so sad. Was there no way this little child could feed herself? What cruel deity insisted that she be born without hands?

Kialessa picked up some meat, and fed the little girl. She chewed very quickly and swallowed it down, as if expecting Kialessa to lose interest in this project swiftly. But Kialessa was not going to lose interest in feeding this poor child. Again and again she fed her by hand.

'What is your name?' Kialessa asked.

                    By Dr Joe Ireland

'Bah!' the girl replied, sounding more like a request for food than a name.

'Her mother never named her,' a woman's voice replied. It was Lossel. It looked like she'd been in a bit of a food fight recently, with something smeared in her hair and arm. But she was smiling in an almost too relaxed kind of way. She sat down, and fed the girl some of the food from the plate she was carrying. 'We were going to feed her, Kialessa. But that gravy's got a very small time limit, if you know what I mean?' she laughed, more to herself. As though she could not help it. It didn't sound like a real laugh.

The girl popped open her mouth.

Kialessa fed her again. 'How'd she get to be here?'

Lossel looked serious. 'Oh, you don't want to know that. But let's face it, she's better off here than … out there, don't you agree?'

Kialessa could see the point, but didn't know enough about where they were to argue it.

She fed herself a small morsel, and looked at the little girl. It was hard to believe she was still hungry. She popped open her mouth and Kialessa began to hand her another piece of food.

'Ahh, I think-' Lossel began to say.

And before the older girl could finish, the little child bit Kialessa on her hand.

It was a very hard bite. Maybe not as hard as the little child could bite, but hard enough to break skin. It really hurt.

Before Kialessa could react the hoof handed child had fled on all fours. She was very fast.

Kialessa could not hold back her tears, 'Why'd she do that?'

'Meh, beats me,' Lossel said, and stumbled away.

Kialessa sat there, despairing at the chaos around her. On only one thing she was decided. *This is not a good place, and I do not belong here.*

Raynah

A loyal sister is worth a thousand friends.
Kapal, scholar of the Academician, 304CY.

Kialessa looked around. It had only been an hour since dinner, but everyone was asleep now, most stomachs visibly distended. She tiptoed amongst the limp limbs, tapping Mak on his shoulder and calling his name. But he was as still as a pile of wet rags.

She sighed to herself. There was no point feeling sorry now. If there was any hope of escape, she needed to begin to explore her options. And the first thing seemed to be finding out about this "Sanctum Brumae".

She looked around. The door to the kitchen was ajar. Something was moving about inside, cleaning dishes. Carefully she walked up. Inside the room was quite clean, and then Kialessa saw the creatures responsible for the noise: Imps.

She gasped. These creatures were trouble. Full blooded demons, they could turn invisible, and loved to trick and lie. Some could turn into other monsters, like miniature versions of herself, or giant boars that could knock a full grown human archmage to the ground – she'd seen one do both. One of them sneered at her; another slapped him on the back of the head and went to talk to her. She ignored it. These creatures could be trouble, and she was already in a lot of trouble.

Outside the kitchen a curving stone corridor led. It looked like it had been forged by magic – too smooth to have been built by stone smiths. There were no chisel marks at all.

The tunnel ran up the mountain, and she followed it. Along the wall lay

By Dr Joe Ireland

several exquisite works of art. Some were truly amazing. Some were even protected behind strange glass or powerful warding stones that pushed her away as with invisible hands. There were carpets woven of infinite patterns, and pictures of faraway lands that moved with magically painted breezes. Each work of art was a creation of passion and beauty.

Yet there were two kinds of art. The first seemed to be a wistful longing for home or people that the artists knew.

The others were works of frustration and horror, depicting death and the futility of existence. Some of these she could not bear to look at.

Kialessa noticed the outside wall. Upon it, every fifty paces or so, a small window looked out. The view was pitch black in the night, so Kialessa could see it fairly well. They were surrounded by a dark forest, many of the tallest trees reaching up half as far as a fortress. Shadowed forms moved among the trees as if they enjoyed the company of the mountain. Whispered messages flittered among them too silent for her to catch, but tempting her with confusion. And far away, at the edge of the forest, a dark wall seemed to loom, like a mirror, deep at the edge of her imagination – it was difficult to describe. It was clearly a barrier of some kind, and it made her nervous. Soon she stopped looking out.

Eventually, after several locked doors, a noise caught her attention. Kialessa estimated she had walked one entire loop of the fortress. It was a significant journey. But she'd finally found a door that was open.

Kialessa crept up. Someone was speaking from inside. 'You need to add the thongsweed now if we want to succeed at this, Peechee. Hurry now, don't dilly dally!'

The voice sounded young, but tense. Like it was always choking back worry. But Kialessa was sure that it was not a voice that she'd heard at the party.

Kialessa tried to listen at the door, pressing in to get a better look. Her heart skipped a beat as the treacherous door squeaked at her touch.

The voice within gasped. Then she spoke, and her voice had a commanding edge to it, like Piex's. 'Go away; we're working on the ice enchantment for the father!'

From the way she said it, Kialessa decided, this person did not like the merchant prince any more than she did. And that meant she might be an ally, somehow. She would have to risk the chance at making this person, whoever she was, her first friend here.

Kialessa pushed the door open.

Inside was a girl, about fifteen years old. She seemed underdressed, but what scant and tattered clothing she had on bore the excellence of magic about it. She had a long, red cloak, and close fitting tights. Her hair was black, as dark as the skin around her eyes and lips. And all up both her arms, and along her hips, some old, deep scars ran.

The girl noticed her noticing, and immediately put on some bracers and wrapped the cloak around her. 'You're new here,' she announced.

Kialessa momentarily wondered who the girl must have been speaking to, but ignoring that she decided to talk to her, trying to be as polite as Allastassia, 'Greetings. I am Kialessa,' she said, surprised herself at how miserable her own voice sounded. It was the first sound she'd made in hours.

The girl seemed to guess her situation immediately. She seemed sad, and looked like she wanted to say something she wasn't allowed to. So, instead, she just bent her head and walked away. There, near the window, was a beautiful barn owl. It was staring at Kialessa without blinking, but stopped to preen the pretty dark girl.

No one said anything for a long moment.

'I'm Raynah,' she eventually replied.

'You don't look tae'anaryn,' Kialessa said, hoping it was the right thing to say.

Raynah smiled sadly, 'Mother and I cut my horns off when I was young. And my wings and tail too.'

By Dr Joe Ireland

Kialessa was astonished, 'Did… I mean… it hurt.'

'I know of no greater agony. Except one.' Raynah replied, but didn't explain further.

'What are those scars you have?' Kialessa asked hoping to prepare herself if something that gave scars like that happened around here regularly.

Raynah huffed, and looked angry. 'I don't like people to see…'

'I'm sorry,' Kialessa replied. This was not something Raynah wanted to talk about. She looked around the room. 'So… you must be a wizard. I know a wizard. They… know a lot.'

Raynah smiled at that. 'Well, adapting *Kreegon's inimitable temperature declivity* to a stable state of primary matter is no small task. And I can't shake the nagging feeling something is missing in *Glacius Maul's third treatise on low temperature magic!*'

'So I've heard,' Kialessa admitted.

'You have!' Raynah looked up with wizard like desperation written on her face.

'Ah, well, not personally, my friend

5 Raynah, wizardess

the wizard, he said something like that too.'

'Did he go into details?' Raynah begged.

Kialessa shook her head. 'Never, he just complained a lot.' Then her heart felt a sudden twist for her friend Piex. She missed him deeply.

Raynah seemed to notice. 'You need to be careful here, Kialessa. Don't trust anyone. And I mean NO ONE. People here are just trying to survive, right? But we've all got this death sentence hanging over our heads and *ulp!*' She stopped talking and sounded like she was having trouble breathing. Her hands leapt up to the iron studded black leather choker around her neck. It was looking suspiciously tight.

Kialessa would have helped, if she knew how.

'Don't bother,' Raynah muttered, again guessing what Kialessa was thinking. 'Our father put it on there a few years ago. It's never coming off, well, at least while he's alive. Probably for the best, but again, a temporary measure.'

The owl looked really worried for her, but after a moment Raynah recovered. She smiled, one of the first sincere smiles Kialessa had seen here, but it was a very sad smile. 'So, this place hasn't corrupted you yet? Well, that's good. Perhaps we can be … associates. I can finish this tomorrow – have they told you where you're sleeping yet?'

'No one has mentioned anything.'

'Father likes us to sort it out on our own, part of the "strengthening",' she muttered, and gulped at her collar. With a mystical wave of her hand the room began to clean itself up. With a year full of magic Kialessa could finally appreciate what was happening. The girl had somewhere mastered tomes of algorithms and programs to be commanding the room like this. It was clearly her private workspace; even Piex didn't have a wizard study this behoven to his arcane will. But Raynah did.

A moment later the owl floated silently through the air and onto her hand.

 By Dr Joe Ireland

'I take it from the silence downstairs that they used the horn at dinner tonight?' Raynah stated.

Kialessa nodded.

'And I take it, from your ability to stand up right now, that you are either immune to the horn's effects, or did not partake?'

'It was not to my liking,' Kialessa said.

Raynah scoffed, 'No mortal so says. But that you have a strong enough spirit to resist its addictive effects speaks well of your ability to survive here. Come, there's much you need to know.'

The older girl grabbed a large book on her way out, weaving some praesidium enchantments on herself as she went. Then, she started speaking. She knew everyone who lived inside the fortress by name, and had some kind of personal dossier about them all – including personal histories, likes and dislikes, and a full list of all manifested powers.

And that was when Kialessa began to realise what a challenging situation she was in. Everyone here was a half demon of unrivalled uniqueness and unmatched skill. Wings, horns, and tails. And those were only the easily observed powers. There were those who could see through stone, and those who could wield fire. Those who were unaffected by acids, and those who could see magic around them all the time. Those who skin did not yield to sharpened blades, and those who could draw weapons directly from the dream realm. They were, each of them, a being of intelligence and power.

And it seemed each year a new batch of children would arrive, usually about six of them.

Raynah then began to detail the most powerful, and had not gotten past the first four when they arrived back at the dining room. She stepped quickly over fallen bodies and twisted limbs. Everyone was asleep, but it seemed the imps had not touched anything other than to clean up the food.

Raynah went straight up to Lossel. She took some dust from a bag at her hip, and sprinkled it in the air. Intoning arcane words the dust became glistening silver, and soon soaked into the blond haired warrioress.

Gasping for air, Lossel awoke. 'Who? What?' she demanded.

'Lossel,' Raynah stated, 'We plead sanctuary for the new students.'

Lossel swore, but then started to stand. 'Gods, I hate that stuff,' she muttered. She looked unsteady on her feet but pushed Raynah's offered hand away. 'Fine. Go wake up Mak. Him, over there, the enhanced wingbreadth standard form.'

Lossel glared over at Kialessa, then got a mischievous look on her face and turned away. Glancing around, Lossel skipped over several fallen students as though trying not to wake them, which really did seem impossible. She unsheathed a sword one of the older boys had, ignoring the blast of electricity that shot out along her arm. Then she snapped it in two with her bare hands. 'Reforge that, Beomith!'

He was apparently very good at dream weaving, and the sword had, apparently, once been very good at entering the dream realm.

Now it lay broken on the floor.

Lossel skipped over another two students and grabbed a strange knife another young man was holding next to his chest while he slept – he looked like a gedzelai tae'anaryn. Its blade was at right angles to its handle, and didn't seem very easy to wield to Kialessa.

Without waiting Lossel threw the knife so hard it embedded right up to its hilt into the wall.

Kialessa had not believed Raynah when she'd told her about Lossel's enhanced physical strength, but seeing it in action, it was clear now why the young woman commanded so much respect here. And snapping a sword bare handed hadn't even pierced her skin.

Raynah was done waking Mak, but he didn't seem too keen on getting up even with her magic.

So Lossel grabbed him and lifted him up off the ground in one arm,

          By Dr Joe Ireland

looking not at all put out by the effort. 'Hurry, Kia. Let's get out of here before the fighting starts.'

Kialessa looked at the fifty or so students piled on top of each other, sleeping soundly. Students that, she still did not want to believe, might all actually be her half brothers and sisters.

She did not wait to be told a second time.

Lossel

Remember to thank your God for everything; every good, and every bad thing. For if He acts first from love, then nothing ever befell you that could not act for your highest, holiest good and greatest happiness. There are blessings that cause us to rejoice, and there are blessings that hurt. Remember to be thankful, even for the blessings that hurt.

Lady Jacinthia, unnamed sermon, 313CY. Cited in Recollections of the Tae'anaryl.

It looked like a church, with pews, bowls, and candles. There were bookshelves lining every wall, and strange symbols – they looked holy, but made her feel uncomfortable. Kialessa did not feel safe here.

Lossel marched up and threw Mak over the altar. He landed in a pile and protested sleepily.

Kialessa wondered what was going to happen.

Lossel looked down at her, and drew a huge broadsword from an impossibly small sheath on her back. When she placed it, tip down onto the ground, it made an unnaturally loud and thundering crack.

'Never play a game of chance in this place,' Lossel told them. 'Or if you lose a bet you may end up being compelled to defend all new students to this college for the rest of your brief, miserable life. Kia, get behind the altar and do not come out. Understand?'

'No,' Kialessa admitted.

By Dr Joe Ireland

6 Lossel, the humanform battle taint

Raynah placed a hand on her shoulder. 'I imagine you've had a very busy day, Kialessa.' That was an understatement. 'And you need rest. This is the safest place, well, for students at least. And once the fighting starts…'

'I estimate we have around four hours,' Lossel stated.

Raynah nodded. 'Agreed. You need time to process all that is happening here. Once the-'

'Fighting?' Kialessa asked.

'That stuff wears off, hard,' Lossel admitted. 'Kids will fight. We stay here, we stay safe. Daygon will be around sometime after midnight, and then he'll take you on the tour. You'll enjoy that. So rest up while you can.'

Mak stood up, looking glum. He put his wings around him, 'Don't know that I'm tired after that nap.'

'Oh, you will be,' Raynah stated, and with a wave of her hand removed the silver sprinkles from inside Mak.

He fell over sideways and started snoring.

Raynah put her hand on Kialessa's shoulder as well. 'You too, newbie. You'll need your strength. Tomorrow is a very big night. We work only at night here.'

Kialessa looked around. She still did not feel safe here. This was a weird place and these two girls were people she'd only just met.

Raynah tilted her head and gave her a kind smile, 'The chapel is sanctuary to Pumos, god of mysteries and darkness. Tyran Noblax built it. Violence is not accepted here. Once the others wake up they will all be in a very bad mood. Most just wander off, some will pick fights.'

'He likes it when we fight,' Lossel explained, 'He thinks it makes us stronger.'

'Sounds cruel,' Kialessa protested.

Lossel laughed.

Raynah spoke slowly, choosing her words carefully. 'We are… here… to learn how to become stronger. He… needs our strength, to make himself stronger. We are… protected here, but you need to learn how to look after yourself. You're new, and I think the new kids need help.'

'Is that why you are helping?' Kialessa asked Lossel.

'Nope. I made an oath, and I intend to keep it. You will be safe in this room tonight Kialessa, you can sleep out the storm. I promise. I give you my oath.'

Kialessa still did not feel comforted. But she did feel exhausted.

There looked to be nowhere to sleep, so she grabbed some cushions off the pews and made herself a bed. She was just beginning to wonder what to use as a blanket when Lossel spoke.

                    By Dr Joe Ireland

'I've been watching the shadows near you, Kialessa. You're a shadow weaver, why not just use shadow?'

Kialessa wondered about that, was it possible? She reached out and was amazing to find her hand in the shadow realm immediately. It was very close in this fortress. She tried to get her dagger from her magical chest in the castle at Lenmer'el, but it seemed blocked to her for some reason. There was no getting to it at this time. But she pulled out great clumps of shadow weave, it was everywhere.

'You shape it with your soul,' Raynah explained. 'Like this,' she reached out, and touching the weave formed it into a tightly woven blanket with complex stitching. It was amazing. 'It will evaporate by dawn unless you take more specific steps, but it'll do for tonight.'

Kialessa nodded, but squeaked in alarm when she saw the creature that was stalking up behind Raynah. It was a curiosity, but so unnatural. It was like… a "bush" of darkness made of tentacles, with two pupil-less eyes of white light. It looked alien and strange, and yet, also … cute.

Raynah turned, 'Oh look, you summoned a shadow tendriculous!'

The shadow creature plodded around, it seemed to be trying to sneak toward her like some kind of lost puppy. Kialessa was struck with fear, she couldn't not be. She'd never seen anything like it, could it bite her?

The tendriculous shuffled around for a few moments, then snuffled and disappeared back into the shadow realm somewhere near the middle of the room.

Lossel hadn't moved a muscle, but watched the whole scene like it was an everyday thing here.

'Oh I'm jelly,' Raynah mused. 'I need a whole three page scroll to achieve that!'

Kialessa wasn't sure what to feel. The creature didn't seem harmful, but it had popped into existence, or rather, into this reality when Kialessa had put her hand into the shadow realm. This was a strange place.

Raynah pointed at her makeshift bed.

Kialessa sighed, and thanked her. Then, because it felt like the only sensible thing to do in a night gone mad, she reached out, and hugged her.

Raynah seemed uncomfortable, and she was all sinews and bones, but she hugged her and patted her on the back.

Kialessa settled down on her mattress, it would keep her safe from the cold stones, and she hoped Mak would be all right. Raynah walked over and placed a cushion under his head as well.

Lossel and Raynah turned away, Raynah sitting on a pew and reading her book, and Lossel standing guard, sword drawn, before the alter.

Kialessa hid under her blanket and drew from under her armour the hidden memento she was grateful no one had taken from her as yet. It was the religious symbol Darrix had given her. She prayed, very, very sincerely. For peace, and safety. Silently Kialessa took her hardened fingernail and drew a rough circle around herself; for safety and faith in a dark place.

After a moment Kialessa felt surprisingly peaceful, as though an unbreakable promise of safety was extended to her. She looked around and noticed that the stones of the shrine weren't black, but a very, very deep purple. It was calming. The symbols still looked weird, but were no longer threatening to her mind. Somehow in her heart Kialessa knew that everyone she loved was alright – Kiel and her parents would be bitterly upset, but they were still as safe as ever. And that was reassuring. King Dunnkan didn't know where she was, or even that she was in any trouble, but he would soon – by next year if not sooner, and his priestess was very prophetic and very powerful. Kialessa took comfort from the old dwarven priestess's words of hope and faith. With a certain conviction Kialessa knew she would get through this one, and maybe even learn a little along the way.

***

                    By Dr Joe Ireland

Several hours must have passed before Kialessa heard Lossel and Raynah speaking. She realised she was watching them from the dreamworld, something her brother Kiel had taught her how to do this year. She wondered where he was, and was heartbroken to find the entire mountain was cut off from the dreamworld outside as well – she would not find Kiel this way. It was still night, and the fortress was still silent. This time she promised herself she would not forget the dream walking.

'Fire tainted shadow weaver. Wingless, prehensile tail, undersized horns.' Raynah listed, describing Kialessa. She was sitting on the floor near Kialessa and Mak, some kind of divination candle on the floor between them.

Lossel nodded, still facing the door as she turned her head towards them. 'Think she'll be trouble?'

'Hard to say. There's some kind of energy field I'm not familiar with protecting her. I wouldn't mess with this one.'

'The merchant prince called her a dame,' Lossel informed her.

'Of a human land?!' Raynah seemed incredulous. She and Lossel were the most human looking of any other children Kialessa had seen in this place. 'A king's prayers? That would explain the energy field. I wonder how that happened…'

'Is that all?' Lossel asked

Raynah sighed. 'Her soul resonance, her religious measurement. I've only seen it once before.'

'Oh?' Lossel asked.

'In the prophet,' Raynah announced.

'Then she's trouble,' Lossel declared.

The Tour.

Don't wait for something outside of yourself to make you happy. Think how really precious is the time you have to spend, whether it is at work or with your family. Every moment may be enjoyed and savoured.

Nemon, 3rd Sage of Lumos, keeper of times.

A loud thump thundered though the ground, and it woke Kialessa up. She gasped; strange noises echoed through the fortress, sporadic shouts, the clanging of steel swords. Then the sudden thunder of crashing pots and pans.

Kialessa sighed; so the fighting had begun.

She was feeling awake now, and stood up. To her surprise two young tae'anaryn lay on the ground where it looked like Lossel had punched them into unconsciousness. A dark, black cocoon was hanging from the rafters now; it appeared that Mak had adjusted his place while he was asleep. Kialessa's blanket was still intact.

It would be around midnight now. Her brow furrowed; it would take time to get used to this new routine.

'Hey, up! Redling,' Lossel called to her. She looked wide awake, and stood ready and alert. 'Get your beauty sleep?'

Kialessa looked around. The room didn't seem as frightening as the night before. There was something peaceful in the darkness, and comforting in the walls and walls of books hidden behind the thick, mahogany curtains. 'Yes, very well. Thank you, Lossel. Thank you kindly,' she said with a curtsey.

'Call me sis,' Lossel replied, but did not smile.

By Dr Joe Ireland

Kialessa wasn't sure what to make of that.

A horn sounded.

'About time,' Lossel muttered.

Mak roused. 'Morning already?'

'Your luck,' Lossel complained. 'We rise at dusk here, brother. You'd better get used to it.'

Mak stretched and grinned. 'Nope, feels natural. All those walking in the day meant danger, better to rest when they were up and about.' He leapt athletically down from the rafters. He was a head taller than she, at least. His stretched his wings out theatrically, as though warming them from sleep, then flapped them downwards with a deep thud that sent dust swirling in all directions.

'Watch that!' Raynah protested. It seemed she'd been napping on the pew, her book fluttering in Mak's breeze. Her owl popped up from where it had been snuggled under her arm.

That was when Kialessa noticed how quiet it had become. 'What now?' she asked.

'Shouldn't be… oh, there he is,' Lossel replied.

It took Kialessa a moment to hear it, and a dark rage settled on her heart. Solid footfalls. Someone confident was walking quickly in their direction.

Sure enough, it was the demon. He looked briefly at the scene then started speaking. 'Sanctuary, Lossel?'

'Raynah demanded it.'

Tyran nodded. He looked at Raynah. 'You have done well to take care of your newest siblings.'

She just glared at him, hatred in her eyes, 'I did not do this for *you*.' She said, and swallowed heavily several times.

He looked sorry at that, but did not say anything further.

'Where were you?' Raynah asked, looking uncomfortable. 'They're *just children*.'

He glared at her, then softened. 'Yes, I know. You're right, you're right… there's … a lot going on the Great Kingdom at this time. You'll hear all about it after the winter festival, if things don't take a turn for the worse before then.' He turned to look around the chapel, but spoke again to them, 'I'm going to be very busy this season. You'll have to learn your way around quickly, Dame Kialessa and Mak, scourge of Nomer'el. I'm sorry for the added challenge, but that's the way it has to be.'

'Why are there only two this year?' Raynah asked, swallowing.

He ignored her. 'So! My children! You have been properly welcomed; I suppose it's now time to show you around. Daygon!' he called.

An instant later the aged, horned tae'anaryn teleported into the room. He seemed to form a portal of some kind; Kialessa had no idea how that might be accomplished. 'You called, Honoured Father?' he said, bowing with the skilled tact of a diplomat.

'Daygon, please show Kialessa and Mak around –'

'Still can't do it yourself?' Raynah mocked.

'**I am NOT here to cross words with you!**' The demon shouted, and at that voice the ground trembled, and the curtains moved as if by a mighty hand.

Kialessa felt her blood pale with fear. It was a terrifying noise, clearly not designed to harm, but a special kind of frightening she'd not experienced before. Something special for Raynah.

She glared back at him – shaken, but refusing to be cowed.

Kialessa was speechless. If such enchantment had been focused on her she was sure she'd be a trembling ball on the floor by now. Mak was already covering his body with his enormous wings.

The merchant calmed down instantly. 'As I've said. There are important things happening. I am going to be very busy this winter.'

For a moment no one spoke.

Then Lossel cleared her throat. 'Even so, father… Rawhawk is moulting, and you know how Flameheart gets near the winter eclipses.'

'But that's not what you mean, is it?' he asked her.

She glanced in Kialessa's direction.

Tyran seemed to think for a moment. 'Would a little challenge lift your spirits then? Combat practice this evening, in the great hall.'

Lossel grinned.

And to Kialessa's curiosity, so did Raynah.

'So let it be; I'll make the announcement.' And with a nod to Daygon Tyran Noblax sprouted a pair of demon wings and flew from the room faster than it should have been possible.

'That does please me,' Lossel remarked, nodding at Kialessa.

'Means more work for me,' Daygon muttered.

'Oh, come on, big brother!' Lossel patted his shoulder. 'All in training opportunities like this are rare.'

The man at least four times her age sighed. Then seemed to cheer up. 'Very well then! Mak *paladinbane*, and Dame Kialessa Tavernskeep, would you do me the great honour of accompanying me on a small tour of the fortress?'

'Why does everyone call me that?' she wondered out loud.

'Tavernskeep?' Daygon questioned. 'Your mother owns a tavern. It's your family name, or a name of convenience at least.'

'Oh,' Kialessa said, wondering why people had only just starting using it this season. Was it her age now? She would be twelve in a few weeks. She should have been back at home to celebrate it. But for now, a tour? Kialessa hadn't wanted to be shown around the fortress until that moment, and now it sounded very exciting. It was an odd feeling, as though she wanted to be afraid, but when Daygon spoke the world seemed normal again.

Raynah nodded her encouragement.

Kialessa went and stood by his side, and though he offered her his hand, she did not take it.

Mak jumped up on the altar, and with another flap of his wings landed in front of Daygon, placing his hand on the old man's shoulder. 'Sup, bro. Right? How is it that we're bros?'

Daygon grinned as though he really enjoyed having the younger man take such person liberties as touching him in such a condescending manner. 'Ahh my youngest brother. We have a lot to discuss. Come, come,' and he started walking. As he did, he waved his hand and the world twisted together again in a dark purple spiral. Within, an image of the feast hall lay. It was strewn with mess and ruin, but the imps were cleaning it at an impressive pace. Daygon kept walking and talking, but stopped to make sure Kialessa had plenty of time to catch up at her own pace.

'I came here, oh, fifty years ago. Your father, our father, has many children. Many, many children. And we are from all over the Great Kingdom! Yes, many, and mighty. But it's only here that we are safe. I'm sorry to admit, not all of our brothers and sisters make it to this fortress. But we're here. And we learn, and then we go out into the world to make it a better, braver, safer place. At least that's what I like to believe!' and he laughed, a happy, convincing sound. They reached some doors at the end of the hall and went through. It led to a wide, impressive hallway with several doors and branches, but alumium inlaid doors as tall as a tree waited at the end. Statues of exquisite work and beauty lined the halls. 'But I'll admit; it can be tough being here. Not everyone had the benefit of at least one good parent like the both of you two have. And sometimes we take in struggling tae'anaryl from around the region, such as Flameheart. Tyran is not the only father around, you know!'

Daygon walked to the end of the corridor where the doors lay. Opening the palm of his hand, he uttered unpronounceable syllables in a language Kialessa had never heard, but knew to be powerful. 'So, yes, we are here, and it is good. Welcome, welcome my family to the *Sanctum Brumae*, heart and home to the most powerful tae'anaryn to walk the lands in living memory – your father!'

Inside an inspiring throne room lay. It was massive, possibly as large as her king's entire inner keep. Elemental fires of timeless power lit the room, while inlaid metalwork of bronze and silver flowed around it as though they spoke in a language Kialessa had never learnt. The room had a dark majesty about it, and a throne of polished brass sat at the end, surrounded by runes of power. It was truly glorious.

Daygon gave them a moment to appreciate it.

'Woah,' Mak said.

'They say,' Lossel began to explain, and Kialessa was momentarily surprised she was with them. She had not seen her journey with them thus far, her feet were silent. And yet she still carried her sword unsheathed. 'That this fortress was forged by dwarven masons of *civit aurea* millennia ago, and fell into ruin centuries later. But then it was repaired and brought here by arts that father keeps to himself. They say he only sits on the throne thrice a year – when the winter eclipses pass over the sun.'

'Why then?' Mak asked.

'Can you not tell?' Lossel asked.

Mak pondered. 'Nope.'

Kialessa felt she knew. 'He worships Pumos, the god of darkness, doesn't he.' They all looked at her. 'It is the only deity with a shrine I have seen here. And Pumos is most powerful when the moon covers the face of his mortal enemy, the sun god Serros.'

'Well done, well done Kialessa!' Daygon complimented her. 'You learn well.'

Mak did not look pleased, but then again, he hadn't had the benefit of a years' worth of formal education, so he really shouldn't have expected himself to know.

'But there is … one thing you need to understand,' Daygon said, almost in apology.

His voice was soft, but it made Kialessa feel uncomfortable as though she'd said something wrong and was about to be corrected for it. She looked at him.

'Two things, actually.' Daygon said. 'First, Pumos is not the god of darkness and never was. He was and is the god of mysteries, and of wisdom that goes beyond mere knowledge.'

To Kialessa it was clear that Daygon worshiped this dark god as well.

'And, secondly. His name it not Pumos. To all who know him we take his true name from the time of the golden city – Ik'skuretza. The Father of Mysteries,' and with that pronouncement, Daygon bowed.

A chilling breeze filled the room, and the flames danced. Soft whispers filled the air, seeming to speak mysteries Kialessa could not quite catch.

Mak braced himself, but Kialessa waited.

Daygon looked at her carefully. 'I see you are one who has already reached up to the divine.'

She looked at him, not agreeing or disagreeing. But he was very right.

Daygon nodded. 'That is a most precious gift.'

They stood there a moment till the whispers subsided.

Daygon bowed his head. 'There is truth in darkness, and you were made to see that truth,' he told them, waiting for a moment. 'Come, we have tarried long enough in this powerful temple.'

Kialessa was inclined to agree. In all her studies she'd learned almost nothing of … Ik'skuretza. The humans she'd grown up with loved the sun god, but now she stood in a hall devoted to his mortal enemy. Yet for all that hatred, Ik'skuretza was still honoured by the humans as the god of nighttime and of the underworld. He was named at every funeral. His symbol was there in every token of the great pantheon of the seven gods that ruled the world. He had an entire day devoted to him – as far away as possible from Serrosday. The more she thought about it, the more she realised that they treated him as unwelcomed, but not necessarily evil. But who was he – apart

By Dr Joe Ireland

from being the sun god's older brother?

And did she really want to know?

Well, she reasoned, *if my enemy worships him, I would do well to get to know him anyway.*

A glint of purple caught her eye, and she wondered if her sight was playing tricks on her. Had a reflection of the strange fires combined with certain angles on the bronze inlays to form an odd… symbol to her mind? Would Ik'skuretza work like that?

It was distinctly possible.

She tried to recall the image but it was already gone from her mind. It made her feel nervous.

'Come,' Daygon offered her his hand, and she eagerly took the comfort. 'Let us see the rest of this marvel.'

They wandered the fortress for the rest of the night. There were scores of rooms, possibly hundreds. Kialessa was quickly lost, but found there was a kind of spiral pattern to it all as most rooms soon led towards the great hall once more.

They were just passing through a black cathedral made of pure stone when a woman's voice shouted from the roof, 'Stay your hooves, for you trespass Shadowmonger's domain!' Rippling fire ran along the roof, and there was a crack as though from a mighty whip.

'Calm yourself, Flameheart!' Daygon replied. 'We take the new ones on a tour for our father.'

The air rumbled. 'He has not place sending them here. Till we die, this is ours.'

Lossel stood forward, looking angry.

Daygon put his hand on her sword arm, and she paused instantly. 'There are other paths,' he whispered.

Suddenly someone jumped down from the ceiling. It was the black boy, with wings of shadow. He rose up, looking twice as tall as anyone here till

Kialessa realised he was levitating.

Lossel stood back, this was not a fight she was going to start. 'Shadowmonger,' she inclined her head.

He acknowledged Lossel, then glanced at Kialessa and Mak. 'So, I get to see the new ones close up, finally. Kialessa Tavernskeep and Mak of Nomer'el.' He spoke the words as though he tested them on his tongue, tasting them for weaknesses he could exploit. She couldn't not feel nervous. He had not participated in the feast the night before. Neither, presumably, had Flameheart. 'Do you like the place?'

Kialessa was silent.

'Seems nice,' Mak said with a cheeky grin.

Shadowmonger looked down at him with gentle disdain. He was not impressed. 'I was asking the lady, sir.'

Kialessa looked up at him, 'I miss my home.'

He bent his head, 'It will do you no good to complain,' he told her. 'Father does not take to such ingratitude.'

The ground rumbled gently.

Shadowmonger grinned, looking at Daygon. 'Ka is also upset that he didn't get to sit at the grownups table last light. I would not go further down this corridor if I were you,' he advised.

Daygon bowed, 'Good Master, please -'

The ground thundered.

Kialessa did not feel like going any further down that corridor.

'I'm game,' Mak shrugged.

Now Shadowmonger looked annoyed. 'That would be because, *caterpillar*, they haven't told you yet: You don't get a room in this fortress – you earn it. You *fight* the previous owner and *claim* your own space.'

Again, the earth thundered. Ka must have been *livid*.

'Sounds fine to me,' Mak said, crossing his arms.

Shadowmonger scoffed. 'Just like all the other caterpillars. So arrogant.

     By Dr Joe Ireland

Just you wait until you learn the full truth about this place.'

'I can't wait to see the look on his face when that happens,' Flameheart uttered from the roof, and it momentarily lit up.

Mak balled his hands into fists.

Lossel put up her hand to keep them from fighting right there and then.

Daygon did nothing, as though this kind of challenging and fighting happened around here all the time.

It did not seem a very well supervised place to Kialessa. Dozens of angry teenagers and next to no grownup supervision? It was the very recipe for disaster.

But Shadowmonger just grinned sarcastically, 'Well, maybe you'll learn some humility during the battle at dusk. Till then, caterpillars.' And with that, he shot up to the roof in a single wingbeat.

Mak waited until they were well out of earshot to reply, 'Yeah, let's see, Mucker.'

Lossel shook her head, 'He probably heard that, caterpillar,' she said with a grin.

'Let him,' Mak muttered quietly.

***

They travelled several more hours. Daygon showed them how to locate the washrooms, several with magical taps and refuse-devouring toilets. But all the best rooms seemed to be higher up. Several even had resident siblings that had to be placated by Daygon in order to let them pass without incident. Aside from the event with Flameheart and Shadowmonger he always seemed to know the right thing to say. But it made a confusing venue into a veritable *labyrinth* with all the no-trespass zones where the other students had tried to carve out a space for themselves.

Then they entered the archives. It was large, but not extravagant. It held at least a dozen roof-to-floor bookcases, laid out in a star pattern around an ornate blue stone summoning circle inlaid with gold and silver runes. Kialessa thought it was very pretty. A dark owl swooped down across her view and flew to the other end of the room.

'You always save the best room for last, don't you Daygon,' a voice called. It was Raynah's.

'We're not halfway through!' Daygon protested.

'Perhaps,' Lossel replied. 'But here is where I leave you. Mak, Kia, good riddance – see you at the dawn battle!' and she walked off.

Raynah walked up, preening her owl. Her bracers and cloak covered her scars already.

'Well, I guess sanctuary's over,' Mak remarked.

'Oh, don't mind her,' Raynah said of Lossel, trying to look unflustered but doing a pretty poor job of it. 'It's her oath. But, yes, now she's… "off duty" I suppose you'd, um. Well…'

'Well?' Mak pressed.

'Let's just say you best don't take anyone here for granted,' Daygon said.

That bothered Raynah. 'She's not your friend, Mak. She's just keeping a promise. Remember that; you can't rely on her.'

'Oh, don't be so harsh,' Daygon pled, making Raynah sound ridiculous.

'You know it's true,' she said with cold conviction, dispelling any impression that her words were ill chosen. 'Remember that, Kialessa and Mak. No one is your friend here despite what *he* says,' she gestured at Daygon.

He glanced at her condescendingly, and she swallowed several times.

Then she huffed, sighed, and continued. 'Well, best to make the most of it then!' She turned. 'Welcome, my brother and sister, to *my* domain. The archives.'

Kialessa looked around. There were more than books; there were scrolls, codices, even clay tablets. Strange rods with elven runes, and dwarven knowledge stones. And on the study desk Raynah seemed to be using an open book and a crystal ball.

Raynah noticed Kialessa looking, and for a moment seemed to forget her distress. 'Some of the most powerful words from this entire world lie in this room, Kialessa of Lenmer'el.'

At that name Kialessa turned to face her. 'Oh, your face makes that little scowl thing whenever anyone calls you "Tavernskeep." I've noticed.' Raynah continued to admire the books. 'I've read every last one of them. It's a goal I had, before I die.'

Daygon looked at her in alarm, but Raynah didn't seem to go into one of her trademarked choking fits.

Raynah caressed a book's spine. 'You'd be impressed. Our father keeps almost all his personal research here, except the business transactions. Those he keeps with his scribes in Emerel, or so I'm told.'

'What does he research?' Kialessa wondered, looking for an edge.

'Oh, not so much nowadays,' Raynah confessed. 'Mostly conjuring, for the hall of trials. But there's a fair bit of inflornum and mentium, from the old days. Last century, I mean.'

It put a bit of perspective on it. Was he really more than a hundred years old? He looked barely in his fifties.

'Do you like books?' Raynah said, looking at her.

'Yes.' Kialessa replied, thinking of someone she knew who liked books a whole lot more than she did. 'But I'm afraid I'm not a very good reader. I only started this year.'

'Perhaps I'll teach you,' Raynah replied, and it made Kialessa smile. 'If you help me out with a few things.' And Kialessa didn't smile so broadly. 'You, Mak?' Raynah asked.

'I can read,' he replied, 'Mum taught me,' and Kialessa couldn't help but feel a little jealous. 'But I prefer it when someone reads to me.'

'Good luck with *that*,' Raynah replied.

Mak grinned.

Kialessa guessed he would not be getting much reading in during his stay here.

'I need… chores.' Raynah replied. 'Favours. Just like everyone else here I suppose – chores run, spell reagents. New ink, that sort of thing. I can help you read and teach you what I know, if you think you can trust me?'

Kialessa was suspicious. Why was she asking for trust? But at least it would fill up her days, and possibly help her find an ally in a confusing and indifferent fortress.

'I'll help you,' Kialessa said, and felt her voice come out surprisingly strong at that promise.

Raynah looked touched.

'Please, wizardess,' Daygon said to Raynah, 'We still haven't picked out a room yet for these young ones.'

'Oh, you're not going to like that,' she muttered, and turned away.

'Come, young ones,' Daygon offered.

'You will give them blankets, won't you?' Raynah's voice begged from among the shelves.

Daygon looked genuinely troubled at that, 'Of course, we're not monsters!'

'Besides, shouldn't there be extras this year?' Mak grinned.

'More than likely,' Daygon replied.

'So… just how many kids usually arrive each year?' Mak wondered out loud.

'Six.' Raynah called from the other end of the room. 'It would be a dozen but the others die before they…'

She said no more, but struggled for breath at the other side of the room.

'Come, children,' Daygon whispered. 'We'd best stop stressing the only capable wizard around with our little concerns.'

Kialessa vowed to herself that she would one day free Raynah from whatever oppressed her, if she could.

***

The accommodations were miserable. Daygon had to take them deep, below the basement and into the cavern below the fortress. Nine rough alcoves were carved out of the limestone and granite there, with a trickling stream that kept the air moist. There were no beds, just patches on the ground where the previous owners had made camp, until they'd secured for themselves better lodgings.

But they'd taken everything with them, except the graffiti on the walls. There were no pillows, no blankets. Not even a mattress.

Daygon coughed uncomfortably, 'Well, um, yes. Not to matter, I'm sure there's something we can do about this. But you'll be pleased to notice the room has… plenty of space, and cold running water. There's a privy at the far end. I'll see about the blankets.'

'No you won't,' Mak pronounced.

'Brother,' Daygon said with indignity. 'I can't leave you like this, I won't!'

'Yeah, you will. You think we're blind? It's every tae'anaryn for themselves in this fortress, and the merchant father likes to keep it that way. He's got fifty plus kids here so there's no time for newies like us. Besides, you said yourself you're busy. You'll forget us, we'll see.'

'Oh Mak,' Daygon said, the pity fairly oozing from him.

It was clear to Kialessa what Mak was trying to do. He was trying to pull at old Daygon's heart strings to take a little extra pity on them. It felt like it was working, but Daygon was too hardened or wise, or perhaps he really was too busy to get drawn into Mak's guilt trip.

'I can't promise you an easy time here. It has to be that way, in order to help you bring out your best! But, yes, if you feel you have any needs, I'll see what I can do. The imps can be very… resourceful.'

'I could use some straw for a bed,' Kialessa thought out loud, wishing they would just let them sleep in the chapel again. But sanctuary was over, and she suspected visitors were not welcomed there any time they liked. She was twice a mind to go and steal some pew cushions from the extravagant chapel. But then again, Ik'skuretza might not be too impressed. And Kialessa was unwilling to upset too many powerful individuals at a time, and if she could, never a deity – the man who called himself her father was enough.

'I'll get the straw, and we have some chests you can keep your belongings in, I'll get it set up right away, you will see. Do you like red? We have several bolts of fabric you can use to spruce the cavern up a little – on loan of course. I'm sorry; it really is the best I can do for you at the time. The other rooms are full.'

'I doubt it,' Mak disagreed.

Kialessa could see his point, the other kids held onto their space like it was all they owned. If they could grab extra space to hold as insurance against losing their domain, all the better. Kialessa and Mak would not be getting any better accommodation than a wet cavern this year.

It pricked her heart with fear. How she'd fought, how she'd borne with every insult and unkindness just to get her own mattress and sheep wool rug! Now it was gone, locked away in a far off castle that might one day forget her name.

She pushed back that thought; it bore with it a dark depression. Daygon was right – the cavern was better than nothing. They could build a fire; the fire pit was still there. And they could find blankets or make them – they would probably have to make them even if all they had initially was shadow weave. They had water on hand at any time. It ran down the cavern and disappeared into the floor at the other end. They would be safe enough in this dingy cavern from any other students coveting their domain.

'It will do,' Kialessa announced.

                    By Dr Joe Ireland

Daygon seemed relieved.

'Do?!' Mak was incensed. He flew around the room, and was very unimpressed. 'We've got no space here, no bedding. This place is a dump Kialessa – it's a dungeon.'

She nodded.

'I'll see what I can do,' Daygon promised.

'Yeah, you do that!' Mak grumbled, and settling himself on a far rock above the stream folded his wings about him.

Daygon nodded to her, looking unimpressed at Mak and sympathetically at her. Then he teleported out and into the kitchens.

Kialessa looked around, wondering where they might hole up. The nearest fire pit seemed the largest and most used, perhaps it would do. She tried to make a shadow blanket, but it just wasn't working in the damp, forgotten cavern.

'This place is a dump Kia. I can't believe we're in here.'

Kialessa thought for a moment. 'He wants us to fight the older kids, Mak. He makes us fight for a place to stay.'

'I suppose it's one way to help us feel like we're not in a prison,' he muttered.

In a strange sense it was relieving to Kialessa to hear that. At least Mak wasn't ignoring the truth. He knew he was a prisoner here too.

'I miss my sewer,' Mak muttered. 'At least it had my reading lamp, and keepsakes. Jasmin wouldn't even let me take them.'

Kialessa felt she knew why, 'So not even your mother could track you by divining your personal items. I've heard it can be done.'

Mak looked miserable, and flew over to sit at the dead fireplace. He just sat there, a bundle of wings. Then he got tearful.

She walked over, but he moved away. Then he wiped his tears. 'We need to start practicing. C'mon Kia, will you be on my team?'

She nodded, grateful for at least one ally in this place.

'They say there's combat training soon. Sounds like fun, well, more fun than fighting for your life which is all I've ever done. You from a college, they teach you how to fight there? C'mon Kia, I need to show you my moves.'

She nodded. Time for combat training.

 By Dr Joe Ireland

Combat Training

But the fight was gone from me. This was not about improving ourselves; it was all about making us fight for a prize that did no one any good. It was madness. This… was evil.

Recollections of the Tae'anaryl.

'Capture the flag,' Kialessa pronounced as soon as they entered the arena.

The cavern was set out with an active volcano in the centre, and Kialessa wasn't sure if it was real or illusionary. The entire scene tilted uphill towards the peak. All other students gathered in groups around the base of that hill. Nine groups in all. They seemed to be arranged in year levels, but it was a bit hard to tell. Some of the students had to be older than their teammates, making things look like they were arranged in alliances more than age. But no group had more members than six, and Kialessa and Mak were in a team of their own. No one joined them. Lossel was leading another group and didn't even look at them.

And at the top of the volcano, looking decidedly dangerous, was the group of the four oldest students at the college. Kialessa recognised them all; Flameheart was a pale skinned tae'anaryn with burning coal wings and fire for hair. Ka was the stone giant tae'anaryn, and his legs seemed to grow out of the stones at his feet like they were carved from it. Rawhawk was odd, he had a beak, his legs and wings entirely hawk like. He wielded twin scimitars that looked far too deadly for any training event. And then Shadowmonger, clearly their leader. Despite the light of the volcano, he was wreathed in shadows, and they danced about him as if they waited eagerly to take any form he desired. He was holding out two swords of gloss black, made entirely from shadow.

And there, in a golden frame suspended above the middle of the active caldera, was the horn of plenty.

Daygon was making an announcement through the air, his voice magically enhanced. 'Last week's winning team hold the high ground, defending their title. Each team has a chance of claiming that ground if they can capture the horn of plenty before they are defeated by the winning team or all pretenders to that prize. If every team surrenders before any have touched the horn the winning team continues to claim their prize for yet another week, as they have successfully managed to do so far all this year! They, alone, will feast on a single drop each in their ambrosial wine. Combatants… begin!!'

A group of students, possibly the second oldest, rushed the hill. Before they were even halfway there a group of youth, possibly the second youngest, attacked Kialessa and Mak.

Kialessa barely had a moment to register their faces before Mak, with a thump of his powerful wings, smashed into all six of them at once. They crashed to the ground, but several recovered almost immediately.

Mak was about to charge the third years who were working their way around the back of the hill towards Flameheart's side when a second year unleashed a scything whip of twisting air that tripped Mak over on his face. Two of the second youngest students were there in a second, punching him fiercely on his back and head. There was nothing dignified about it. They were brutish, cruel attacks at an already fallen opponent. If they'd had knives, they probably would have used them.

Kialessa's raced to protect Mak, her only weapon her whip. She set it on fire, and cracked it above their heads. They backed off.

Mak got up, his lip bleeding black blood. They stood back-to-back as the other students surrounded them, though one seemed to have lost interest, and another seemed knocked out cold by Mak's initial charge.

'We need to hold back, sit this one out,' Kialessa told him.

'Nope, won't be doing that,' Mak replied.

She grinned. But she knew they had no chance. She didn't even know what other powers these four possessed, apart from a blind rage right now.

She turned aside to watch a student feint an attack, and as she guessed another student charged her. She back-flipped over them and with a kick sent them both into the soil. The second student just lay there, crying.

This was not like combat training at the college at all. There were no healers. Indeed, there seemed to be almost no rules.

Another student attacked her with a club, and the glancing blow hurt. She wrapped her fire whip around his leg intending to trip him, but he cried out in pain. With a stab of regret she realised he was not immune to fire, as she was.

Quickly she dismissed her magic and helped him remove the whip. He was hurt. She tried to apologise but he slapped her on her head, and then he curled up in a sorry looking ball. He looked like a child. A helpless, outclassed, lost child that was not supposed to be in this sort of situation.

She felt sick in her stomach. Kialessa just looked around. The battles were heading up towards the summit. Mak was still wrestling with two of his assailants, and they seemed much more evenly matched now. Rolling and punching like kids in the dirt. It might have even looked like Mak was holding back.

But the fight was gone from Kialessa. This was not about improving themselves; it was all about making them fight for a prize that did no one any good. It was madness. This… was evil.

She looked up at the hill. The younger students weren't even trying, but the second oldest students were pushing the middle aged students right into the fray.

The battle was joined. It was fierce, and fast. They fought with elemental prowess Kialessa had never before witnessed. Lighting flew through the air from someone's sword. Someone tried to slide through the stone, but with a twist of his foot Ka sent them flying up into the air and they rolled painfully down the mountain. Flameheart breathed fire on half a dozen more, some shielding others with their wings or shields enchanted from the air.

But it was clear the oldest students were just toying with them. Within a few moments the middle students were retreating.

And that was when the second oldest students struck. *That* was fierce. This was the **real battle**. Rawhawk swooped among them with fevered haste, exchanging blows that were too fast to see. Flameheart let out a billowing plume and it just kept on growing. The fire turned into wild beasts; posks, drakes, hounds. They leapt about on their own will attacking the second year students. Ka slipped into the mountain and began to punch out from the solid stone.

But the second year students were holding their own. Lossel was among them, cleaving up flame beasts with her broadsword even as the any others her age fled. Ka took a hit and was thrown out of the stone and onto his back. Rawhawk was suddenly wrapped up by conjured leather ropes. Flameheart's hounds were doused with glacial winds, and many died.

Then Shadowmonger acted. The entire volcano was wrapped in shadow weave. Great fronds of it lashed out at each and every combatant, even his own team. The second year students battled bravely on, but were forced back. In the flurry of dark tentacles Shadowmonger's allies stood up.

And by the time the enchantment was spent, the oldest students stood, ready again to fight.

Everyone else looked exhausted from the climb and their battle. Almost as one, they lowered weapons.

Flameheart screamed in victory and hefted the horn from its stand with a twisting whip made of air. The other students applauded politely, or glared at them with hatred in their eyes.

     By Dr Joe Ireland

The battle was won.

***

The mood was much more subdued at the dawn dinner. People were very bruised. The boy that Kialessa had burned glared at her fiercely, but seemed too scared to pick any more fights about it. His leg was bandaged but it looked poor. The second-year students were, clearly, under resourced.

Lossel's group, the seventh years even though she was supposed to be a sixth-year student, seemed quite hale. Kialessa's best guess was that there was a healer among them. She did not know who it was, but there was some fifth-year gnome tae'anaryn boy with antlers who seemed overly fond of unctions and potions, and she had to assume he was an alchemist of some skill perhaps.

She looked at the younger students again, the boy picking at his bandage. If there was any way Kialessa could have helped that boy – maybe put some ice on his leg or anything. But she had nothing to give. Only fire and the promise of more pain. There was nothing she could do to help him.

Or, she feared, anyone here. Some of them were truly dangerous. But the oldest students weren't here tonight; they feasted at the demon's table.

Kialessa was poking at her steak, wondering if she could find the courage to ask someone to pass the salt, when there was a small, 'Bah,' at her feet.

She looked down to find the six-year-old sitting there.

Unconsciously she flinched away; that child had very sharp teeth.

The little girl wined like a puppy, she looked so very pitiful. She put up her hooves like a dog begging.

Kialessa wasn't sure what to do.

'She always tries to bite the people who feed her,' a second-year student claimed. Most weren't watching the scene, but the students at this end of the table were.

'Like this,' another girl said, with purple skin and sharp horns. She put a small plate on the floor next to the child, and dumped a potato and some pumpkin on the plate.

The child bent down and ate it, not caring at all if she knocked it onto the floor. If Kialessa hadn't seen her face, she might have mistaken her for a young goat with a dress on.

Students laughed to themselves.

'So,' a third year addressed her. 'You're a mean shot with that whip, Tavernskeep. That was pretty impressive stuff.'

Kialessa did not feel impressive. She felt robbed. Robbed of a normal life and dignified childhood.

Things seemed to get uncomfortable for the other students.

'That word you used,' a second year student said. '*Ignis*. Dragon speech. I didn't know sorcery used language like that.' She seemed sincere. She was the girl who'd stopped fighting once Mak had wacked her with his wings.

'It's not. It's wizardry.'

'Flames, you're a wizard too!' another student said.

Kialessa shook her head. 'No. But I learnt a little.'

'Is it true that you went to the college at Lenmer'el?' A boy with red horns asked.

She wondered how he might have heard that. She nodded.

They seemed impressed. 'Like, actual real college? Almost no one gets that, 'cept Lossel.'

The warrior seemed to have heard her name, and looked over. But the other students pretended to have not said anything.

But their curiosity kept them talking. They wanted to know all about the college, and the king, and the training. They seemed amazed, even jealous. Even Mak kept silent to learn about it. They laughed when she told them about the time Posk tamed a drake, or when Allastassia almost levelled the college hall. They were most impressed to hear about battle training, and Kialessa wanted them to know about the priests of faith who would heal them.

'Oh, we need more of them!' a boy again said.

'Yeah, well, the prophet – ' the burnt boy started to say, but was soon shushed down.

They continued eating for a moment. Kialessa took the chance to look at the boy she'd burned. 'I'm sorry I burnt your leg,' she apologised.

He huffed, chin up. Then he put his foot on the table and pulled down his bandage. The skin underneath was red and raw, but the burn was not too deep. 'This'll only make me stronger, you will see. One day, when I am covered with these scars, I will be immune to fire. Like you.'

Kialessa wasn't sure that was how it happened, but it might be possible. Even so, it was a brutal way to develop fire resistance. 'Very well,' she tried to agree.

Kialessa looked down, and noticed the little girl had stopped eating. With almost prescient instinct Kialessa moved her leg out of the little girl's clenching mouth as she lunged forward and tried to bite her. Missing, the little girl scurried away into the darkness.

It made Kialessa cringe, and the other students laughed.

It was hard not to smile, though the situation was very, very strange.

They ate on, and Kialessa slowly began to feel she was gaining a little respect. But they were not her friends.

***

Kialessa and Mak walked into the damp, dripping cavern.

Amber, one of the third year girls from the dinner table, was carrying a lantern and a blanket for them. 'It's not much, but I wasn't using it anymore. I hope you'll be all right.' She was a tallish young girl, with leaf and vine motifs embedded in her skin, green eyes, and long, soft green hair. She had angular features, pointy ears and pointy edges to her eyes, like most beings with fey or fairy heritage. Small patterned wings emerged from her back and fluttered in the dimness.

Kialessa looked at the dank cavern. One blanket for them both would not be enough.

She wished for the sanctuary of the strange god's chapel again.

7 Amber, the moth winged fey taint

'I'm sorry,' Amber muttered, somehow guessing her thoughts. 'You can only claim sanctuary once a year.'

'We'll be fine,' Mak promised her.

'You can sleep in the kitchen, if you get too cold,' Amber explained. 'The imps aren't too bad if you command them to shut up. At least you won't freeze to death, like you will sleeping all day in here.'

Kialessa nodded. It still felt so strange to her body to be trying to sleep now as dawn was bright over the horizon. And it would be no easier in this

By Dr Joe Ireland

wet, damp cave. But she yawned anyway, she was exhausted!

'I hope you'll be all right here,' Amber whispered to them.

Kialessa looked at her. Her eyes were a strange, iridescent colour. Maybe part dryad? It was hard to tell. 'Thank you for your kindness,' Kialessa said.

Mak looked at her, as though she'd said something wrong.

'People aren't kind here, Kialessa. You'd best watch yourself,' Amber said, though it seemed to make her sad.

Kialessa sat in the dirt. Daygon had made good on his promise for a small pile of hay and some firewood, but it would not last the day. Mak sat down beside her. 'Would you like me to light it?' Kialessa offered, hoping her wizardry could be useful tonight. She'd forgotten Amber was carrying a lantern.

'I got this,' Mak boasted. He ripped up some wood to make some kindling using nothing but his claws, and split apart a few twigs to make some workable kindling. Then he took two of the smoothest pieces of wood and rubbed them fiercely together. She'd never seen anyone do it by hand before, but within moments they were smouldering, then the kindling burst into flames.

Amber looked very impressed, and a little worried.

Mak kept the fire burning like an expert. He clearly knew fire, though was not immune to it. The logs would burn well tonight.

Amber sniffed. 'It's just so unfair,' she muttered.

'What'd ya mean?' Mak asked.

She sat down daintily. It seemed she'd been well trained in manners somewhere. She was… delicate. 'Some of us tae'anaryn… you're just so talented. Skin that does not burn and superior strength. But what do I get? Nothing. My bones break as easily as anyone's. Wings that don't work. I'm not smart like Raynah, and I don't just reach out like Shadowmonger and find a sword in my hand! I'm going to die in this place.' And she sniffed.

Mak looked over at Kialessa.

She slid closer, willing to put an arm around Amber if she'd let her. 'What makes you say that?'

Amber looked at her, but said nothing.

Kialessa tried to say something helpful, 'A wise man once told me that there's no one of insignificance, we can all make a difference.'

Amber was tearing up now. 'I miss my mother,' she said, and burst into tears.

Now Kialessa hugged her. Mak went to pushing the logs in the fire. He did not scowl or leave, but stared at the fire as though he knew Amber's feelings all too well himself.

Suddenly Amber seemed angry, and stood up. Kialessa immediately felt the twingle of magic as it worked its way from the fey tae'anaryn. It felt like an enchantress's talent – unworked, and unskilled. 'But our mothers aren't coming for us, Kialessa, and we are not getting out of this fortress. So I have to make it on my own!'

The change was so sudden, and abrupt. It reminded Kialessa of something she'd learnt about fairies long ago – that they are so small they only have room for one emotion at a time, and they always feel that emotion very powerfully.

Without another word Amber swept up her lantern and stalked to the door. 'I'm sorry, I … just… go and see Raynah tomorrow, Kialessa. She has a fire spell that sets on stone. It will keep you warm.'

Kialessa thought that sounded like a wonderful idea. But she was still hurting. What was she supposed to do to help Amber be her friend? She was already too upset to help.

'Like I said,' Mak repeated, 'We'll be fine.'

Amber's lip trembled and her eyes filled with tears. Then swinging around she walked quickly away, almost as though she regretted helping them in the first place.

The fire was cheery, but the room was far too large for the heat to make

By Dr Joe Ireland

a meaningful difference.

'I don't mind sleeping in a kitchen,' Kialessa told her brother. 'I grew up in one.'

He spread his wings. 'We're not sleeping with those… creepy little imps tonight. I have never needed a blanked in my whole life.' He spread his wings wide. 'C'mon sis, there's room for one more under these wings.'

She was too cold and too tired to care.

Mak spread the blanket on the ground. They snuggled up beside the dancing flames, Mak wrapping his wings about her. They felt like cured leather, and seemed to pulse with his heartbeat. His body was warm, but so large were his wings she didn't need to press up against him. She hoped he would be all right, pressed between cold stones and a sleeping tae'anaryn.

She snuggled down, trying to dream about her family and her friends. Trying to dream about anything. It took her an hour, till the realisation dawned on her that there were no dreams in this fortress. Dimly she wondered if it had been closed off to the dream realm somehow. It made her so terribly sad as she fell to sleep, *Not even Kiel can find me here…*

Favours for the Wizard

I needed a favour from this wizard as well, and carrying a little box would make me more a servant than a helpful friend. But I couldn't back out now. How was I to ask a favour? How to point out the task was beneath my dignity as a friend, and that I was not a servant?

From 'The Year in Jail'.

It felt strange to be having breakfast at sundown, but that was the way it was. Students were feeding themselves in orchestrated chaos, and Kialessa found she had to wait quite a bit to get a chance to eat. Yet she had to admit, the food was quite excellent.

She sat near Mak while he chatted with the others, and she nibbled miserably at the sour dough bread she'd buttered, when suddenly there was a stir at the other end of the room. In walked at least four of the older students, their leader a hulking, half-bear tae'anaryn of some kind Kialessa did not recognise.

Amber called him an eighth year student. 'They've been hunting all day,' the part fey girl explained. 'Father expects it of the older students to help supplement the food supplies over winter.'

The older boy stalked to a large chair and threw his bow on the table in disgust.

'Aww, things not going so well for you, Plough?' Lossel teased.

'Shut up,' he told her.

'He's just remembering that stag you took down last week,' Lossel's

By Dr Joe Ireland

friend teased the older boy as well.

He glared at them, 'Where's the food!' he shouted at the imps.

'This is all your fault,' another of the older boys accused him.

Plough said nothing, but glared at his hands.

'Go on,' Lossel's friend said.

'Bear boy gets all caught on a scent… says we need to get it. Turns out to be a dead end, the creature got clean away long before we even got a glimpse.'

'Would'a been worth it if you'd just shut up,' Plough said.

'Yeah, right,' the other boy protested, he was a tall boy with Kudu horns and four bat wings.

Plough just simmered.

Lossel looked at him sincerely, however. It seemed she believed the story, 'What got you so interested?' she asked him.

'The fortress is sealed with powerful protections,' Plough seemed to say out loud to no one in particular, 'a dark prison. Space bends back in on itself. That creature should not have been able to escape that way at all.'

'Father will not be pleased if something is breaching the protections on his sanctum,' Lossel's friend noted.

'What do you suppose could have accomplished that?' Lossel's other friend asked. Kialessa wasn't sure if she was curious, hopeful, or afraid.

One of the bear tae'anaryn's friends hit him, 'Go on, tell them your theory.'

Plough seemed reluctant.

'Well?' Lossel demanded.

The older boy muttered, 'Unshod hooves, deep set, wide stride. It should not have been able to get out that way. It's a unicorn. I know it.'

Some students seemed amused, but none mocked him. One or two whistled as though impressed.

'Would have to be a very powerful one to get into and out of the fortress grounds with such ease,' Lossel muttered. 'Father will need to hear about this.'

'Already knows,' the older boy muttered, stretching out and leaning backwards, 'What's the keep up!' he roared at the imps. They scurried out almost immediately with a big plate of meat.

'Strange omen,' Amber muttered.

'What do you mean?' Mak asked.

She paused. 'Why would a unicorn come so close to the fortress? And why in winter when there is such little light for them to draw upon? Unicorns are very magical, and very powerful. But I have never heard of any that could match the power of our father.'

Mak shrugged, and kept eating. 'You know, I think my mother actually loved him, once. He built her a home and everything. She tells me he was great for the first season. But after that he never stopped by. I saw him, once, when I was four. I heard them argue. Next day, mum just takes me away and we run. I honestly never knew we were running from him. Guess I now know why.'

It was a strange confession, Kialessa thought, but valuable information.

Suddenly there was a mighty booming noise from the entrance, three times as if someone was knocking.

Students ran. Kialessa followed along with the others to see what was happening. They reached the front doors and she scurried up with the others towards the freezing barbican. She had to run to keep up, and had never wished she could fly more than right now among all the other tae'anaryl. Some even seemed to be able to run up stone; they were so fleet and athletic.

She ran up the stairs to the inner wall, peering up, trying to see who had knocked on the front gate. To her surprise, it was an old man. He looked human, with a thick travel coat and broad rimmed, pointed brown hat.

'Ahoy!' the old man shouted.

She gasped. She knew him! It was the old storyteller. The old man who

By Dr Joe Ireland

stopped at the inn each and every winter just before the eclipses. She could not believe he was here.

'Ahoy! Good folks of the fortress!' he shouted.

'Shove off!' Rawhawk replied from the gatehouse. 'We don't need your stories this season, old man!'

He looked visibly disappointed. 'Please, I really must! There's an old story I never had the chance to finish-'

He was cut off as the dark skinned Shadowmonger, with black feathered wings enlarged with shadow weave, leaped down from the tower in front of him.

The old man stumbled backwards. 'A thousand apologies, good master. I do not mean to intrude-'

'Get out,' the young man told him.

The storyteller bowed his head. 'Shadowmonger… please… have mercy. You would not turn out an old man in this weather? I'll write my death of cold in this winter!'

Shadowmonger glared at him. 'You know father does not welcome the presence of your kind, or your tales, in this place. Get out, before you upset him again.'

The storyteller nodded sadly. He glanced around, as if looking for someone. 'Very well, very well, I know when I'm not wanted.'

He turned to leave, and her heart went out to him. If she called him, he might know her voice, and he might be able to tell her parents. But if he did, then his own life might be in jeopardy, and she did not want that. Then again, if he knew where the fortress was, and if he came by to tell his stories once in every while… there might yet be a chance to escape, or at least get a message to her king.

Her knuckles turned white as she watched him walk away, her heart breaking, desperately hoping he could at least feel her pain, and know she was here.

'What is it, Tavernskeep?' A cold voice said.

Kialessa turned, and gasped. It was Flameheart, up close. She was a pretty young elven woman, with dark orange hair and wings made of smouldering rods of black coal. Her body was a snake from the waist down. She glared at Kialessa, as if almost begging her to give her an excuse to attack.

Kialessa pressed her back up against the wall, keeping a very close eye on the towering woman.

Mak stood up to the older girl, looking unafraid. 'You turn an old man away from shelter? He'll die out there.'

She just glared at him. 'If he lay on a bed of broken glass, one such as he would wake well rested in the morning,' she replied cryptically.

'Flameheart, you coming?' Rawhawk called. The older girl sneered at them condescendingly, and stepped back. Then her wings burst into flames, and she few away.

Mak and Kialessa shared a look, but neither dared press the point.

Kialessa stretched up the tall crenulations to see the shadow of the old man walking down the darkened path, desperately hoping she might see him again. But dusk was here, and she needed to get to work.

***

'Why aren't there more wizards here?' Kialessa asked.

Raynah was putting the finishing touches on a scroll she'd been writing all night. Even her owl looked tired. 'Lazy,' she proclaimed. 'Tae'anaryl. Well, most tae'anaryl, are lazy. They prefer the "effortlessness" of enchantments that flow directly from their soul. But my mother taught me reading, and arithmetic, and astrology from as early on as I can remember. I like to keep things organised. I like to know *why* they work, and *how* they work. *That's* why I'm a wizard!' She said it proudly, as though it was one of the few treasures she could hold on to in this place.

                     By Dr Joe Ireland

Most other students were milling about the fortress. There were hundreds of rooms to explore, and board games in the main hall. Kialessa had found none to her liking, though Mak took to the card games with great enthusiasm. Kialessa felt there was a more pressing problem to attend to.

She'd slept adequately well under Mak's wings, but she was too afraid to turn for fear of waking him. It was very kind of him, but he smelt… like *boy* – all sweat and dirt. And he was warm; too warm. Her magical night dress was enough to keep her comfortable and modest, but still, Kialessa needed blankets and a mattress. And she needed a fire.

'Why aren't you with the other students in the hall?' Raynah asked.

'Their games were not to my liking,' she confessed.

'Tavernskeep!' Raynah said in false disdain. 'You need to make quick alliances here; keep your friends close and your enemies closer, that kind of thing! Board games have a very real purpose in prison… *gak*… I mean, in a place such as this.'

Kialessa looked at Raynah's necklace. It made her feel uncomfortable just looking at it.

Raynah continued, 'So, I need to get these reagents to the icebox. Perhaps you might carry them for me?'

Kialessa leapt at the chance to help, but her heart fell when she saw the task. It was a very little box, and there was no reason Raynah could not carry it herself. Her owl could have probably carried it.

'Come, come,' Raynah hurried her.

Kialessa grabbed the box and started following Raynah. Immediately she regretted it. She did not want to be taken advantage of. She needed a favour from this wizard as well, and carrying a little box would make her more a servant than a helpful assistant. But she couldn't back out now. How was she to ask a favour? How to point out to her that the task was beneath her dignity as a friend, and that she was not a servant?

'Thank you, Raynah,' Kialessa said after a few moments of silence, 'for letting me carry this little box for you.'

Raynah seemed embarrassed. She knew she was taking advantage of Kialessa's friendship. 'Oh, well, that's all right. Maybe I can return a favour to you, one day.'

Kialessa smiled to herself, it had worked. And the only reason it had worked was because Raynah was a kind, empathetic person at heart, and didn't want to take advantage of other people. She was a good person.

And Kialessa did need a favour. A really big favour only a busy wizardess could provide. Learning a new wizardry spell? That took days, and Kialessa did not have a book of her own to write down spells. But she really needed to make a sleep-time fire of her own.

'I am not lazy,' she announced.

Raynah looked at her, considering. 'You think you can learn some wizardry?'

'*Didgitis Ignis*,' Kialessa proclaimed the only spell she knew, but she prepared it every single day, just in case she needed to set fire to something, like a cooking fire, or a circus ribbon.

Raynah actually looked unimpressed. 'Finger fire? Gods, a child can learn that. *Rageperatus!*' Raynah shouted an activation phrase, and unleashed a blinding fan of orange flames that would have engulfed half a dozen people with ease. It was military quality; thick, scorching flames that danced about for several moments before dissipating. The heat was impressive.

'Oh,' Kialessa said, wishing she had wiser words to say.

'My *stone on fire* program, if that's what you want to call it-' Raynah began, and it took Kialessa a moment to realise Raynah did know exactly what she'd come to her for. '- is among the more "simple" of wizardry processes. But you'll need to know the basics and I suspect no one ever taught you. Can you multiply?'

'I have learned all the basic tables, up to twelve times,' Kialessa boasted. It was more than some students at the college had learned, and they'd been there for years.

Raynah scoffed. 'Unless you can do seven digit multiples in your mind in real time, you'll have to do it all on paper. That means it's a ritual, ten moment casting time, minimum. By Halm, I hope you're not lazy. Listen up; I'll give you the basics:'

Kialessa listened. She really tried to listen. But Raynah was moving fast. The spell apparently didn't use real fire at all, but converted the local matter into raw energy somehow, which unleashed enormous heat – like fire. Contained, it was apparently quite safe, and even used for cooking. Uncontained, it was the very heart of the *fiery conflagration*, apparently capable of levelling cities under the strictest of conditions. It sounded amazing!

But she really only needed it to make a fire burn all night.

By then they'd arrived at the kitchen. The imps, one and all, hid at Raynah's presence. It seemed they had already reached some kind of arrangement where they dared not bother her.

Kialessa noticed one peering out at them, mischief written on its face. She wondered if they were really afraid of Raynah, or just pretending to be so that she felt more in control. It was a dangerous, cunning game, very much like the kind of game an imp would play.

She wondered if any of them were like… the one imp that she'd met before. He had been nice, and saved her life. He'd then hopped on the arm of an angel and gone to meet Serros the sun god, apparently.

No, Impy was a rare one. Impy was the prisoner of an evil archmage. These imps probably worked voluntarily for a wicked merchant demon. None of these imps had been bound by a chain of goodness for decades, and none would likely have the spark of kindness in their devil hearts. Kialessa chose there and then to have as little to do with these imps as possible.

Raynah opened a trap door in the floor. Within there must have been the chill room; it was cold.

Kialessa joined her as she walked down.

Inside was a small room, clearly recently enlarged. It was stacked to the rafters with barrels and food.

Next to the ladder was an imp at a desk, wrapped in a dozen blankets till it looked like a small ball, trembling with the cold while holding a quill. 'Business!' it demanded.

Raynah glared at it.

'*Business*, I have my t…ta…tasks to attend to!' it insisted.

'Slavery,' Raynah replied.

The imp gave a tsk, tsk, then it breathed fire on the ink pot at the desk. 'Ungrateful,' it muttered, and began to write on the paper. It seemed to have the job of writing down everything that went into, or out, of this room. That, and not dying of the cold.

Kialessa had never liked the cold. It was not good for her. She usually kept warm by sitting inside a fire. The cold always seemed to get to her when it was around, though. She was always trembling long before her adopted brother would be.

Raynah pulled out her scroll. She was about to cast when she noticed Kialessa looking.

'I had to invent several of these runes myself,' she explained. 'Most wizards do. Our concepts are … subtle. Sometimes only a new word will suffice.'

Kialessa nodded.

Raynah intoned the activating words at the end of the scroll. Kialessa didn't have time to read them properly, but Raynah seemed to get it all right. Then, from her left hand, a frigid blast of ice emitted. The temperature in the room fell dramatically.

She aimed the spell at the barrels at the far end of the room. They began to split and splinter as ice formed inside them, freezing the water within. The blast lasted several moments, but by the end the entire far end of the room

By Dr Joe Ireland

was a cragged barrier of ice.

'That should suffice him,' Raynah said with a snarl.

'Hmff,' the imp protested. It had rugged itself up to the point that its eyes and mouth were invisible. It looked like a twitching, complaining ball of fabric. 'I'm *sure* he'll be pleased you broke the barrels.'

'Oh no,' Raynah protested, oozing sarcasm, 'You mean I was not supposed to do that? Oh no, how silly of me!'

Suddenly the trapdoor slammed shut.

'What!' Raynah screamed. She ran up the ladder and bashed on the door.

Imp-like giggles emitted from the room above.

The imp in the bundle of fabrics muttered, 'Serves you right, disrespecting the-'

Raynah raced down the ladder and grabbed the imp by its neck, scattering the rags everywhere. It was scaly, like a lizard, and ugly. Perhaps that was why it had the least popular job among its peers.

'Get them to open that trapdoor *now*!' Raynah screamed at it. She did not seem to like being trapped in. 'Or this one *pays* for your stupidity!'

'Squish his neck!' an imp called from above.

'Ice him to death!' another demanded.

Raynah seemed annoyed that the threat wasn't working.

The imp shrugged.

She threw him to the ground. He landed safely and scurried back under his blankets.

Raynah ran up the ladder and banged at the door. 'Don't make me come up there and blast my way out, so help me! I'll curse you all!'

There was silence for a moment.

'You do it,' one imp muttered.

'No, you do it!'

'You let me out this instant,' Raynah demanded, 'or I'll melt all the ice down here, *right now!'*

There was a metallic click as the latch slid away from the door.

Raynah threw the hatch open.

Kialessa wanted to say something diplomatic, something like, *Don't worry about it, it's not worth it.*

But Raynah clearly wanted a fight. Her owl was all puffed up and angry.

As soon as she left the trapdoor Raynah cast another spell, a complex set of clear armour formed around her and then turned invisible. The imps scurried in panic and fright. One tried to hide on the stove using a frypan as a shield. Another jumped into a ceramic container of pasta.

Six *Magus Spherae* appeared, floating above Raynah's hands.

If she wasn't so afraid of how Raynah was going to use the lethal weapons, Kialessa would have had time to be very impressed.

'Please, don't!' the master imp begged her. 'He'll be upset! He'll make you clean-'

Raynah was done casting, and began attacking. The ceramic pot blasted apart, the pan went flying from the little imp's hands. Whatever they were cooking was knocked right off the stove, and red soup went everywhere. Imps were crying out and scurrying in all directions.

Then Kialessa noticed the lead imp. With a horrifyingly evil look in its face, it was reaching into a knife drawer. It pulled out a very sharp looking knife with a polished handle, looking much more like a weapon than a kitchen tool.

In the midst of the chaos it threw the knife with impossible strength at Raynah. It would have hit her right in the arm.

But Kialessa had learnt all about catching knives from a travelling circus. She grabbed it mid-air, just before it would have spun around blade first. The imp was strong; the weapon bruised her hand even though it was only the handle, and knocked her against a very angry wizard's elbow.

Raynah glared at Kialessa, death in her eyes. She was still holding a

Magus Spherae. Then she saw the knife. Then her eyes followed the direction the knife was now pointing.

With a word that seemed impure to Kialessa's ears, Raynah shot the lead imp with the sphere. The little demon crashed against a spice rack spilling things everywhere.

The room fell silent.

A moment later a few students poked their head into the kitchen. 'You're in so much trouble for this,' one of them teased her.

Raynah stormed out, no one stopping her.

Kialessa scurried to follow her down the hall. They walked in silence for a few moments.

Eventually, Raynah spoke, 'Hurry up, Kia. We'd better get started quickly if you're going to learn any wizardry in this place.'

***

As it was, Raynah was actually an amazing teacher. Piex always seemed to start at the complex ideas and try and get more complex. Raynah was gifted at teaching. She took it easy, used clever analogies to help things make sense, and gave Kialessa time to make sense of the new ideas before moving on.

Around midnight Daygon arrived in the wizard's archives. He said nothing, but stood at the door.

'You keep learning these runes, Kialessa. I will be back within the hour,' Raynah said, voice choking.

She left with Daygon, and did not take her owl.

When she returned, she was subdued, but would not speak about what kind of punishment she'd had to endure. She just went right back on teaching, as though being tortured was no worse than being made to live in this place each and every night.

Chapel

Did any of them know who they were, or what they were truly worth?
Did they all think they were bad, and that they were made evil and that there
was no good in them? No wonder bad things happened in this place.
Kialessa, the Tae'anaryn, in report to king Dunnkan, Winter 313.

Kialessa was scribing the circle Raynah had taught her around the fire pit. They were going to sleep warm tonight!

Mak walked in, pillows and blankets overflowing in his arms.

'Where'd you get those?!' Kialessa asked him.

'Second years were hoarding them. I asked nicely, and when Broose said no, I punched him in the nose. They seemed to lose interest in holding on to so many blankets after that.'

Kialessa wasn't sure what to think. Was it stealing? Was stealing all right if the other students were being greedy? Was it a way to make them respect herself and Mak, or did it make other people hate them even more?

'I don't think we'll need them,' she said out loud. 'You just need your wings, and I have a new spell to try.'

He dumped the blankets on the floor, looking like he didn't care if they used them as bedding or fuel. To Kialessa's eyes they really weren't the best blankets around… more like… large rags. 'Yeah, I noticed you were up to something. What did that wizard teach you?'

Kialessa pointed at her growing rune circle. 'I'm copying the image here.' She held up the spell book Raynah had given her. She'd let her pick from the dozen or so sitting around, and Kialessa had chosen a blue cover with golden embossing on the front; the colours of Lenmer'el. It already had

By Dr Joe Ireland

a spell or two inside, but most pages were blank. It probably belonged to some lazy wizard student who gave up years ago. Raynah assured her it would take years to learn the other spells properly, but *stone on fire* was apparently a fairly simple one.

'Reckon it'll work?' he asked.

She shrugged and kept on drawing with the sharp stylus in the stone. 'I got it to work at least twice today already. I think it will work.'

'You missed one,' he pointed.

She glared at the book, then at her rune circle. Then back at the book. It really didn't seem like she'd missed one. She looked up at him to ask what he meant but saw he was grinning cheekily.

She went to play hit him but didn't have the courage to touch him, but he cringed anyway.

He laughed, then flapped up to a stalactite, looking around the cavern. 'I never leant any wizardry. Don't think I will – priests of faith can command you to silence, kinda kills the magic don't ya think?'

She knew what he meant. But she'd also seen what power a trained and focused wizard could wield. Truly, they could bend reality itself to their whim. She was glad she had her own spellbook now; she had some surprises for Piex next time she saw him.

Ecce, Kialessa whispered, calling the magic around her. Mak seemed to notice, turning his head. Kialessa began intoning, very carefully, the runes in a clockwise direction. They were more than words; it was a program – an algorithm that told reality what Kialessa wanted to accomplish.

Et num, she said, informing reality it was time to enact the program. To her relief and delight, the stone in the centre of the circle began to glow and soon burst into bright, orange flames.

She sighed with relief. 'We will be warm tonight.'

Mak shrugged. 'Speak for yourself. I was warm enough last night.'

'For the both of us,' she muttered.

He laughed, yawned, and stretched out his wings. They would be far more comfortable not keeping her alive tonight.

'Thank you, Mak,' she said.

'For what?' he dismissed her gratitude. 'We gotta look out for each other. This place… it's not good.'

She nodded. 'I think you are good.'

He huffed, and looked away. 'Don't get hung up on that,' he said. 'I … I did what I had to do to survive. Bah! I'm not *good.* Don't go saying things like that, Kia. That's why I'm here, trapped with the rest of them.'

She frowned. 'You think I am not good, then?'

He leaped down, apologising immediately. 'No, no, you're good. Nicest person I know, except me mum. No. *You* don't belong here.'

'But I am here, with you.'

'Everyone knows it. You freak them out, you realise. You're not like … I don't know. "Dame"? The other kids, they're talking about you. They don't know what to think and I think you make them nervous – you kept out of the fight, and you just spent the whole day with the wizard and she has, like, NO friends. I asked. NONE. You even make the big kids nervous.'

Kialessa frowned. She didn't know what to make of that. Once more, everyone was talking about her, and no one was talking to her.

A year ago, before college, she would have curled up in a corner and cried for days. Now, she'd learnt who she was, and that she was a good person, intended for great good, with a body that was worth protecting and goals worth fighting for.

Did Mak know that yet?

Did *any* of them know who they were, or what they were truly worth?

Did they *all* think they were bad, and that they were made of evil and that there was no good in them? No wonder bad things happened in this place.

'You don't say much,' Mak grinned.

By Dr Joe Ireland

She smiled, people said that to her a lot. 'I just… well… if my thoughts would turn into words that'd be great.' She sighed. 'I guess I'd better get to know some of the other, I mean, our… siblings, I suppose.'

'Can't hurt,' he patted her on her shoulder, he was quite tall for his age.

That was when Kialessa noticed his bare chest. There was not a single scar or scratch on it. He never bathed, that was obvious, but the injuries from combat training? Completely gone.

He noticed her looking. 'I guess I heal pretty quickly. Mum said so, but I'd never noticed it till last yesternight's battle. Gosh, that was fun; I can't wait till next week!'

Every week?

'Welp,' Mak said, and with a dominant flap of his wings landed on a tall stalactite and began to look for somewhere to hang from. 'There's some choir on tomorrow we're supposed to attend. Could be fun. Something to do with Iki's religious services or something, I couldn't really make sense of it. But I'll go if you go - there we are!' He leapt up to a wooden beam stretched between two stalactites, 'Someone here had some class,' he muttered, and latching his knees and tail around the beam hung downwards, his long wings dragging in the water far below.

She stared a moment, and he stared back at her and yawned. Then he began to fold his wings around his entire body until he just looked like a caterpillar within its chrysalis.

She shook her head – boys sleeping upside down with their wings as their only blanket – NOT the weirdest thing she'd seen here.

Choir. Kialessa enjoyed singing, very much. She could not match Allastassia's range or tone quality, but she did like singing. And this dusk, when she awoke, she could keep fit and practice her own enchantments by dancing inside her little circle with a *stone on fire*.

She lay down, using the blanket as her pillow, her orange fire flowing up around her stomach and curling around her arms. It was a welcome, warm comfort after a long night of wizardry.

She sighed. What Raynah might not have known was that the circle of runes was, to Kialessa's heart, also a circle to her god. She thanked the Eternal for her safety, for Mak's company, for her sister's gift of teaching. And she thanked the Eternal for a fire tonight.

***

Kialessa's voice rang high, along with the other sopranos. She could hold her part, but the harmonies were complex and strange. They made her feel weird, but also curious – enchanted. Either the choir could not master Pumos' dark mysteries, or he really was a very strange deity who liked dissonance very much.

'No, no,' Lossel insisted. She was not the most musically talented, a quiet fourth year kept correcting her. But she was the most revered sixth year, and everyone shut up when she told them to. 'First sopranos, you have the 7th of the chord. It's *vital* you get it right. Sing it, sing just that chord. Starting at the second altos.'

Everyone held their notes for the chord Lossel indicated. As it built, Kialessa felt a strange welling inside. It was as if some mysterious truth was trying to speak to her, but she didn't know the language yet. It was something between the twingle of magic and the exultation of religious conviction. When the first sopranos hit their note, of which she was one, the energy struck her powerfully. Purple fire burst around her.

She squealed, and ducked down onto one knee.

Everyone stopped to look at her.

Lossel conferred with her music master, and then they looked at Raynah sitting in the pews of the chapel. The wizardess didn't even look up, but an odd, purple symbol formed in her hand and she said nothing.

Lossel nodded, 'Kialessa, you're moving to third soprano.'

 By Dr Joe Ireland

And, just like that, she was demoted. Or moved. She knew she wasn't supposed to consider it a demotion because every voice was needed in a choir.

Then Lossel continued, muttering, 'Can't have you channelling an avatar of Ik'skuretza during services, can we.'

Kialessa didn't know what she meant, but from that point on the magic was lost, and it was just another song.

As soon as the rehearsal ended Kialessa tried to speak to someone, but they all seemed to have someone else to speak to.

Then someone grabbed her hair and started platting it.

Kialessa turned, and was relieved to see it was Amber.

'It's good you already know some music,' Amber muttered. 'It always helps.'

'Why are only the girls singing?' Kialessa asked.

'Boys have different jobs,' Amber replied, tying her hair with a piece of string. She was excellent at it, making it look far easier than it really was to tie up hair with string. She must have practiced a lot. 'Perigaul will be teaching some swordplay and unarmed combat, down in the hall again this dawn,' Amber informed her, thinking out loud a moment. 'Our father expects us to teach each other, I think he hopes it will help us gain the mastery ourselves. Will you be coming?'

'Kialessa!' A commanding voice echoed through the chapel. It was Raynah. 'We go.'

Raynah was walking briskly out, and Kialessa knew she'd have to run to catch up.

'Go,' Amber spared her a long farewell.

Kialessa opened her mouth to speak.

Raynah did not wait, 'Kia!'

She ran out after the wizard.

***

Four more nights flew by.

'How are you doing, Kialessa?' Raynah asked.

It took her a moment to dislodge her mind from the runes in *Academiclees Guide to Modern Magic* that she was studying. It was a difficult book, but it was finally beginning to make some sense to her. 'I'm all right.'

'You work very hard,' Raynah complimented her for the first time since they'd started working together.

'Thank you. I… have a very good teacher.'

Raynah smiled, but it was still her small, hurt smile. Her owl puffed up happily.

'Much more than your broad winged brother,' Raynah protested.

Mak had spent the last four days talking and tussling with all the other young kids. Kialessa had the sneaking suspicion that he was holding back now, trying to get a sense of their powers and limitations.

'I'm glad Lossel is here.' Kialessa confessed. 'Just yesterday Mak and Arbour were getting a bit rough and she stepped in before they broke anything.'

Raynah nodded. 'She's a treasure, that's for sure,' she said while still working on her unguents.

A silence fell, and Kialessa wondered why Raynah had interrupted her study. 'Was there something?' she asked.

As if in reply the great gong sounded.

'Ah,' Raynah replied, 'Right on schedule.'

Kialessa stood. Was there a meeting of some kind?

Raynah guessed her thoughts; she was very wise like that, often. 'It's Ik'skuretza's night, what we call "Reveal". They'll be expecting us to attend the chapel now. I find it's easier to just wallow in silence for a few hours than upset everyone; it gives them all a reason to make your life miserable if you don't attend church once in a week.'

Kialessa nodded. Raynah was very practical like that. But she was also very dour, and Kialessa hoped the religious services weren't all that boring. Then again, Serros' services were. But then again, again, Pumos was the god of mysteries, apparently. It might be enlightening. But then again, again, (again), Serros was the god of light itself.

She sighed. How she missed her own church to worship in! But she could keep that faith in her heart. Getting to know this deity might be useful in this place.

They made their way to the little chapel in the centre of the mountain. Most other students were already there. Ik'skuretza didn't seem to mind much decorum, however. Several of the winged students were perched on the rafters, and a few others clung to the statues or bookshelves. And when they got tired, they stretched out on the floor.

Raynah sat in the back corner, so Kialessa sat with her.

'Hey,' Flameheart's voice ordered from somewhere up at the roof. 'By year level. Now.'

Raynah gave her a dark look, but moved several seats up. She pointed to the front where Kialessa was probably supposed to sit.

Mak shrugged, looking cheeky, but not yet willing to pick a fight here. Everyone was about, all the other tae'anaryl and even most of the servants. Kialessa gave a start as several ghosts floated in, but no one seemed bothered in the slightest.

Another gong sounded, and everyone fell very silent.

Daygon approached the podium. He glanced up at Shadowmonger who seemed to have a rafter all to himself. Daygon gave him a questioning look, and Shadowmonger gave him a rude sign in return.

Daygon cleared his throat, and in a singing kind of voice intoned a line in some language Kialessa did not recognise. The room vibrated slightly with a mystical energy. He looked up, and spoke a rhyme in yet another language, but by some power Kialessa understood it all,

Shadowed god of mysteries, we implore you.
Teach us of your darkness, the wisdom of your silence.
Bring truth beyond light, mystery beyond knowledge,
We implore you, we implore you.

'We implore,' everyone intoned.

Mak looked at Kialessa, and shrugged. 'Here's where things get weird, right?' he whispered with a grin.

Someone slapped him gently on the back of his head, and he smiled.

A blinding, dark purple light erupted from Daygon's hand, and his eyes went a kind of pearlesque white. A book flew from the shelves as though it had selected itself and landed in his outstretched hand.

He put it on the lectern and it snapped open. He started reading the first thing his gaze fell on. Fascinatingly, it was a lecture by the first priests of Serros – all about how vital the sun is and how plants need the light to grow. As it ended, Kialessa was sure Daygon was about to discredit the words of a priest of his god's nemesis, but fascinatingly, he did not. He approved them all, adding great insight and information. It was fascinating.

And it might have continued to be compelling, but Daygon went on, and on, and on. His voice such a droning monotone it was a wonder no one fell asleep. Most of the other students, however, seemed fairly interested.

Kialessa wondered if there was something she might be missing. She tried to listen harder. But it was really boring. She sighed, thinking how this was exactly like Serros' meetings, only not as well lit. Almost a week and she was still not used to staying awake all night and trying to sleep all day.

Quietly she touched her little scripture, the one hidden away in the folds of her college day clothes. She'd been given it by king Dunnkan when she

By Dr Joe Ireland

was a prisoner of the trolls – for comfort, and guidance. It contained the one and only speech given by the Eternal himself, at the founding of a golden city thousands of years ago. It was so little to go on; there were books, entire libraries devoted to making sense of that one little speech. So as Daygon droned she prayed in her heart for peace, and patience in this prison, and power for the strength to go on and to make sense of whatever opportunity lay in this weird experience.

'Stop that,' Daygon suddenly stated with great force. He was glaring at her.

Kialessa glanced around. Everyone was staring at her. She looked, and could see nothing that might have made Daygon stop his lecture.

He leant over the podium at her, 'No other deity but Ik'skuretza may be called on in this place.'

Kialessa gulped. Everyone was watching her.

She wondered what to do. It was the easy thing to stay silent. To not pray.

But that was one freedom she did not know that they could ever take away from her.

One freedom she never wanted to lose.

Ik'skuretza hadn't seemed to mind when she'd encircled herself on the night of sanctuary, and every night in the damp cavern. And if he loved mysteries as much as he loved wisdom, then the Eternal and he would no doubt get along.

And if he was not an evil god, then he would not mind her praying to another of the acknowledged gods of good.

She might be silent, but she would not stop praying. But that didn't mean she needed to be rude about it.

She stood up. 'No,' she said, bowing politely.

Daygon's eyes flared with bale purple light. 'How DARE you risk offending the god of death and night! How *dare* you come into this sacred sanctuary and profane it by uttering *any other name!* How-'

There was thunderous thud as someone interposed themselves between Kialessa and the priest. Far more than the ground shook; it was as if the shadows themselves rippled in the presence of this semi divine power. Kialessa had only felt it once before, in the beast that Darrix had tamed.

She looked up, trying to hold herself together. No one else seemed as affected as much she was.

It was Shadowmonger, and he was facing Daygon. He turned and glanced over his shoulder at her. To her surprise he did not seem angry, or even amused. She was not sure what he was thinking.

He held out his hand and his eyes turned white. Suddenly a book flew from its place in the shelves and he grabbed it. A podium of raw shadow wove itself from the shadow realm, and as Shadowmonger placed the book down it sprang open.

The tall, dark boy read the first things his eyes saw, 'Upon the rooftops, and in the closets. Over the fields, and over the flocks. In places secret and in places most public. In times of peace, and in times of war. Let them pray. My people will pray.'

Shadowmonger closed the book, reading the title, 'Of truths and aspirations, Zingal, priestess of Xin, avatar of Annas.'

No one spoke.

Shadowmonger glared at Daygon.

The old man stuttered and lowered his eyes. 'The spirit of Ik'skuretza has left me, I will stop speaking now.' He moved to his seat, and sat down.

Shadowmonger turned to face them all, and glared at her. Then he spoke one of the most memorable sermons Kialessa would ever hear.

'The greatest thing,

   you'll ever learn;

is just to love,

   and be loved in return.'

With a flap of his wings, he was gone.

The Treasury

Oh, there is some good in everyone here!

Kialessa, the Tae'anaryn, in report to king Dunnkan, Winter 313.

They nabbed her after the service was over. All the younger students clustered around her, speaking at once as they walked along.

'I can't believe you stood up to Daygon like that!'

'Yeah, it was amazing!'

'Showed him, eh! Even Shadowmonger got involved.'

'Hey!' Lossel warned them from up front.

They looked at her, but kept whispering belligerently.

'I think,' Kialessa pondered, 'That that might have been the most profound speech I've ever heard.'

'Meh,' Broose said, 'That's all Shadowmonger ever says.'

Kialessa was a little disappointed to hear that, but felt it did not diminish Shadowmonger's wisdom at all.

'I guess you got permission to pray to who you want,' Amber muttered with a frown.

'How'd Shadowmonger do that?' Kialessa asked, missing her chance to ask Amber what she was thinking about.

'He's a chosen,' Amber answered. 'Chosen of Ik'skuretza.'

'Isn't Daygon a priest as well?' Kialessa asked.

'It's not like that,' Broose explained. 'Daygon is the highest-ranking priest of Ik'skuretza in the fortress, after our father that is. But Shadowmonger is a chosen. He's gifted, a prodigy. He can do stuff that Daygon still can't master, he knows stuff that Daygon still doesn't

By Dr Joe Ireland

understand. Ik'skuretza and Shadowmonger, they got this thing going on. Like, like an avatar.'

'It's nothing like an avatar,' Amber interrupted.

'Yeah, I know,' the boy agreed. 'But like it, sort of … I don't know.'

'To be the chosen,' Amber added, 'is to have special access to a deity's powers, and their thoughts. Shadowmonger can ask favours of Ik'skuretza that Daygon wouldn't even dare. Chosen are rare – one in a generation. It's probably why he's such an amazing shadow weaver.'

Kialessa nodded, thankful for the information.

'Kialessa!' Daygon called.

She turned, and the other students left her quickly.

It seemed to be the thing to do, so she walked up to the old priest.

He looked meek, but there was still a raw power about him she did not want to contest at this time. He may not have been a chosen, but he was still a high-ranking priest of the god of darkness and mysteries. He bowed, and spoke, 'I do apologise. Many students think to cheat fate at this college by allying themselves to any other deity than he who rules this land by right and power. I beg your forgiveness.'

She nodded, 'Their fate?' she asked.

'Indeed. All must die, that is long decreed from before the world was organised. This is a special place; it protects the tae'anaryl from an outside world that would hate them. I hope… you have found some friends here?' He looked kindly, and harmless. Like the nice uncle everyone wanted to trust.

She sighed, and stepped back. She was not ready to trust him, or anyone here, just yet. Except Raynah maybe. And Mak. And maybe Amber a little. And that child with the hooves. *Oh, there is some good in everyone here!* she protested against her own distrust.

'Come, Kialessa. Would you like me to show you the treasury?'

'You have a treasury?' she asked, sounding much more enthusiastic about that than she meant to.

He laughed, and placing a hand on her shoulder began to walk through the fortress. 'Truly, there are more than a thousand rooms in this labyrinth. Some new ones too, with Ka's favourite hobby! But having mentioned, yes, and your father would have you select any weapon you need for your safety. I think we can trust you now.'

She nodded, silently wondering what price would be paid for the weapons tae'anaryl had forged.

He smiled. 'Two provisions. You must never take these weapons from the sacred ground of this fortress.'

'Why-' she interrupted, thinking better of it as soon as she had, '…sorry.'

'No, no, go on.'

She bowed. 'Will the weapons cease to function once they leave the fortress?'

'Oh, no, no. Nothing of the sort. But they are for the protection and development of those who live here. You may take freely of any weapon; they are for the use of everyone here!'

'I see,' she said, not committing to any promise.

'Second, you are required to forge one of your own to leave here, before you move on. We all need to improve the world, Dame Kialessa. To make it a better place before we die. And to that end, we leave a tool, a weapon of protection and self-defence behind, to help protect those who must come after us. Do you understand?'

'I do,' she replied.

'Excellent.' And at this, he teleported them, or whatever it was that he did, to a steel banded stone door deep within the fortress. She did not know how she would have gotten here on her own. Runes of mystery and power were carved deeply into its foreboding stone surface. Daygon read them, thinking for a moment, absently muttering the astrological dates and times, depressing several runes in a confusing order. They began to light up. 'Oh, and another rule. Well, more a rule of the fortress, well, of life itself actually!'

The door began to swing outwards, but it was thick, massive. Truly unnecessary thick – at least ten paces of solid stone. He kept speaking. 'We're trusting that you will not kill anyone here.'

She looked at him, wondering why that was a rule.

'It's a weapon Kialessa. They can hurt people. Our father does not mind conflict – he teaches us that it can bring out our best. But to kill anyone here is a crime of the most, deepest severity. Remember that. He can bring someone back from the dead too, I've seen it happen. But the punishment of those that caused the death… it's too horrible to mention.' He was actually turning pale at the thought. 'Ghastly… don't, don't ever kill anyone here Kialessa. Not even by accident.'

Accidents did happen, and the weapons they used in battle training and carried around every day were all very real. It seemed an odd thing to be telling an almost twelve-year-old. But it was not the first time she'd been told it, they lived in a dangerous world. Everyone older than eight held a dagger in Lenmer'el. And she was a being of innate power.

'I will not kill anyone here,' she promised him, wondering if that was really a promise she could keep, and wondering if that was really a promise she should be making at her age. But she had to try, if only to get a weapon herself! Her acid dagger was far away now, and her only weapon was her father's unburnable whip. It was useful, but had its limitations.

Daygon entered the room, and a massive spectral guardian rose to greet them. Kialessa gulped, but it only glared at her. He was an enormous djinn ghost; an undead demon of the blithling lands, with a gold and bronze turban around his head. He had twin, see-through sabres at his hips, and another two held out in his two of his four arms. He had a bare chest of demonic tattoos, and his waist below tapered away into mist instead of legs. With a start she realised it was the merchant's man at arms, the one she'd seen at the pre winter festival. How he'd acquired, or reacquired, his physical

Choice, set free   127

body for the event was a miracle beyond imagining.

Daygon raised his hand in a special greeting, and spoke in a language she did not know, but it sounded Blithling. The being nodded, and glaring raw threat at her, slowly floated aside.

Kialessa watched the guardian warily as she passed. It glared at her with the hatred of undeath in its evil eyes, and the world paled and chilled in its presence. Only the most evil of beings would keep a demi demon of fear and undeath on as a servant – they may have kept their oaths, but its very presence exuded hatred of all things living, loathing of every good virtue, and vile commitment to wickedness. She kept close to Daygon.

They entered a mighty chamber, easily ten times the size of the treasury at the castle of Lenmer'el. Gold was laid up in great heaps of coins, jewel encrusted crowns dangling on masterwork swords of inestimable value. The room was neat, clean, organised, and indescribably wealthy.

Daygon gave her a moment to appreciate it. 'Little trinkets of the master, I assure you,' he promised.

She nodded, impressed at the wealth around her.

'Come,' Daygon offered, 'we best shop from this lower platform. The best treasures must be earned. But here we are sure to find something that suits you.'

He turned her to face towards a massive alcove, the size of a room. The treasures here were less impressive, the coins of silver and copper. This alcove was truly less than half, less than a tenth, of the treasury at home.

But the variety of weapons here was unsurpassed. There were swords, and glaives, cruel metal edged gloves, and several bows. Kialessa was sick of bows; they had not served her once in a real battle. They were unwieldly, lost their spring, and took too long to load. And they had an annoying tendency to get caught on her mount's back when she was supposed to be shooting troll griffins in the heart. Oh, they were great for practice, and shooting annoying boys with blunt arrows in combat training. But for real

By Dr Joe Ireland

battle? Next to useless.

Then she noticed there were even spiked wrist bands too small for any wrist here.

'Horn spikes,' Daygon nodded and pointed at his head.

She nodded, it made sense now.

She continued to look around. There was a full table of even stranger horn spikes – blades, and hammers. They had long, thick handles.

'Tail weapons,' Daygon explained.

'Oh!' she muttered. *Tail weapons, what a great idea!*

'Only one,' Daygon repeated. 'All here must be earned except the first.'

'Has Mak been here?' she asked.

'Ahh, not yet,' Daygon replied. 'Bit… rough around the edges, don't you think? Can't risk arming him *just* yet.'

She nodded. It was a sensible precaution.

She looked around. Much here did not seem like a weapon. Necklaces and headbands, footwear and cloaks. It was hard to choose. With only one option what was best for her? Something of greatest value that she could trade for her freedom, perhaps? Then her eyes fell on what looked like a shoe string poking out from under a shelf.

She bent down, and pulled at it. Something was stuck, and she had to move a shelf to get it, the jewellery jiggling so that Daygon lunged forward to help keep things stable. But then she pulled out a long sling.

'Oh!' Daygon said in surprise, 'I was wondered where that had gotten to, haven't seen it in forty years!'

Kialessa hefted the long sling. It was a little long for her, but its saddle was weighted as though with lead, and the entire device was of exquisite make. Its thongs were strong and expertly platted. And in the centre, within a circle, was a small symbol to Annas – goddess of love and war.

It seemed a fitting gift; since Annas had stood up for her during the chapel to Ik'skuretza.

'I'm thinking this one should have been several tiers up,' Daygon pondered out loud.

She looked at him, hoping he would not take it from her.

He sighed, 'But… best not to deny destiny twice in one day! It's a rider's sling – for use while mounted. Very, very powerful, though I suppose you can use it while standing, with practice. The weight in the saddle uses a powerful prayer to push against the ballast, greatly increasing its accuracy and force. Go on, try it. Swing it against the air.'

She did so, and to her amazement, just as she released a leather plat at the height of its swing, the entire saddle gave a loud thud and flung itself backwards. The whole effect jerked at her arm.

'It… may take some getting used to,' she admitted.

Suddenly the djinn spectre rose up towards them.

'I suspect our time is spent,' Daygon muttered, looking nervous. Kialessa wondered how much authority the old man really had around here. Was he really just a student like the rest of them? One who'd been around a lot longer, and was supposed to know a lot more?

But she did not argue, and left quickly. She was late for wizard training.

By Dr Joe Ireland

Unsupervised

'She will outlive most of you, if she chooses wisely. She has the potential to be an old woman.'

The Prophet, cited in recollections of the Tae'anaryl.

As it was, Raynah was not at the archives. Kialessa found a note telling her to come to the toy room. But she had no idea where that was.

She went into the main hall, seeing if there was someone to help her.

At least a dozen students were milling around, looking like they had nothing to do. Mak and several other boys seemed very intent on some kind of game that involved pushing each other off a log. They'd tied Mak's wings behind his back, but he was still winning. They were arguing about tying his hands behind his back too, to make it fair.

Lossel was sitting, talking to some of the other girls at the main table. They didn't seem interested in what the boys were doing, but were looking over a detailed map of the Great Kingdom, checking trade routes and the genealogies of various nobles.

Kialessa approached the table carefully, not sure what to say. The girls were all a lot older than she. She'd never spoken to students so much older than her, at least without friends by her side.

But she could wait forever without their help, and be called lazy by Raynah. Or she could swallow her fear and ask for help.

She walked up to the table, and thankfully the girls all stopped.

'Hey, what up, Redling?' Lossel said to her.

Kialessa didn't mean to find them terrifying, but they really were. They were tae'anaryl just like her, that wasn't the problem. They were all the older students. She held out her note and tried to speak, but it was all a whisper. 'Raynah wants … I'm supposed to meet her… I mean I just…'

They just stared at her.

Kialessa took a breath, and tried to speak clearly, 'Can you help me find the toy room? I'm to meet Raynah there.'

They looked at her. Lossel seemed to be making up her mind, as though wondering what she could get Kialessa to do as a favour in return. 'Sure, Redling.' She seemed to take pity on her, and Kialessa felt the fear in her stomach leave. 'I'll take you.'

Lossel stood up, the bench she was on tipping three other students to the ground, though one managed to leap back and land on her feet.

'Sorry girls!' Lossel gave a casual apology, as if what she really wanted to do was remind them that she had superhuman strength. *'Sprigiti, fanciuletta,'* she said in eastern elven, hurrying Kialessa along.

Kialessa looked at the students, their unfriendly faces glaring back at her. She was about to leave when she noticed Mak staring at her. Someone hit him on the head and he fell off the log, laughing as the other boys cheered.

Kialessa shook her head. She turned away and followed Lossel, wishing she knew what the other girls thought, and wishing she had some way of getting to know them all better so that they could see there was nothing to fear from her. But she could not think of anything to say to them, so it was just easier to use study as an excuse to skip socialising. So she did.

***

'Bah!' A young voice warned them rudely as they entered the toy room. This was the Child's domain, clearly. The room was large, and very well lit. A painting on the far wall glowed with magic as though it was daylight. The pillars of the room were hewn wood, and the floor polished oak.

And then there were the toys. Racks upon racks of some of the most

By Dr Joe Ireland

skilfully made toys Kialessa had ever seen. Toy soldiers, and rocking posks. Magical rocks that changed their colours every time you spoke to them, and a spinning top that only stopped spinning when the Child stopped it. Towards the corner a bundle of brightly coloured rags lay, and next to it an empty bedpan. Kialessa had to assume the Child lived, and played in this room.

As if on cue the Child scurried passed her on all fours, stopping to hiss at her like a cat. It was clear that, if the Child could, she would chase Kialessa from this room right now.

Raynah spoke from the back, 'She can't speak, Kialessa. Her gullet is all fish. I wouldn't look if I were you, it's disgusting.'

Lossel stomped away ignoring her thanks. Kialessa entered, looking for the wizardess.

She sat at a small table, a clear, rhombus shaped stone in hand. Raynah held it up to her eyes. 'You can learn more of the science of magic from toys than books sometimes, Kialessa. Can your eyes see magic?'

Kialessa shook her head, but it was a kind of magic she wanted to learn, very dearly. 'My friend gave me a scroll of *mage sight*. I would very much like to learn it, and scribe it into the spell book you gave me.'

Raynah huffed. It must have sounded like work. But she, for her own reasons, sighed and said, 'Well, where is it?'

Kialessa looked down. 'When the merchant took me, I didn't have time to get it from my… hiding place. Now the shadow realm is closed around this mountain, and I can't get to it.'

Raynah looked, pondering for a moment. The Child scurried up to her and she patted her absently. 'I think we can get it for you, for the right price. The barrier of the shadow realm is very 'thin' around this fortress; you may have already noticed – sacred to Ik'skuretza and all. I suppose I can help you get it.'

'How?' Kialessa wondered, secretly hoping it might provide a way of escaping, but fearing it might not.

Raynah stood, and with commanding words fashioned a glowing violet rune circle on the wall. The lighting in the area dimmed. 'It is possible… we cannot leave the fortress, it is true. But we can… stretch out… the shadow realm here because it is so very powerful. I think we can build a tunnel of sorts, if my maths is correct. I can get all the way to the castle of Lenmer'el, if that's where your cache is hidden?'

Kialessa nodded, thinking it very clever that Raynah had already figured that out.

'But not the keep,' Raynah apologised. 'It's disconnected from the shadowrealm somehow, I don't know how.'

'The enchantress Greens'holm did it,' Kialessa informed her.

'Really? I did not know that. Dryad work… difficult to replicate. So where is your treasure hidden?'

'At the foot of my bed, in a chest in the girl's dormitory.' Now she was feeling a light of hope growing in her chest.

'I don't know where that is,' Raynah informed her.

'If you can get me to the castle, I'm sure I can find it.'

'You can see in the shadow realm?' Raynah queried her.

'Easily.'

She huffed with envy. 'Never mind, I cannot send you there. Just… your hands. Do you understand? The tunnel is going to be very small. You could not crawl through. Understood?'

Kialessa nodded.

Raynah pushed a small, wheeled wagon absentmindedly. Then she grabbed up a scroll and started writing, 'Fifteen hundred leagues… carry the four… midwinter but before the eclipses so we should not have to worry about…hmm.'

Kialessa left her to her thoughts.

Then she spoke, 'We need to talk about remuneration,' she informed

 By Dr Joe Ireland

her.

'What do you mean?"

'Payment. What will you give me for this service?'

Then Kialessa's heart dropped. What could she give a wizard? 'I have a hundred gold coins. I could… you could have all of them if you wanted.'

She didn't even look tempted. 'Gold. What good is it in this place? No. We work on a different currency. We do favours for people around here; a life debt.'

Kialessa was incredulous, such a high price? Her very life? That was ridiculous. 'I already owe you more than I own for your kindness. What could you ask of me more?'

Suddenly a gong sounded, and Raynah looked surprised. 'This is unusual.'

'What is it?' Kialessa asked, hoping at least this was not too much of a favour to ask the wizard such knowledge.

'A meeting. We are not expecting a meeting at this time. Come, we'd best get to the chapel. Child! Move!'

The belligerent youngling didn't seem interested in coming along, but when she looked at the seriousness in Raynah's face, she scurried out.

Raynah looked tense.

***

Kialessa entered the chapel, feeling her heart knit in the same irrational, dark hatred of the man who'd imprisoned her here. Lady Jasmin stood by his side, looking glorious. Daygon was at his other side, looking concerned.

The students gathered with impressive haste.

The merchant demon spoke, and he did not mince words. 'Children. I am going away.'

Everyone complained, though a few looked pleased.

He continued, 'As I have warned you, Emerel embraces a time of deep change. I need to be there when those changes come. My business requires me to be away from the fortress for a few days, at most. I expect to return by the midwinter festival, just before the eclipses.'

Children murmured in complaint. The older students didn't seem fazed at all.

'I'm sorry; this is just the way it needs to be.' He held up his hands for silence against their protests, and the room fell quiet immediately. 'Daygon has the care of you all – obey his words as you would my own. Understood?' He glared at them. Then he spoke softly once more. 'Take good care of each other, my children. I want you to feel safe here. I want you to be safe here. Will there be any questions?'

There were none.

'Safe journey, father,' Lossel spoke for them all - well, almost all of them.

'Go eat a tiger, dad!' Mak spouted an old saying for good luck from Nomer'el.

The merchant glared at him to show he felt it was a disrespectful saying, but did not punish him.

Then the older man nodded. 'Good. Very well. Lady Jasmin, we'd best hurry away!'

She grinned and took his arm.

The ground shook as a massive, and highly complex rune circle erupted from the stones around him, and in a blinding pillar of light, they were gone.

For half an instant, no one moved.

'Now - ' Daygon began carefully.

Chaos erupted around her. Raynah grabbed the Child and they *ran* out. Lossel drew her broadsword and held it out against any who threatened the cluster of second years who cringed behind her. Fire exploded from the roof, and shadow tendrils erupted around them as Shadowmonger fled.

The next thing she knew, someone pinned Kialessa's head to the floor.

     By Dr Joe Ireland

It looked like one of the fourth years, the fifteen-year-olds. She heard Mak fighting, screaming, 'Let her go!' There was a deep crack as Lossel's sword hit the ground, and the room fell silent except for the scurrying of a few feet retreating.

Kialessa's assailant spoke, 'Keep out of this, Lossel! You know as well as I do that we don't have the measure of this one. She's *dangerous*. "Dame" indeed. Luck I say, luck or far more destiny than either of us combined.'

'Then you would not want to make an enemy of her,' Lossel replied.

Another spoke. One of the fourth-year girls. 'I don't like her. She doesn't even have any wings.'

'And is that such a problem, Rankbreath?' Lossel insulted the girl.

He shoved her head down, and it was hurting. Kialessa's heart pounded in her throat. She didn't know what to do.

'Stop! What are you trying to do?!' Mak screamed.

'Shut up, shut up!' the assailant said, and the room began to quiet down again. 'I'll tell you what we're going to do. We're going to take her to see the prophet. Let us know her through his eyes. Then you'll see, this little weakling is going to cause us trouble, and she needs to be taught a lesson soon so that she knows who she'd better respect!'

His allies cheered. She was dragged to her feet, and they held her arms behind her back so far that they hurt. It felt like there were at least a dozen of them.

Lossel looked very busy protecting almost a dozen second and third years. All over the room fights were breaking out. Mak was pinned by an eighth year student who looked on with dark curiosity. And Daygon just sat down, looking worried and helpless.

***

They blindfolded her. It was completely unnecessary, but they seemed to want her afraid. There were at least twenty or so other students with her now. She wasn't sure how many. Lossel and Raynah weren't there.

She didn't speak as they dragged her along, unkind voices muttering hate. They moved deep into the fortress, passed the damp cavern, even lower. Her heartbeat thundered in her ears, and she could not still her fevered breath. But she did not speak.

After at least ten moments they unlocked a heavy iron portcullis, screeching as it rose. Then they forced her to her knees.

She allowed it. What perverse kind of "initiation" this might be she did not know. But she wished she'd tried to find out more about this "prophet" before today.

The blindfold was torn from her eyes and she blinked in the dim light. There pale moonlight shone from a single window, and it silhouetted a young boy. He looked about thirteen, with large ram horns and a small frame. There was a great aura of peace and calm around him. He wore tattered sheets as clothing, and he looked underfed.

Everyone fell silent. Only two boys were with her in the room with the young prophet, and they held her down. Everyone else stood outside the iron bars, saying nothing.

'Well!?' one of her captors demanded.

The boy did not turn, but kept looking out the window. 'Winter will be brief this year.'

A captor stood, and menacing up on the young boy slapped him hard across his head. He stumbled, but did not fall. 'You want to eat tonight? Do you!?'

The prophet stood tall.

'Then you tell us what you see. And you tell us NOW!'

Without acknowledgement he turned to face Kialessa.

She gasped, his pupils were covered with a smoky white cloud – she had to assume that he was completely blind.

     By Dr Joe Ireland

He smiled, and knelt down on the floor in front of her. It looked like there were tears in his eyes. Then he put his hand on her face and touched her cheek with the most gentle respect. 'So much nicer, in real life.'

Her captor shoved her suddenly, and she half squealed.

'Are you SURE you want to know!' the prophet demanded, very forcefully.

'No tricks this time, seer,' the boy who had slapped him demanded. 'Just give it to us, straight.'

The prophet sighed. 'There's really not much more than you can already see. Female. Undersized horns, no wings. Fire taint, shadow weaver. She has the potential to be a chosen of Ik'skuretza if she'd like.'

'NO!' the boy roared, and struck him again. 'You know what we mean. The real information. Tell us about her destiny. Tell us what you see in her *fate.*'

The prophet looked at her, and for just an instant Kialessa recognised a flitting of fear in his expression. He did not want them to know the answer to that question.

And she saw in his calm manner – he would suffer most horribly before he'd ever tell them. She doubted he would ever tell them.

'She will outlive most of you, if she chooses wisely. She has the potential to be an old woman.'

Students seem displeased by that. Why was growing old such an envious thing around here?

'You'd better do better than that,' the boy threated.

The prophet sighed, and paused a moment before revealing; 'She also has a dream guide.'

She gasped. She did not want anyone here to know about her brother's rare talent. This was not the kind of place were that information was safe.

Students protested while her captors suddenly laughed and cheered.

The next thing she knew, the blindfold was back on. They were dragging her out.

Someone shouted, 'Tell the alchemist! We need Marebane toxin now!'

They dragged her along another ten moments, saying almost nothing now. Then there were more shouts, and arguments. Most of the other students had left by then.

She could hear they'd entered a large cavern now, and there was the familiar damp air, the recognisable trickle of water.

She was thrown to the ground, and could finally remove the blindfold herself. She was in her damp cavern again, lying in the centre of her fire circle. There was no light.

And no-one except the three older students remained in the cavern with her.

Kialessa stood.

They looked at her, cruelty in their smiles.

'Decorum surely does disintegrate quickly without the firm hand of the father to guide us,' one of the boys said.

Kialessa did not reply.

His companion, the one that seemed to enjoy hitting people, took out a blowdart and dipped it in a pouch at his belt with great care.

There was nowhere to run. The cavern was a wide-open space, and there were three of them. She had no weapons, no allies, and nothing to defend herself with.

'Oh, don't cry, little Kialessa!' the girl teased her.

It just made her even angrier.

'You're not the only one with magic around here, Kialessa,' the first boy threatened her. 'And you need to know just how powerful we have become.' He spoke some dark words of power, and his eyes became glowing orbs of shadow, as did the other boy's. 'We're going to find this dream guide of yours, and tell him his services are no longer required. When you dream, from now on, you answer to *us*!'

                    By Dr Joe Ireland

She did not know what he meant, but it sounded awful.

'You get used to it,' the girl stated. 'One day, you watch, these two are going to get enough dream power to escape this hell hole. Maybe even kill our father. I breathe and live only to see that day.'

He nodded, 'Well done, well done, Tetrarch. You see, even now her entire conscious and unconscious soul bends to *my* will alone. The day soon approaches -'

He said more, but one glace at the girl's look of hatred and disgust at her brother told Kialessa that she was in no way his minion. She was just letting him believe that.

'You still don't have to do this,' Kialessa argued. 'You would not want someone to do this to you.'

He glared at her, 'Sometimes it's not anyone's fault when bad things happen. They just do; it's pure, random chance. I didn't always get a say in what happened to me, but I have made powerful decisions on how I choose to react to it. So you will sleep now, Kialessa, and enter the dreamworld. Then we will meet this little "dreamguide" of yours and find out just what they're capable of.'

They laughed, and seemed wickedly pleased with themselves.

She didn't even move.

The dart hit her with little more than a pinprick, but the poison was unnaturally fast. She barely had time to register her hand beginning to feel cold, when the floor rushed up to greet her.

Nightmare.

They are not yours. They are all broken. All is broken. You cannot own
them. They don't c– they cannot love you the way you need to be loved.
Cited in Recollections of the Tae'anaryl.

Kialessa felt herself dancing. She was back at the inn, by the well, for some reason. It didn't matter.

Then she heard a voice. It was her voice. 'Ahoy!' it called, 'is anyone here?'

Kiel, her brother, appeared in a glistening of golden sparkles. 'Kia!' he shouted with joy.

For reasons she could not explain, she was not happy to see him. Not at all. 'You need to get out of here, Kiel. It's not safe here.'

'Kiel, my beloved brother,' her voice spoke from the sky.

Kiel looked confused. 'I've been looking all over for you. I keep losing you at the fortress gate; the dreamworld seems broken away around the fortress.'

Suddenly the world snapped into focus. Kialessa realised she was in the dreamworld – forced there by her siblings so they could frighten or harm Kiel.

And he'd run straight into the trap.

'Kiel!' she screamed, desperately hoping he would get the message in time, 'Kiel, run! Get out of here, it's a trap!'

He just looked confused.

'I'm glad you're here,' her voice crooned from the sky.

Kiel looked around. His eyes glowed golden.

        By Dr Joe Ireland

The images of the inn and well evaporated, leaving him standing beside her prone form in the damp cavern.

'What did they do to you?' he asked.

'Run,' she begged.

Dark, bat like shapes swooped in on the world.

A golden sword appeared in Kiel's hand. It didn't even materialise, one instant it wasn't there, and the next moment it had always been.

Kialessa tried to move, but found her hands and ankles chained to the ground.

Three figures appeared. They felt to Kialessa like her three rude captors, her siblings. But they looked like arch-demons of nightmares and pain.

This was their domain, and this was not a fair fight.

None of them were, in this hellish fortress.

'So, Kiel… a brother, perhaps?' the tallest one said.

'Not much to look at,' the other demon crooned.

'Please, let him be,' Kialessa begged, finding her mouth gagged. She was unsure if anyone had heard her.

'Kiel, I want you to go away. You are not needed here anymore,' she heard her voice say.

Kialessa screamed, but no sound came out.

But Kiel cringed as though he'd heard her. The gag snapped away, and with a crack the chains broke away from her limbs.

She stood with him, back to back. A whip of magic and fire danced in her hands.

'Oh, a little fight, I enjoy those!' the girl teased them.

The shadows attacked in one moment, suffocating them in blackness. Kialessa immediately forgot who she was, and what she was doing there. But a golden light exploded around her, and then she remembered. Fire leapt around her, and a shadow ducked back, screaming. The other grappled with Kiel, who with multiple arms growing from his back kept beating the shadow demon down. Monsters formed from the shadows, but Kiel burned them with his eyes.

'Help me here, Beomith!' the demon screamed, and the darkness left Kialessa.

She was about to help Kiel, when someone stabbed her in the back. Her entire legs fell numb. She dreamed the paralysis away, but found herself tied down by thorns. She fought them, but they kept growing.

'You really are afraid of being tied down, eh sister,' the other girl teased. 'Always the last to know, the last to be helped. You can't even read properly yet!'

The thorns grew and grew. Kialessa saw how they fed off her own hidden fears; they were the embodiment of her own self-imposed limitations. They held her captive in the other girl's will.

She watched helplessly as Kiel battled on. He was powerful, a true prodigy. He kept coming up in an instant with new ideas to confront powers the others had developed over years and years of practice.

But he was only one boy, and a very young, and very frightened boy. He could not prevail. Dark chains wrapped around his wrists and held his neck back.

'Kiel, only brother of the tae'anaryn. You were abandoned. Your mother and father don't even know your name, and the two who own you don't even care about your life. You are alone, you are abandoned, you are forgotten.'

Darkness wrapped around Kiel, and his eyes filled with tears. The darkness began to dissolve his body.

'You should watch,' the other girl stated. 'This spell usually kills them. It's only fitting you should watch your only brother die.'

Blinding rage and fire burned through Kialessa's veins, igniting the thorns, and the girl screamed. The shadow was on her in the next moment, and again she could not move; he was so powerful.

    By Dr Joe Ireland

The darkness spread around Kiel, swallowing him. The last she saw was his lonely, tear filled eyes.

The shadow released her.

'She is broken, now,' the girl muttered.

The darkness was reaching into her now, filling her. Taking away the pain, taking away the hate. Taking away everything. Every memory… something was wrong, but most of her didn't care.

Then she saw it, the little golden light. Something was glowing in the distance.

'What?' a boy's voice protested.

'Hurry!' the girl demanded.

But the golden light filled her with hope. She'd seen that light before. She reached out, and it looked like a heart. A tiny, human heart. It was beating, strong and steady. From it veins grew, then lungs, then ribs.

'Stop it!' the shadow demon demanded.

A shadow raced to the heart, but could not touch it. It reared back, screaming.

'Hurry, hurry!' the girl demanded.

The shadows stabbed deep into her, but she resisted them. Again and again they tried to take away who she was. But she remembered it all. She remembered her father's irreverent sense of humour, her mother's endless complaints as she kept them all clothed and fed. She remembered getting water from the well each day, so they could care for their guests. She remembered Kiel, seeing his face written with concern as the guests would tease her again and again.

She saw her family.

Again and again the shadows stabbed at her, 'They are not yours. They are all broken. All is broken. You cannot own them. They don't c- they cannot love you the way you need to be loved.'

In those words she heard it; the pain in the boy's voice. This was not her fear, it was *his*.

Golden fire filled her soul, and in that moment she felt such utter, overwhelming compassion and sympathy for this young life. She didn't know what his family was like, but she knew he was just as frightened a prisoner of the fortress as she was. And he was turning to pain and fear and tyranny to fill the emptiness in his own soul. But he was afraid. And he was alone. And he was terrified that no matter what he ever did… no one would ever love him the way he needed to be loved.

Her love swelled for him, wanting in that pure, precious moment to be the friend he had never found in this hell.

Suddenly the world jolted sideways, and she momentarily felt the ground where her body lay shudder as the entire fortress was struck with some incomprehensible power.

She turned, and with growing dread saw an adult man, of perfect proportions, dressed in nothing but servant pants. It was the golden man that had saved her from Allastassia's nightmare, and it looked like a grown up Kiel.

Dread sympathy and compassion flowed from the golden man. Kialessa knew with perfect certainty that he was about to do something terrible.

His hands shot out, one grappling the shadows to his left, the other reaching several paces to grab the shadows by her. In that instant the shadows coalesced into the struggling forms of her two brothers. The light cleared, and she was back in the cavern, but still in the dreamrealm.

Her sister cringed by some rocks.

I bet you're glad he's only using two hands right now, Kialessa thought with uncharacteristic cruelty.

The girl's face was a mask of terror and confusion. One look and Kialessa realised the seriousness of their situation.

The golden man held the boys by their throats.

'Please,' one coughed, 'spare us.'

     By Dr Joe Ireland

'No,' the man said.

He waited only a breath more, then in one move crushed both their throats instantly. They would have died barely knowing any pain.

Black light flowed around the edges of the golden statue, then the light fled. 'Judgment is passed,' he spoke.

Her sister screamed, and Kialessa heard that scream right through the dreamrealm and out into the real world. But she still could not move her body, or escape this nightmare.

The golden man walked towards Kialessa, looking expressionless.

She tried to move, but could not bring herself to believe that Kiel would harm her.

Then as he looked down at her, his face seemed… distraught. Forgotten. Betrayed. That somehow, she'd brought this danger into the only safe world he had… and now he was no longer safe here either.

She knew right there and then – he was leaving.

Her heart leapt in panic, 'No, Kiel, don't leave me! It's not my fault … and you only did what you had to do – they would have killed you, and me! You can't go… you can't…'

He didn't even shed a tear. 'You should not have told them where to find me.'

'I didn't, I promise! It was the prophet.'

He looked up, then down again, 'Either way, I am no longer safe here. I cannot be safe here with you. I have to think about this for a while.'

He turned his back on her.

'Kiel!' she begged.

He didn't even glance back. Once his mind was made up in his golden state, it was unbreakable.

Perhaps that was what had saved his life.

She could only hope he heard her. 'I love you, Kiel!'

***

Kialessa heard someone praying,

Ik'skurteza's light, light divine.
Restoring truth, breath in kind.
Purge this vessel, make crooked straight,
Free this soul by wisdom's gait.

Something tore away the poison, and she sat up choking. Then she started crying. The demon who called himself her father was holding her in his arms, uttering prayers. Lossel was there too, perhaps. And some dark tendrils… Shadowmonger?

Then Kialessa realised the demon father was holding her. She screamed, and kicked out at him, pushing herself away for all she was worth. If she'd had the presence of mind, she would have kicked him in the face.

She found herself backing up against Mak, lying in the circle she used to keep warm. There were at least a dozen others there now.

Then she saw the bodies. The two boys were lying, unmoving on the floor, their bruised necks glistening with golden soot. Their eyes were open, and unmoving.

The demon father glared at her, but spoke instead to Daygon, 'Priest! Gather the bodies and bring them back to life this hour.'

Daygon turned pale, well, paler. To bring one back from the dead was a terrible ordeal, and took great focus and commitment.

'I would not bother,' Shadowmonger said, voice grim.

'Why!' the demon father demanded.

'They will not hear his voice, or any. Their time has come.'

The demon father stood, and glared at her older sibling. Shadowmonger did not look proud, but he did not back down. It was as if he was simply

     By Dr Joe Ireland

stating a fact.

The demon father looked angry then, and glared at Kialessa, his fists clenched.

She glared back, trebling in fear and pain.

'What happened,' he demanded of her.

Her sister spoke first, 'I tried to stop them!' she begged, held back in Flameheart's arms. 'I told them to leave her alone, but they insisted!'

Kialessa was incensed. That was a bald-faced lie.

But her sister continued. 'Drake and Beomith insisted on trialling her in the dream realm. They meant no harm, they-'

'Then why did they use Marebane?' The merchant demon accused her, holding up a dart he had probably taken from Kialessa's hand.

Tetrarch, was that her name? She looked worried, but recovered quickly, 'Marebane? Unbelievable!'

Kialessa scoffed.

They glared at her.

Then the demon turned to face Kialessa. 'Two of my sons are dead tonight, and I've yet to decide your part in this-'

'Have mercy,' her evil sister begged, 'she did nothing wrong.'

'Tetrarch! Your lies are as apparent as your forked tongue!' He roared, and the lights fell dim.

'If you had been here, this would not have happened,' Mak accused him, being characteristically bold.

Kialessa sat up, giving Mak some cover.

The demon father seemed to be holding back some powerful rage. 'You have no idea how much you have inconvenienced me, Kialessa.'

At that, her rage boiled. She stood. 'Me? You blame *me*?' Why was chaos so swift to blossom in his absence? Was this what it was to be like for most of the year? She would not survive that time in this prison. She would not survive the winter. But he was swift to leave. Swift to make them fight for food he himself did not touch, swift to let them fight for basic necessities, like a bed or a few blankets. 'You want us to fight each other, all the time, in this place,' she accused him.

He looked at her, and what was it, admiration? 'Two of your brothers are *dead*, Kialessa! You think that means *nothing* to me?' His voice broke. 'We will mourn. A day each of silence on the mountain for of them. *Ad'dendium*!' He spoke a word of power, and all noise dissipated from her. Not a sound. Nothing.

Two days passed slowly. No one spoke, they could not. She read with Raynah, and ate bread with Mak for they were given no other food in all that time. But the unnatural silence was restful. She knew she had done nothing wrong.

The third day, as dusk dimmed in the far horizon, she was awoken and taken to the funeral. There, they wore deep robes of purple, and burned red wax candles in abject silence. Only Daygon spoke.

Because the demon merchant wasn't there. He had "business" to attend to.

They'd tried to kill her, and died for it. Yet she was made to mourn them. In her heart, she did feel sorry for them. Terribly sorry. In a sense she was glad they did not heed the call to return. In a sense, they were now free.

But she was not, and she had to light a candle and wear purple and mourn without complaint at the command of a man who couldn't even be bothered attending his own sons' funeral.

As the services concluded, her voice returned. No one seemed to be bothered talking.

But there was something she needed to say.

Walking up to Daygon, she demanded in the newly broken silence, 'Where is he?'

Daygon took a moment to reply, barely whispering. 'If you must... see him... you will find him in the upper study. Come, I will take you.'

     By Dr Joe Ireland

She and Mak walked without talking up to the office. There were voices behind the door. Daygon knocked gently, but there was no reply.

Kialessa hit the door fiercely.

'Come in, Kialessa,' the demon father's voice replied. He seemed unimpressed.

She marched in.

There, to her horror, she recognised the man the merchant had skipped out on his own sons' funeral for. A man she would have never expected to see here, but on thinking about it, it was really was no surprise.

Dog, Cruel voice and assassin of kings. The man who she'd only barely stopped from killing her king back at the start of the year.

Her whip was in her hands, and burning, before she could have possibly realised it.

Dog stepped back, hands up.

The demon father held out his hand, but Kialessa was not going to strike just yet.

'You always going to greet me like that, Horns?' Dog joked.

'Kialessa, do not harm my guest unless you wish to feel the sting of *my* whip against *your* back,' the merchant warned her.

It was almost comforting to think he realised she was willing and able to do it.

She spoke to her "father", 'You weren't even there. Why weren't you there?!'

He didn't immediately reply, and Dog chose to fill the silence, 'I think you need to be more careful about what you assume your father knows, and where he may be found.'

She glared at the assassin. 'What are you doing here?' she demanded.

He laughed, but it was not with the childish mockery she was used to. He seemed subdued in the merchant's presence. 'Well, business has been very good this year, trading furs out here in the western and all, *you* know.

I was just… checking in on a few of my investments, getting the best returns, you understand,' he winked.

If she wasn't sure the demon father was ready for it, she would have lashed out with her only weapon right there and then.

Tyran Noblax leaned forward, 'I see I've been too indulgent with you, Kialessa Tavernskeep. But no more. If you wish to learn the hard way, then so be it.'

'Where were you?' Mak asked.

The merchant glanced at him, grinding his teeth with anger.

'Mum's in jail. I know you can get her out. But you never come by. You're never around. We needed you… dad.'

Dog raised his eyebrows in an, *Oh boy, here it comes*, kind of way.

Tyran glared at them. 'You are, both of you, lucky to be alive because of me. I give you this fortress to hone your skills and develop your talents-'

'You give it to make us fight!' Kialessa screamed. 'You are a demon and you are a monster, and I want to get out of here!'

Tyran stood, Dog scurrying to the far edge of the room and cringing down like his namesake. The table the merchant was sitting at split in two in the aura of his indignation. When he spoke, dark magic wallowed in every imposition of his will, 'How *dare* you speak to your father that way! I give you *everything*! I work day and night for your welfare, and *this* is how you thank me; with sedition and riot?'

Kialessa felt her heart dying, crushed by the indignation of his words, her hands tingling… no, twingling. Then her mind snapped clear again – he was using magic.

Summoning every energy from deep within her stomach, she screamed at the demon father. The magical energy shattered in her voice, scattering in every direction. Mak stood up straight.

The man who called himself her father gave her a wry grin, 'Not bad, Kialessa, not bad. But you really need to be taught some manners. Perhaps a

By Dr Joe Ireland

day without food and water will teach you?'

'Let us go,' she demanded.

He scoffed, utter conviction in every laugh.

She summoned her courage, 'Let us go. We do not want to be here. We do not belong here.'

'And have you bring my enemies to this place? Kialessa. There is something you need to realise. You have nowhere to go.'

'We want to go back to our families.'

He looked at her with pity in his eyes, pity, and disgust. 'Kialessa, that's not what I meant. You don't have a family to go back to.'

She sneered at him.

'My mother and father-'

'He is not your father!' The demon merchant roared, and the ground trembled. Even in the shadows of the fortress, there seemed to be terrible truth in those words. He continued, stabbing his words into her like knives. 'You have no family to go back to. Your mother sold you to me the day you were conceived, because the man you call father is too drunk to even try. Just lovers at some rundown tavern at the edge of the smallest kingdom of the entire realm. Your brother is some orphan they bought to wash their dishes. Your mother and father *aren't even married.*'

His words smashed into her. Not married? It was a crime to have a child outside of marriage in their culture, had they simply never told her? Could it really be true? It was the most unimaginable way for her to find out, from a demon who wanted to hurt her in the worst possible way. Her thoughts fell apart. If it really was true could she go back? Should she? What would she find there? And what right did she have to go back if they … weren't really… a real family…

Mak spoke, 'Mum and I did all right.'

The demon father glared at him, and Kialessa grinned. Yes, she was still part of a family – a broken one, but perhaps, with help… they could be a family to each other again. More of a family there than he had ever been to his children held prisoner here.

But she still wanted to ask them about it.

'So help me,' the demon father sprouted wings, and a black crown began to form from the shadows between his horns, 'if you don't give me honour, I will beat you till you all beg for mercy!'

He raised his fist. Kialessa wasn't sure what magic was invoked, but she didn't wait to find out. She lashed out with her whip, hoping to catch him in the eye. Hoping to stop him, or at best, to get away.

But faster than she could imagine he whipped his fist around and caught it in his hand.

She pulled it back, but it was stuck there as though embedded in stone. He twisted it around his fist, and it yanked on her hand.

She squealed.

He gripped it with his other hand, and reeled it in. Hand over hand he pulled with irresistible might. She may as well have been trying to push the entire mountain as to stop him gathering up her whip. He dragged her along the floor right to his feet, and held her up off the ground as though it was no effort at all.

'Three days in the dungeon, Kialessa, to rethink your gratitude. And lest you think there is anything you can do to stop me getting the respect I deserve in this place from my own children…' and he snapped her coiled whip in half.

She screamed, falling at his feet.

Again he coiled the broken fragments around his fists, and snapped her father's treasured whip again. Then he took the handle, and what tiny pieces he held in hands, and snapped them all too.

Forty or so pieces of cured, faithful leather fell broken at her knees, mingling with her falling tears.

Then he stood up, straightening his coat. 'Consider your rudeness.'

With a wave of his hand, the shadow realm lifted itself up and into the normal realm, grappling her. She fell in dark shadows that not even her eyes could piece. Screaming, she fell into a pit of blackness.

She knelt, sobbing on the floor. Broken whip lay about her, the only defence she'd known all this past year.

Reaching out, she took hold of the split remains of the broken hilt. In the darkness, she pressed the hilt to the floor, and began to scribe a rough circle around her with trembling fingers.

Then she wept.

Revelations

Whether your life is supposed to be like this or not is not going to have

any bearing whatsoever on what your life now actually is. Being upset is not

going to change it.

Kialessa, cited in Recollections of the Tae'anaryl.

Kialessa didn't know how long she lay on the floor. She was already hungry from the funeral, but now the thirst was burning in her throat. It must have been hours, but she did not know if she'd slept or not.

What am I to do? she wondered.

Nothing she'd ever experienced was darker than this dungeon. It seemed especially designed for those who could see in the darkness for she could see nothing but black in here. *This must be what it was like for Piex,* she wondered. It was terrifying. She would have to be kinder to him, next time they met.

She cried again.

This is not how my life is supposed to turn out, she told herself, and her heart twisted in bitter knots.

But this is how your life is, her heart replied. Or was it her own heart? She did not know if some god heard her, or if she was just talking to herself.

*What's **that** supposed to mean!* she demanded to know.

For a moment, no thoughts came. So she waited.

Then the thoughts arrived: *Whether your life is supposed to be like this or not is not going to have any bearing whatsoever on what your life now actually is. Being upset is not going to change it.*

It sounded like the least compassionate thing she could possibly think

                    By Dr Joe Ireland

now… but then again… it felt true. Well, actually, it kind of was true. What could she change about her life right now?

She could stand. She could find water.

But she could not change her venue.

And, if she thought about it, demanding life be anything other than what it was right now would only make her more upset, and less likely to do anything about changing it.

Strange how 'this is the way life is' can be both depressing, and hopeful, she realised.

Yeah, that's one of those weird things, isn't it?

All right, who am I talking to! Kialessa demanded.

The thoughts, however, did not reply.

At any rate, they'd been distracting, and she wasn't so upset now. What could she change? Could she get home? Could she get her parents married so they could be a "real" family? None of those things could be done right now. So there was no power in worrying about them.

But there were some things she could do right now.

Carefully, she felt around her way in the darkness. Not seeing was a very unnerving experience. She was in some kind of small cave, by the feel of things, with a doorway that led to a corridor.

It seemed she would have to feel her way along it, when she suddenly felt a familiar presence. Familiar, and unwelcomed.

She sat up just as a swirl of grey sand coalesced into the form of a young man. The entire room began to glisten with light and colours, scintillations of mica in the stones around her. Then he appeared, grinning obnoxiously, a curious wreath of deep green ivy leaves and fine spun gold around his head.

'Well, you recovered sooner than we expected,' the man said.

'Dog,' she muttered, intending to fling a whole host of curses his way, but finding too many to get them all organised in time.

'My name's not Dog!' he insisted, flinging his arms. He sat on a nearby outcropping of stone, looking visibly upset. His behaviour was still so strange; conversational, simple. Almost immature. Almost as if he was in reality not a day older than she was. 'My name's Jerik. *Jerik*. You could at least call me by my real name; you're one of only a handful of people who know it.'

She had no weapons, no idea where she was, and no idea how he had arrived here. However he'd done it, it was making the rocks glow with internal lights, like iridescent gems.

He noticed her looking around, and pointed to the wreath. 'Borrowed this. Need to give it back in ten or so.'

She looked around, the entire cavern pitch black except nearest his person.

'It's the fey realm,' he explained, ever conversational. 'Coterminous, like the shadow and dream realms. And the first layer of the afterlife, but you should know all this. I only ever had tutors.' He sighed, almost regretful.

'Who *are* you?' she needed to know.

He huffed. 'I serve a powerful master. Tyrannical, but powerful. That's why I couldn't kill you, Kialessa! You just got in the way, but it's nothing personal. I quite like you. Only you can understand…. anyway. That's why I couldn't kill you. And your father, what a man! Wise, smart, strong. I just didn't want to upset too many potential allies, you know what I mean? I didn't want you dead; you were your father's child. But you just got in the way.'

She stood back. He was no threat to her right now. 'You have me. Is this what you wanted me to know?'

He looked at her, as if thinking deeply. Kialessa was again struck at how young he seemed to be in the way he moved and the way he behaved. And yet his body was at least in his thirties, maybe more. In fact, if she didn't know any better, she'd say he'd actually aged visibly since she'd seen him at

By Dr Joe Ireland

the start of the year, holding her upside down so that everyone could laugh at the fact she had a tail.

And now he was here, in a dungeon, using the fey realm just to chat.

'I don't understand you,' she admitted.

He huffed. 'You're the only one who can,' he told her. 'I just wanted you to know that I respect your father greatly, and that was why I couldn't kill you that day out on the rope when you challenged me, backed up by all the might of Lenmer'el. I've never failed my master before. I was willing to take them all on. But you reminded me of your dad, just so fearless and committed, and I realised if I hurt you, I'd upset him. A lot. So I let you go. Oh, it got me a beating! Like I've never had before, I could not stand for a day!' He laughed, like it was some kind of perverse joke. 'So I guess what I'm trying to tell you is; if anything ever happens to your dad, the deal is off. I have no reason to spare you again. My master wants you dead, and soon.'

She glared at the cowardly assassin, 'Then why not kill me now? You know I will stop you, and I will not let you harm my king, in life or death!'

'See, that's the trick,' he muttered to himself, but she still felt compelled to stop and listen. 'People don't change, and death doesn't change who people are. Sometimes it's better to let them live so they can make up their minds to be something else. I'd rather you just got out of my way. You could do that, you know? You can be very rich here. You can be very powerful. Change is coming to the Great Kingdom and you can be a queen, not a servant to a petty king at the edge of the greatest kingdom-'

Kialessa stood. 'He is no petty king, and you are no hero of a rising order! You are a murderer and an assassin, and I am going to stop you!'

He sat back, eyes wide. He seemed afraid, even transfixed. It was as if no one had ever flatly denied him in this way before. He broke out in sweat, and looked away. 'Oh. All right. All right then. If you must. I guess you must... I guess there really was no other way.'

The knife appeared in his hand, but he did not use it.

Choice, set free159

She knew he would not.

He let it disappear again. 'You're no threat here. None at all. You're as good as dead now that your dad's got you, and I will never have to worry about you getting in the way of my master's plans again. So, I guess what I'm saying is… goodbye Kialessa. I… I wish we could have been friends.'

She wanted to snarl at him, but she froze. Was he actually being sincere? Was he really a … nice guy… down at heart? Who was he, really? And was there something deep down in that heart that she could use to free herself now? Or to, perhaps, help save her king one day…?

He seemed to guess her thoughts, 'No, there's not. I may have my faults, but rebellion is not one of them. However, it is written all through and over you, and the king you protect. Oh, we could have had such fun!' he sighed. 'Things are very busy now. They're happening so fast. I gotta be back in a few hours and I don't have time for this chat. But if there's one thing I wanted to say… it's nothing personal. It's just… business –'

He looked to the side. Kialessa heard it too.

Someone was shuffling up the corridor.

With a smug grin and casual salute, the assassin disappeared, and the world was cloaked with impenetrable darkness once more.

The soft footfalls made their way tentatively up the corridor. There seemed to be something gentle about them. She tensed; unsure of who it could have been that would drive off the assassin.

A light rounded the corner. It was a pair of white glowing eyes. Actually, the whole face was glowing. It was the young boy, the one they called the prophet. 'Hmm,' he pondered out aloud, 'I heard voices…'

'I was … talking to someone…' there was a distinctly notable aura of peace that surrounded him. 'Were, were you the one that was speaking to my mind a few moments earlier?'

'No, but I recognise the auric energy of the One here. Perhaps it was him?'

  By Dr Joe Ireland

'The One?' Kialessa asked.

The prophet nodded. 'Him. He does not tell me his name, for his voice is a deafening thunder. I cannot see his face, for I am blinded by the lightning. I see the work of his hands, in every stone, in all life. It is Him to whom I worship, and him to whom I am Chosen.'

She looked at the boy, noting that he was getting brighter as he spoke, or her eyes were adjusting to the unnatural dimness. His whole body seemed to be made of light.

'You speak of a god I do not know,' she admitted.

He laughed, and looked as though he did not believe her. 'But you are more full of his light than any other being I have ever encountered.'

She wondered what he meant, till it dawned on her. 'You… worship the Eternal. You mean, you're a Chosen of the Eternal!' Her heart lifted in hope. Even if she died here, this was important! There had never been a Chosen of the Eternal, not to her knowledge. 'You… I don't believe it.' Without thinking, she jumped forward, and held his hands.

He winced, as though the experience was very new to him.

Then she noticed his eyes grew moist with tears, 'What is it?' she asked him.

'I just… I've never known anyone who has met my god… You have been washed? Your energy, it's so clear. I've never seen anything like it. He promised me he would send a messenger with his words one day, and I felt that day drawing near. When they brought you down two days ago I thought my time had finally come. You cannot believe how heartbroken I was when they took you away. Kialessa, can you help Him keep His promise? Will you teach me about our Eternal?'

She felt very unsure of what to say. Was this what it felt like to be Darrix when she'd asked him the same request? And what a strange and eclectic series of conversations she was having in one day!

'I'm sorry if I rush you,' he apologised.

'No, no, it's all right,' she said, unsure of what to say, or where to begin. Of all the places to begin sharing one's beliefs, why here? And of all time times, why right now?

'Your light darkens, you are confused,' he told her.

'How is it you can see?' she asked.

'Fate sight. I am blind, but I can see the souls of living, and unliving. I see the soul of Mya, and can walk around these caverns without trouble. But when they brought you to me…'

Her heart was momentarily angry, but she didn't dwell on it. This boy's words had cost her dearly. They had brought down two monsters who were willing to hurt her. They had tried to hurt her brother.

'I am sorry,' he said, looking at her. 'You need to understand, Messenger. When they brought you down, seeking excuse to harm you… I could not tell them what I really saw. I did not tell them what I really saw.'

'What do you mean?' she asked.

He looked at her, seeming for the first time a little uncertain. 'They knew I saw more than I told them. Telling them about your dreamwalker was the only way I could keep them from a far deeper truth. When I see other people's fate, Kialessa, it seems to be far more than they are usually ever able to see for themselves. You have the writing of destiny about you unlike any other person I have met, my sister. I dare not speak it, not even to you.'

'What?' she did not understand him.

He might have said more, but something stopped him. So instead he said, 'Your power is something that the father demon will covet dearly. He will not wait to claim that power from you, once he realises what it is. You will not survive that process.'

She was stunned, which was saying something for a very dark day like today. 'What does he do?' she asked.

He was quiet for a moment, thinking. 'You will know, in time. Can you not share your message? I have been waiting for a long time, and we don't have very long here.'

She wanted to ask more, but suspected it was very important, and would have to wait.

And how did her father have the power to claim her fate?

What did that demon want with her?

And why was this kind-hearted prophet locked in this dungeon with her?

She was certain that any truth or happiness they found here would work against that evil demon's plans and desires. He would have to be a full-blooded demon – it was why they were all tae'anaryn after all. But they had their own choices about what kind of creatures they as children became, whether they embraced their demonic heritage, or their true.

She sat down, probably still in her circle, and the boy sat down too. Reaching in, she took out her scripture, the one the king had given her.

'But I cannot read in this darkness,' she told them.

'Truth can shine in darkness,' he told her, and his entire body burst into silent flames.

She saw him clearly; he was clear like a ghost. In the flames she got a sense of his soul, an incredibly pure and innocent soul. An astonishingly wise and patient soul. A soul that seemed, in part, to carry within it a portion of the Eternal's own presence.

So she read, and he listened. She could not see the words on the pages, but it was as if the words were written on her heart, and she could read them as if she could clearly see them on the page.

He listened an hour without comment, absorbing every word.

When she finished, he was silent.

She wondered if he wanted her to explain it some more.

Then he burst into tears, 'Never, never, have I heard such truth!' he spoke then, words in a language she'd never heard. But it was a beautiful language, and his voice was with such depth and sincerity. She felt the light explode out from him, and watched in fascination as it seemed to be hidden in the darkness. They were surrounded by twelve beings of unimaginable depth and wisdom, but they did not speak to her or the prophet, they only bore witness, and prevented every darkness on the mountain from perceiving the sacred truths being shared in its inaccessible depths.

Truly, great light could shine in darkness.

Then the young prophet prayed,

Everlasting Eternal, Sacred is your unspeakable name,
Your kingdom stands, your desire to fulfil,
In this cavern, as at your throne.
Care for us, and deliver us please.
And forgive us, we pray,
As we plead for the strength to forgive our captors.
For yours is the Kingdom, and all power, and all light,
Forever and ever, so be it.

Tears filled her eyes as he prayed with a power and humility she had never before felt. Nothing sounded more pure than a young man's first prayer.

Then he slumped forward, and appeared to fall asleep.

'Prophet?' she asked him.

He did not move.

'Prophet?' she nudged him again.

That was odd.

She wondered what to do, and a particular peace filled her heart. He would be safe, and probably communing with her Eternal some more. Perhaps through the dream realm? It was probable.

She adjusted his position so at least he looked comfortable. Then she waited ten moments more, maybe twenty. Then a whole hour. Nothing changed.

He seemed quite at peace, however, and she was beginning to feel curious. Looking around, she found a dim light, and it seemed to beckon her, and she felt renewed. She wanted to explore the cavern some more.

She stood, only briefly noting she did not feel tired or stiff or even upset, not even a little.

It was time to explore the dim light.

She turned to the prophet, still burning from the inside with white fire. Only then did she notice that he was in the centre of her crudely wrought circle, scratched imperfectly from a broken tool never designed to write such sacred things.

Yet, somehow, even that had been enough.

Undercrypt.

'You're each so unique. So amazingly different and special. Everyone in
this mountain has a totally unique and wonderful story to tell, and I want
to hear them all. Will you tell me? I would like you to tell me.'
Recollections of the Tae'anaryl.

Kialessa wandered in the darkness. Ten moments or more passed as she made her way through its labyrinthine depths. It was impossible terrain, inexcusably dark, made of up unwelcoming stone that was cold to her touch.

Suddenly something lunged at her in the darkness. She screamed out as bestial claws scratched at her armour, but did not penetrate it. The claws ground against the stone, throwing up red sparks. In their light Kialessa saw her assailant was a giant rat of some kind, filled with demonic hatred. It was trying to press itself though a narrowing of the passage, but it could not get anything more than a single claw though. She crawled quickly out of its reach.

She stood, and it sniffed at the cavern, but did not threaten her further. Stilling her fevered heart she crawled quickly on.

Soon she was drawn to some movement in the distance. She felt her way along the stone, till at last she saw the flickers of shadows on a far wall. Some creatures were speaking. They seemed other young tae'anaryl, like herself.

'No, put the rock back on your grid, Arpil. You can only move up to six squares in any direction.'

'She's still not going to listen to you,' another voice replied.

'I'm sure she gets it, look, just, oh!' the first voice protested.

And a third voice laughed.

                    By Dr Joe Ireland

Kialessa turned a stone corner, and found three tae'anaryl crouched in the darkness. They seemed to be looking at a game of some kind that they'd made up on the floor, with crudely carved figurines of stone. They were lit, only, by the dim grey fire that burned from one of their tails. The flames were very poor, it was not much more than the size of a torch light and far less bright, but it did not go out. In that light she could not make out their faces very well, but their forms were clear enough.

'Hey, the weeper awakes!' the boy with the burning tail spoke. He seemed to be doing most of the talking. 'Welcome to the undercrypt - what have you done with our prophet? He's not usually gone this long.'

'He's praying,' Kialessa replied.

The stone girl laughed. She was a terranoid tae'anaryn, made from earth and rock, including her wings. Her face looked human, her body too, but her hair was jagged stone and crystals. She looked pretty, and was stoutly build like most of her race.

'Arpil thinks you have a nice voice,' the boy smiled. He was human, with bat wings and scorpion claws and tail. He looked rough, but spoke well. 'Anyway, what's your name? We don't get to meet the new kids. I'm Pain-in-the-butt. Though my mothers call me Ipi. You should probably call me Pain.'

'Oh, don't be like that Ipi,' the third child protested. She was a dwarven tae'anaryn, with dark fangs and glowing green eyes. 'I'm Parrow, by the way, and if it's all good, we are the lowest of the low, the prisoners of the imprisoned. Is that what brings you here, redling?'

Kialessa looked at them. They seemed friendly enough. But they looked rough. Their clothes were rags, if they wore anything at all. She did not feel very comfortable, and it was still unnaturally dark in the cavern.

Arpil nudged Parrow, and she stood up.

'It's all right,' Parrow said, taking a step toward her. 'We're just… um… won't you sit with us?'

Pain, or Ipi, jumped up. 'Hey. I'm here because I spilt wine on dad's stupid business lectures. *Total* mistake!'

'Yeah, right!' Parrow disagreed.

'Tis true!' Ipi insisted. 'Parrow here just refuses to play by his rules-'

'He is a demon who stole me from my family, and I'm going to escape and get home.'

'Like thus,' Ipi nodded, 'And Arpil here… much the same. Won't speak to anyone, tries to kill the merchant every time she sees him. Can't seem to get along with him, eh? So we're all stuck in here for a few days, years in Arpil's case. So what he get you in here for? What'd you do to upset Noblax?'

Kialessa couldn't help but smile at their rebellious camaraderie, 'I tried to hit him in the face with my whip.'

They congratulated her. Arpil just grinned.

Then a lump grew in Kialessa's throat. 'Then he caught it with his bare hands, snapped it into a thousand pieces, and threw me down here.'

They didn't laugh at that.

'That's one more point against him, that demon,' Parrow shook her fist.

Arpil grunted.

'Oh, we'll get out of here, one day!' Ipi promised her. 'Just you wait and see.'

Arpil grunted again.

'Long before you're dead, stoneface!' Parrow said, and started shoving Arpil.

Ipi scurried over to Kialessa, 'So, you got any food on you?'

She shook her head. He looked famished, like he might try and eat her if she wasn't carful.

He nodded, 'Dad only feeds us once a day. Can be rough.'

'Do you have any water?' she asked.

'There's a pool over here,' he said, pointing into the darkness where she could see nothing.

By Dr Joe Ireland

'He doesn't like us to have light,' Ipi explained. 'I think he hopes it makes us too scared to stay here for long.'

'Well, it's dark, and I'm cold,' Kialessa said. 'Does anyone mind if a light a fire?'

Arpil and Parrow stopped shoving each other then, and looked very curious, 'Not much burns down here,' Parrow explained, 'shadow realm too thick.'

'I think I'd like to try,' Kialessa said, 'Do you have anything I can write with?'

Ipi looked around for a stone, but Arpil handed her a sharp stylus immediately. It was as if she'd been holding it the whole time.

Kialessa nodded, wondering where the implement had come from. She bent down, noting dark scratches in the stone ground.

'Not there,' Ipi protested, 'that's where our game is happening!'

She moved over to where there didn't appear to be any further writing, and knelt down. There she began to inscribe her magical circle, the *stone on fire* spell. It took almost ten moments.

'You know wizardry,' Ipi informed her.

'I don't have my spellbook with me, so I'm really hoping I got it right. I think it's right.'

'What if it's not right?' Parrow asked.

'Well,' Kialessa admitted, 'there's a very small, small chance it might blow us all up.'

Ipi took one step back.

Kialessa began to intone her program.

Ipi took several more steps backwards.

She finished, intoning the action sequence, and to her delight the large rock in the centre burst into flames. Her hands lit up with warmth and light, but the dim fire could barely reach anywhere past the edge of her circle.

The other three pressed in closer.

'I have not seen light in over four weeks,' Parrow mused. 'You've got to teach me how to do that.'

Kialessa wasn't sure how it was done herself, even with Raynah's amazing teaching. She did not think that she could not pass on that knowledge effectively yet.

But it would be worth the time, seeing the look on Parrow's face. It was one of wonder, and respect. Her irises were fully extended as if desperate to grasp any remaining tendrils of light. In that light, Kialessa saw her clearly. She had somehow sewn her own clothes together from whatever grew in this darkness, or the sacks they'd thrown in.

Arpil looked oldest, maybe eighteen. Her face was kind, but her eyes were so terribly sad. It was clear she did not sleep well, and had not eaten properly in all her time here. Kialessa knew terranoid needed crystals to fill out their diet, and it looked like Arpil hadn't received nearly enough.

Ipi was the youngest; a bright-eyed young man of about fourteen. His eyes were a deep, welcoming red, but his features betrayed the look of a man who would rebel no matter what his circumstances. His hair was a mess and his teeth so unwashed several had already turned dark. He looked like a troublemaker, it was sad to say. But he stared at the fire as if enchanted.

'Pity you can't do anything about this shadow realm,' Parrow mentioned. 'I've always wanted to get the height of this cavern.'

They looked at her.

She didn't know anything about "pushing back" the shadow realm. But that didn't mean she couldn't try.

She sat down, her feet in her little, welcomed fire. 'I could use a drink of water,' she mentioned.

Arpil ran, and brought her a large drink in a wide stone cup. It looked like it was made out of the same material as the walls and floor, something some other hapless prisoner might have made once. She took a long drink. It would help.

					By Dr Joe Ireland

Kialessa liked enchantments. Allastassia made it look very easy. She stood up. 'Do any of you know music?' she asked.

Arpil grinned, and thumped the floor. The entire room shuddered. Then she thumped it again, adding a simple, driving rhythm.

Parrow sung, her deep dwarven voice a thundering bass that shifted in perfect time with the beat.

Ipi scurried away and returned with a stone pan flute. He added in a lilting melody that seemed to be an improvisation of something she'd heard before.

And then she danced, just like for her king. But this was more; she was calling on her enchantress's powers now. There was a purpose to this dance; a wish, or a prayer. Fire was the science of magic to her, but to weave the shadows, Kialessa needed something more artistic and improvised.

Wordless tunes worked their way around the cavern, echoing against distant, invisible walls. Shadow weave clung to her outstretched fingers, toes, and the tip of her tail. But she pushed them back, again and again. They seemed clingy in this place. But shadow weave was not like normal threads; it responded to her heart, it could be shaped by her will. Again and again she pushed it back, till as the song began its final chorus she set a burning fire in her heart, and the weave rushed away and beyond the walls.

Their music stopped as the others oohed in wonder. The entire cavern lit up wonderfully in the light of her single fire. In the darkness, it looked as bright as day. The room was quite large, with several pools of water, and an ornate entrance at one end that appeared to lead up – perhaps the way out? And high in the roof gems of light and colour glittered.

Suddenly Arpil cried out, and rushed towards the far wall. She seemed to move through the stone as she ran, the floor shuddering as she went. Reaching up, she grabbed some glittering gems with what might have been a squeal of delight. She tore them from the wall without any apparent effort, and began munching on them.

Parrow laughed.

'She's been looking for them the whole time we've been here,' Ipi pointed.

Kialessa smiled back, only then noticing the wide welts of several whippings across the young man's back. There were layers of welts, years.

He saw her noticing, but made nothing of it.

Parrow's voice broke as she spoke, 'Oh, Arpil,' she rushed to the terranoid's side. It looked like the older girl was sobbing. It was as if this was her first meal in years.

'We have to get out of here. *All of us*,' Kialessa promised.

***

They relaxed an hour more in the light of Kialessa's fire, teaching Parrow on basics. Kialessa learnt a bit more about their past, and their hopes. She tried to learn their game, but it was very complex and seemed to require a lot of imagination; the kind of game you really needed to write things down to play properly.

Then she heard a shuffling.

'Ah, the prophet finds himself!' Ipi grinned.

Sure enough, the young man soon walked around the corner. He was still glowing white, but it was not quite so obvious in the light of her fire. After a while, she hardly noticed it at all.

The prophet bowed, and sat down.

'You all right?' Parrow asked. She didn't seem to like him very much, but they were all in the same boat down here in the dungeon.

He didn't speak at first. Then all he said was, 'I have never before considered such things. Never.'

Ipi stood up and grinned, 'Oh, oh! Did you hear that Kialessa! Did you hear that! It is a new day, folks, *a new day!* The day the prophet finally admits he does not know everything!'

Ipi danced about with glee, while Parrow grinned. The prophet gave them an apologetic smile, and they all laughed some more.

'I still don't know who you are,' she told the prophet.

'Oh, this, this is-' Ipi began.

Kialessa held up her hand for his silence, and he honoured her immediately.

The young boy spoke, 'I am Charl Greymonger, of the southeastern nomads. My mother brought me to the fortress the day I turned twelve.'

'Oh, he has a name,' Parrow seemed surprised.

Charl continued, 'As I foresaw, the father demon did not take to my gifts with kindness. They vastly excel his own, and he knows he cannot claim them for they reside in my soul, and not my physical form.' He turned to face the fire. 'Thank you, Kialessa, I think I had forgotten what fire looked like.'

'I'm beginning to think the demon leaves the nicest children in the dungeon,' she pondered.

'As far from himself as possible,' Parrow agreed. 'How do you propose we escape? I'm hoping you have a plan.'

Kialessa thought for a moment, but none came. She did not know her father, or what kind of demon powers he had. That was something they needed to know. Then they needed to find a way to foil his scrying on them, so they could not be found once they escaped. In all, it seemed very hopeless, unless the demon died somehow, but that was not looking very likely, or possible. She realised this was going to take some time, and there were things that needed to be accomplished before she could set everyone free. 'I wish I did,' she said.

'You will,' Charl the prophet said. 'I have foreseen it.'

It gave her hope, but the others groaned.

'Don't suppose you got any clues about how she'll do that?' Parrow almost demanded.

Charl shook his head.

'This is why dad threw him down here.' Ipi explained. 'Always knowing about the future, never giving anyone anything actually useful to prevent it, or change it.'

Charl looked annoyed, 'I told you, I-'

'Yeah, yeah, we know. Whatever,' Parrow told him.

Charl said nothing more.

They listened to Arpil chomping on stone.

'I suppose we have a few days together,' Kialessa pondered.

'Two, father comes to claim you on the dusk of the second day,' Charl said.

Kialessa nodded, it was easy to trust his words as he spoke with calm conviction.

'And he takes Arpil as well,' the prophet said.

The others looked at him.

'Why?' Ipi asked.

He shrugged. 'I do not have that knowledge,' he replied. 'But I have a favour to ask you, Kialessa, my half-sister? If I may?'

'Say on,' she told him.

'Take me with you,' Charl asked.

The others protested, 'Why not us too?!' Parrow demanded.

'Your time has not yet come!' the prophet replied. 'But I am only down here for my … misbehaviour. If I offer to behave myself and keep silent I know he will allow me back.'

'Tired of being in the dark and hungry?' Parrow teased him.

He glanced at her, allowing her to see his blind eyes. 'The days of my fast are ended now I have feasted upon the words of life. So, yes. Kialessa, the Eternal requires that I submit myself to you. As you command me, so will I do.'

     By Dr Joe Ireland

Kialessa wasn't sure what to make of that.

Neither, it seemed, did the other students. Except Arpil, she seemed very busy right now.

'I've seen our prophet wipe out toxins, and put a kid's arm right back on after it was cut clean off and heal it,' Parrow boasted.

'Ain't no one tamed the prophet before,' Ipi muttered. 'This'll really freak them out,' then he grinned.

'I will come back for you two,' Kialessa promised, 'or I will send help. You will not stay in here.'

Ipi waved his hand, 'I already know that.'

She wondered what he meant.

'Yeah,' Parrow explained, 'Prophet told us.'

They nodded.

She looked at Charl. He looked very calm, sitting on his seat, warming his face by the fire. They all looked very calm, hidden in the darkest room of a fortress prison.

'Tell me your stories,' she begged them.

They looked at her.

'You're each so unique. So amazingly different and special. Everyone in this mountain has a totally unique and wonderful story to tell, and I want to hear them all. Will you tell me? I would like you to tell me.'

'This part of your plan to escape?' Ipi asked.

'Not sure,' she admitted. 'But… it's a start.'

Ipi nodded, and sitting down to warm his hands told her everything about his life and how it had led up to this point. The story was funny, and heartbreaking, and full of the occasionally very, very stupid things he had done.

Then Parrow shared her story, and how her mother and she had sworn to fight the demon and protect each other no matter what. They'd survived a whole year before he'd tracked them down in the Feuerdrache. It was a compelling, heart wrenching tale. Kialessa knew Parrow's mother was still looking for her, and hoped that they would find each other again.

Then the prophet told his story, and it was the most unique. His mother, a caprivald prophetess, had actually sought out the demon to bear him a son. She'd raised Charl in full awareness of his talents, his limitations, and his fate. It was an incredible life. His prophecies were most accurate in the short term, with the people he knew best and could observe, but his long term prophecies also seemed freakishly accurate. His was the kind of talent that kings sought and would pay a high price for, but he was the kind of man who would never sell his talents. He worked, and lived, and would gladly die only for a higher cause.

Arpil would still not speak to anyone, though the others insisted she actually could. Almost no one knew her story; she had fought the demon ever since she'd arrived, and no one here knew a day that she was not in the dungeon. The demon came at least once a year to offer her freedom, and she would always use it as a chance to attack him again. It was not her time for her annual offer of freedom, which made the prophet's words curious, so it would be interesting to see how it worked out.

The two days passed quickly, and Parrow learned her spell adequately well, writing it down in several places just in case the father demon didn't like the light. To Kialessa, this was a precious time, and the first time that she really began to feel a kinship with her strange, diverse, and occasionally very dangerous siblings. But she promised one day she'd write a book about it, beginning with these three. She would share their stories by name, and share their thoughts without names so that everyone would wonder which tae'anaryn came up with what wisdom.

And that book would be called; 'Recollections of the Tae'anaryl, by Kialessa, of Lenmer'el'.

By Dr Joe Ireland

The Beginning

You can pray to whomever you want to, no one can take that right away

from you. Just be prepared for an answer, that's all.

Kialessa, cited in Recollections of the Tae'anaryl.

Light burst in through the doorway as the appointed dusk drew nigh, followed by a somewhat surprised voice, 'Oh.'

Rawhawk stalked down, his massive clawed feet clicking on the floor. His huge, feathered wings were folded along his back, and his muscular, toned arms were folded across his chest. He had feathers instead of hair, and they flowed down his back to a hawk like tail. He was almost twice as tall as a normal adult human when he stretched himself up, and his feral eyes held a bestial dangerousness that made Kialessa gulp as he glared at them. He was holding an old hessian bag.

'You keep surprising us, Tavernskeep,' he told her. The room was well-lit from one end to the other, as they had renewed the enchantment every dusk. She stood at the step below the ramp, Charl at her left, Arpil at her right.

Rawhawk glared at her. 'Arpil, the master wishes to see if you are ready to consider civilising your manners.'

Arpil nodded slowly.

Rawhawk raised an eyebrow at her, as though quite surprised. 'And what is this? Charl, what are you doing waiting here?'

'I wish to discuss my release with the father.'

Rawhawk shrugged, 'It's your death. Whatever.'

'Reckon we could get some of that chow?' Ipi begged.

Rawhawk scoffed, tossing him a bag.

Parrow and Ipi ripped it open.

'Crusts and cheese? There's not enough here for an afternoon!' Parrow complained.

'Should have thought about that before you caused over eight hundred platinum coins' worth of damage to the master's business!'

Ipi glared at him.

Charl was already there. He took the bag, and gave thanks. When Ipi opened, it was overflowing with full bread loaves and ripe, saporous cheeses.

Ipi and Parrow laughed, and thanked the prophet. He tried to tell them not to thank him personally, but they were already eating their fill.

'Guess you prisoners won't need any food tomorrow then?' Rawhawk threatened them.

They stopped dead.

'While they remain unjustly in this dungeon, the bag will never fail,' Charl informed Rawhawk without a hint of boasting or pride in his voice.

Rawhawk looked livid. 'While you live, prophet… this is *exactly* the kind of trouble that got you in here in the first place!'

Charl did not reply.

Kialessa curtsied at the tall young man. 'Thank you, Rawhawk. Please, if you may release us, we wish to speak to the father now.'

He looked at her without much expression. 'Whatever,' he muttered.

They walked up the very steep slope.

'See you in a few years!' Parrow said cheerily.

Kialessa shook her head. It would not be a few years; it would not be a few days if she had the power.

Suddenly the ground started shaking in a weird, unnatural manner.

Kialessa turned to see Arpil growling. She'd grown up some very sharp looking crystals from her hands and back. She was glaring up at the creature

     By Dr Joe Ireland

who was holding the door open for them – Ka, the stone giant tae'anaryn. He glared back at the much smaller terranoid tae'anaryn, hatred in his eyes.

Rawhawk just laughed. 'They have history,' and left it at that.

***

They sat at the dinner table. They were early.

Mak burst in. He was with the second years. He ran up, trying to ask all his questions at once, though the second years paused when they saw the company Kialessa kept. 'You're alive! You all right? How was it? What did you eat? Who are these guys?'

She laughed. 'Mak, meet Arpil, the terranoid tae'anaryn.'

He looked her over, 'Never seen a terranoid before. How are you doing, Arpil?'

She said nothing.

'I don't think she speaks,' Kialessa explained. 'And this is Charl, though they call him the prophet around here.'

Mak sat back. 'Oh! Him… hey, look. Anyone stuck here is a brother to me, put it there blind boy!'

Charl looked over, nodded, and reached out his hand carefully. The other students watched him warily. 'The pleasure is mine,' he said.

'See!' Mak told the other students. 'he's cool. Hey, prophet, can ya tell me what my fate is?'

Charl looked over at Kialessa. She hoped he didn't say anything too upsetting, or weird. 'If you are kind, you will find kindness,' Carl said, and Kialessa sighed with relief. Charl continued, 'and if you show mercy, you will be shown mercy.'

Mak nodded, 'Cool, cool. I'll get back to you on how that goes.'

The prophet nodded seriously.

'So how'd it go?' Mak asked, the other students crowding in.

'Dark,' Kialessa admitted, 'but full of light. Alone, but very, very friendly.'

Mak gave her a sideways look. Then he nodded, 'Clearly, it drove you insane.'

They laughed.

'Did you see dad?' he begged.

She nodded, 'Rawhawk took us. I secured a tentative release for Charl here, and for reasons of his own the father demon allowed Arpil out, as long as she doesn't try to kill him. But no matter how I begged he would not let the other three out.'

'Who?' Mak asked.

Amber replied, 'Parrow, the dwarf. Hates him too much. Ipi, human, full of mischief, loves causing trouble. Blak the giant rat shifter is just too wild; I don't think he'll ever get out of there.'

Mak nodded. 'Weird you get put in there anyway. That's just not fair. That was just mean.'

She nodded, but was long over mourning her father's whip.

'We need to get you a new weapon,' Mak said.

At that, the prophet twisted his head suddenly sideways, as though listening. She noticed, but he said nothing and made no indication he had anything he wanted to say.

Everyone chatted about events for a half hour or so. Raynah hadn't been seen at all, and apparently Lossel had broken someone's nose when they'd been "slacking off at training", but other than that there wasn't much news.

Soon the other students began to arrive for dinner. The imps set the table. Some of the older students, particularly the fourth years, gave her some very dark looks. Shadowmonger, Flameheart and Ka did not come to dinner, leaving Rawhawk the apparent master of ceremonies.

'Let us feast to the master's good health,' he said.

Charl interrupted everyone's half-hearted toast. 'Ghap, the imps have

By Dr Joe Ireland

poisoned your food with swamp spider venom, in retribution for your "rudeness" to them earlier this morning.'

The room fell dead silent.

A sixth year stood up, grabbed his food and shoved it in front of the alchemist's nose. The gnome nodded.

Everyone groaned, and the boy called Ghap stormed into the kitchen. There was a smashing plate, several shouts, and the sounds of some imps getting thrown around the room. Then silence. Ghap stormed out with an entire chicken carcass in his very angry hands.

Several students giggled, then the eating started.

Rawhawk glared at Charl, but only Lossel spoke to the prophet over the dim of noise, 'This is the kind of behaviour that got you in trouble last time, *prophet.'*

Charl seemed to ignore her.

Kialessa wondered about what had just happened and she nibbled on her food, and how upset people had become when the prophet had used his gift. He'd done nothing wrong, actually, he'd been helpful. But somehow, he'd still managed to upset several people. Was it inevitable to upset people when you could tell more about them than they could?

Kialessa looked at him, leaning over to speak to him. 'Charl, why did you do that?'

He looked confused. 'To, protect Ghap, of course.'

'No, not that,' she asked. 'I mean, out loud. Tell everyone. Make sure everyone knew you had protected him.'

Mak seemed to be listening, 'Yeah, no one likes the imps. But like you could have just snuck over there and whispered it to him.'

Kialessa was still curious, 'Why'd you set him off in front of everyone like that?'

Charl looked genuinely surprised. 'I… don't know… I suppose you have a very good point. Why *did* I do it that way?'

But she thought she might know. She'd seen that smug look before. Ghap was a bit of a jerk, and getting him upset made him look out of control and foolish. She wondered if this was Charl's true intention, or was he really not thinking it through? Having a seer's sight did not always mean he came with a seer's wisdom, that would still have to be learned. Putting Ghap in his debt was not wisely nor necessarily done as a public affair – it could make everyone afraid of poisoned food, even if the imps did deserve it.

'You make a very good point, Kialessa,' Charl repeated.

Amber's jaw dropped when she heard that, but she said nothing more. After eating for a few moments she moved her plate over to Kialessa, helping to feed the Child carefully. She whispered to Kialessa, 'I have been thinking about what you said to Daygon on the day of chapel. I've been begging the moon I would serve her forever if she'd only get me out of here, but she seems to just ask patience. Now you get to pray to anyone? I've been feeling prompted to talk to Planas, god of plants. My family are related to the goddess Appleblossom. I think I might try. Do you think I should try?'

Kialessa could think of at least one other deity more worthy. But it would be a start, for a frightened young girl in a difficult place. 'You can pray to whomever you want to, no one can take that right away from you. Just be prepared for an answer, all right?'

Amber grinned conspiratorially, and kept on eating thoughtfully.

Charl refused the delicacies and ate only the bread and vegetables. Arpil ate happily, so happily that after she licked her plate clean, she ate that too. Mak kept this end of the table quite entertained with his adventures in Hamelthorpe, several probably quite embellished.

Most students left after dinner, but the conversation continued. Arpil curled up into the floor and seemed to doze off. Charl walked over to a corner and knelt down in obvious prayer. Then, at a lull in the conversation, Kialessa announced the first part of her plan.

'Everyone,' she said. The room fell silent and all the other students

 By Dr Joe Ireland

looked at her, all the second years, and most of the thirds. Lossel was there with her two friends from the seventh year, but most other students weren't there. 'I want to hear your stories.'

'So you can figure out how to defeat us?' Lossel's friend accused her.

'No!' Kialessa protested, trying to put her feelings into words. 'I just… you all… you all need to be remembered. Don't you realise? You're all just amazing! You can do so many things, and you have overcome some of the worst things I can ever imagine.'

They looked at her, seeming unsure of what to do with her statement. It was as if kind, sincere words didn't belong here.

But she had to try, 'You all… are made for great good. You have bodies that are worth protecting, and you have goals that are worth fighting for.'

The older girls laughed, and the younger students followed.

Kialessa's heart fell, were they really so hardened?

'I'll tell you my story,' Lossel bragged, and everyone shut up. 'Mum didn't tell dad I wasn't his, and we only found out when that… man turns up at our mansion five years ago and informed us he was taking me away. I had never heard them fight until that day. Can you imagine it? I was a nobleman's daughter with weird strength powers one day, and a child of a demon the next.'

No one spoke. No one dared; Lossel was something else in this place. Her eyes had tears in them, but her face was hardened. 'I did ballet since I was four, and had to keep my power under control or I could throw myself though the roof! I did it once! Oh, how they freaked out!'

Her friends cheered her on, but she got sincere again, 'So, yeah. My life got turned upside down. You must think it's all so easy being the only tae'anaryn who looks like a human, but let me tell you, it is the *worst*!'

'How did you survive?' Kialessa asked.

'Yeah,' Mak backed her up, 'you so motivated Lossel!'

She almost snarled at them. 'Bad things happen, and sometimes, there's nothing you can do about them. So why worry?'

'Easy for you,' Lossel's friend protested.

'Look at it this way,' Lossel said as if continuing a discussion they'd had before, 'Sometimes bad things happen because some people are jerks; live with it. It doesn't mean I need to become a jerk as well. There are always going to be people that are going to try and hurt and destroy and control you, but you can rise above their intentions.' She sat back, thinking. 'Be stronger, and leave the world a better place than it found you.'

People nodded as if thinking about that. Lossel was known for hitting things; Kialessa felt it did them all good to hear her story, her pain, and just how deep her thinking really was.

They went then, from the oldest to the youngest. They all told their story. It went long into the day, and would have kept going if Daygon hadn't put a stop to it so they could rest. Kialessa, Charl and Arpil went down into the damp cavern, and a few moments later Mak, Amber and another boy joined them, bringing handfuls of blankets to make it comfortable. Arpil formed cots for them all, inexplicably comfortable for solid stone. They all slept the day out peacefully.

The next night the stories continued, and she wrote what notes she could in the only book she had. Word had gotten out that Kialessa wanted to hear them, and that she'd tamed the "prophet", and somehow that gave her a credibility everyone trusted. No one asked about the two dead boys her dreamguide had slain. But most people had seemed to have lost interest in hurting her, even though the father demon was far away again by now.

But she still didn't have a way to escape, or a way to keep everyone safe from the demon that imprisoned them here.

The Unicorn

Death holds no pain for me. It is but another part of the story we all must journey though.

Man'yifikanse, prince of unicorns.

'The unicorn has been sighted in the forest!' Lossel shouted.

Several weeks had passed, solemn rituals to Ik'skuretza each Pumosday, studying with Raynah most nights. Kialessa was gathering stories in the dining room when Lossel had run in shouting.

Everyone grabbed their weapons and stood up cheering.

'What is happening?' Kialessa asked Amber.

For some reason the older girl was just sitting there, unlike all the others. She looked sad, 'I don't think you want to know.'

Kialessa looked around. It was if a hunt had just begun.

Amber was already tearing up.

Kialessa suspected it was probably the kind of hunt she did not want to be a part of. 'What is it? A unicorn?'

Amber sniffed, 'Just more treasures for the demon. A unicorn horn is a rare prize. They are going to kill it.'

'What?' Kialessa gasped. It made no sense. Unicorns were sacred to Annas - who would dare risk offending the goddess?

Apparently, everyone.

She grabbed Mak's arm, 'We have to protect it.'

'Why?' he asked.

'It's a unicorn! They are...' she didn't know what to say.

'Purity incarnate,' Amber explained. 'Killing one is a deep crime, one you might never receive forgiveness for.'

Mak looked serious, and put away his knife. The other second years didn't look as enthusiastic either.

'We have to save this unicorn!' Kialessa announced.

No one moved.

She pulled out her only remaining weapon, the sling. 'Mak, get me out there. Amber, where will we find the unicorn? We're going to help it escape.'

Broose, whom she'd burnt early this season, looked at her, 'That horn's worth at least six thousand gold coins, Kia. You'd be rich.'

'While your soul remains dead? That is no prize,' Charl argued.

'Help us,' Kialessa asked the prophet.

'I think I need to sit this one out,' Charl argued. 'I can't be seen to be partial.'

'Seriously, dude!' Mak chastened him. 'Pick sides when it's convenient to *you*!'

Charl glared at him, as much as a blind boy with fatesight could. 'Oakwood. Follow the fighting. The unicorn can run on light so it won't be where you would expect. But don't worry; it will never leave this mountain.' He glared at Broose, 'It has come to die.'

Amber gasped, and standing up drew a dagger with a small rune to Planas on it. 'Not on my watch.'

'That's more like it!' Mak said, spreading his massive wings.

Kialessa looked around for ammunition. Stones were plentiful, but they could kill, and she only intended to target her siblings at this point. So she grabbed up as many raw potatoes as she could fit in one hand.

Mak leapt up, grabbing Amber and Kialessa in one arm each. Somehow he lifted them both and swooped across the room. 'Let's go, ladies!'

Within a moment they stood at a window, looking out into the forest. Ka was crashing through the trees, splintering the smaller ones with deliberate recklessness. Rawhawk was leading a wing of at least four other

     By Dr Joe Ireland

talented flyers in the air. All over the fortress young tae'anaryl were running into the forest in small groups.

'They're in year level groups still, more or less,' Kialessa noted.

Amber studied the land. 'Look!' she shouted.

Rawhawk was diving down, leaving the others far behind. Ka turned his rage and thundered in the same direction, as if trying to beat his flying sibling.

Mak shoved off the ground with violent power, jarring Kialessa's arm. But she held herself together. Amber seemed to be doing a better job of it. They skimmed the top of the trees.

Suddenly a javelin flew through the air and almost impaled Mak's wing.

'Just like in combat training,' he muttered, taking them a little higher in the air.

Suddenly there was a screech, as though Rawhawk had just sighted his prey. Ka shifted his charge and headed towards the sound.

Mak ploughed on.

'There!' Amber yelled, she was pointing.

Mak looked down to check.

'The Oakwood. That old tree, chartreuse green. There, there! See it!'

'Sure,' Mak shrugged.

There was a thunderous shuddering that shook the trees, followed by a blinding plume of fire that would have incinerated several large buildings. A vortex of wind formed, and was torn apart moments later by dizzying bouquets of lightning. All the action seemed to be happening far away from the tree they were sending Mak towards.

Suddenly a spinning twist of trip wires flew right up into the air, pinning one of Mak's wings to his side. They were plummeting down. Kialessa turned, trying to see what was happening, only to notice Amber was way ahead of her and cutting the leather thongs from Mak's wing with her dagger. She had him free only moments before they hit the ground in a struggling heap of limbs and bruises.

'What was that?' Mak asked, checking out the trip wires.

Amber held them up, showing him how they'd spin.

'Wicked,' he grinned. 'I want one.'

Six students entered the clearing, mostly fourth years.

'Go!' Mak said, 'I'll hold them off.'

Kialessa armed her sling, wondering if it could be used in any way other than lethally.

Amber hit the ground with her fist, and Kialessa heard her mutter, 'Appleblossom, hear my prayer.' A tiny tsunami of vines and clover flowed towards the other students.

'I didn't know she could do that!' one yelled as the plant life covered him, pinning him down.

Another tried to get away, but was soon wrapped in vines. Kialessa downed one with a potato to the head, hoping he was all right, though he lay there not moving. The sling was eager to reload, finding its own way into her hand by the time she'd grabbed another potato. She loosed it, slamming an armed fourth year in the solar plexus and he collapsed. Kialessa armed another potato.

'No, I got this,' Amber grinned.

One of the fourth year students burst into flames, breaking away from the vines. Then she threw three sharp daggers toward Amber.

Kialessa didn't know how anyone could throw three daggers at once. She caught one, Amber dodging another. But the third one embedded itself in the older girl's shoulder.

She cried out in pain, her leaves almost evaporating, but she kept her fists on the ground.

Mak deflected the next three daggers with his wing, and with a deep thud charged the fourth year. He smashed his wing onto her chin, knocking her unconscious in a breath.

     By Dr Joe Ireland

He limped back, holding his wing. 'Amber, you all right?'

Amber looked pale, but did not let up on her task. Mak tried to stop the bleeding around the knife.

She didn't let him. 'Get out of here, Kia. Get to that tree. Save that unicorn!'

Kialessa prayed over the wound, and it seemed to stop bleeding, but she didn't feel she could remove the knife without causing some serious damage.

There were voices in the forest.

Amber glared at her, fierce anger in her eyes. 'Mak, get my cloak. Grab that log. Fly west, try to draw some of the attention, go!'

He paused a moment, but acted quickly. He was up in the air less than a breath later.

Amber turned her fierce gaze on Kialessa.

She did not wait to be told twice. In an instant Kialessa found herself at the far end of the clearing, wondering how she got there so quickly. But she had no time to ponder it.

Kialessa ran. The forest seemed to dash past her, filled with magic and fear. She heard the fighting far away, voices sounding confused. Something dreadful filled her heart; like a broken dream.

She stumbled down a steep ravine, pressing away a mouth full of dirt that tried to climb into her. The entire forest seemed alive, wilful… slightly unkind. It didn't like her, or rather… it was curious, and wanted to test her, and didn't mind hurting her. Like a fairy. Like… Amber, just a little. It was trying to speak to her, but it wasn't using words; just feelings, and images.

Kialessa looked up, the serenity of the scene momentarily disarming her. Dappled light filtered through the benevolent bows of a magnanimous Oakwood tree. He seemed huge, and ancient. And at his feet, lying on its side, a dying unicorn lay.

8 The dying unicorn

Kialessa gasped. Something horrible was happening. Everything alive in the forest recoiled at this terrible sight. The unicorn had the form of an enormous stag, beautiful and muscular. Its horn was a pure alabaster white, glowing gently from between its bone white antlers. Something indescribably pure and innocent tugged at Kialessa's heart. And on the unicorn's side, a deep gash ran. Iridescent purple blood ran onto the ground, turning it white with indignation.

Several fey lights appeared in the air above the unicorn, mourning the loss of the one of the goddess of animals' choicest servants. They seemed to sing a sad song, pouring misery into Kialessa's heart.

Gently she stood, and took a faltering step toward the dying creature. It

 By Dr Joe Ireland

stiffened, as if it might run again, but could not move.

There was nothing she could do for the unicorn now. It was already too late to save it. At best… all she could offer it was a merciful death.

Her heart retched at that thought. *No one should kill this pure being!* It was more than an animal; it was a spirit of innocence and power. It was sacred to a goddess. Whoever had wounded it might pay for this with their very soul.

She found herself at its trembling hooves. Its breathing was ragged, but quickly becoming more and more shallow.

There was nothing she could do for it now. As tears stung her eyes, she reached out and patted its neck. It twitched in fear at first, then relaxed.

'If only I had a knife,' Kialessa mourned, 'you would not suffer a moment longer.' Even as the words left her lips, she felt a wrongness about them.

Her eyes met the dying unicorn's, and it spoke inside her mind, *You think I fear dying? And that my life was somehow robbed? I have lived a good life, and die a warrior's death. I am Man'yifikanse, a stallion of the goddess of the hunt. None have tamed me in six hundred years. I have run the rainbow falls of the infinite cliffs; I have stormed the waters of the undying seas. I have fathered a dozen brave colts of both wisdom and power. I do not fear death.*

Images of his incomparable life flew past her eyes; he was a kind of demigod, an exemplar of all unicorn stallions. He took a shuddering breath, his pain flowing through her. Then he continued, *Death holds no pain for me. It is but another part of the story we all must journey though. The life beyond holds no pain, no weariness. There is no fear in Annas' light.*

He trembled, and as he did, his hooves turned dark grey, as a normal stallion's. Kialessa heard voices in the trees, but they had not found them yet.

Child, he said, addressing her. *You have wished kindness on me in the hour of my last breaths. So I offer you a gift, a prize highly sought after, but which I know you would have traded willingly for my life. I must go toward the light now, but from this bright place I can watch over you. Please, if you will, take a hold upon my horn.*

She hesitated.

Hurry, Man'yifikanse told her, *I do not have long.*

She did as he told her, letting her tears fall freely. 'If you must go, brave soul, go in peace.'

He sighed, *I have looked my whole life to find a maid of your purity. Please, receive my final gift.*

With that, he breathed his last. His light gathered toward his horn. With a stab of horror, Kialessa watched as it clicked off his brow and remained in her hand. Then her horror turned to fascination as his great mane began to weave itself from that horn, twisting and curling around with gathering light and power as though the unicorn's spirit had not left this world at all.

Let this serve you well, Man'yifikanse's voice whispered to her heart.

A moment later she stood, a blinding white cord stretching from the unicorn's horn in her hand. Its complex platting ended in what looked like a hardened, sharpened tip.

It was a whip, and it was a long one.

A moment later Ka charged into the clearing, stopping dead when he saw her. He roared in frustration and punched the ground.

Then Rawhawk landed in front of him, digging his claws deeply into the earth. Ka stepped back.

Rawhawk glared at her, his neck feathers rising in bitter rage and anger. His brown eyes glowed a feral red, and he screeched at her with deafening rage. The forest quivered, leaves scurrying to the ground in the sound.

Rawhawk summoned his two blades from the dreamworld, menacing up on her.

White rage rose up in Kialessa. Those blades, those claws, they looked very much like what might have wounded a unicorn.

She returned his screech with a deafening cry of her own, and he looked surprised, but did not stop.

                    By Dr Joe Ireland

She swung her new weapon above her head, and it circled as though it had a spirit of its own. It circled her, sparkles of white light floating down around her and the body of the slain unicorn. It formed a perfect circle of blinding white light, shimmers of light reminiscent of sunbeams glowing up from the ground protecting her.

Rawhawk stood for a moment, then he charged.

She didn't wait to see how badly he intended to harm her for the crime of claiming his immoral kill. She lashed out with her whip. It flew to an impressive distance, twisting of its own accord. It struck his ankle, and he fell on his face.

Before he'd had a chance to recover, and before the whip had the time to be pulled backwards, she struck out at him again. With supernal power it twisted about, tearing one sword from his grip, and snapping the other sword in two.

He roared, and sat up in fear and surprise.

Even Ka looked weary about attacking her now.

Dark light engulfed the clearing, and in the next moment Shadowmonger stood there. He was glowing with dark fire around his skin, two dark blades of pure shadow weave in his hands. Dark shadows moved about at the edge of her vision within this realm, and within the shadow realm. Shadowmonger regarded her with impassive disdain.

Then he stood back.

It did not look like he was going to attack.

As her rage subsided, a painful sorrow filled her heart. It was as if the entire forest, or perhaps the entire world, mourned for the loss of Man'yifikanse. She threw herself onto his still warm body, silent, and unbreathing. If she could have reached into the afterlife and dragged his noble spirit back into his body, even if it meant giving up her new whip, she would have gladly done it.

There was shuffling around her, and she turned to see Shadowmonger allowing Amber and Mak to join her. Kialessa didn't even notice the bandage on Amber's shoulder. But she noticed her tears.

Amber looked confused at the whip, but burst into sobs as she came into the region of the unicorn's lingering personal energy, joining her in the sorrow.

Mak tried to stay back, but with a single step fell on his knees and choked back tears.

Something terrible had truly happened. How Rawhawk could be so hard hearted to the event was impossible for Kialessa to imagine. Even Ka seemed untouched, perhaps actually annoyed. Only Shadowmonger seemed to have any respect.

There was a cry of dismay, and Kialessa turned to see Arpil joining them. Sharp crystals formed on her, and she roared at Shadowmonger. His dark tendrils closed in as if in automatic defence, but he did nothing more, and Kialessa dimly wondered if he wasn't keeping their mourning private from the other students.

Arpil stood by her, not daring to touch the slain unicorn. Then she started to hum, an inaudibly deep noise. The tree seemed the echo the noise, or harmonise with it.

Then the earth beneath the unicorn began to sink.

'No!' Rawhawk protested, but Shadowmonger held him back.

The sorrow seemed to lessen as Arpil buried the unicorn. She took him deep, deep into the soil.

Summoning petals from her hands, Amber began to throw them into the still deepening pit. She handed some to Kialessa.

A dark shadow tendril reached out then, and she tensed. But it took up a handful of dirt, and added it to the grave.

Mak joined them; his tears still not dried, and added more earth to the grave. Sorrowful lights floated above; fairies mourning an immortal's death.

'Yes, I agree,' Amber told the dancing lights.

                    By Dr Joe Ireland

The ground closed over the grave, and immediately the tree's roots shifted with deep, creaking sounds.

'He guards the grave.' Amber informed them. 'The others will not be able to disturb the unicorn's rest,' she placed her hands on the soil, and grass grew up from the area in moments.

Immediately the deep sorrow passed, leaving Kialessa feeling tired, but deep inside also very, very hopeful. A warrior had earned a warrior's death, as if this was not a sad thing, just a necessary one.

Amber looked over at her new weapon. 'You could only have that if he gave it to you.'

'Man'yifikanse,' Kialessa muttered his name, confirming Amber's guess.

'That was… yeah… phew!' Mak seemed unable to make a joke of things right now, and therefore, was lost for words.

She smiled at him. She thought about gathering the whip, and in that moment it curled up of its own volition and rested in her lap. She could feel a portion of the mighty unicorn's spirit flowing through it, but he was gone. He would have to watch over her from far, far away.

Amber looked thoughtful through her tears, 'I wonder if… maybe… Nothing is ever innately good or bad, it just is. A unicorn has died, but you have a new means of protection. Under other circumstances, sparing his life might have even been the 'bad' thing. Fear and regret will not change what is, but it might stop us from making things better now.'

'Thank you,' Kialessa replied to Amber's new conviction.

Amber held out her hand, and Kialessa allowed her to touch the whip. 'It is sacred,' she confirmed.

Mak held out his hand, and touched it too. 'Smooth,' he pronounced.

But when Arpil looked over, an indignant sentiment filled Kialessa's heart. The terranoid seemed to feel it too, and appeared unwilling to test if the whip was something she could touch.

Shadowmonger, watching them this whole time, didn't even try. 'You're in very deep trouble with this one, Tavernskeep,' he whispered.

***

No one else touched the whip. As soon as Daygon saw it, he pronounced, 'You need to take that to the treasury as soon as you can, young dame. If the father sees it, he will not take kindly to it.'

'Then I will not part with it forever more,' she told them, rebellion or righteous indignity in her heart. For she finally felt she had, now, a fitting replacement for her true father's love and protection. She had a weapon that could threaten, and maybe even one day defeat, even a prince of demons.

 By Dr Joe Ireland

The God of Darkness

If you lie today, you can give up lies tomorrow. You succumb to greed, you can exercise self-control tomorrow. What you are now you might not be in a year, or a decade's time. It is a wondrous, magnificent, powerful thing - and we gods fear and love you for it.

Ik'skuretza, the god of mysteries, cited in 'The Year in Jail'.

Two weeks passed. Kialessa gathered all the stories she could, scribing whatever meagre notes she needed in order to help her remember the details in the only book she had – her spellbook.

'People are beginning to consider you quite divisive,' Mak told her later that dawn, as they snuggled down for another rest in the damp cavern. All the second years were sleeping there now, and two of the third years. 'They say you're gathering all the power to your throne, and intend to overthrow the Father one day. Is that true? So what's your plan?'

Kialessa didn't know what to say. What plan could she have? She was the smallest, youngest, and probably the most vulnerable of them all. She couldn't even fly and most of them could, and could do so with great skill.

What could she possibly do to help them all?

She didn't know what to do. So as dawn began to silence another night in the fortress, she prayed.

Yet she felt very uncomfortable in the cavern, which was unusual. She prayed there every night. Many other students had asked her about the Eternal, and while she'd told them all no one asked any more questions than those they needed for information. Not even the prophet, with his insight or wisdom, could ply any more curiosity from any of them.

Yet a nagging feeling tickled at Kialessa's neck as she tried to pray, and she could not cast it off: She needed to pray in the shrine of Ik'skuretza.

She sighed, and stood to leave.

Charl watched her go, looking as though he might ask her business, or to see if she wanted his company, 'I go to pray at the shrine of Ik'skuretza,' she told him.

He looked a little unsure, but nodded.

As soon as Kialessa reached the exit, she was surprised to find Lossel and the two seventh years standing there.

'Oh, hey, redling,' Lossel said, still the apparent boss, though the youngest of the three students, 'Just, um, checking up on you younglings. All hanging out now. Gett'n kind of sweaty in there now, eh?'

Kialessa disagreed, 'It's quite pleasant. The air flows out with the water. It's renewed all the time. It can get cold, but my fire is warmth enough for us all.'

Lossel gave her a strange look, as if she'd just answered a question she hadn't actually asked. Then the older girl walked in, and the younger students fell silent. 'Oh look, you got girls on one side, boys on the other.' She seemed to approve.

Everyone just waited on her.

'Well, all seems to be in order. You little ones keep out of mischief, you hear!'

'Be good, or be good at it!' Mak teased her.

She pretended to find that tasteless, and several students jeered. Then Lossel fell silent. 'You kids let me know if you need anything, all right?'

They were silent in reply.

'We'll be all right,' Amber told Lossel.

She nodded, and walked out.

                    By Dr Joe Ireland

Amber gave Kialessa a, "what was that about" look, and Kialessa shrugged.

She tightened her new whip. It was very content to be a belt, and turned a very natural brown when it did. It was a kind of "off" mode, because when it stared glowing white it would not let some of the older kids touch it, and everyone in the room began to feel the need to be quiet and respectful. Most people didn't seem to like the sensation. It could define the entire mood of whatever room it was in.

The imps, naturally, loathed it. They refused to serve dinner if it was in the same room. And when it was in the damp cavern they never went in.

Kialessa thought it one of the nicest gifts she'd ever received. But it seemed to only increase the growing hatred of some of the older kids. The fourth years had started a campaign of hating on her every chance they had. With two of their numbers down, their entire year level was at a distinct disadvantage now. They would never, ever win the horn at battle training, not even in their ninth year, unless they managed to kill of a few third years before that time. It was a very dark thought.

Kialessa put them out of her mind and walked on. She had no trouble finding the chapel; it was a very familiar sight. Prayers each day, and religious services every seven days. She entered the room, circling her heart, then making the correct obeisance Ik'skuretza apparently required towards the altar. It was amazing how much it looked like the chapel to the sun god, except everything was dark and black and purple. She enjoyed the singing, and the feeling in the room. It was nice, a soft blend of informative and inspirational, but at times a little dry. Ik'skuretza seemed to like it that way.

'Oh, you judge me so harshly!' a young man's voice accused her.

Kialessa's heart leapt into her throat. She did not expect to find anyone here. But it was more than that; it was more than the fact that it was a voice she did not recognise. There was something different about this voice. It was confident... powerful. As if it could speak vast oceans of knowledge but preferred simple conversations.

She dreaded to know who was speaking to her.

She walked toward the window where the voice was coming from. The sun had not yet lifted over the horizon, but the sky was already noticeably bright.

And standing by that window, leaning comfortably against the sill, was a young man. He looked about seventeen, but he was ridiculously handsome. Not a crazy, heart crushingly handsome, but more a soft, attractively confident kind of handsome. His hair was black, deep purple in the light, and his eyes vivid lilac or dark sapphire blue, it was hard to say. He was wearing the clothing of a traveller or a priest; she could not tell from the unusual cloth. His cloak was of the darkest purple.

And on his left shoulder a deep white dove sat, a moment later it flew off, disappearing out the window. He watched it as it went.

She looked at him. There was a most remarkable sense of… unremarkableness. He looked, like, normal.

He laughed, as if to himself, 'Seem I so plain to your eyes, Kialessa?'

She knew who he was, but still just had to ask, 'Are you… are you the god Ik'skuretza?'

He nodded as if to say, you already know this, and returned to staring out the window. 'Does that surprise you, child? That I have lived more than six thousand years but appear to you as a cousin? I rule over all the darkness, and every truth ever spoken on this orb and all others in this realm. Yes, I am Pumos, I am Ik'skuretza. And it is a kind honour to finally meet you in person too, Kialessa, Dame of Lenmer'el.'

She felt quite shocked. He looked, acted just like a teen boy. A very confident teen, perhaps. But just another person.

'Would you prefer to see me in the thrall of my deepest powers?' he teased her. Such things had the reputation for devouring mortal folks such as herself. She shook her head fiercely.

　　　　　　　By Dr Joe Ireland

He kept looking out the window, 'I'm glad you can finally see me,' he said.

'You have been here before?' she asked him.

He scoffed. 'I am here every hour. This room is sacred to me, as was once this whole mountain, and as it will be once again. I like scholars. But not when they get too arrogant, eww.'

He made such a silly noise, a little laugh escaped her.

He smiled at her. Then he seemed sad, 'I wish we could have talked before, but you have your tasks to attend to. Do you want to know what we gods envy most about you mortals?'

She wasn't sure what he wanted, he seemed to be changing topic of conversation a lot. But if he wanted to tell her what gods envied, why not?

She nodded.

'Your ability to change. It makes you powerful, more powerful than we gods in many ways. Oh, we can shatter mountains, it is true. But choose to alter our destiny? Not a chance. Be something today that we weren't yesterday? Never. What we cannot achieve in six thousand years, you can do in an afternoon. How I envy you!'

He looked at her, seeming sad, and not at all dangerous. As if though envious, he did not have the will or power to claim her coveted ability from her. The power to change? Was that really such a great capacity?

He continued chatting, as if explaining. 'If you lie today, you can give up lies tomorrow. You succumb to greed, you can exercise self-control tomorrow. What you are now you might not be in a day, or a decade's time. It is a wondrous, magnificent, powerful thing - and we gods fear and love you for it.'

She was beginning to suspect he was actually going to ask her to change herself in some way. She wasn't sure how she'd react to that. She was honour bound to serve another god, the Eternal. Would she do what Pumos asked? He was powerful enough to demand anything of her, right now, right there.

Choice, set free 201

He could probably force her to be anything he wanted, turn her into a mouse, or make her a murderous monster at a simple whim. Why was the god of darkness chatting to her by a window?

He laughed, 'It's a wonder you get anything done with such a busy mind!'

She had to laugh too, no one had ever told her *that* before.

He seemed serious, and kneeling down lay a hand on her shoulder. It felt solid, like any other hand. She'd expected it to be bursting with power and magic. It had, after all, helped make the universe. But instead it felt like any other hand. 'Please don't ever think that we, the seven Elder gods, don't know what's happening in this mountain, Kialessa. We do. But even we are behoven to powers greater than ourselves, to deal with this situation with a certain… delicacy, and compassion. It has to be in time.' He paused, as though thinking.

'You sound like Lumos,' she said with a smile. Kialessa felt like he really liked her.

He laughed, and looked out the window, 'You hear that, sister! Ha, yes. Yes. You mortals can't assume because my sister exemplifies patience that the rest of us don't have any, you know!'

He poked a finger out towards the moon, and Kialessa couldn't help but smile, he seemed so indignant.

He sighed, and seemed to be waiting on her.

'What brings you here, god of darkness?'

He smiled out the window, 'I was never the god of darkness. Not at the beginning.' His eyes glowed white, and a book flew into his outstretched hand. He flipped it open so she could read it, and he quoted from it without even looking. She could only just manage to keep up, but miraculously, she did.

Pumos was not the god of darkness, the mysterious author wrote. *Not at the beginning. He was the god of truth, which ascends beyond mere information, beyond*

By Dr Joe Ireland

*governing principles, even beyond intuition and understanding. Pure truth speaks of that which **is** regardless of time, place, preacher or personality. Within truth is the wisdom to know when to save life, and when it is time to die – for neither life nor death are any good or bad thing in and of themselves. For each must come upon all, but that we might prepare for and act within each of them wisely. Indeed, as the god of truth Pumos gained wisdom far beyond the other six Elder gods, peering deep into the very edges of reality, into primordial powers none others could comprehend and remain sane. Thus, of truth, he became also the god of secrets none others could contain. And, over time, the god of secrets became known as the god of darkness, where all secrets lay. But he was not the god of darkness, not in the beginning.*

'I am preeminent over all other Elder deity,' Ik'skuretza told her. 'For I must be. Yet I do not answer to them, but to those far worthier and higher than myself. Do you understand what I mean, little Kialessa?'

She did not, not really.

'I was there,' he mentioned casually, 'when the green star fell to earth at the hour of your birth. I saw it split into two, one trailing to the capital at Emerel, one to the little village in the Wintervale, south of the castle at Lenmer'el. Only two other mortals know this. But I think it's best if I tell you. It's something you ought to know.'

She was stunned. A star, split in two? The green star falling to earth was Mya's sign that a protector had been sent to guard the king. Why did no one else know it had been split into two?

And what on Mya could that mean?

Ik'skuretza continued, as if that was in no way the most important thing he had to say while he was here. 'And what does it mean to have a father?' he asked.

This was something she really wanted an answer to.

He filled her silence, 'What makes a family, Kialessa? A commitment, a promise? A marriage, perhaps? Is it just several people hanging out together? You do realise the power in a promise, don't you? Demons are most powerful when they work *within* the promises mortals make to each other, Kialessa. Even an arch demon will feel compelled to respect that promise, for through such they may bind mortals with their own words, and they would hate to be seen as truth breakers themselves. A sacred promise between any two mortals is a very powerful thing. Even the least of the gods can bind a pact no demon king can sunder.'

She looked up at him, desperately trying to catch every subtle nuance and meaning in his seemingly casual sentence. It seemed profound, even lifesaving, but she wasn't sure what he was getting at.

He laughed, gazing out the window, then looked back at her. 'I would have liked to have made you one of my faithful, Kialessa; my friend. But you have sworn your allegiance already, and that is a promise not even I would dare transgress!' he sighed, and looked at her. 'The Shadowrealm is but a small part of the entirety of reality. You cannot master it all in one mortal life. But will you tell my child, tell Peyter, my Shadowmonger... tell him that I *am* pleased with him, will you? He's been trying to ignore me for several years now.'

The words seemed to genuinely hurt the god. As if Shadowmonger was actually someone very important to Ik'skuretza, the... god of truth, and mysteries, and darkness, and the dead. It was very touching to see.

She wanted to say something nice about her half-brother. 'He protected me when I ... when I tried to save the unicorn.'

Ik'skuretza looked sad, then grinned, 'Annas is not to be ignored, is she!' the god sighed. 'Man'yifikanse is a great being, Kialessa, and a very kind heart. Even I did not foresee his sacrifice. It's really something; that weapon is one of a kind. I doubt we will see its equal in the lifetime of this world.'

She looked at her belt. It seemed to be glowing with pride. 'How do you always seem to know what I'm thinking, yet seem surprised when I say it?' she asked.

He smiled at her. 'You do not understand, I am effectively omniscient,

By Dr Joe Ireland

compared to you Kialessa. Almost each and every choice that you could make is present before my eyes constantly. But I'm never quite sure which reality you will choose to manifest in this world, so it's always a kind of nice surprise when you say something like that.'

Then he was gone.

It was so abrupt, no goodbye, no farewells. She looked around, hoping he might be hiding somewhere, but even the feeling of his presence had retreated. She figured that if he was aware of everything that happened in this room, he was still sort of here. But he felt so far, he felt like he was not here anymore.

She sighed. What would she tell the others? Should she tell them anything? And had he even answered her question about what to do to help everyone get away from the demon?

She walked slowly back, pondering deeply about everything she'd heard and seen.

The Heart of Fire

Who cares who you hurt when you are hurting!
Flameheart, cited in Recollections of the Tae'anaryl.

A few days later Kialessa was sitting through another somewhat confusing and mostly boring Ik'skuretza night lecture, by the ever-devout Daygon of course, when she began to fall asleep. It was something about plants this time, and seasons. Hard to follow. Kialessa had to admit, her mind was beginning to wander. Her eyes began to droop.

She heard a voice then, as clear as if she was standing next to her, 'Well I like her,' it said.

She glanced around. No one else seemed to have noticed. Had someone just spoken? It sounded strange… like… a dream.

Kialessa began to wonder if the god of truth and mysteries was not trying to tell her something again. The dream world was closed around the mountain, but that didn't mean they could not dream about things *inside* the mountain. It was one of its most agonising dangers; she had learnt that the hard way.

But she felt safe now, and safer that she had the courage to pray to whomever she wanted, *Eternal, and his servant Ik'skuretza my friend, if you will, grant me knowledge.*

She felt very sleepy suddenly, and went with it.

 By Dr Joe Ireland

She was watching a young man, beautiful, with jet black skin. In his arms a gorgeous young woman lay. She had red hair touched with glowing embers, and black wings of made of rods of coal. They seemed so happy in each other's arms, and it took Kialessa a moment to realise she was looking at Shadowmonger, and Flameheart.

9 Shadowmonger and Flameheart

'Well I like her,' Flameheart smiled, snuggling into Shadowmonger's arms.

He seemed completely immune to her fire, and Kialessa noted the malachite ring he wore, glittering brightly. He spoke, 'She's just a child. Don't underestimate her. Little kids grow up.'

Flameheart pouted, and stroked his face. 'I still can't believe there are only two kids this year. Your father's losing his game.'

Shadowmonger laughed, but held a finger to her lips to indicate she should not risk saying such things here.

She kissed his finger, and snuggled in his arms. Then she looked up into his eyes, 'When will we escape, my love?'

Shadowmonger looked to his left, shuffling among his papers, 'During the second eclipse. There are three every year, but the second is the strongest. The days of partial eclipses the week before and after will not do. The machine is ready, it just needs power.'

She nodded, looking afraid. Their eyes somehow met her even in the dream.

Suddenly Kialessa woke up with a start. The entire roof of the chapel was ablaze with fire.

Everyone ducked down, people screamed.

Daygon looked up, looked down at Kialessa, rolled his eyes in frustration, and said nothing.

From that fire Flameheart's form appeared, and she glared at Kialessa angrily. To her left, Rawhawk grinned malevolently, and Kialessa had the distinct impression that he'd spotted her dream walking into Flameheart's life, or her dreams.

Kialessa gulped, and sat up. She waited out the rest of the hour in silence, awaiting Flameheart's judgement.

When services ended, she kept seated. She knew the older girl would not take kindly to having to chase her down.

Mak and some of her closest friends offered to assist but Kialessa sent them on, she needed to see this through on her own.

Flameheart waited till everyone else had left, and made a point of it by standing over the door, glaring at Kialessa. No one spoke.

Eventually there was just Daygon, herself, and Flameheart in the chapel of Ik'skuretza.

'I don't know what's upset you so,' Daygon said to Flameheart, with perhaps a touch of falseness. 'But I trust you to honour her father's wishes?'

She glared at him. 'As he will, no doubt, honour all his promises to me.' She hissed, and the ground shook.

Daygon spoke again, 'Please, there's no need for harm. Kialessa I'm sure meant so little by it, and she is one so young.' His voice sounded so sorry, so pitiful. It was almost impossible to ignore.

'Spare me your witless enchantments,' she swore at him. 'And spare me your wanton affectations, old priest!' Then she seemed to calm down. 'Nevertheless, fear not. I only want to speak to her. She is safe, I assure you.'

He looked genuinely relieved.

Kialessa wasn't feeling relieved. Flameheart was patient. She was cunning. Kialessa was sure the older girl wouldn't kill her, but that didn't mean she was safe with her, not at all. Everyone had left now. Kialessa had allowed no living being to stand by her.

Flameheart slithered up on her snake tail, and held out a jewelled hand with bright red fingernail polish over her wickedly sharp claws. 'Come, little one. I just want to speak to you.'

Kialessa hesitated. But she needed Flameheart, or at least she needed to know where she stood. And if this was her chance to hear Flameheart's story, it might be the only chance she'd get.

Flameheart bent down, and asked her, 'Would you rather speak in here?'

Kialessa wasn't sure.

'Come, come to my domain Kialessa. I think you'd like it. Only ones like us can truly enjoy the Heart of Fire. Come, let me show you.'

Daygon shuffled, 'A rare privilege, to be invited to another's domain.'

'Shut up, you spineless coward,' Flameheart swore.

Daygon left, and Flameheart offered Kialessa her hand again. She took it, but let go as soon as they left the chapel. Kialessa watched Daygon's form as he left, feeling terribly disappointed for him. He never seemed to make any real difference in a fortress full of frightened, violent youth.

They walked, or in Flameheart's case, slithered in silence for several moments. Eventually Flameheart spoke, 'I was eight when I was brought here. I don't know who my father is, some unfortunate elf I guess. My demon mother brought me here to the care of the merchant simply for convenience. They told me I was free to leave at any time, but I knew that to be a lie. I will die, soon enough, just like all the rest of them.'

Kialessa listened quietly, 'What happens to them, to us?'

Flameheart laughed. 'You still don't know? We die. We all die, Kialessa. Unless the father demon thinks he can use you in some other way.' She twisted around her, looking falsely apologetic, as though she enjoyed the sport of mocking others with their impending deaths.

'Is that why Daygon is still around?' Kialessa wondered.

Flameheart huffed, 'He's a Living. He has a talent your father still thinks he can use, so he spares his life, for now. Daygon is able to sense the emotions of others, and uses it to control us. Your father uses him to keep the others sedated. Daygon used to try much harder, now he only panders to his father's whim. He is beginning to lose his usefulness, and when he does, your father will murder him.'

Kialessa looked at Flameheart. This was not the kind creature willing to love that Kialessa had seen in her dream. What had changed? Or was it a vision of the future? She glared at the older tae'anaryn.

Flameheart slithered up, and held her chin, 'Fascinating. I see no fear in your eyes. Only compassion. You are not like the others here. Not like any of us at all.'

'Who is Shadowmonger?' Kialessa asked. She knew it mattered to Flameheart.

The woman stopped, and looked away. 'Blunt… yet observant too.' She slithered to a window, out towards the mountains and the castle of Lenmer'el, far away. 'It looks so far, doesn't it? But you cannot get out that way, especially at night when everyone thinks the darkness is their ally. The

By Dr Joe Ireland

darkness currently serves only one master here, and answers only to him. You cannot get out that way, Kialessa,' she said, pointing out the window. She turned back, 'But why would you want to, when everything you need is here? Friendship, and enemies. Food, weapons, challenges on every floor. Something to do, and someone to hate,' her fists burst into flames. 'And we're all dead one day anyway, why not die for a higher cause, no? Makes life worth living, don't you think?'

Kialessa didn't know what she was driving at. Death... and love... Shadowmonger, and a way to escape...

'You want to take him with you,' Kialessa assumed, then pondered, 'in fact, if he did not come with you, you would never leave.'

Flameheart looked at her with a stony face, then grimaced, 'Shadowmonger? Full of his own glory, arrogant. What a pest! Bossy demanding... mmm, but have you seen those biceps!'

Kialessa had to grin. And if she could see emotions, Flameheart's light would have turned a rosy pink. Of few convictions she could be in this place, but this drove her; Flameheart would bear him their child, if she ever had the chance.

Flameheart grinned, opening a bronze door. Wild heat fled out, burning flames of white and orange.

'If it gets too hot, you let me know,' she teased.

Kialessa put down her whip, and entered. One day Piex would make that whip permanently fire proof as well. But not today.

The blazing room within was something else – bronze and basalt structures of great art and beauty adorning a giant hall of blistering heat. An entire wall was given over to gently flowing lava.

'How?' Kialessa wondered.

'Your father has some portal to the heart of the dwarven Feuerdrache somewhere, some unused volcano. I think it's simply gorgeous.'

Flameheart reached out, and put her hand in the flowing stone, running patterns in the lava. She offered the same to Kialessa.

It felt like treacle, running and oozing all over her fingers and unburnable armour. It cooled quickly, turning black, and she returned it to the wall.

'Go on, make something,' Flameheart suggested.

Kialessa tried to form the stone into something meaningful. A cube perhaps? It was more of a challenge to make lava into art than she'd ever imagined.

Flameheart grabbed a handful, and skilfully twisted and pulled it into a magnificent model of a unicorn. She smiled at Kialessa.

Then Flameheart took her unicorn and smashed it cruelly into the wall of lava. It began to dissolve in moments.

Kialessa could not hide her disappointment.

Flameheart snarled, 'Good things die in this place, and you have to look out for yourself Kialessa, or you will die too.'

She looked up at the giant snake fire woman with coal for wings. Kialessa knew she could not fight her way out of here, and she knew she could not hope to slap some sense into Flameheart either. She was being unkind, and cruel. Not like she *really* was, not in the dream. It seemed the waking Flameheart was already resigned to an inevitable death, and might have given up choosing to live already. Kialessa wanted to say something wise, something like, "Isn't Shadowmonger worth living for?" but she didn't want to get beaten, and Flameheart already looked angry. Kialessa looked at the lava, wishing she had Arpil's gift. She would reach in, and bring out the unicorn. And take it away, alive, and whole.

'I'm sorry you feel that way,' Kialessa admitted.

Flameheart grew angry, flame leaping up and growing brighter about her body as she spoke. 'I know you've been asking everyone about their stories Kialessa, and you will NEVER know mine. So stay out of my head, out of my dreams, and out of the shadow realm when you're around me,

By Dr Joe Ireland

child, for there are worse things than a slow death by fire…'

Kialessa's next words fell from her mouth before she had the sense to stop them, 'Isn't Shadowmonger worth living for?'

Suddenly, instead of slapping her, Flameheart fell on the ground. Her fire died, and the light in the room dimmed. 'Curse you,' she said. 'Curse you, Kialessa, "Tavernskeep". Curse you forever.' Her shoulders suddenly wracked with heavily bridled sobs.

Kialessa knelt down, and tried to say something.

When Flameheart looked up, her face was strewn with glowing tears of lava. She wiped them away, and they turned into stone as soon as they hit the floor. 'I am going to die before the end of the year – it is your father's promise to me, and to every twenty-year-old who ever set foot in this … prison. Some fight, and he likes it that way. They die stronger. You should get away too, Tavernskeep. If you ever get the chance to escape; you take it, Kialessa. You get away, and you run as far away from this hell as you can! Bad things happen in this world Kialessa, and you need to look after yourself – who cares who you hurt, when you are hurting.'

Flameheart sobbed. 'And you forget everyone and everything you ever saw here… because if you don't, he will find you. The demon will find you. He can hear your fear, and he will find you anyway. And you die here, fighting, or die far away, cowering. This is our fate; this is the destiny of all the children of the *Sanctum Brumae*.'

Kialessa didn't know what to say.

'Get out,' Flameheart ordered.

'I –' Kialessa began.

The burning woman grabbed her so fiercely it was like a punch in the stomach. And then she threw her out of the bronze doors like a doll. Kialessa hit the ground in the sudden chill of normal air, stealing away her breath and leaving her gasping.

'GET OUT!' Flameheart roared as searing fire burst from her domain.

Choice, set free   213

Kialessa could only snatch up her whip and cover it.

A moment later she looked up, and saw Raynah and the Child. She was surprised, till it dawned on her that they must have been looking out for her. Without asking she ran up and wrapped her arms around the bony wizardess.

'Flameheart will not help us,' Kialessa told them. She clutched her aching stomach and held back her own tears. Then they ran away.

*****

The fourth and fifth years battled it out in the jungle clearing. The sixth and seventh years tackled the powerful four ninth years at the top of the illusory pyramid. The eighth years held back, biding their time.

Lossel was shouting. Her team weren't putting in their best, it was clear. They knew they were battle fodder for the eighth years. But Lossel still wanted something from them they just refused to give – she wanted them to care.

And the second and third years, along with Kialessa and Mak, simply kept out of all the conflict entirely.

'I don't think father will approve,' Amber said with a grin.

They milled by the jungle's edge, a steep mountain wall defining the edge of their mock battle ground. Kialessa looked out at the fighting students. It was in no way a fair combat. It was simply melee; pointless, violent conflict. And it was for such a poison prize.

'He just likes to see us fight,' Mak pronounced of their father. 'No point even being here.'

'Look up,' Charl suddenly shouted.

Kialessa looked to where he was pointing. It seemed the fourth and fifth years agreed with Amber, and taking matters into their own hands had decided to attack.

By Dr Joe Ireland

Cowards, Kialessa thought.

The younger students quailed in fright.

'Back against the wall, defend yourselves!' Kialessa shouted, her whip trailing out from her. She ran to defend the other younger students, Mak, Amber and Charl standing back to back against her. She swung the whip in a circle, and it glowed a brilliant white as its circle of protection surrounded her. A fourth year tried to fly past, and she grappled him from the sky. He hit the ground hard, twisting his wing and curling up in pain.

The other students, eleven of them, menaced up. Tetrarch was among them, hatred in her eyes.

'I swear,' a boy said, 'if it wasn't dad's rule to not kill anyone, I would kill you now.'

Kialessa looked at him, not sure if he really knew what he was saying. But he looked pretty serious, as if he'd conceived himself.

'Why?' Mak teased, 'What would that achieve?'

'Vengeance for the fall of Drake and Beomith!' Tetrarch shouted.

Kialessa's heart pricked. No one mourned their deaths more than she, and no one had suffered more. Why did they keep playing into the demon's plans, wallowing in hatred and fear? Could they not see she was only trying to free them all?

'You are a great person,' Kialessa told her, 'with a body-'

Suddenly, with a move faster than she could see, the young man lashed out with his fist and punched her in the mouth. It stung, but it did not drop her. 'Shut up, Tavernskeep!'

Mak moved to attack, but Charl held him back.

She wiped the red blood from her lips. 'All right then,' she said, 'you learn the hard way.'

Without intending the circle burst out from her, staggering the fifth years for a moment. Kialessa lashed out and snapped the curved knife in his hands right in two. Before she could act again, Mak swooped over her head and bashed four of them in their faces, knocking them to the ground. Wild vines grew with supernatural haste, grabbing the other four students, pinning them to the ground.

The younger years cried out, and Kialessa turned to see the remaining three fourth years menacing up on them. Then the younger students charged. Kialessa did not like the wildly outnumbered fourth year's chances at that point.

Suddenly a tae'anaryn erupted from Amber's vines. Sharp knives sped towards Kialessa's throat, and she evaded them only at the last moment, knocking one away in the air. A fifth year slammed Mak in the chest, sending him flying into the jungle. Kialessa wondered how he would ever rise from such a deadly blow.

With a sinking feeling she began to wonder if they weren't a little outclassed by the fifth year students.

Then Charl stood forward, bursting into a blinding white light. Several sharp knives sped toward him, but they all simply missed and he didn't even dodge. Someone tried to club the side of his head, and the weapon slipped from its master's hand before it had even connected with the shield of white light around him.

When Charl spoke, it was with a thundering condemnation that took the fight out of the whole arena. 'Fools! Children! Serve you a dark master with this violence! Your ignorance is your only chain in this place! Put down your arms, or let your fingers burn till wisdom compels you!'

No one moved, his voice shuddering through the jungle with resolute indignation. Everyone seemed either unwilling to break that silence, or unable. A long moment passed.

'Woo hoo!' Rawhawk called in the silence at the far end of the illusion, 'We won again!'

No one joined in his celebration. The older students looked angry. Mak stood from among the giant fronds, brushing himself off and limping up. He patted the prophet on his shoulder, 'Thanks, friend. I'll have to remember that one.'

Charl still looked angry. 'This violence is exactly what the demon father seeks.'

***

Dinner was subdued that dawn. It was as if people were embarrassed. Daygon was trying to liven up the conversation at the table, but with Kialessa's whip, or perhaps just the prophet's presence, no one dared.

Then a group of fourth and fifth year students grabbed their plates and left the room.

Lossel marched down to join them, her two friends joining her a moment later. 'Kids. You got a situation.'

She sat down next to the prophet, at Kialessa's right. Charl had to move out of her way or find her sitting on him.

No one spoke.

Lossel ate something else. 'You're going to get us all killed, you realise this Kialessa? Charl? You don't play the father's little games he's going to get very, very angry. Next time you cancel training on us like that, he's going to put you right back in the dungeon.'

Kialessa nodded, but looking around the table it seemed most other children didn't want to play these games any more either. Several other students joined them, though Daygon still held court with the eighth and ninth year students, and several of the others as well.

'They're going to start calling this "Kialessa's conspiracy",' Lossel mentioned, casually gnawing a root of some kind.

Kialessa looked around; the other children did seem worried. This was a dangerous situation, and it needed to be dealt with using a certain… delicacy, and compassion.

'What can we do?' she asked Lossel.

The older girl seemed to like the question, grinning to herself. 'Pick a fight or two, Kia, ones you know you can win. You know this mountain is a treasure trove? There is no end to the rooms you can find here. You should go on an adventure.'

That didn't seem to help much. 'Will it help if we fight during battle training?'

'Yup,' Lossel said, the older girls nodding their agreement.

Kialessa hated the suggestions. 'It's all one sided. This is not a fair fight. The teams are not built for diversity and power.'

'No one says you have to fight in year levels,' Lossel claimed, pointing at her two older friends. 'And team sizes are all arbitrary.'

Kialessa pondered that revelation. 'And what of the prize?'

Lossel stopped eating, and looked at her. 'There is no rule saying who you have to share it with. Just… the winning team. But I know for a fact that horn makes enough in a week for everyone here. I know it.'

Everyone looked at her, but Kialessa could only grin as a certain catchy idea worked its way into her heart.

***

The plan was hatched that morning in the damp cavern. Most other students were asleep or dozing in the dawn.

'We're going to get that horn,' Kialessa said. 'And we're going to share it with everyone. Then we can all be stronger.'

'Strong enough to take down the demon?' Mak asked.

'Maybe not, but at least we won't be fighting each other anymore. That's half the problem here. He keeps us fighting each other, all the time. I'm glad he's away right now, this place is worse with him in it.'

The others said nothing.

Eventually Charl spoke, 'Who will you want on your team, Kialessa?'

'Everyone,' she replied. 'But even so, we'll need a core strike force, half a dozen or so. Most of these kids can barely defend themselves and they've never been taught to fight properly. We need to change that.'

'Can I be on your team?' Mak begged.

'What do you think?' Kialessa asked Charl.

'I am not told. I think we're meant to figure this one out on our own.'

It saddened her, but she'd felt as much herself. 'We can't take those fifth years yet, but the fact is we don't have to. All we need to do is get to that horn. Amber, Mak, Charl. It's us four. And then we just need a few surprises. Charl, you're a priest of exceptional faith. You think you can pray up some unexpected, um,' she wanted to say "tricks" but hated when people said that of her.

'Tricks?' Charl offered.

She laughed.

'Yes, we need some new tricks, things the older students haven't seen before. And that's why we're going to get Raynah.'

Treasures

What are our truest treasures? What can we honestly say we get to keep
forever? For where our treasures lie, there our hearts will journey always.
The Eternal, in the sermon at Civit Aurea.

Early the next night Kialessa stood at the Toy Room door. It was very
quiet inside. She'd tried to find Raynah at the archives but she was nowhere
to be found. So she'd come here, but it was so quiet inside. Carefully, Kialessa
pushed the door open.

She saw Raynah lying on the floor, the Child tugging at her shoulder.

Kialessa rushed in. As soon as she touched Raynah the older girl took a
struggling breath.

The Child looked up at Kialessa, a worried expression on her face.

'Raynah, are you all right? Raynah, what happened?' Kialessa shouted.

The older girl rubbed her eyes. Her bracers were removed, which what
looked like a sharp letter opener in her hand. But there was no visible
damage. 'Oh, nothing, just decided to … take a little nap, I suppose!'

Something was very wrong about this girl. It was almost as if she was
trying to harm herself, and the necklace was stopping her somehow. Kialessa
didn't know what to do, was she supposed to say something? Was she
supposed to not mention it? She felt afraid, and filled with a burning,
helpless pity for her older sister. Kialessa looked hard at her, trying to see
what she could do to really help.

Raynah sat up, 'Oh, don't look at me like that, Kia. It's pathetic. I'm fine.
I'm always fine.'

She helped her sit.

                    By Dr Joe Ireland

The Child ran away, apparently she was going to ignore the whole situation.

'What can I do?' Kialessa asked her.

Raynah took her time to reply. 'While the demon lives, we cannot remove this collar. And… to be honest… I would not want you to.'

Kialessa did not know what she meant, but Raynah did not look like she wanted her to press the point.

The wizardess looked hard at her, 'What do you want, Tavernskeep? No one comes looking for me this time of night unless they want to beg another favour.'

It was a poor way to start a conversation.

'What's your story?' Kialessa asked.

Raynah laughed, 'I hear you've been interviewing everyone. That you cancelled battle training with your prophet, and convinced all the second and third years to stay with you in that damp first year cavern with your new whip. You're trouble, Kialessa. More than I could have ever imagined!' Her voice trailed off; as if she wished for a favour of her own that she could not speak out loud.

Kialessa waited. It was the best way she'd found to get people talking.

Raynah eventually spoke, 'My mother hid me, for twelve years, in the wilds of Nomer'el. She hoped she could use magic to keep us hidden. She was a wizard too, and a good one… but not good enough. Somehow, he pierced the illusions. He sent Shadowmonger to get me, and mum didn't have the heart to kill him. She still wouldn't… I miss her… I miss her so much.'

Kialessa wondered – Raynah was a wizard, they had ways to talk to people on the wind, people far away. Was her mother still hiding?

'The dream realm is closed around this mountain. I cannot get a message out. Now, if I could use the shadow realm that might be a different story! But I don't know how.'

'Maybe Shadowmonger can help you?' Kialessa offered.

Raynah scoffed. 'He spends all his time with his girlfriend Flameheart. It's a wonder they just haven't eloped together. Oh, yeah, that'd get them both killed. It's their ninth year here, you know Kialessa. They're both going before the end of the year.'

'Where … will they go?' Kialessa asked, hoping Raynah meant they were likely to become the 'Living'.

Raynah begged her with her eyes, but did not reply. 'Shadowmonger will not help me, and I have nothing to offer him. He's already the best shadow weaver in the entire fortress, probably the entire continent. He's a prodigy, did you know? Chosen of Ik'skuretza. He'd know how to get out… Did you know the entire mountain is a nexus, a powerful connection to the show realm? But it is magically fortified somehow. Some kids have tried to fly away only to find themselves flying back in. They call it the Dark Trap. You'd need to disarm or destroy the Dark Trap if you wanted to fly away. I just thought you should know that.'

So that was what Flameheart was talking about, Kialessa realised, and remembered the strange, mirrored walls above the forest she's seen her first night here. 'And you think Shadowmonger can do that?'

'I know so. But he won't. He'll just wait…' she sighed, 'and it's not like I have the *Liber de nocte Tenebrosi* in this archive. The last copy sold out midyear at Emerel, we missed it by a few days. I could throttle whoever took it from me!'

Kialessa gasped.

Raynah noticed, 'What?' she demanded.

'It's funny that you should mention that book…' Kialessa admitted.

Raynah lunged forward, eyes glowing with academic lust, 'What - what do you know, Kialessa!? Tell me!'

Kialessa would have told her immediately, a year ago when she was younger and more afraid; Raynah looked so fierce. But she had learnt to not give into the self-serving demands of even her very best friends. 'I have a copy. The king gave it to me, as a reward for saving his life.'

'Where is it?! I will get it for you!'

Kialessa paused. 'Raynah, I -'

'You need a favour,' Raynah proclaimed. 'Fair enough. I can… curses! Anything. *Anything* Kialessa. You just don't know how much I need that book *right now!'*

Kialessa smiled, those words giving her more courage than she'd come with, 'We're forming a team for combat training, Raynah. We're going to claim that horn and we're going to share it with everyone. So we need a new team of our own, and it needs a few surprises…'

Raynah glanced at the Child, poorly stacking blocks with her non opposable hooves. 'I thought we had to be arranged in year levels?'

'Lossel says we don't have to.'

'Well, she would know,' Raynah muttered more to herself. 'You'll need a strike team, five or six. The younger ones will have to hold back. You and Mak are powerful enough, and the prophet is the highest-level cleric in the fortress at this time. Maybe Amber, I don't know. But you wanted a surprise? You get me that book, and I will get you several surprises.' She turned to glare at her. 'There's a reason I keep finding excuses to keep out of combat, Kia. Surprises are my *specialty.'*

The Child looked up over at them then, her face a solemn expression Kialessa had never seen on her before. It was a kind of mature wisdom she did not know the Child possessed. It was clear this was one of Raynah's … surprises.

Raynah grinned, 'You like being trouble for the demon father, and that makes you valuable to me. Now, *where is that book!?'*

***

Mak shielded them from the light with his wings. It hardly seemed necessary, the art in the toy room could apparently be turned down, but Raynah was attempting to minimise "extraneous variables", so the shadow of his wings would have to do.

Raynah worked the strange runes on the wall. They moved and twisted as though they were some kind of complex machine made out of words and light. It was fascinating, and something Kialessa really hoped to master someday. If only she'd learned to read six years ago!

Raynah spoke, 'You have a talent, Kialessa. And if we're going to get past Shadowmonger, you're going to have to learn how to enter and exit the shadow realm at will. It should be easy in this place; the veil between the realms is so very thin in the fortress. But to do this, you're going to have to learn how to shadowstep, and to help you, we need some of the equations in the *Liber de nocte Tenebrosi*.' She stood back. 'Try again.'

Kialessa put her hands up to the circle, glowing against the wall. Then, instead of pushing them up against the stone, she pushed them into the shadow realm. She felt her hands reaching out, leagues and leagues, right to the castle at Lenmer'el. It was a strange sensation. She bent down to peer into the other realm, guided only by the shadow weave that clung around her hands. The area was bright and clouded, so she reached out towards a shadowy area. 'You made it! I'm in the courtyard by the horse's field!'

'What's a horse?' Mak asked.

'Pah!' the Child stated, holding up a little brown female unicorn with its antlers and horn snapped off.

'Oh,' Mak said.

Kialessa was concentrating. 'Left a little. Left a lot. All right, move in.'

Raynah spun her lights on the wall. 'Remember you don't have to follow the paths, Kia,' she instructed her. 'You can travel through stone in the realm'

Kialessa tisked, she'd already been doing that.

'I've had to compensate for the slight curvature of the world at this point,' Raynah boasted, just a little. 'You would not think a thousand leagues would be much at this scale, but it's still appreciable – forward is really, "East and down a little". So, where to now?'

Kialessa was still trying to get her bearings in this strange hole she was reaching across the country through. Lenmer'el was the smallest nation in terms of population, but one of the largest in terms of sheer size. 'I can see it now, the dormitory. Oh, how I miss that place! Forwards… not so far… oh, my lambswool liner! All right, left, not so far. Right, forwards, no back a bit. All right, let me try.'

She could see her chest now, the magical silver locket guarding it. She reached out, pressing her shoulders up against the edges of the magical circle Raynah had conjured. It was barely enough. Her hands were inside the chest, they would have seemed shadowy and spectral to anyone who saw them now, which seemed to be no one. Everyone was on winter break, and the old lady was probably off cleaning something, doing the paperwork, or finding old cats with patterns like socks to tell off again.

She felt around, laying aside her three beloved dresses the king had given her. Carefully, Kialessa removed her dagger and its sheath.

'Woah,' Mak said as Kialessa placed it on the floor. It really was an excellently made little sword.

'Acid taint!' Raynah said in surprise.

Again Kialessa reached in. The pouch of gold she left there. Then, silently, she slipped a piece of parchment out of her sleeve. Gently, she placed it down in the dark chest. When they realised she was missing next year, they might come looking in here for clues. And they would find a message she'd written herself, however poorly. They would come looking for her again.

Then she grabbed her first ever book. Gently, she removed the *Liber de nocte Tenebrosi*.

As soon as it was out, Raynah snatched it from her hands. The runes on the wall slowly faded, disappearing as the light touched them again. Raynah was caressing the cover.

'You're going to give that back, right?' Mak asked her.

She glared at him, and walking to an oak podium grabbed up an inkwell and quill she'd already prepared. She intoned magic, and the quill started moving about on its own, copying the book. 'Yes, you can have it back. Once I'm finished reading.'

Raynah said nothing more. She didn't speak to them all the rest of the night. She did not sleep that day, nor speak to anyone the next night. By the time she was done, she'd amassed at least a hundred parchments of copious notes, equations and diagrams. It wasn't until she'd slept the second day right through that she approached Kialessa and Mak in the cavern, along with the rest of the strike team that had allied themselves with her. She'd brought the Child with her.

'It's time for some surprises,' Raynah announced.

***

Again the dream hounds charged. Amber held them back with her vines, springing even from the dark cavern's floor. Kialessa hit one, hard, with her new whip, and the hound shattered into glass shards. Mak grappled one, somehow holding its jaw agape, while Arpil stabbed it in the side with a crystal dagger.

The battle was over in moments.

'Good, good,' Raynah complimented them. 'But still not Flameheart good. You've got to gain ground when you take out the flame beasts she conjures or you'll never get to Shadowmonger in person.'

'We don't want to get to him in person,' Mak protested, bandaging his arm. Even though the dreamhounds were only quasi real, they could still kill someone. And Raynah was a very demanding teacher. 'We only need the horn.'

'And no one gets to that horn but by Shadowmonger. He's their … goalkeeper.'

She sat down, and they all rested. 'I got Rawhawk; he relies too much on air and wind, which is his weakness. Flameheart is arrogant, easily drawn out. But Shadowmonger is smart. He's calm. We're just going to have to battle through the hard way. And Arpil, you need to handle Ka, you're the only one with his talent.'

Arpil grunted, looking annoyed.

'Still, we'll need a dependable front line,' Raynah muttered to herself, looking over at the Child.

Staring at her.

The little girl had been watching with unusual focus, and at Raynah's questioning look, nodded fiercely. 'Ah!' she affirmed.

Raynah shifted. 'Very well. Start easy. The goat.'

The little child stomped her feet, and knelt down. As she leant forward and by the time she was there, her horns had straightened, her legs had shortened, white fur had broken out all along her body. She had become a goat, all except for a very brown peacock tail.

'Excellent, well done!' Raynah complimented her anyway.

'We'll be working on that one,' Mak huffed.

'Now, cat!' Raynah said.

The little animal shook itself, pawed the ground, then bending its head tried to turn into a cat. It seemed a difficult shape to get in to, but when she was done it was a very convincing job. They were just about to compliment her when she sprang out of the form, a child once more.

'It can be difficult to maintain certain forms on certain days, naturally,' Raynah explained. 'Come, do a lion. The day is right.'

The child yawned and stretched a moment. Then she bent forwards on all fours. Then she gave a cute little 'rawl'.

'Aww,' Mak squeed.

Then the child gave a positively terrifying, lion like roar. Far more powerful than any lion should be capable of.

They all jumped back.

She was trembling. Her hands suddenly turned into lion-like paws, and desert coloured fur sprouted all along her back. She grew, almost a head taller. She was twisting and roaring, trying to squeeze herself into a new body that wasn't quite sure what it wanted to be.

'Come on, you got this!' Raynah muttered.

'Yeah!' Mak shouted, 'You go girl!'

The half lion roared again, enjoying Mak's encouragement. She tried again, and again, and then she fell face forwards onto the ground. Raynah ran to cuddle her.

Softly, the little child's features turned back into her own, her hoof like hands reappearing. She mewed softly in Raynah's arms, her eyes half shut. She looked exhausted.

Raynah patted her. 'She's been trying. She's been trying so hard!'

'That would be an awesome front line,' Mak admitted.

'How did you get her to do that?' Amber asked. 'She's never been able to do that before.'

Raynah gently turned the little girl over, and lifted up the back of her shirt. There they notice was a highly detailed grid, with ornate symbols in every cell. It seemed to be glowing with fading magic.

'What is that?' Mak asked.

Raynah grimaced. 'A complete transformation grid. Four gods, seven days; twenty-eight beasts in the ancient astrological calendar. I've been wanting to try it for years. It turns out that her amorphous physiology actually makes her more ameliorable to Firmiantic magics than normal beings – a natural polymorph, a transmutation taint, if you will. We've been researching it for days now, just as a hobby.' Raynah looked up at them as the Child rolled off her and stretched out like a cat, complete with licking the back of her hand.

'Poor child,' Amber muttered an all too common epithet toward her, having nothing she could do to help.

'How can we help?' Kialessa asked.

'Practice will help, but her own natural enchantress powers are too latent to be successful, as you have seen.' Raynah seemed lost in thought a moment. 'But there is a set of coloured inks, kept in the treasury. If we can break in somehow, get past the djinn, I could redo the image in permanent, magical, colour. I know it would be enough!'

'What's a djinn?' Mak asked.

'They're like demons, but they are not necessarily evil.' Amber explained. 'They originate from the Blithling lands, from before the second demon war. Some are fire spirits, others natural shape shifters. But the djinn guarding the treasury is a particular case as an incorporeal. He was once a human man; cursed for breaking an oath, now long dead but in no way at rest. Now he is compelled to obey the demon father, and protects his treasures. I think it gives him a sense of dignity he lost in his past life.'

Mak nodded. 'I still haven't gotten my gift from the treasury, we could just walk in. I'll get those paints.'

'That's very kind of you, Mak,' Raynah said. 'But you will need your own items of power to survive this. You may have a battle taint, but there is armour for winged creatures such as yourself, it can increase your stamina, your command of the air around you, and harden your wing edges for battle. Rawhawk made his own; I would not risk facing him in the air without one.'

Mak nodded. 'Seems we need to make a trip to the treasury then.'

'We will need to practice some more, the guardian is quite formidable, though I suspect he has never met the likes of Charl here.'

Charl nodded.

'Even so,' Raynah muttered, 'it would be ideal if the Child could get some more practice before-'

Suddenly the stone they'd placed to hide their training at the front of the cavern was tossed aside.

'Maybe she gets to practice right now,' Mak pondered.

In walked Lossel, her two friends in tow. She glared at them all, noting the presence of Raynah. 'We know you're up to something, redling, and we want in.'

'Oh, you're already in,' Mak joked.

Raynah held up her hand. 'I'll be honest; we could use your help. But this is kind of… um… how do I say this. We're still in the early phases of planning and wanted to keep this on the low.'

Lossel glared at her. Then she turned her other friends, 'Girls, push off. You're not needed here.'

One of them shrugged and left, the other glared at her. 'So quick to dismiss us for the redling?'

Lossel shrugged, 'She's ambitious. I like ambition.'

They stalked out.

Lossel sealed the door without much effort. 'They'll be fine.'

'Lossel will probably tell them all about our plans as soon as she gets out,' Mak whispered so only Kialessa would hear.

'No, I won't,' Lossel replied as though she'd heard him easily. 'They're nice girls, but they're not warriors. Most don't start trying till their eighth year because the horn motivates them, and by then it's too late. If you're planning on getting out of here, you need to focus every day. I know the father won't tell you, but one or two have escaped here over the years, some lived their whole lives and he never found them. It can be done. I want to know what you're planning on doing.'

They all looked at Kialessa. 'I don't know if we're planning on getting out just yet. But we need to get everyone on the same team. We're going to get that horn, and then everyone can benefit from it.'

Lossel whistled, 'That's bold, I'll give you that. I don't think anyone's tried that before. Gotta admit I don't like it, but then again, you got the prophet and Arpil out, so that's something. But you want to beat the ninth years you're going to need something *extra special*.'

'Oh, we have a few surprises,' Raynah grinned.

'Not enough,' Lossel shot her down. 'This isn't the games room. Rawhawk will kill you if he considers you a serious threat. I've heard him say as much. Your situation here, Kialessa, is a lot more precarious than you realise.'

She looked up at the older girl. 'Would that all might realise our situations are precarious – none of us should be here.'

'Oh, I don't know about that.' Lossel grinned at her. 'Rawhawk is a murderer, he likes it. A place like this keeps him in check. Ka is just an idiot. You want to beat them, you gotta bring something a little more than your A game, first years.'

'What did you have in mind?' Raynah asked. Kialessa thought it was rather noble of her to ask for help when Lossel just seemed to want to insult everything they'd achieved so far.

'Dad approves of feats of power, I can promise you. Take only one thing each, you'll be clear.'

'What *exactly* do you propose?' Amber queried.

Lossel grinned, 'We break into the treasury.'

Mak grinned, 'Already our minds are becoming as one...'

Of greatest worth

He looked right into me as he spoke: 'I deserve this, as do you. For we are all slaves to our hungers, trapped in a cycle of death and life forever until we learn for ourselves what true treasures compel us. It was my greed, my insatiable greed in my past life, that drove me to steal and rob and murder. And for this I am rewarded… hungering for food I cannot eat, surrounded by coins I cannot spend, craving impermanent things forever.'

The guardian djinn, cited in Recollections of the Tae'anaryl.

The collapsing treasury wall made a noise like thunder as Arpil tore it down. All the lights within suddenly went out.

'Watch yourselves,' Lossel instructed, and walked into the darkness.

Their focus over the past two days had shifted from beating the ninth years, to taking out a dark spiritual entity; the guardian djinn.

The room was dark. Faint dust drifted past Kialessa's little light, the magical lantern that Amber liked to use. Kialessa held up the lantern, pouring her enchantress' powers into it in an attempt to push back the darkness, but it did not succeed.

She took out her whip, and it glowed gently.

Lossel and Mak went first, followed by Raynah and the Child. Kialessa went last, sling and whip in hands, flanked by Arpil. The stone trembled gently as she resealed the wall. She smoothed it over till it was almost impossible to tell it had ever been broken down.

'Try it again,' Raynah ordered Kialessa.

By Dr Joe Ireland

She held up the lantern, but it could not push back this darkness.

Dark laughter filled the room, and the torches suddenly burst into light.

'We can see really well now, thank you,' Mak joked.

A dark mist wallowed among the mounds of treasure. 'Children of the Master, you should not be here. Leave now, before I decide to sate my boredom on your cries of panic and fear.'

'Get back, you ancient evil, lest a fate worse than undeath greet you!' Lossel shouted.

The djinn laughed, forming up before them, four arms folded across his excessively muscular chest. 'You think yourself so wise as to instruct me? I deserve this fate, as do you. For we are all slaves to our hungers, trapped in a cycle of death and life forever until we learn for ourselves what true treasures compel us. It was my greed, my insatiable greed in my past life, that drove me to steal and rob and murder. And for this I am rewarded; surrounded by mounds of treasures and gold I cannot own or need, or touch.'

He glared right at Kialessa, 'Are you any wiser than me? Is the freedom you crave any more a blessing than the structure and stability of this fortress you claim is a prison? Can you teach me to transcend all worldly lusts and hungers, when you, too, are just as trapped as me by the illusions of freedom and wealth and power that compel us? I do not have the wisdom or light to free myself from this hunger; hungering for food I cannot eat, surrounded by coins I cannot spend, craving impermanent things forever.'

Lossel had promised to try diplomacy, 'Stand *down*, djinn! We come to claim but one treasure each, for our training. You will not stand in our way.'

It laughed as it disappeared, its voice echoing around the walls. 'You already have one, child. Think you I will allow an instant simply because you ask it?'

Lossel marched them into the most open area, standing back to back. She held up her blade, a translucent green.

The djinn drew a sharp breath.

'Yes, you know this, don't you, soul lost to undeath! Pachah was only too happy to loan this to me.'

The voice that replied held no mockery within it, 'You could only mean business to bring such a blade in here, tae'anaryn. Are you truly ready to die?'

Lossel swung the blade with ease. 'Only if we must.'

The djinn did not laugh, 'So be it.'

There was a moment of silence.

'There!' Charl shouted, pointing at the floor.

Lossel swung, hitting the stone the very instant a hand reached out in an attempt to grab her ankle. She struck it poorly, yet drew green blood from the incorporeal wound. The sound of the strike rang through the room.

Undead figures of mist charged them from all sides as the ghosts of fallen warriors attacked them. Lossel cut two down, while the sharp, cracking fireworks from Raynah turned another two into harmless mist. Charl held out his hand, and a pure white circle glowed there, sending another two fleeing from the light. Kialessa managed to keep the last at bay with her own strongly presented symbol Darrix had given her, but the remaining undead did not flee till Lossel charged them.

The djinn rose from the floor again, but was held at bay by a hissing cat. The Child was putting her hidden talents to good use.

Lossel slashed out at the djinn and it deflected the blow with its own saphirum blade. But it adjusted poorly for her inhuman strength, and the edge of her jade blade cut it across its brow.

The djinn dodged, hiding in the stone. Lossel swung downwards with a powerful blow. Too powerful – Pachah's sword blade split in two as it rammed into the stone.

Lossel swore, and Arpil grabbed the blade, trying to mend it. Kialessa was sure Pachah was not going to be very happy – he loved that blade, and he'd really not been pleased at all to "loan" it to Lossel.

Suddenly Lossel's body drew rigid.

'Oh, no, no!' Raynah mourned, 'the blessed water was supposed to prevent that! How is this happening?!' She rushed up, drawing a bottle to anoint Lossel again, but the possessed warrior shoved her effortlessly away. Raynah hit the ground hard and fell limp.

Suddenly a ghost rose up and pinned Arpil in the air, the sword shards falling to the ground. The Child hissed, but the few remaining ghosts were too many.

'Told you I'd be useless,' Mak protested.

Kialessa nudged Charl. 'You're up.'

He stepped forward, and praying, exploded with blinding light. Arpil fell on the floor, and Raynah awoke.

But Lossel still acted possessed. When she spoke, her voice was not her own, but the djinn's, 'You will pay for the loss of my servants, mortals! How foolish of this woman to bring her own sword into this fray, did she not think it's only use would be against her own allies!'

Lossel began to draw her own broadsword slowly. It looked like her soul was battling the djinn, who was trying to control her.

Charl stepped forward, at first he held out his holy symbol. Staring at the man with blind eyes, he stopped, and lowered his spiritual weapon. He spoke, gently; 'Old man, how long you have languished here?' His voice was not angry, or threatening. It was not like the exorcisms of Serros. It was… conversational… gentle… almost compassionate.

Lossel choked, but kept drawing her sword.

'This is not your house. Come out of her.'

Lossel's eyes turned up, and she began to convulse.

'If he can't control her, he will destroy her,' Raynah reminded them.

Charl held out his hand, and touched Lossel's arm. 'Enough, old man. Too long you have waited here. Do you remember your mother's face? Go, go to her. May the Light release you from your service and guilt. Go, and take your rest in peace.'

Lossel opened her mouth, and a gut-wrenching wail came out. It sounded like a hundred lifetimes of sorrow and regret tore at the air. 'I am… so tired…' it muttered.

Kialessa felt her heart drawn out with compassion for this hungry soul.

'Look up, old man,' Charl said. 'And go to the Light.'

Lossel suddenly collapsed. She looked exhausted.

The lights burned dimly, but the room was silent.

'Right,' Lossel said, drawing herself painfully to her feet yet saying nothing more of it. 'Let's get what we've come for.'

For a moment Kialessa waited, but no ghosts returned. Apparently; that was that.

Kialessa took nothing. Charl claimed a gleaming crystal he seemed to like. Mak took the armour Raynah indicated, and another green jade blade they all hoped Pachah would accept. Kialessa worried Mak was being greedy and took the jade blade off him. Arpil grabbed up a large diamond, and promptly ate it. Raynah grabbed a thick book, and hid a small wand under her owl's wing. Amber took up an oaken wood staff with a wooden sphere, uttering thanks in some language Kialessa did not know. The Child ran all over till she found her paints in a closed box, grabbed it in her teeth, and ran back over to join them.

And Lossel grabbed up an armour stand from the highest tier. It had what looked like nothing more than a metal bikini on it. Without warning anyone, she physically tore off her old clothes and started putting it on.

Mak was blushing and trying to look away. Charl made no indication he'd noticed anything at all.

'You're not going to wear that, are you?' Kialessa worried. It was, well, 'You can see your midriff entirely!'

'Actually, you can see a lot more than that,' Amber added.

		By Dr Joe Ireland

Lossel just laughed.

Raynah grabbed up a crystal, and held it up to Kialessa's eyes. It was a rhombus shaped *magesight* crystal, just like in the toy room. In the radiance of the crystal, Kialessa could see the metal bikini was a very small part of the actual armour. An entire set of full plate completely surrounded Lossel, but the invisible armour of force did not impede her movement in any way.

'The undergarments,' Raynah explained of the bikini, 'are just the superstructure from which a really rather exceptionally well designed *mage's inertial bodily armour* is projected.'

'Whichever of our sisters originally made this, designed it to be intimidating.' Lossel boasted. 'Can you see the banding? The strongest points of the inertial field are where the metal plates aren't. Besides, it's actually quite comfortable.'

'Will you be warm enough?' Kialessa asked.

Lossel shrugged, then she strode toward the front door. 'Cold is a state of mind. This is the best suit of armour in the kingdom. You're going to love it,' and with that, Lossel punched the stone doors. One split at her touch and she shoved the rest of it out of her way with a thunderous rumbling.

'I guess they'll know we broke in,' Mak said.

'Just letting 'em know.'

'Oh yisss,' a voice said.

Everyone turned. For a moment Kialessa wondered who might have spoken. It looked like it was Arpil.

'Finally,' the terranoid celebrated in a gravelly voice. 'Now I finish you, my beloved.'

Kialessa looked, and saw Arpil heft a strange, enormous broadsword over her shoulder. Its blade was rough-hewn and cut from raw obsidian. It was deep black.

'With this,' the terranoid announce, 'I will finally kill the stone giant.'

10 Arpil's Blade

***

Arpil's blade was strange, and simply impossible to lift.

'Glad you're talking now, girl,' Mak complimented her.

Arpil grunted, 'I've been making this for the past six years. No one else is supposed to be able to wield it. Even Ka is going to be allergic to it.'

Mak whistled. 'Neat.'

Lossel went to the hilt, 'May I?'

'Please do,' Arpil grinned.

Lossel hefted the blade, twisting it down onto her shoulder.

Arpil looked very disappointed.

Lossel swung it, and it seemed very heavy. 'Acts more like a club than a sword,' she said. She lowered the blade gently to the ground, several other smaller rocks exploding as she crushed them. She looked at Kialessa. 'Remember you cannot hold that blade when you stand on soil, or you'll sink though like a rock into water, understood?'

Kialessa nodded, unsure if Lossel was trying to make some kind of joke. She tried, but could not heft the blade at all.

Mak had a go, straining with every muscle. It lifted up a few paces before he dropped it on the floor. The entire room shook.

'This is what I use to destroy Ka,' Arpil repeated.

'Yeah, we're still not on kill mode here, dusty,' Lossel told her, clearly having nominated herself the leader of the group. 'Could have… unhealthy repercussions…'

Arpil gave her a dark look, 'When he charges the ground attuned to this blade, he will trip and fall. He cannot use it, lift it, or wield it in any way.'

'Nice, very nice,' Lossel agreed. 'But can he stand far off and smash us with boulders.'

Arpil looked like she'd never thought of that, and didn't look pleased.

Lossel sat in front of her. 'Arpil, even Ka is a prisoner here too, you can't afford to kill anyone today. Understood?'

Arpil did not look impressed.

Lossel continued her motivational speech. 'You ever been thrown, Arpil? Let me tell you, it hurts, you get all turned around. You use this sword, and you get one chance to throw Ka to the ground. You do it right; he's not getting up for the rest of the day. I seen those stone giants heal, it's slow!'

Arpil grinned. 'Teach me how to throw people,' she begged.

'I think we're almost ready,' Lossel grinned.

11 Amber grows in power and confidence

 By Dr Joe Ireland

Kialessa's story

Speak the truth, even if your voice shakes.
Aarg'gon, dwarven sage and scholar of the Delge'um.

'Where is everybody?' Mak asked.

They'd sent him to get some food from the kitchens. Amber was late for practice, and combat training was only two nights away. But even Kialessa had noticed that the fortress was strangely silent this night.

Then the gong rang.

Lossel rose, still wearing her wildly immodest armour. She swore. 'All right kids, I think we're up.'

'That's not possible,' Raynah protested. 'Combat training is two days away.'

'Where's Amber?' Lossel said darkly.

They looked at each other.

'Get your weapons,' Lossel ordered.

***

Amber was waiting in the combat arena, along with everyone else. Her face was strewn with tears, and she knelt at Shadowmonger's feet, a black chain of darkness wrapped around her arms and neck.

The entire arena was set out like a giant desert, hot sands stretching away into the far distance. Several tall columns of yellow sandstone dotted the landscape, and a large pyramid dominated their view. The four most powerful students stood alone at the end, and at the apex of the pyramid the hated horn of plenty stood at the top on its usual stand.

And at the entrance to the desert, each and every other student of the fortress waited. Their expressions a mix of concern, disdain, and raw loathing.

Someone waved, and Kialessa looked over to find even Ipi and Parrow were here, hands tied. Truly Shadowmonger held all the power at the fortress in the absence of the merchant.

Daygon stood with the youngest students clustered around him, looking indignant and sympathetic all at once.

Kialessa was astounded at his ineffectiveness once more. 'Again, you do nothing,' she muttered to herself, but he looked like he somehow heard her.

Everyone stood back as Lossel strode forward, her broadsword drawn. 'It seems we stand in the presence of the *true* lord of the fortress, in the absence of the demon,' Lossel accused them.

Rawhawk hissed, but most other students looked scandalised.

'What did you do to Amber?' Lossel glared at them.

'Next to nothing,' Shadowmonger boasted. 'Truly, she told us the whole story at nothing more than a few threats.'

Amber wept.

Kialessa did not believe Shadowmonger's story, and she was deeply stung at his treachery.

Flameheart danced forward, 'We knew you were up to something, redling *Tavernwhelp!* You think you can take our horn from us!'

Kialessa leapt up. 'Share!' she demanded, and students actually laughed. She looked around, 'Don't you get this? This is what the demon wants, war and us fighting each other. Life does not have to be like this!'

They laughed some more, but fell silent when Mak suddenly spread his huge wings and shouted, 'Bugs in a jar! That's all we are, kids. Bugs in a jar!

And he just shakes us, and pokes us, just to see us fight. Why we all got to play *his* game?'

No one answered him; it seemed the analogy was quite adept to even the least intelligent among them, perhaps even more so to the cruellest among them. Perhaps they all felt like bugs, trapped and tortured in a glass jar they had no hope to escape.

Flameheart burned with rage, 'You will not take our prize from us.'

'We wouldn't need to, if you shared it,' Amber muttered, and Ka hit her. It must have felt like being punched with a brick. Everyone gasped in horror, even the students that hated Kialessa. Amber was just a nice, harmless, agreeable girl most people liked.

Ka made no friends with that attack.

Flameheart glared at them. 'We're not going to wait to find out what "surprises" you have for us, Rebellion. So if you want that horn, you're going to have to get through us first.'

Lossel turned, and they conferred.

'Now what,' Mak asked.

Arpil pointed with her head at the other, younger students.

Mak agreed, 'Let's take this chat away from the other students, I don't trust them.'

Lossel agreed.

Raynah interjected, wringing her hands. 'The air will carry our words to Rawhawk's ears, there isn't any time for a new plan here.'

'Plan A then?' Lossel said.

They nodded.

Carefully they stepped into the arena.

The Child turned into a bear, and everyone oohed. No one expected it.

Then Lossel tore off her cloak to reveal her… armour. People cheered. 'Flameheart, we call you out!' Lossel shouted.

The fire weaver humoured them. She screamed, fire bursting out along her serpentine body and wings of coal rods. Ka and Rawhawk covered their faces. She charged them with flashing blades of fire.

Charl blessed Lossel with some fire resistance, and she met her mid-air. They exchanged blows faster than most could see. Just before they hit the ground, Raynah tried to blind Flameheart with flashing lights, but she seemed barely concerned.

Kialessa took the front line, trying to stop Flameheart from getting to the Raynah, but she could not fly like the older girl could.

Mak had his trip wires out, he'd been practicing non-stop. But in the heat of the moment his aim was poor, and she didn't even need to dodge them. Flameheart flung sand at Lossel, forcing her to cover her eyes, and lunged towards Raynah.

The frail wizard calmly reached into her spell pockets, but Kialessa lashed out with her whip. It caught the end of Flameheart's tail, and pulled her off balance. She crashed to the ground just as Arpil leapt up and pummelled her. Mak tried to join in, but then Flameheart exploded. Arpil hid inside the ground for protection. Lossel raced to protect Raynah as Flameheart breathed white fire on them all.

For a moment Kialessa moved forwards in the flames, then she felt a strange, stinging, hurting sensation. She looked down, and found the end of her armour on fire.

She was burning.

Squealing in surprise and pain, Kialessa fell prone, and rolled frantically. All her skin hurt, and her hair was badly singed. She felt her mouth dry with raw panic.

So this is what it felts like to burn? It was perhaps the worst experience she had ever had. She could barely rise.

Then she heard Flameheart scream. Plumes of white steam were billowing up in the air all around her. Someone had conjured a great body of water and dumped it on her, and, apparently, it hurt.

                    By Dr Joe Ireland

Mak did not waste a moment, but with prescient speed charged her, and knocked the older girl out with his wing. He turned, limping.

Kialessa could not move for the indescribable pain. The next thing she knew, Charl was there.

He held her and Mak by their shoulders. Then he seemed to take their agony into his own body. He trembled under the pain, but Kialessa's burnt skin healed in moments, and Mak's wing popped back into place.

'I didn't know you could do that,' Kialessa told him.

'Until this moment, neither did I,' Charl said, drenched in sweat.

'They have a healer with them,' Rawhawk informed Shadowmonger.

The oldest boy looked livid with rage. 'Get them,' he ordered the taller boy.

Rawhawk looked disgusted, but obeyed.

A dozen blinding vortexes suddenly exploded into existence around them, kicking up so much sand it was impossible to see.

'To the east!' Charl called through his fatesight.

There was a sudden violent jingling of chains, and Rawhawk cried out in pain.

'Surprise!' Raynah called. The vortexes died, and they saw Rawhawk caught in a *golden shackles* spell, except Raynah had done something different to this one – it was anchored in the air itself. More and more golden chains wrapped around the older boy, throttling him. This was not a spell Raynah had discussed in combat training.

Rawhawk struggled violently, and Raynah clenched her fist. Students threatened to race onto the field, but others held them back. It looked like the eighth-year students were siding with Kialessa's 'rebellion', for the time being. The battle between the wizard and the dream weaver intensified.

But Raynah won, and Rawhawk passed out in the ever-contracting chains. If she wanted to, she could probably strangle him with them.

Now Shadowmonger looked blindly upset.

'We're coming for you, 'Monger!' Lossel boasted. 'And we're sharing what you covet!'

Students cheered.

And then a thought struck Kialessa. What was it that they were cheering for? The addiction of more poison? Would it only serve to make each of them more powerful, and more greedy? Or was that simply a side effect of being the most powerful in the fortress, and not of the poison? What was the long-term plan here?

Shadowmonger pointed at Ka, and he roared. Kialessa advanced with the others as Ka charged downwards. Arpil surged forwards.

'Not now, they know the plan!' Lossel told her.

Arpil ignored them with rock hard obstinacy. Sure enough, the moment she thrust her blade into the ground, Ka leapt up. It was amazing, Kialessa had never seen him fly so high in the air, like a boulder granted flight - he looked like a small moon.

He landed on the ground on the far side of Arpil, hard. The terranoid would not get her chance to throw him this time.

'Back up against the pyramid,' Lossel shouted, getting them closer to Shadowmonger and their goal.

Then Ka picked up a stone obelisk and threw it at them.

It was a killing move. Kialessa didn't know how it could possibly be allowed. All six of them could die.

Lossel grabbed Arpil's sword, and leaping up against the pyramid flew through the air. With a scream she smashed the end of the sword against the centre of the flying obelisk, and the rock split in two and shattered into dust.

Students looked like they might have applauded if they could believe what they'd just seen.

Lossel stood on the sand and sunk to her knees, Arpil's sword in hand.

Then Shadowmonger attacked, from behind. Dark tendrils flurried around them. Pinning them to the ground.

By Dr Joe Ireland

Blackness surrounded her. Kialessa pushed it back, and found it surprisingly easy. She stumbled around, trying to find someone else to free. It sounded like Lossel was still battling Ka, and a bright burst of light indicated Raynah's position. Kialessa tried to make her way toward her, hoping the others would be as well.

A moment later a three-meter ape tore itself from the shadow tendrils near Kialessa, and loomed up above her. The creature was massive.

It looked down at her with gentle kindness.

'Get it!' the child's voice bellowed from the monster. She scooped up Kialessa, and ran.

They must have made it at least half way up the pyramid before Shadowmonger realised his mistake – for some reason he'd not supposed the Child could be a threat. But as soon as he did, flailing tendrils of darkness lashed out, tripping the Child. She landed almost face first, slamming her wrist painfully on the stone but turning her fall into a roll. The tendrils were all closing in. Suddenly they shuddered, and Kialessa looked up to see a small forest of vines and lianas battling the shadow tendrils at the summit. It seemed Amber had been cleverly biding her time to help out.

'Get it!' the Child shouted once more, and threw Kialessa toward the summit of the pyramid.

Without waiting another moment, Kialessa focused on everything Raynah had recently taught her and then took her first shadow step in battle. With only an act of will, she disappeared from the normal realm and entered the perfect silence of the shadow realm. She turned and looked at Shadowmonger while her momentum carried her towards her goal, the dim light of the horn of plenty.

He looked horrified at finding her here, as though the entire shadow realm was his own personal world and she'd just invited herself in. Making a pulling gesture he directed several dark tendrils into this realm, making it look easy. They rapidly moved to block her path.

She held out her own hand, commanding the shadow weave around her. Dark shadows parted at Kialessa's touch. A moment later, she found herself flying over Shadowmonger's head, and she slipped back into the normal dimension. He looked up at her with horror in his eyes. Desperately he tried to cover the pyramid with his darkness, shifting illusions of the horn appearing all over the summit.

And as soon as she pulled out her whip, it lit up like daylight. Illusions dissipated in its light, and she lashed downwards toward the horn. Time slowed down as dark fingers of shadow tried to stop the whip, melting in the sacrificial light of a unicorn's life. The whip grappled the horn and she pulled it toward her flailing fingers. It flung clumsily in the air toward her, and she twisted around to grab it. The very tip of the horn nudged the edge of her fingers and kept falling away.

Yet as she spun around her tail reached out and grabbed the horn mid-air, seemingly of its own accord. With a grin she hefted the prize into her hand.

'No!' Rawhawk shouted from the far end of the desert, struggling against his bands.

At this point Kialessa realised she was still flying along at incredible speed, threatening to overshoot the pyramid. She prepared to step through the shadow realm in the hope she might land safely on the apex instead.

Yet in the next moment the shadows around her appeared, and a hand of darkness caught Kialessa in the air. It lowered her safely to the summit. Shadowmonger looked darkly pleased, almost proud. He nodded.

She held the horn up. Everyone cheered. Even from its touch she could feel it emanating health and power; intoxicating health … and illusionary power.

Then she realised what she'd really come to the summit to do. She held the horn up and they cheered. And she shouted, 'This! This is what he uses to keep us all prisoners here!'

And with that, she threw the horn on the floor. As it touched the stone, she stomped on it with her left heel.

It split instantly.

Their cries of jubilance became cries of betrayal as the life enriching oil spilled on the stone. The gold trim became rusted iron, and the sapphire gems evaporated into grey dust. She had intended to make a speech of it, telling them how they all had to fight together to get out of this place. But she suddenly found she could not move, and it was very, very hard to think.

Dark magic worked its way up her left leg, and her muscles seemed to want to stop working. She looked up as Rawhawk slammed into her, grappling her by her throat. He lifted her up off the summit of the pyramid.

'Why?!' he demanded. 'That was the only thing worth living for in this hell!'

She struggled for breath, but even though she knew his claws were digging into her skin she felt no pain. None at all. Even fear seemed to be a distant memory. Nothing was moving the way it should.

The arena fell silent. No one had expected the surprise of her destroying the horn. Not even herself.

She struggled for words even as her vision began to disappear at the edges. She'd wanted to say more, to say something profound. But only nine words escaped her fading mind, 'Because there are things worth saving in this place.'

***

When she woke up she still felt no pain. Her left leg refused to move, and even though she hoped it wasn't permanent, she could feel no fear about losing it.

'Look on me,' the demon father's voice demanded.

At best, all she could manage was mildly annoyed. She struggled to raise

Choice, set free   249

her head, finding her hands were tied to some kind of pillar of stone, so tight that they could not move. It took her a moment to realise the sun was shining brightly on her face.

'Again, you inconvenience me, young Dame. This is not a habit you'll want to get in to.'

'Where are we?' she asked, dimly wondering why nothing more profound was in her thoughts.

'The highest point of the fortress. You caused trouble in the lowest; I thought it was only fitting.'

She nodded, there didn't seem to be anything else to do.

He seemed annoyed. 'I see my master Ik'skuretza has visited you. Why you? What have you to offer?'

She said nothing.

'That horn is irreplaceable. It will take me decades to make a new one, and what will happen to those here? You make it hard for me. They will be unhappy now, because of who you are, and what you did.'

'Who…' she muttered, 'who will have to die so that you can make your poison?'

His body stiffened at this offence, but he did not answer. 'Three days, to sort out your allegiance. You have no friends here now, Kialessa. No one will speak for you. You have betrayed their alliance with you, and promised you would make them full and instead delivered a hunger no other feast can fill.'

He turned to leave.

'You are a demon,' she pronounced.

He turned back.

She continued. 'Let your children go. If you love us, as you say. Let us go. But you make us fight, over food. Over a place to sleep. Over the weapons we need to protect ourselves in *your* home. If you have any real love for us, then, please, let us go.'

He did not reply, but she saw him glare at her.

                    By Dr Joe Ireland

'My words are wasted on a monster,' she muttered, and passed out again.

***

The first day and night were a blur. Kialessa slipped in and out of consciousness. Her first clear thought was watching the rising sun on the second day. She thought it beautiful, and thanked Serros for his warmth. Day was delightful; Kialessa's skin did not burn in a day's worth of sun.

But the second night was torture. She found could not keep her heat. Perhaps because she was so tiny, she had always been sensitive of the cold? She used to sleep halfway in the stove fire to keep warm some winters. She shivered the second night away in gathering horror, begging each and every god she knew for deliverance.

But none saved her, as if they simply needed yet one more reason to condemn the demon who called himself her father.

Around late dusk she began to realise she was in some very real trouble. If she didn't find a way to warm up, she would die.

She was almost tempted by the thought, but wanted to help the other children to escape first, if she could.

But she was getting colder and colder. The tight ropes had cut off circulation to her fingers, and they were darker than they should be. Desperately she tried to wriggle them, but they'd stopped moving now.

She wondered if this was what Darrix must have felt like, tied to a pole.

She kept praying, trying to sing hymns to keep herself awake. But soon her body began shivering constantly, and she could not stop it.

She looked out at the darkness. Something had to be done.

Then she remembered that the entire mountain was a fortress built on a nexus of the shadow realm.

And that place was never cold.

Summoning all her power, she tried to shift her entire body into the shadow realm, and to keep it there. She tried twice, failing completely, and then on her third attempt it was almost too easy, as though someone had pushed her here.

Again, it was a surreal beauty. Massive monsters of pure shadow circled in the air around the fortress. Tentacled leviathans as large as a sailing ship hung in the air, tendrils wafting effortlessly in the shadow breeze. She'd never seen anything like them; they were majestic, silent and beautiful. Bright eyed shadow deer ran through the air like dreams, and little shadow tendriculii clustered around her, giving her company if not warmth. The entire mountain seemed to be a haven, and fortress of sorts, of all the shadow realm in the nation. It was glorious; a fitting footstool for the god of truth and darkness.

She looked at her limbs, finding them still tied up with ropes even in this realm. The demon father had done a very thorough job. But it was easier to move her fingers here, and they returned to their correct colours in a few hours, but her toes were still too dark.

She did her best to sleep against her bonds, and still dawn came soon, melting the shadow realm away from her. By then she was starving hungry, and prayed for food, and the strength to make it through her third day.

There was a flutter of wings, and bird arrived on her shoulder. It looked like a little white dove. And in its beak, it held a small berry.

Trusting in fairy tales, she opened her mouth. The bird hopped over, popped in the fruit, and fluttered away. The berry was surprisingly filling, and sated her thirst. It returned twice more, and then was gone.

Too soon the day was past, and the third night began. She tried again to slip away into the shadow realm, and it took several very sincere prayers, but eventually she managed. A wondrous night flew by as shadow leviathans swum in the air around her: A distracting beauty despite the agonising pain in her limbs.

    By Dr Joe Ireland

It gave her time to think. Who was Tyran Noblax, and why did he keep everyone captive here? It was not for their protection; that was abundantly clear. He could disguise them all and have them attend any college in the grand kingdom; he could afford to bring tutors of skill and discretion in from every county in the land. But he did neither.

He wanted them dead. Violent, and dead. He took their powers… what kind of a demon was he, and how had it all come down to this?

The lone solider

Because there are things worth saving in this place.
The lone solider.

Around midday of the third day, Kialessa awoke with a start. Her arms hurt beyond imagining, and her feet were completely numb.

She looked around, curious to see what had awoken her so suddenly, and her breath was taken away to see an old man standing in front of her. He had a crooked staff and a battered old grey traveller's hat. His cloak and robes were thick for the winter, and well-worn from traveling.

'Storyteller?' her voice choked with incredulity. She could not believe he was actually here, talking to her. Was it an illusion? Or a fevered vision?

He looked at her, compassion flowing from him. He stepped up, and without permission somehow loosened the magical ropes around her angles and wrists, allowing a tiny bit of movement, but still not enough to escape. 'How you get yourself into these kinds of situations I may never believe,' he muttered.

'I am glad to see you,' she admitted, wishing he was here to free her, and maybe even take her away.

He shook his head, 'Sorry, I am not permitted to free you.'

'Is there nothing you can do?' she asked, wondering herself what an old storyteller might be able to do.

He smiled at her, and patted her hair and polished her horns. 'I wanted to apologise,' he said. 'I did not tell you the whole story of the Khozmoh Djinn last time.'

 By Dr Joe Ireland

'That was over seven years ago,' she laughed, feeling strangely buoyed up in his presence.

He laughed, and nodded, 'True, true, oh, how I lose track of time sometimes. Ahem, anyway. Would you like to hear the rest of the story?'

'I'm not going anywhere,' she joked.

He grinned sincerely, 'Indeed! Not until dusk today, at least. But anyway… I wanted to tell you the rest of the story. Let me see… let me see… Ahh! Yes! The lone soldier, on a bridge. What a courageous man! Twenty companions running for their lives, a hundred slavering demons bearing down on them. Now the river was blessed; the demons could not cross it. They needed the bridge. Now if there was time the soldiers could have pulled down the bridge, but there was not. So someone had to remain, and hold off the demons long enough for the rest of them to get to the fort. Can you see it?'

Strangely, she could. It was drawing itself on her mind, like a dream. It was almost as if she was somehow actually there, watching it, being a part of it.

She saw a young man, about twenty years old, muscular yet narrow chested, with dark black hair and a sunburnt complexion. He did not belong in the desert. His clothing was Emerellian, but old style. His eyes, brave, but hurt. Young, but having seen too much. Yet within them there was so much light. He was here for a purpose. He was here to save lives. 'Go, go!' he roared.

'Don't, fool!' his wounded commander shouted in the growing gloom of dusk, 'They'll kill you!'

'They'll kill us all if I don't! Go, get back to the fort! Go!'

The older man did not outrank the young solider, but he knew he was right. 'You're a braver man than me, Kilpoe.'

The young boy nodded, and the older men stumbled away.

He did not have to wait long. Within moments, the howls and heckles of the demons could be heard. They threaded their way out of the trees.

Then, for some reason, they stopped. It was as if something was holding them back. Was it fear in the presence of such courage? Was there something about a righteous, powerful decision that made even demons afraid?

They waited till their leader came, a Baradgule, a hulking form with thorns for armour, and leathern skin like an ox. He held a blithling desert blade, forged light and cool for battle under the unyielding sun. The demon commander looked out at the young soldier. 'Run, little mortal. Run for your life!'

But the young man did not run. He stood there, tightening the grip on his sword. It was a good sword, his uncle had made it. Three demons already it had slain, a hundred more would suit it. 'Why, are you afraid?!' he shouted at the demons.

They roared and heckled, but did not attack.

Their leader pointed to two little chekkel demons, winged, and clawed. They charged.

The young man wondered if this was it. Chekkel could gnaw through chains. They could go years without water, and lived only for the suffering of others. They never retreated in battle.

But the young soldier had already made up his mind to die fighting. So instead of fleeing, he stepped toward his attackers. The first impaled itself on his blade as if it knew not what else to do. The other cut at his leg grieve, and then the soldier beheaded it.

The demons roared.

'Right, who's next!' the soldier shouted.

Demon after demon was sent to destroy the young man, and one at a time he slew them all. Each took their toll, each a little scratch or bite. He was growing weary. But on he fought.

Twenty demons later, they fell silent.

He stumbled to one knee. When he looked up, the leader demon, the

By Dr Joe Ireland

Baradgule was standing in front of him.

'Give up now,' the Baradgule demanded, 'your strength is spent.'

But again, the soldier stood. The demons hissed and stood back.

But their leader held his ground. 'Give up now!' the demon demanded.

The soldier charged.

The battle was pitched, and the soldier exhausted. But on he battled, on and on. Suddenly the Baradgule tripped him. His head hit the hardwood bridge, and his vision turned. He wondered why the demon did not finish him there and then. He looked up to see the monster had tried to, but had swung so hard its sword was stuck in the planks of the bridge. Still, he only had moments to live as the mighty demon hauled at its sword.

Then he looked across to his right. There, under the panel work of the bridge, he noticed a small rune, glistening light blue in the dusk light. It was a fey symbol, for breaking. Someone must have put it there when the bridge was made to allow it to be taken down in haste!

He struck the rune, and half the bridge crumbled. The demon stumbled on its feet, then clawed out at the soldier. He swung around to avoid the blow and allowed his sword to swing out against the right side of the bridge, hoping to find a rune there too.

Just like in the old stories, his sword found that rune, and the bridge collapsed.

He found himself clinging to the wood, dangling in the dangerous, rushing waters. He heard demons crying out, and looked up find them lifting their leader to the safety of the far side of the river.

The solider looked above him, and found no one supporting him. Despair filled his heart.

But then he remembered why he had done this. For whom he had risked his life: His mother, his father. Every man and woman and child on this side of the river who might never know his name, or the sacrifice he'd made to keep them alive long enough to choose the kind of life they had before they too died.

Hand over hand; he reached up, pulling himself up the fallen bridge. It was a ladder to him. His weapon was gone, but it was only weight. He pulled off his helmet, and his broken greave. Two ribs hung out of his chest, and his arms burned with agony.

Jeering and mocking the demons tried to convince him to give up.

But in his heart, he'd already won.

Clawing, slowly, he climbed back up to his side of the river. The demons mocked and threatened him, but they had lost this battle.

But they all fell silent when their leader roared, 'Why!?' the Baradgule demanded to know, 'why did you not give up!?'

The soldier looked at the demons – lost souls driven by regret, determined to make others suffer rather than face the challenge of their own repentance. And he told them why, he told them, in only nine words which he knew they'd never, ever forget; 'Because there are things worth saving in this place.'

***

When she woke up, the storyteller was gone, with no trace he'd ever been here, and she was left to wonder if it was only ever a dream.

It was dusk, and someone approached.

It was Lossel.

Kialessa looked the older girl in the eyes.

'I think you're very brave, Kia,' Lossel admitted.

A moment later Mak arrived, and cried out in distress. He began tearing the ropes from her arms.

Amber arrived, and burst into tears also. 'I'm so sorry, Rawhawk put something in my mind, I couldn't help… so sorry!'

'It's all right,' Kialessa muttered. She tried to stand up, noticing that her legs had stopped working altogether.

Mak carried her. She could barely put her arms around his shoulders.

They took her down into the fortress, through silent halls and deserted corridors. They went through the unattended dining room, no one was there. Then they entered the damp cavern.

Over thirty tae'anaryl were there, of all ages. They looked at Kialessa with concern and indignation.

Mak put her down, and helped her stand.

An older tae'anaryn, one of the eighth years, approached her. He was Plough, the hulking, bear type with tiny bat wings that still let him fly somehow. He glared at her from under his elk-like horns. 'We're prepared to fight,' he stated. 'We need to get out of here, Kialessa. Together, all. You were right.'

Kialessa's Conspiracy

These seven years have ye mourned unto us, and these seven years have ye spurned our council! I cannot change your circumstances until you change what is in your hearts!

Annas, to the starving vethras of Dell.

They spent the next hours planning their escape, with few honest plans engaged because they did not know who could be trusted, and who could be compromised.

On one thing they did agree. 'The ninth years are our biggest problem.' Lossel summarised. 'They answer to the demon for their lives. They're willing to hunt us down. Now, if we leave all at once it'll be harder for the father demon to track us. So we got to co-ordinate this. You showed we can take Rawhawk down. Ka has his own limitations. As for Flameheart and Shadowmonger, we either need them on our side, or we need to get rid of them.'

'No,' Kialessa ordered. 'No death. No killing, else we become the demons ourselves.'

Most seemed to agree, reluctantly.

'We just need to stop the father demon, somehow,' Kialessa said.

Plough, the bear tae'anaryn, grunted, 'Impossible. His blood is venom now, his skin harder than steel. There are no weapons at this fortress that can harm him, and he makes sure of it.'

'You sure about that?' Mak asked.

By Dr Joe Ireland

Plough glanced at him, but did not answer, 'At best all we can hope for is enough chaos to get everyone away. We might not all escape, but enough. Spread the word, spread the rumours. Let the priests of Serros know – he has the care of youth, I am told.'

Lossel nodded, 'Serros may yet step up with Ik'skuretza's indifference. I know the priests care, but don't know where to find us. Even if just one of us gets a message to the High King, or any king, it's going to make this a lot harder for the father demon to keep up his lifestyle. Once they know who Tyran really is, it'll severely curtail his business opportunities.'

Several people nodded.

'It's something,' Amber agreed.

Kialessa looked at Charl; he was staring away as though he did not hear. He noticed her looking, and people fell silent. 'I think it's a good plan. If the demon cannot stop himself, perhaps kings and queens may yet prevail against him.'

It seemed to give everyone courage.

Raynah stepped forward, 'Then it's a plan, or at least the beginning of one. First, I'm going to feel out Shadowmonger, and Lossel, you talk to Flameheart, she still has some respect for you. Keep the prophet in here - they both want him dead.'

Everyone agreed. Charl had conjured the water that had taken down Flameheart, and she still did not forgive him. Shadowmonger had healed her by his faith in Ik'skuretza, and Rawhawk was patched up by the alchemist, as usual. But neither had forgiven Charl for his role in their failure.

'Get to work, folks,' Lossel ordered.

People set off around the fortress to prepare for flight, or to battle the other tae'anaryl still loyal to the father demon.

Then Lossel sat down in front of Arpil, and glared at her, hard.

The stone girl seemed to want to avoid her gaze.

Kialessa joined them, and the others gathered around; Amber, Charl,

Mak and Raynah. The Child seemed content to be practicing being different coloured birds, while a few others hung around, preparing things or sharpening weapons.

Salt water tears began to glisten in Arpil's eyes, and she wiped them away. Actually, it might have been actual salt from the way it smeared.

Lossel spoke, 'Arpil. You've got to get over your vendetta with Ka. It's clouding your judgement. You almost got us all killed.'

Arpil wiped her face.

Lossel glared at her. 'You've got powers, everyone knows that. But you can't expect-'

Kialessa was wondering what Lossel was trying to do – stab her with her words? She held up her hand, and the older girl suddenly stopped. Kialessa was secretly very glad.

'Arpil. You're speaking now. What happened?'

'Oh,' Raynah began, 'when she was younger-'

Kialessa looked at Raynah, begging her to stop with her eyes. She understood immediately.

Silence lay in the cavern for several moments.

Arpil sniffed. 'When I was younger… I almost got away. I kept getting thrown in the dungeon every chance I could. I was digging my way. The Dark Trap makes it hard to get away. But I was succeeding, I could feel it! But so could Ka… he found me… and he dragged me back to this prison.' She wept. 'I almost got away. I almost got *home!*'

Kialessa's own eyes filled with tears.

'Years… wasted,' Arpil muttered.

Kialessa could not imagine what that was like. Years, working in the darkness every day, getting into the worst kind of trouble again and again just so that she could dig and dig and dig. And then to fail? It would be heartbreaking. It would be a soul-destroying failure. She didn't know what to say.

     By Dr Joe Ireland

'So!' Arpil muttered, putting on a brave face she didn't really seem to believe herself, 'when I get the chance, I'm going to kill the giant. Then nothing will be stopping me from getting home again.'

Kialessa doubted the giant alone was responsible for her failure. That their father could know many mysteries was apparent, it was probably not Ka who'd found out. But as the hand of the oppressor, the father knew Arpil would hate her brother all the more, and that hate might help her study how to become more powerful, and then the demon himself would somehow claim those powers for his own. It was truly the heart of evil incarnate.

But it would not do to have such blind hatred guiding a key ally. It had indeed clouded her judgement in the surprise combat training; she'd bargained every victory on a single tactic that had most probably, and indeed, been compromised.

'Killing Ka will not solve your problem,' Kialessa advised her. 'Being motivated by vengeance will… allow your enemies to control you, even in their deaths,' she quoted the wise words of a woman she greatly admired.

The others just looked at her.

Kialessa sighed. 'We just need to escape, Arpil, and we need everyone's help to do that. Everyone… including Ka. I mean, think about it. Isn't he just a victim of the demon as well? What about his family? Why is he so afraid of that monster that he would want to make your life miserable?'

'Yeah,' Mak agreed. 'Take it out on the father demon; he's the real enemy here.'

Arpil seemed to think about that. Her face hardened, 'I don't care. He's a monster. If I can take the demon out, I will. But Ka… well, I can forgive him maybe one day, but I will never forget. I will never forget what he did to me.'

'As stubborn as stone,' Amber muttered.

Arpil looked pleased with herself.

'Ka is not so bad, once you get to know him.' Lossel counselled her. 'Bit simple, perhaps, but he does love a joke, and evoking magic into stonecraft as you well know. He just seems to get dragged along with all of Rawhawk's schemes. I know he's not evil at heart. Just don't forget the big picture here.'

But Kialessa wasn't satisfied. 'Arpil. Please, don't be like this. Don't let your hatred of Ka destroy you as well! We need each other; we need everyone to escape here. Even Ka. Ka is a victim as well.'

Arpil looked at her. It was as if she wanted to forgive the giant, as if she deeply wanted to. But she just didn't know how.

'Even Ka,' Lossel agreed.

Arpil gripped the hilt of her impressive sword, and looked away.

'Give her some time,' Raynah asked.

Kialessa had to agree, Arpil really did seem to want to be alone. And she knew herself forgiveness took time, and was so very difficult if the other person felt they had nothing to apologise for.

This would take time.

And Kialessa desperately needed rest. She put herself on the cot, letting Charl pray over her as she praised her God for his deliverance, and beg for their safety, and freedom. Every one of them.

By midday Kialessa was well rested, and completely healed. The Eternal had heard Charl's prayers, the colour returning to all her fingers and toes. It was a miraculous deliverance.

But she was not looking forward to her first task this afternoon as part of the conspiracy; she had to see Shadowmonger.

***

Kialessa walked up to Shadowmonger's domain alone, Raynah's last counsel still echoing in her heart. 'I can't get through to him, Kialessa. Perhaps you can come to reason with him? He has a certain kind of ... affection for you, as the only other shadow weaver he's ever met. I think he

By Dr Joe Ireland

will open to you more than he opens to me, even though I've told him everything I know from the *Book of the Dark Night.* '

But now that Kialessa was here, she was beginning to doubt the wisdom of this task. She had betrayed him, and had defeated them. Could he forgive her just because she was a shadow weaver as well?

She entered the vaulted room, many hours before anyone was supposed to wake up for the night. But she knew he was watching her.

Holding her breath, she stepped into the shadow realm.

To her surprise, he was standing right in front of her. All around him, dozens of shadow beings floated. He seemed a master of his own zoo of creatures. Shadow tendriculous crawled along the ground, and hulking beetles of darkness stood guard over the young man. And there she noticed, made only of shadow weave, a short metallic crown of glossy darkness.

He grinned down at her. 'You really ticked me off, Kialessa. But you are right. He is using the horn to control us, and keep us in conflict and oppression.'

She breathed a sigh of relief – it was clear he was not going to attack her at this time. But it made her grin, 'You once told me to not risk saying such things.'

He looked annoyed. 'I don't care anymore. I know Flameheart tried to tell you, but it's like you still haven't figured it out, Kialessa. How all the ninth years vanish over the year? Do you know what happens to them?'

She wondered, unsure if she wanted to know. They couldn't all become Living. But that meant the others didn't... live.

Shadowmonger continued. 'Have you noticed the red gem he wears around his neck? Do you know what that is? It's the Blood Heart, a device from the ancient city. We understand it was once an implement of healing, until it was perverted by demon prayers. Now it serves a far crueller purpose.'

'What is he going to do with you?'

He looked at her, his face a strange mingling of disdain and pity. 'You'll figure it out, all too soon. Come.'

The shadow realm bent at his will, and it moved around them as though they stood still, and it was the world that moved. A moment later they were floating high above the fortress, looking out at a darkening land.

It seemed the first of the winter eclipses was about to begin.

'You have chosen a curious time to seek my council, gifted one. I wonder if you meant it?' he said, gesturing to the darkening day. 'Feel. Look inside, Kialessa. There is a power only we were made to feel. Notice… embrace…'

She did feel an odd swelling in her chest, she'd been feeling it grow silently for several days. But it still seemed distant… indistinguishable.

'Here,' he offered, 'let me show you.' Calmly, he breathed in raw shadow, then began to glow with power. An ornate circle of shadow weave symbols coalesced before him, as though it was were composed of a hundred thousand prayers. He presented it to her. 'Claim this,' he instructed.

She wasn't sure what he meant, but she tried to absorb it into her soul using her enchantress powers. As soon as she did, the symbol diffused into her, and a moment later, raw power exploded from her body.

He laughed, 'You've talent, little one. Talent to master everything I've learnt! Talent to challenge even me… I wonder-'

She breathed heavily in the growing power within her, and the eclipse hadn't even begun yet.

'You have much to learn, little one. And you will need to be prepared. Did you not figure it out for yourself? What does the father demon want from us? Nothing less than our power, our talents, and our very lives. With his amulet, he has the power to do so.'

'Is that why there are so few older students?'

'He never lets any live to twenty-one, that he cannot compel to serve him the rest of their lives. Spies, all over the Great Kingdom, placed in some of the highest positions of power, all tae'anaryl, all his children. So many

By Dr Joe Ireland

admire the merchant's wisdom, his great depths of knowledge. All lies, all just his spies who answer to none other but himself. Lies… and that's why he makes us fight, to gain power he can use, or to gain power he can claim.'

'He… kills us?'

'If only… he claims your life and powers and fate, and then makes them his own, usually destroying your body in the process. In the past century and a half he has grown mightily, and soon he will become unstoppable. But Flameheart and I are going to escape this world together. We cannot help you in your little revolution.'

'But won't he just keep on killing his children?' she begged. 'Is there nothing you can do for us!?'

A deeper darkness suddenly fell over the land as the eclipse officially began. The shadow realm itself suddenly filled the normal reality. Various rifts flowed across the mountain, shadow beings popping into and out of the realm at will.

'Never is our kind more powerful than during the eclipses, Kialessa Tavernskeep!' Shadowmonger roared at her. 'And tomorrow is this day that I choose to fight for my life! Tomorrow -'

Suddenly there was an explosion from the roof of the fortress. Orange and white flames lit up the sky.

'Flameheart...' Shadowmonger whispered in fear.

'Go, save her!' Kialessa screamed.

But he was gone before she could finish.

She knew she had to help. Somehow, she teleported right back inside the fortress, into the main hall. It was empty. All over the fortress the ground shuddered. Some epic battle was taking place on the roof.

Kialessa ran, feeling the dark powers of the eclipse flowing through her, enhancing her every power, making certain abilities… limitless. She shadow stepped through the realm and simply teleported into the dining room. No one she cared for was there. So she teleported into the damp cavern. Lossel and Mak, and a dozen other students were all resting, but had been woken by the battle and looked about warily.

'Hurry!' Kialessa screamed. 'The demon is attacking Flameheart on the roof, and Shadowmonger is trying to save her. We have to help them!'

They didn't move.

'This isn't our fight, Kialessa,' Lossel told her. 'This is our chance to escape.'

Kialessa looked at her with disgust, 'And this is why the demon will always win. Because he can rely on us never sticking up for each other.'

'I'm up,' Mak told her.

Lossel drew her sword and prepared to leave, 'You cannot hope to help - they are both shadow weaving masters, and that is just the beginning of their powers!' She ran away from them, almost tripping on the trembling ground. Whatever battle Shadowmonger was putting up, it was tearing holes in the fragile boarders of their reality.

Kialessa grabbed Mak by his shirt coat. This time it was her time to carry him. She pushed him into the shadow realm and it parted easily. He looked blind, but she could see. She teleported them up to the pathways along the outer fortress walls, grateful for Shadowmonger's blessing. A huge cloud of dangerous shadow tendrils covered the upper level, making it impossible for her to get them up there. They would have to fly.

She pushed them back into the normal realm. Mak looked up, swallowing hard. A huge leviathan roared in the air. It struck out at the burning flames on the tower.

She held out her arms for Mak to carry her, 'Let's go.'

He adjusted her position, grabbed her, and just as he was about to leap off the stones, they heard Shadowmonger cry out in mortal agony. Immediately the dark clouds around the fortress began to dissipate, the shadow beings turned to flee.

A moment later a dark shape was thrown from the tower. It was a young

 By Dr Joe Ireland

tae'anaryn man. Mak swooped out, and grabbed him, barely slowing his fall as they crashed to the pathway.

It was Shadowmonger. He was burned badly, in a manner terrifyingly similar to Flameheart's own whips. But his skin was also sunken and drained as though the very life had been stolen from him. His breathing was ragged, and shallow.

She ran to him, pressing her hand to his chest and praying for his deliverance.

Shadowmonger just laughed, ending in a fit of coughing. 'That bastard Ik'skuretza. He told me I'd die here. He could have stopped it. I begged him to stop it. But he just didn't care.'

Shadowmonger coughed grey blood. He held Kialessa's hand as Mak cradled his head on his lap.

The older boy spoke, 'There's nothing you can do now. The demon used Flameheart's own powers and knowledge against me... it was a rigged battle from the start, the eclipse just a ruse to give me the courage to attack.' Shadowmonger's breath shuddered as an inevitable death drew nigh. 'And now the demon rests to contemplate his newest acquisitions...'

In her arms, the older boy seemed so young, too young to be broken. He had a good heart. He should not die so young. There was so much he had yet to give!

There was a demon that should be dying in his place today.

Despite her courage, she still cried. It seemed to be the right place to cry.

Shadowmonger reached up, and wiped away a tear. He looked at her. 'You're a fool for trying to help me today, Kialessa. You're a fool for trying to help any of us. Just, if you can, get away. Just get away.' He trembled, his voice struggling for enough time as whatever death the Blood Heart brought slowly claimed him. Then his eyes flew open. 'There is a text, a small book. Bound only in shadow. It's in my hearth, in the attic of my domain. Only you should be able to open it. I give it to you, Kialessa. It has all my personal research inside, things the wizards don't know, things the wizards could never know. Things only Ik'skuretza told me. Use it, Kialessa. Use it, and break the Dark Trap on the mountain during the eclipse one day. I was always too selfish to use it to help the others escape. But you have the talents, and the winter eclipse in this hallowed domain will give you the power. Get the text, Kialessa! Get the text.'

'I will,' she promised.

He reached for his left hand, and removed a deep malachite ring. Carefully, as though in great pain, he pressed it into Kialessa's hand.

'What is this? Why are you giving this to me?' she pled.

'Flameheart's greatest gift to me; a ring that protects its wearer from normal fire. And it is not for you, but for the person you will one day love…' His voice began to fade.

'Peyter,' she called to him, and his eyes flung open again.

'How did you know my name?' he asked her.

She cried. 'He told me to tell you that he was proud of you, Peyter. He's proud of you.'

Peyter, Shadowmonger, lay silent, 'Why isn't he here then?'

The entire world fell into a dark purple, the sky trembling with primordial power. Shadowmonger's breathing steadied. A brilliant purple lightning scarred the ground few paces away, and Kialessa gasped with surprise. And from the lightning stepped Ik'skuretza, not the chatty teen by the window, but Ik'skuretza; the god. His eyes blazed a deep purple, his hands glowing with black power. His ebon skin glistened as though forged of pure obsidian. When he spoke, the earth trembled, and every shadow in reality stopped to listen. 'Peyter, my chosen,' his voice was sad, and deeply touched.

Shadowmonger choked back his own tears, torn between rage and forgiving.

Ik'skuretza spoke to the broken boy, 'Peyter… did you learn to love?'

     By Dr Joe Ireland

Shadowmonger wept, 'Her touch was fire. He heart … unquenchable. Yes. Yes, I did.'

Tears flowed freely down the god's face. 'And, Peyter, did you learn to *be loved.*'

Deep sobs filled Shadowmonger's dying form, and he spoke like a broken child, 'Yes, yes I did.'

The god held out his hand to his friend. 'Then, come, she is waiting for you.'

Shadowmonger smiled, weeping for hope. He reached out his arm and took his god's offered hand. In that instant his body fell limp, slumping to the floor. But his spirit rose out of his body, and in a second bolt of brilliant purple lightning he had disappeared with Ik'skuretza, god of darkness, truth, and of the dead.

The eclipse suddenly ended, and a moment later the sun shone out of the daylit sky. The world seemed to drink in the light with desperate fervour.

Then the father demon arrived. He looked sad, but nodded with righteous sanctimony. He was wielding two whips of fire.

Flameheart's whips.

Kialessa glared at him.

He levitated up Peyter's body, and spoke with devoted fervour, 'We will bury him in the crypt of the honoured dead. He fought as the best of them. I will miss him, deeply.'

Her blood boiled at the hypocrisy and self-deception that flowed through every vein of this demon. Without waiting to see to Mak's safety, she leapt back into the shadows and disappeared, teleporting through the tower and directly to Shadowmonger's old domain.

She leapt through the rafters, finding the old furnace high in the roof, locked in securely with shadow weave hardened stronger than steel. She switched realms again, and searched frantically. Soon she found a dark, mahogany chest. She tore it open without waiting to see if it was trapped.

Inside she found a few trinkets, several letters and a locket that no doubt once belonged to his beloved Flameheart, and a small bundle of papers securely tied with shadow weave.

She ripped up the bonds, and opened the text. She could not read well, and the entire text seemed to be written in some kind of unique code she would need Raynah's help to decipher.

So she teleported into the archives, grateful for the power of the eclipse and the nearness of the shadow realm here. She was beginning to tire using her enchantress powers; the eclipse was long over.

But she had only one day, at best two, to find out what the text was trying to tell her.

The

Dark Trap

'Brother… young or old, we all die. And, perhaps, your day to die is today. You might not get to choose that day, but you can choose what kind of story you leave behind. Are you going to help a demonic murderer hunt us all to death one by one? Or are you going to be the very reason every one of your brothers and sisters live one more day?'

The Prophet, Cited in Recollections of the Tae'anaryl.

Raynah copied the text in its entirety in less than an hour. 'I think I can make sense of it. Look, Shadowmonger was kind enough to leave a code here, translated into his script. I can write it out if you need, but it is very odd writing. Much of this won't make sense, even in Emerellian.'

They were in the archives, just herself, Mak, the Child, and Plough the bear tae'anaryn. They were ignoring the funerals for Flameheart and Shadowmonger. Everyone was looking out for her now. They had a goal. After this, the others would be milling about the fortress, trying to make everything look as normal as possible.

Kialessa turned to Raynah, 'Can you just find the part that talks about taking down the Dark Trap?'

Raynah flicked though the text. 'Yes, I think so. Can you believe it? I wondered why so many of the first attempts ended in failure, a shadow realm spatial recurve, I did not know! See this image? There is some very complex machinery the size of the fortress itself that bends real world space back in on itself. But Shadowmonger appears to have developed some kind of device made of shadow weave that if you wedge into these gears here the entire Trap will tear itself apart. Shadowmonger has saved us all! But it's not going to be an easy task, the energy required is immense. Did he *really* think the eclipse would do it? Give me an hour; I'll see what I can do.'

Kialessa waited, trying to understand the text herself. She felt pressed for time. If the demon found out, or one of his deluded allies, the quest might be over in moments; the research lost until recreated by Kialessa herself, and that would take years. She memorised everything she could, scribing all of it into her own book. Raynah even lent her the quill to speed it up. But it was strange, complex work.

'Get some sleep,' Raynah suddenly told her.

Kialessa scoffed. 'How?'

'All the action starts tomorrow afternoon, right when we're supposed to all be asleep. The demon will be meditating during the eclipse in another vain attempt to force Ik'skurteza's allegiance. It will let us get started. Take a nap, Kia. I'll keep at it.'

Just then a huge yellow lion walked around the bookshelves. Kialessa was too surprised to be worried, and by the time she decided she might need to be worried she realised it was probably the Child. The lion seemed placid. It was purring, and then yawned. It sat down next to the pillows, and dragged over a blanket with its teeth.

Kialessa sat among its paws, hoping the Child would not suddenly be taken by her habit of biting everyone. But it seemed she was going to behave herself, and meant well. Kialessa looked at her allies. 'Are you all right?'

Mak grinned at them, 'Amber is off to set the kitchen on fire in a few hours. Yeah, keeping it real. Get a nap sis, we got this.'

She sighed. It would do. But would a sleep be enough to get the massive machinery of the Dark Trap tearing itself apart? Only time would tell.

***

 By Dr Joe Ireland

Mak shook her, and she woke up with a gasp. She tried to remember her dreams, but then she remembered there were none in this place; at least, no good ones.

She wiped the sleep from her eyes. Apparently, she'd slept very deeply for almost one entire day, but still felt tired. Everyone looked tired; it was about mid-afternoon, several hours before they usually woke up.

No one would be expecting that they were planning.

'Let's go,' Mak whispered. 'Raynah got the device to work but she needs you to power it from the roof. We're ready. Let's go.'

They ran to the height of the fortress, Raynah unlocking a rune encrusted door with magic. They waited, and looked out, darkened clouds and a fierce breeze seeming to herald an event of great portent. There was only a moment or so till the second eclipse began, and Kialessa could feel her powers growing.

'Oh, by the way,' Lossel told them. If this works, and we get away. I don't know any of you, right? You tell anyone about who I am, and where I've been these past six years, and I will personally rip your throats out.' She grinned, but looked deadly serious.

'All … right … then,' Mak muttered, looking like he didn't believe her.

But Raynah nodded, standing up to Lossel's face. Then she spoke, 'Lossel? Never heard of her. Doesn't even look tae'anaryn.' She sounded quite convinced.

Lossel grinned, and waited for everyone to agree.

'But we're still friends, right?' Amber almost begged. 'We're the strike team. We're… family.'

'Not if we win,' Lossel told her.

Amber looked upset.

Kialessa held her hand. 'I am your sister,' she told her. 'And sister to all of you, and if that means keeping your secrets, so be it. But I'm also going to tell all your stories, as much as I can. I will not forget you.'

'Touching,' Mak grinned.

'Whatever.' Lossel rolled her eyes, looking out on the roof. 'Today looks as good a day as any to die. Ready?'

They nodded.

Lossel lead the way with her favourite broadsword, followed by Kialessa and Mak. Raynah rode with the Child in lion form, still one of her favourites, and Arpil ran last, turning the steps into rubble as she went.

They ran out, the wind whipping their faces and hands. Kialessa looked around; there was a strange mountain perched on top of the dark fortress where none had been before. Then it moved.

She only had a moment to scream before a giant club of stone and hate smashed down upon them. She could not have dodged it if she'd tried, but it did not strike for her. Lossel could have held it off, but she was too busy studying the eclipse. It aimed entirely for but one person.

Arpil disappeared under the club of hardened jasper, glowing brown runes indicating its bane of all things terranoid. When the weapon lifted up, Arpil's hips and legs were completely shattered into dust and stone, and she screamed in agony.

Raynah's fireworks thundered, and Ka was forced to pull back. He was wearing some strange, stone giant armour, his wings augmented by some power she'd never seen before. He was wearing a military helmet. He was ready for a fight.

He knew they would be here.

But then, he stopped, and dropped his stone club on the tower. He looked at his own hand, seeming ashamed.

They ran to Arpil. Her breathing was ragged.

Lossel and the Child guarded them.

'No, not you too!' Raynah wept.

Arpil tried to say something. Then she tried again, 'Lossel!'

By Dr Joe Ireland

The warrior turned, and jumped to the ground. 'Hey, up sis. You got this.'

'Just a scratch,' Mak promised.

Ka was studying his hands.

Arpil shook her head. She wanted to speak. There was clearly so much that she wanted to say. But, instead, she hauled her sword over, and placed its hilt in Lossel's hand. 'Yours!' she stated.

Lossel looked angry, then turned so they could not see her tears.

'Yours!' Arpil demanded. 'Go, go… set them all free… even… even… Ka.'

Lossel looked speechless. 'Even… Ka?'

Arpil nodded, looking up at her murderer. 'Prisoner,' she proclaimed, breathing in her last breaths. 'Even … Ka.' And her eyes became gems of quartzian white.

Lossel drew the blade, the roof creaking at her feet.

Ka leaned backwards.

'We don't need to fight you, but we *gladly* will!' Lossel screamed at him.

'I'm… sorry…' he muttered, 'my sister.'

Lossel closed in.

He growled.

'We need to break his connection with the ground,' Mak told them.

Kialessa glanced up at the sky – the sun and moon growing dangerously close. They would not have much time to solve this problem, and they would only have one chance to try. 'Enough!' she demanded. 'Ka, please. Mighty Ka, you alone can save us all. Have you come to this place to die?'

He unfolded his arms, and held out his hand. It was as if he was no longer pleased with it.

Charl spoke, thunder shaking the sky with the power of his words. 'Brother… young or old, we all die. And, perhaps, your day to die is today. You might not get to choose that day, but you can choose what kind of story you leave behind. Are you going to help a demonic murderer hunt us all to death one by one? Or are you going to be the very reason every one of your brothers and sisters live one more day?'

Ka looked at them. He opened his mouth as if he was about to speak.

'What are you waiting for!' a voice roared from behind them.

They spun around. It was Rawhawk. He was floating in the air. Raynah armed her spell but Lossel told her to wait – he was likely to be ready for it this time.

Lightning suddenly split the darkening sky.

Rawhawk was very ready this time, and he was not holding anything back. 'Remember your oath, Ka! Remember who you serve!'

Ka glared back at him.

'Remember,' Rawhawk threatened.

Ka looked down at Arpil's shattered form. He looked at the sword now in Lossel's hand, designed specifically to defeat him. Then he looked at his hand. And then he looked angry. 'I am a murderer in my father's name *no more!*'

They attacked each other at the very same instant. Two rows of deadly, spiked stones rose up and rushed towards Rawhawk, who swooped down on Ka. Dozens of feathers fluttered as the stone struck both of Rawhawk's wings, but he still ploughed into Ka's chest. Ka grabbed him, and they wrestled violently. But the momentum of Rawhawk's charge had destabilised even the massive stone giant. He stumbled at the edge of the fortress, grappling Rawhawk by his clawed legs. Ka reached for his club but his grip fell a mere hand width short. They stumbled over the edge even as it began to crumble under the giant's feet.

'Free us!' Ka begged, and plummeted off the edge to Rawhawk's desperate screeching.

'For Arpil!' Lossel shouted, turning around to guard the entrance. 'Go, the others are coming!'

 By Dr Joe Ireland

They ran to the centre apex of the fortress. Raynah held out Shadowmonger's text, holding her right arm to the right, palm down. She intoned the first of his sigils, and a bright purple rune circle appeared at her feet. The last of the sun disappeared behind the moon, and the wind suddenly whipped up around her. She levitated up, reading the text from pure memory.

The entire sky turned deep purple.

Shadow weave wafted out from the writing, forming a strange device in front of Raynah.

'Now, Kialessa!' she screamed.

Kialessa held out her hand, and the device floated there as though it only needed power to expand a hundred thousand times larger and animate.

'Here come the company!' Mak shouted.

Raynah floated away from the rune circle. Kialessa ran towards the circle, then she heard screeching in the sky. Seven or so of her siblings were in the air, and they looked ready for a fight. Suddenly, one charged his neighbour, breaking their formation.

Trust no one, she laughed inside.

'Go!' a voice shouted. It was Amber. Spiked vines twisted in the air, shielding Kialessa.

White fire sprung up, and she turned to see Charl summoning divine power to protect her.

Kialessa wove her own enchantment, and suddenly six shadow tendriculous leapt into this realm. They could not speak, but she could feel the rage and power flowing from them. They would fight for her.

She stepped into the circle.

She was momentarily dazed, suddenly filled with an intoxicating flux of raw shadow power unlike anything she could have imagined. She knew she could rip the whole fortress to shreds, if she had time and knew how.

All around her the fighting intensified. She could feel them battling. But she could not risk distraction. With a screech, she tore apart the barrier between reality and the shadow realm, and hundreds of shadow beings burst in. Most would not serve her, but they might choose to, if only for Shadowmonger's sake.

'Don't waste the energy!' Raynah shouted, desperately struggling to balance the enormous power being channelled through Kialessa.

12 Battle at the *Sanctum Brumae*

Kialessa closed her eyes, and feeling her power stretch out through the shadow realm. The Dark Trap was enormous; a twisting of realities that didn't need to be. She saw the dark machinery that made it possible, and she was disgusted. It was a cruel bending of the world she loved.

 By Dr Joe Ireland

It was just too easy; she simply untwisted the shadow realm and let it flow back the way it was supposed to be.

'You did it!' Mak's voice shouted.

But Kialessa was not done. She glanced at Raynah. Still she held her pose. The realm was healed, but the machinery was still a problem. With it, the Trap could be reset.

Suddenly a dark screech echoed through the entire realm, it would have been heard at the other edge of the country.

The father demon was coming.

She knew she only had a few breaths to solve this problem permanently. She took hold of Shadowmonger's device, made of little else than conceptions, shadow, and desire. She held it up, speaking in her heart to the denizens of the shadow realm.

The leviathans were the first to respond, pouring their will and magnificence into the device. Then the tendriculous. Then all the others, some like posks who ran on the air, snakes that flew, glowing balls of dark fire. She felt their indignity and rage at the desecration of their world by the Dark Trap. They filled the device with their power and hate.

The device primed, then it struck.

There was a thunderous crash none would hear but in the shadow realm, hitting the machinery that ran the hated Trap. It shattered instantly, tearing itself apart. Large chunks of the fortress fell away, thundering down on the mountain.

'Flee!' Lossel screamed. 'All of you, flee!'

Just then a being screamed and Kialessa fell to the ground, forcibly torn out of the shadow realm she loved. She'd never heard any sound like it, and all the strength failed in her legs. Looking around, she saw every other tae'anaryl had suffered the same fate.

She looked up, and saw the father demon, dark wings silhouetted by the pure eclipse. Then everyone froze in fear.

Choice, set free

It was already too late to flee.

By Dr Joe Ireland

Retribution

What makes a family, Kialessa? A commitment, a promise? A marriage
perhaps? … You do realise the power in a promise, don't you? … A sacred
promise between any two mortals is a very powerful thing. Even the least of
the gods can bind a pact no demon king can sunder.
The god Ik'skuretza, cited in Recollections of the Tae'anaryl.

The demon father floated himself above the tallest tower, in the mystical powers of the deepest eclipse of the year. Kialessa looked up at him, wreathed in the power of the darkness. She realised there was no way she could challenge him in combat at this point.

'Get out,' he told everyone. The others scurried away, except for Kialessa's closest allies; Lossel and Raynah, the Child and Mak, Amber and Charl.

He was a tapering wisp from waist down, his body seemingly transparent. He was wielding two curved swords of glowing blue metal.

'He's a djinn,' Kialessa finally realised.

Lossel helped Raynah up, and they armed themselves once more.

Kialessa stared at the demon who called himself her father. A djinn. A semi demon… an undying spirit, who broke his oath… a man who took lost children, and they were never heard from again. 'You… you are the Khozmoh Djinn,' she pronounced.

He glared at her, brow furrowed in concentration. 'The storyteller,' he announced, realising who had prepared her to know.

She gave him a wry grin. She knew who her father was; a fallen hero.

The demon snarled at Kialessa. 'Do you really think this is going to be the first time I have had to kill everyone, and start again? You've achieved nothing but sped up their deaths, and I will gain little from it.'

She looked up at him, suddenly feeling tired. She was tired of fighting him, tired of being afraid of him. 'I'm going home now. I'm going home, and you're going to let everyone go now. You will no longer slake your thirst on our fear for our lives, and sate your hunger on our powers.'

He laughed at her. 'So you want to see for yourself what the Blood Heart can do?' He pulled the amulet from his shirt. 'Who will be first? If you all die here, I promise to allow the others to live, for now.'

'Until you hunger for their lives as well!' Raynah shouted, though her voice broke.

He glared at her. Then he turned to Lossel, 'You could have lived a long life, Lossel,' he said.

She actually saluted him. 'And live a coward? No. Sorry, dad, that's just not me. That will never be me.'

He looked at her, angry, but also … almost… with respect.

Then he turned at Kialessa again. 'So who's it going to be first, Tavernskeep?' He raised the amulet, and a dark red light hit Mak in the chest.

Raynah screamed, trying to block it, but it ignored her. The beam levitated Mak up into the air while he grunted in pain.

Kialessa looked, tears in her eyes. But she'd seen enough of his murder to prefer death than further torture by this being. If she could not choose the day she died, she could at least choose how.

Her whip was in her hand before she could reach for it, swinging in a circle it quickly protected her, breaking the dread beam on Mak's chest. Everyone rushed to join her, and they armed themselves against the man who called himself their father.

'Curious,' he pondered, thunder rumbling as he drew in power from the eclipse. He levitated further up.

Quietly Kialessa began to fear that not even a unicorn's sacrifice could stop a skilled sorcerer during a shadow eclipse.

'So, Kialessa first then!' he roared.

'No!' A voice called from the shadows. 'I am!'

They turned.

It was Daygon. He glared at the master, walking forwards. His lip was bleeding, and he held his arm as if wounded. 'Enough, father. Don't delay any further. You hunger for blood from your slavery to that device? Then take me!'

The demon father glared at him. 'Don't be ridiculous –'

Daygon held out an empty vial, and dropped it on the ground. 'Veretheium. I will be dead in less than a few moments.'

'What have you done?!' the demon hissed.

'Enough!' Daygon roared with unexpected power. His voice was old, and strong. There was some hidden might in him yet. 'I am *no longer* your slave! I tire of you using me to keep these innocent children placid and obedient! You've relied on my skills for four generations - well now it's time you claim them for yourself.'

The demon glared at him.

Daygon clutched his chest, and fell on one knee. The Child reached out to bring him into their circle, but Raynah prevented her.

Daygon smiled at them, a wry smile. As if he knew something they did not. 'Well, demon! Are you afraid of what my fate may require of you!?'

The father demon roared, tears glistening in his red eyes. 'I *like* you, Daygon. You had many years yet!'

'No!' Daygon shouted, coughing up pale blue blood. 'Now take my fate, or watch it fade before you!'

The father demon teleported onto the rooftop. He hauled Daygon up by his coat. The demon was… crying. 'You have been my only friend in the past half century, why? Why did you do this?!'

Choice, set free

'You are a murderer,' Daygon replied.

It touched a sensitive spot in the demon. His face hardened, then twisted in vile hatred and agony, 'So be it, mortal fool!'

'Father, no!' Raynah screamed.

A rune circle of profane power suddenly surrounded the demon and his aged son, a glistening light forming a barrier around them, and then turned invisible. Lossel slammed the sword up against the field, but could not break it.

The dire red light shone from the amulet, flooding over Daygon. He looked old, and tired. The demon still held him up in the air by one arm as if without any physical effort.

'Goodbye, my son,' the demon said.

Daygon did not reply.

The light suddenly intensified, glistening sparkles of life lifting up from Daygon's chest and face, and flooding into the father demon's. The father's expression became calm as he contemplated another man's being, drinking in his life force, his very fate.

All the blood and vital fluids drained from Daygon, leaving him a hollow husk. Then he seemed to evaporate, his clothes fluttering to the ground.

The lion stood back within the circle, her eyes filled with tears. Lossel gripped the weapon tightly in her hands.

Then the father demon turned to glance at them. The rune circle disappeared. He stood to face them. 'Now… oh!'

Unexpectedly, the father demon clutched his chest and fell on to one knee even as it materialised beneath him. He trembled, then looked up at them, and his eyes were filled with clear tears.

They looked back at him.

He clutched his chest again. 'I can… I can… *feel you!*' he muttered.

They looked at each other.

                    By Dr Joe Ireland

He continued, 'Your … fears… your hopes… is that what it was like to be Daygon! Oh, he wanted to protect you all! Oh, how *he cared.*'

'Run,' Lossel commanded, sprinted away.

'No, wait!' the father demon begged, holding out his hand towards her. She leapt from the edge of the fortress, and he did nothing. It was not that he could not; he simply couldn't bring himself to.

They ran.

'Wait, no! Please!' the demon begged.

Kialessa ran toward the edge of the tower, wondering where to go next. They had some kind of plan, but it seemed far away. Too impossible to imagine it might have actually worked, she'd never prepared her soul for actual escape.

'Kialessa,' Raynah begged, 'Get me to the archives!'

Kialessa grabbed her around the waist and shadow stepped there.

A golden cricket jumped from Raynah's shoulder, becoming a lion.

Raynah spoke sharp words of power, and the entire room full of shelves suddenly twisted along the ground and piled themselves up in a tight bundle in the circle at the centre of the room. Raynah's owl landed on her shoulder, and the Child turned into a snake around her arm.

Kialessa looked up as Raynah levitated to the top of the small mountain of books. Magic twingled in the area, leaving Kialessa far from its effect.

Kialessa realised Raynah meant to escape without her.

'I'm sorry, Kia. There's no room. Take care!'

She was wounded, not sure what to think, 'Raynah, where?'

13 Raynah and the child

Raynah looked sad, but determined, 'To mother. Goodbye, my sister.' She threw Shadowmonger's text at Kialessa, and in a white bolt of fire she teleported them and the entire archives to somewhere else, far away.

Kialessa felt such sorrow, but was glad that the Child would be all right. Kialessa listened. All over the fortress, fighting was on. She did not know what it meant. She felt her way into the shadow realm, her powers waning in the dying eclipse.

She had to get away too. She'd done her part to help others, now it was time to help them by making it hard for the demon to find them all.

She was just about to leap away, when she found herself thinking of Mak. She felt up, and through the mysterious powers of the shadowrealm

　　　　By Dr Joe Ireland

saw him flying away from the fortress at a desperate pace.

Then, ploughing down on him with silent swiftness, was a battered and beleaguered Rawhawk. Mak hadn't even noticed.

Kialessa sighed – without help Mak was going to die.

Without another thought she shadow stepped up to the air high above the fortress and grabbed hold of Mak's arms. He shouted in surprise, but she didn't wait an instant. She took him far away, right to the edge of the fading eclipse, more than halfway across the country, just a breath before Rawhawk would have impaled him with six deadly claws.

Mak sighed with relief, then reached down and caught her. The air here was high, and cold, but he seemed fine. 'Sis! I did not expect to find you here!'

She tried to speak, finding the cold stealing away her breath. He wrapped her in his arms, still so strong she seemed a little burden to him. She pressed against his chest, using her tail to help hold on. He was the only warmth she could feel up here, high in the winter air.

This was a very stupid idea, she thought to herself.

He pulled a blanket from his backpack, 'Didn't know why I brought this, but now I do!'

She snuggled as best she could, with nothing to prevent her plummeting to the ground but his amazingly powerful arms. 'Please,' she begged, suddenly filled with arcane exhaustion that felt nothing like physical exhaustion. The eclipse had ended. 'Please,' she could only whisper. 'That way, southwest. Towards the long road… do you see it?'

'Think so, near that city at the seaside?'

'North… north of that. Oh, Mak, please. Take me home.'

Home

We all come from somewhere,

We carry that place within us,

It never leaves our hearts.

Elven Queensage – Sagesse L'aimé.

Her strength returned as dusk lit the sky. Mak's strength was just beginning to slacken. She guided him down toward the little town, to the large inn that was her home. He put her down next to the old well, grappling the chain he drew up the bucket, and drank the frigid waters quickly, giving himself a head-freeze.

She held the bucket, warming it with her wizardry. He drank again.

'Now what?' he asked.

She looked around. The inn was as decrepit as ever. 'I need to find my family.'

He looked at the inn, 'We won't be safe here, Kialessa. The demon lives. He's coming.'

'You leave, if you must,' she said. 'I need to find my family.'

They hurried to the front door, and pushed it open. It was not locked; it was not even latched. She stood in the doorway.

'Kialessa?' a young boy's voice asked.

'Kiel!' she screamed, running in. He was hiding behind the counter, and he leapt up to hug her. He looked tired, as though he'd been trying to run the place single handed since she'd been taken. The serving girl was nowhere in sight, and it looked like no one had cleaned up in all that time. Tables and chairs were still toppled over.

Then he took one look at Mak, and didn't even seem worried in the

By Dr Joe Ireland

slightest. 'This is your brother?' he seemed to announce it.

She nodded.

Mak held out his hand.

Kiel actually took his hand, and shook it. 'He's hot,' Kiel explained.

'High air flying, very good exercise,' Mak replied.

Kiel nodded.

'Where are our parents?' Kialessa asked. She did not know how much time they had to sort things out, and, perhaps, to say goodbye again.

'Mum's out back, Dad hasn't left the cellar since you got taken…,' Kiel replied.

'You get Dad,' she said, and started to run out.

'Kia!' Kiel called, his voice choking with emotions.

She turned back to him.

He looked small, and pale. 'Did I… was it…. your brothers…'

She walked over, and put her hand on his arm.

He started to tremble. 'They're dead, they're dead. I killed them. I killed them both!' he curled up on the floor, rocking backwards and forwards.

She tried to comfort him, not knowing what to say.

He shook his head and refused to look at her, squishing his face onto his knees. 'No, no, no, I'm bad, I'm bad.'

'Kiel, you … I mean…' she tried to say.

Mak pointed at him, 'Him?' he mouthed, looking very surprised.

She assumed he was asking if Kiel was the dreamguide. She nodded.

Mak took a step back, looking at the crying, groaning boy with awe, almost fear. Then he looked a little frustrated.

Suddenly Mak picked him up off the ground with one arm, and dumped him on the table with almost no effort. Kiel looked a bit surprised through his tears.

Mak placed a hand on both his shoulders and stared him in the face. 'Listen, kid,' Mak said in a firm voice. 'You think that's the first ever time you're going to have to fight for your life, or the last? You got a talent, and you need to use it right. So don't feel bad about saving your sister's life. She does not deserve that.'

Kiel looked at her, ashamed, and still deeply upset. 'I would not have hurt them if they… they were trying to rewrite you… I've seen it done. It's very evil. I had to stop them. I had to.'

'That's right, you did.'

'And I wouldn't have if they'd just left us alone.'

'It's true,'

'But why does it still hurt?'

'Because you're a good kid,' Mak told him. 'And you don't want to hurt people. It's good, means you still got a heart. Unlike those two. I hope you never forget how bad this makes you feel. It means there's still hope for you. It means you can still tell right from wrong, even in a cruel and difficult world.'

'Where'd you learn that?' Kiel wondered.

'Me mum,' Mak boasted. 'And I'm going to break her out of jail soon, *without* killing anyone. So here's to leaving the world a better place than it found us, when we can,' and he fist bumped Kiel.

Kiel didn't know what to do with that, and blinked. Then he sniffed. 'But it's not over, Kia. It's never over. If not this, then something else. One day this whole inn will probably burn down and I just… why do bad things happen to good people?'

Kialessa was momentarily surprised at that question; it was the very question she was wondering about. But Kiel needed an answer, and she felt she finally had one, 'Why? To help you become a stronger, wiser, kinder person.'

Kiel thought about it, sniffed, took a deep breath. He glanced at Mak, and then gave her a hug. He nodded, 'Come on, we better go get Dad.'

'Right!' Mak said.

Kialessa ran out, thankful for her two brothers. 'I'll find Mum!'

The fields behind the house had never had a fence, and she never knew where their land ended and the valley began. She looked around for her mother, but could see her nowhere.

She ran to the sheds, to the vineyard, looked in the barn. She was nowhere. She called, and called, but no one answered.

Then, as she began to despair, she heard an older woman crying by an old Winterwillow.

She ran, and there, sitting on the ground, covered in dirt with her hair unwashed and unbrushed in what looked like several weeks, was her mother.

She looked up at Kialessa, eyes red with tears.

'Oh, Mother,' she said.

Her mother sobbed, 'Horns! Ye canna be here! You were gone… he took you away.'

She sat by her mother. Rage boiled in her heart; this was the woman who sold her, who lied to her about her family. Who taught her nothing but to distrust everyone, or how to steal from them.

The old woman looked truly distraught, and Kialessa's heart melted. She was not shouting at her now, or swearing. She was sad. She was, probably… regretting.

'Mother-'

'Don't call me tha!' the woman shouted, pulling away, weeping more. But she did not flee.

'What happened?' Kialessa asked her, simply to keep her talking.

She wept again. 'Yer father… the drink… he canna have children. When the merchant came to the inn, alone… I knew what he offered. A child of my very own to love. I sent yer dad to fetch bread at the bakers, knew he'd be gone long enough. Soon as the merchant is done, he tells me he's coming for you when you're twelve and that I was to keep you safe and healthy until then, or he'd burn the whole inn down around us and kill my man!' then she cried. 'I knew it was wrong. I knew I should not have given myself to that man. But until he threatened me, I did not know I was making a deal with a demon.'

She turned, and looked at Kialessa. 'Then, when I saws you, I knew. I really knew. You were so different from a normal child. But … I still loved you, Kialessa. You were mine. You were always mine.'

She cried some more, Kialessa's own eyes filling with unbidden tears yet again. Then she put her hand on Kialessa's face. 'So you see? I don't deserves you. You got to go away, and forget this old *witch*!' she sobbed. 'You were such a good kid; I always knew you were never a demon on yer heart. But then you up and saves the king? Get out. Get out Kialessa, and leave me forever.'

Kialessa cried too. She did not know what to say. If she fought her to stay, her mother would fight. She always did. And if she showed her any softness, even a hint of forgiveness, her mother would ignore it. She always did.

But she did not want to leave her mother.

'I… can't…' she said. 'You are my mother. And… and… and I still love you!'

The old woman wept, and wrapped her fat arms around Kialessa's neck. She muttered something Kialessa could not hear.

'What?' Kialessa demanded.

'I said I never deserved such a kind heart. You've the kindest… but he's coming back, isn't he? The demon. He's coming, and there's nowhere that we can get away from him.'

Kialessa grabbed her hand. 'We don't need to run to be safe from great evil. Come, come, let me teach you.'

She pulled the old woman up; it was not easy. Then they ran into the house.

     By Dr Joe Ireland

They found her old man sitting in the main room where Kiel and Mak had brought him up from the cellar. He looked blind drunk. Kiel was there, trying to talk even a thimble of sense into him. But the old man looked like he hadn't shaved in weeks. He had probably not moved in weeks.

Mak shook his head, indicating that nothing could be done.

Kialessa did not believe it. The alcohol was poisoning the old man. It had poisoned him her whole life.

And that gave her an idea. Taking out her holy symbol, she pressed it up against the old man's chest. He gasped, and looked down.

She prayed,

Eternal light, light divine.
Restoring truth, breath in kind.
Purge this vessel, make crooked straight,
Free this soul by wisdom's gait.

She wasn't sure if she'd gotten the prayer right, but at least it was sincere.

The old man looked down at the symbol, then at her hand, then at her face. 'Kialessa!' He gasped in wonder, and wrapped her up in his arms, kissing her again on her face and head and horns. 'We thought we'd never see you again! Kialessa, how can this be? How are you here?'

She eventually pushed his face away. 'Father, father... how did you let this happen?'

His face twisted in agony. He looked at his mead cup, then threw it away in disgust. He sat up on his chair. 'I don't really know. And I don't have any excuse. I am not worthy to be called your father-'

She hit him, throwing herself into his arms once more. 'Don't say that!' she begged. 'Don't ever say that again!'

He started crying too.

Then their mother came over, and sat down. She held his hand, and for a fleeting moment Kialessa wondered if she'd ever seen them hold hands before.

Then she turned to Kiel. 'You too.'

He looked sad, then angry. 'No. You got your family, I lost mine. They don't need me, and I don't need them. I am going to be fine on my own.'

It stung her heart.

But Mak was the first to speak. 'Doesn't work like that kid,' he said, looking at Kiel. 'Never did. You want to spend your whole life wondering why love never seems to find you; keep thinking like you just did. These folks are offering you a family, Kiel. Don't… don't let that go. Don't walk away from that.'

Kiel looked at them, and his lip quivered. 'Where'd they go?' he asked. He looked at Kialessa, 'I cannot find them, and I've looked *everywhere!*' she knew he meant the dreamworld as well. 'You got your family; I need to find my own.'

She held out her hand. 'All right. All right. But that doesn't mean you can't be my brother. Won't you be my brother, Kiel? We need you too. You're a part of us too. And I know you don't think you can see it yet, but we're not a complete family without you.'

He burst into tears, and ran to them. They all hugged him.

'All right,' he said, 'you can be my family too!'

'Aww, that is so sweet!' Mak said.

'Isn't it!' an old man said from the corner of the room.

They looked around in surprise.

It was the storyteller.

'You?' Kialessa wondered.

He smiled at her, and tipped his hat. He righted up a chair that looked like no one had picked it up since the battle, and sat down.

'Storytella?' her mother asked.

     By Dr Joe Ireland

'Yes, yes. It's me. I heard you praying and thought I'd get it organised, finally.' He sighed. 'The solstice is only days away, and then I must rest. But I have a little time left.'

'Who are you?' Kialessa finally needed to know.

The old man sighed, calling her over. They all joined him. She knelt on his cloak that was spread out on the floor, just the way she did as a child to hear his old stories.

14 Old man Winterwillow - the Storyteller

'I suppose I can be totally honest with you. I am older than this inn. Older than the valley it resides in. I have told the king about you ever since your star fell to the earth, Kialessa, and I know where to find it. I am old man Winterwillow; the breath in their leaves, the depths of their roots. I am the Winterwillow, I am all the Winterwillows.'

'You, you're…' Kiel stumbled to explain.

'He's a god,' Mak finished for him.

The old storyteller nodded. 'Ever wondered how I know so many stories? Well now you know. I have seen the castle at Nomer'el being built, I have walked the streets of *Civit Aurea* when they were once paved with gold!'

'Woah,' Mak said.

'I can't believe we only offered you mead,' Dad said.

'I can't believe we made 'im pay! Why didn't you say you was a god, old man Winterwillow!'

The storyteller laughed, 'And further disgrace your pitiful income from this under-loved, broken-down inn? No, I could not do that.'

Her mum sat down, 'Well, I is sure glad you're by, Winterwillow. I, um, as you know.'

He finished for her, 'You have a three-ton demon prince bearing down on this place, and if I'm not mistaken, he should be here in about two moments.'

They tensed.

'Right,' Mak said, unfolding his wings.

Old man Winterwillow stopped him, 'This is not your fight, young man. I would recommend in the *strongest possible terms* that you take your flight. **Now.**'

'I can't leave these people,' Mak said courageously.

'Not even in my care?' the storyteller cocked an eyebrow at him.

'Maybe for that,' Mak admitted.

'Go, your mother is waiting for you,' the old man said.

Mak looked at them all, taking a step towards the back door. 'Kia, fam. See you round all right? Look me up if you're even in Nomer'el, steady? My sewer's not got many chairs, but at least it's not a jail!'

'We'll be there,' Kialessa promised.

Mak ran to the door, opened it, and rocketed away.

Old man Winterwillow sat down, looking tired. They clustered around him.

He massaged his forehead with his fingers.

'What do we do, storyteller?' Kialessa begged.

'You mean you still don't have any idea?' he said, looking very tired.

She pondered her options. Her blood father, the infamous Khozmoh Djinn itself, was bearing down on the home in only a few moments.

'Can we, just, not open the door this time?' her dad suggested.

The storyteller replied, 'Real demons, yes. But he was born a man. That rule does not yet apply to him.'

Then their mother cried, and begged more sincerely that she'd ever in her whole life, 'Please, please, old man. We'd do anythings!'

They nodded.

'There is one, little thing I might be able to do,' he admitted. 'When people love each other, and promise to take care of each other, and keep that promise… it can be a wonderful power, stronger than hell itself. Can you make that promise? Can you … *belong* to each other?'

They all nodded, very enthusiastically.

'Then we need to make this formal.' Chairs and tables scattered at his will, a single little table that once housed the donations to the goddess of trade scurrying to stand in front of him. Beautiful wreaths of pine and willow nettles wove themselves in the air and affixed themselves to the furniture. It was looking more and more like his claim of divinity could be very well substantiated.

'Hold hands across this altar,' he told them.

They, all four of them, gripped each other tightly.

A deep rumbling echoed through the forest, startling Kialessa.

Calmly he sat up, and cleared his throat. 'Day Armstrum, Jewel surnamed Tavernskeep. Kialessa, Dame of Lenmer'el, and Kiel. Do you all promise to be a family to each other?'

'We do,' they said.

'Yup,' her dad agreed.

Old man Winterwillow glared at them each. 'Do you promise to care for each other, to be honest with each other? To make up when you fight, and to do the very best for each other no matter what?'

A nearby tree shattered. The old man seemed to be dragging this out unnecessarily long.

'Yes, yes we do!' their mother shouted.

'Will you love each other?' The world was silent.

'Yes,' Kialessa promised.

'Yes,' they all agreed.

'Well!' Old man Winterwillow sat back with a grin as trees creaked and split in the forests, 'By the authority granted me by the goddess of this world and the king of your land, I proclaim you… a family!'

Kialessa threw her arms around them, and they held each other close.

The ground outside shuddered.

'Now,' Winterwillow pondered as though he had all the time in the world. 'A name. What name for this new family? A name all four of you can take.'

'Happy to take your name,' her father said. 'I have brought no honour to my own.'

Winterwillow looked displeased at that, but then spoke. 'A new name? A new name then, one for just the four of you? What name could that be then, a name that keeps you safe from harm in the depths of a demon cursed winter. Oh, I know – I name your family; Winterhaven.'

Winterhaven? Kialessa marvelled. *The very meaning of the title "Sanctum Brumae."* She smiled at the irony.

'Kialessa Winterhaven,' she said.

They all grinned, and shared their new names.

 By Dr Joe Ireland

Then a demon prince roared from just outside their inn. Windows shattered, the sound echoing across the entire valley. No one in the whole entire town would doubt the presence of a demon here today.

'Oh, yes,' the old storyteller said, 'That. We'll, I guess we'd better go deal with that thing now.'

He led the way outside.

The Dishonoured Soldier

… death doesn't change who people are. Sometimes it's better to let them live so they can make up their minds to be something else.
Jerik, assassin of kings. From 'The Year in Jail.'

Kialessa was grateful to walk behind the storyteller. He started glowing, calling to himself the powers of the valley he dwelt in.

Because beyond the old man there stood her biological father – a demon in its full strength. He was the height of three men, the tallest of his six horns easily more than the top of the tallest trees. He had six arms, the largest ending in vicious crab claws. He had six wings; a shield for his back, another for his feet, and with two he could fly. Into his hands, a whip of blazing fire ran – Flameheart's power. And in his left arm an immense, gloss black sword of shadow floated – Shadowmonger's talent. His eyes were burning coals of darkness. His skin was a mottled red patchwork of a thousand different skins; bull, elk, crocodile – the stolen powers of the children he had slain. His very aura was terror.

 By Dr Joe Ireland

15 Kialessa versus the Khozmoh Djinn

But his face looked … weak. He was still conflicted, and Kialessa had the distinct impression that he had taken his true form just to give himself the courage to kill again.

The arch demon stepped back in the presence of the old storyteller. When the demon spoke, the depths of hell uttered their hatred at every good and generous thing. 'Stand aside, old man. You think I have not killed your kind before?'

'Yet you did not claim their powers?'

'Not yet,' the demon huffed, glancing down at his glowing red amulet. 'But soon.'

'Oh, you can't deceive me, young man,' the storyteller chastened him. 'It's not a matter of physical barriers, but moral. You can't bring yourself to do it.'

The demon roared, and trees shuddered at the sound.

Kialessa and her family could only cringe behind the storyteller.

Old man Winterwillow straightened his robe. 'Get out, demon. This family is no longer yours to claim.'

The demon growled. 'You can't tell me what is mine,' he threatened.

'Can, and do,' the storyteller mocked.

'We will see!' The demon roared, flaring his whip. Then he looked beyond the old man to Kialessa's home. 'Burn!' he demanded.

Suddenly there was an explosion from behind them. They turned, and Kiel shrieked.

The inn was on fire.

Then the demon charged.

The storyteller ran forwards, tripling in size. Within an instant he had turned into a giant ice posk with eight huge limbs. The two creatures collided with each other, and old man Winterwillow pushed the demon back past the tree line, disappearing into the forest below.

Kialessa ran to the inn, her father gathering up the bucket as fast as he could. Her mother ran to the home, but fell back from the heat.

Kialessa raced to the door and threw it open. Everything was burning, and the fire was spreading with supernatural hunger. Nothing they could do would stop these flames.

Kiel broke a window, and her father threw in a bucket of water. The water actually started burning before it hit the ground.

'It's no use!' Kialessa shouted, 'the curse is too strong!'

 By Dr Joe Ireland

'The papers!' her mother screamed. 'Git the papers from under the till!'

Kialessa knew what her mother meant – the land rights, and the birth certificates for them all, even if one was very fake. She rushed, and grabbed them up. Upon them lay the sprig of "very expensive herbs" the storyteller had used to buy his wine with, and the papers did not catch fire. She rolled them all up together and ran outside, and with the rest of her family watched her home burning.

The entire valley shook with violence as the god and the demon battled nearby. White lighting split the sky and the demon roared, then a plume of red fire and the trees themselves cried out. Rocks as sharp as diamond rose up from the ground, and with a deep thump disappeared again. Thunder and earthquakes rumbled around the valley. Then, suddenly, all was silent.

No one moved.

They held their breath.

Suddenly leaves fluttered about them, falling from many of the nearby trees; soft memories like tears trailing in their mournful wake.

'The Winterwillows are dying,' Kiel announced.

'No!' Kialessa mourned.

Dark, hooved footfalls approached the inn.

'No,' she whispered, falling to her knees.

A moment later the demon emerged from the tree line. He was bleeding under his left ribs, and it looked as if his largest set of arms had been torn off entirely. He walked with a painful, pronounced limp.

She couldn't speak. She could not believe they were left with only their family to face even a wounded arch demon. She gripped the horn of her whip, and called to her the acid blade. But violence hadn't stopped the demon in almost two centuries, and violence hadn't stilled the rage of the last djinn she'd battled. Her family held on to each other tightly.

He stumbled forwards, shrinking in size. Painfully, as though it took great effort, he began to turn back into Tyran Noblax, the merchant prince.

His clothing was tattered, his jewellery rent. He stumbled forwards, seeming a broken man, clutching the Blood Heart in a bleeding hand.

He looked at the four of them, kneeling on the ground. 'I'm sorry, Kialessa,' he whispered in a false apology.

'No,' her dad said. 'This is *my* daughter. You *cannot* have her!'

Tyran glared up at him with blood-soaked lips. 'You honestly think you could stop me! A *god* could not stop me!'

Kialessa stood in front of her family, and put away her weapons. 'You won't take me. You can't.' She let him feel all her emotions – her fear for her own life, and theirs. Her undying love for them all. Her desperation to be safe again.

He glared at her, then his face twisted in anguish.

She tried to convince him to stop himself, 'You don't … *have* to do this.'

Suddenly he screamed, beating the ground. 'Where were you?!' he shouted to no one they could see. 'Why, why did you give me so much power, and then leave me all alone!'

Kialessa saw the woman in the reflection of the fallen bucket water before she appeared in reality. She was gorgeous, simply flawless. A woman of singular, enviable perfections. She had long antelope horns and huge, black wings from her muscular back. She looked every bit like Kialessa had imagined her from the stories. She was wearing something that looked blithling, like the demons of the desert he had once tried so hard to stop.

She appeared, but ignored them. 'Soldier, you called?'

It all seemed so real to Kialessa. Tyran was the soldier from old man Winterwillow's stories, this was the disgraced solider. He took children, mostly his own, to his hidden fortress and stole their powers to fuel his own semi-immortal life, and stole their fate and powers so that he could become richer and more influential than any mortal man ever could by their own honest means. She was one of those children, and he… he was… once a very good man. He was once a hero.

                    By Dr Joe Ireland

He glared up at her, still a powerful arch demon in his heart. Then he glanced at his demoness, 'Why, why did you do this!'

'Do what?' she teased him.

He glared at her, loathing and hatred in his eyes.

She laughed, 'I didn't do **anything**!' she screeched at him, a whole new force of terror Kialessa had never experienced before. 'I kept my *promise*; I gave you your life **back**! And look at what you did with it! You hunted down the Blood Heart of your own volition. You killed your best friend just to see what it could do. Then you, you… *demon*. You bred thousands of bastard children over almost two hundred years and you murdered them! You killed them, *you **killed them!**'*

'No, no!' he screamed. 'You made me do it, you took the heart out of me and you made me a demon!'

'No, she did not,' another woman said.

It was his woman, Jasmin. She looked, different, purer. Her blithling garments were gone, replaced with strange robes of exotic cloth Kialessa had only seen once before.

'You?' Tyran gasped. He looked up at her, 'Who … who are you, really?'

The illusions melted away from Jasmin. Great, bronze wings folded from her back, and her copper adornments became gleaming gold. A glowing halo appeared over her head, and a terrifying power flowed around her.

The demoness stepped back, trying to look unruffled.

'No!' Tyran begged, falling at her feet.

'You see, we never left you.' Jasmin said with such gentleness. 'Serros, god of the sun, knows the name of each and every child you harmed. He inspired you to write their names. For every maiden you defiled, a hundred more were protected from your lusts. Every child you killed was prepared, and watched over, and steps into glory before you. But you were not abandoned. You were never alone.'

Choice, set free

'You… let me…'

'She stood by you, while you slew your own offspring,' the demoness teased.

'Why?' he begged lady Jasmin.

'Because I volunteered. I saw what you had become, and I knew that you were once a very good man.'

The demoness seemed disgusted, but Tyran looked awed, then again he grew upset. 'No, no… it can't be true. I was forced to do those things, and limiting it to my own children was the only way to curb that *thirst!*'

Neither woman replied to what was clearly a long-repressed lie.

He started to tremble.

'Look!' the demoness shouted, and Tyran's face sprung up, his gaze fixing on Kialessa. 'Look closely, Khozmoh Djinn. Use the *fatesight* you stole. Tell me what you see about *her.*'

Kialessa stumbled back, into the arms of her family, yet knowing there was nowhere she could run now. The world itself was not large enough to hide her from this man.

Tyran seemed to want to resist, but it was as if his lust still drove him somehow. His eyes flew wide.

'Yes, you see it, you see it now! The talent. The fate. Every life stolen by the Heart resolves to you, and you see it now, don't you?'

The angel Jasmin spoke, almost sadly, 'Every life, every soul of the Great Kingdom, and many beyond. All touched by this woman's young life. All of them can be yours. You have the power, you have the wisdom. With this fate, you will be greater than any king in all the world, and you *know* it.'

He trembled, his fingers clutched around the amulet, he began to raise his arm as if unwilling.

Jasmin put her hand on his shoulder, and his arm stopped. Neither woman strove against each other, they barely acted as if the other was here. They never even looked at each other.

 By Dr Joe Ireland

Jasmin spoke, 'But, please. Please don't do this. This has to stop.'

'You never stopped me before,' Tyran demanded. 'Your god, Serros the Sun, has never stopped me before. Why? Where was he when the children cried?'

Tears filled Jasmin's eyes, gazing away as if at memories none others shared. 'We tried, *every day* we tried. But not even death would change who you had chosen to become, so you had to be left to choose to change yourself. The children - their tears are counted, as are yours. They rest in glory now, but you cannot rest until you are released from your thirst, and while that amulet controls you, your own guilt will not allow you to be brought back into their presence.'

'Don't believe her,' the demoness whispered. 'You need never see them again, and you know it. You are immortal. You knew the price. You deny yourself one single victim, and the Blood Heart will die within you, and you will burn forever in hell. Unless you claim her fate today, mighty Djinn, your powers are *forfeit*. Your treasures are *lost*, and demons will *mock* your fall!'

This time, Jasmin did face the demoness, 'Demons are not the only ones who speak, and there are those who will rejoice at his freedom from thirst. The power to kill is nothing without the power to protect the ones you love. And what greater treasure is there than those we have learnt to love, and to be loved in return?'

Then Kiel spoke, words she too had learnt in a tower far away, a soft and gentle wisdom she did not know he knew; 'Heaven would not preach forgiveness… if they did not offer it.'

Tyran looked at them, and grew angry again. But he could not move.

Somehow, she had to turn the battle. Somehow, Kialessa knew she had to win this man's heart, and set him free from his thirst for power and blood and death. She had to help him let himself be forgiven, or he would continue to murder if only to justify it.

'Father… Kilpoe… there are things worth saving in this place,' she begged him.

He wept. Deep tears of wracking sorrow.

'No, mighty Djinn,' the demoness demanded, 'do not forget what you are, do not deny what the gods *wanted* you to become!'

'No!' He roared, a lingering torment of almost two hundred years of pain and regret. In a single moment Kialessa could feel him own his own mistakes. He had never been *made* evil; he had *chosen* it.

And now demons mocked him for making the mistakes they'd tricked him into blaming them for.

The demoness grabbed for the dagger at her hip.

He clicked his fingers, and white flame blasted up around the demoness. She screamed in agony as her physical form twisted and marred, and then she disappeared.

Only then did Kialessa realise Jasmin was gone as well.

Tyran knelt there, looking up at them all. His face was ashen, no trace of the mighty sage or merchant prince that had once deceived kings into trusting him.

He said nothing, but stumbled to his feet, and turned to leave.

Nobody moved.

He made it all the way to the far end of the street, then fell on his knees once more. 'I'm…. so… sorry….' she heard him whisper.

Yellow fire exploded from the heavens, and he threw his arms back. The Blood Heart lifted up into the air, drawing all his life and fate from him. He began to glow with dire light, his skeleton becoming clearly visible as flesh and cloth burnt away, two hundred years of death cascading upon him in a moment.

Tyran Noblax, the Khozmoh Djinn, was no more.

The King

Add not to your sufferings by wallowing in regret, expecting no greater good, not even if you are the very cause of your pain. What'er befalls you speaks nothing of what you deserve, or who you are. But what you chose to become will determine if the affliction takes you higher, or holds you down.

Nemon, 3rd Sage of Lumos, keeper of times.

For the longest time, no one moved. What they had witnessed, what had just happened… no one knew what to say.

'It's over,' Kiel pronounced.

Kialessa pushed back sudden sobs that threatened her. Walking up, she looked at the burnt and blasted ground where a demon had died – her father. Ashes and dust lay there, but nothing that would not fade in a few days. There would be no grave marker, no tomb to mark the passing of the greatest murderer in hundreds of years.

It almost seemed too much to believe.

She knelt at the site. He had been a mighty man. A very, very evil man. But a great one.

'Come on,' her mother said, placing her hand on Kialessa's shoulder. 'This mess'll take more 'n a day to clean up.'

Kialessa looked at the ash. She thought about all the people he'd hurt in his life, and all the knowledge he'd kept to himself. But he'd also run great businesses, and been a teacher to kings and princes. What words were to be spoken that might guide him to his afterlife? There seemed to be none.

'Good luck, dad,' was about all she could manage.

Kialessa turned, and looked at the inn. It was almost all ash and rubble now.

'Wonder where the others are?' her dad said. 'They'd see the smoke; we lads all have an agreement.'

'Seriously, dad,' Kiel protested. 'Ain't no creature in the valley that don't know a demon battled here. This whole place feels wrong.'

'And poor old Winterwillow,' her mother muttered.

'At least he'll be back,' Kialessa promised. 'Gods don't die, they can't.'

'Yeah, but these townsfolks.' Kiel protested, 'How are we supposed to winter in someone's barn now!'

'Now you listen here son!' Dad chastened Kiel with a wide grin. 'Them folks is good! They'll likely billet you and Kia till spring, then we can get to rebuilding. You'll see. They'll all come.'

Kiel shook his head, and dad shook his finger.

Then Kiel got a strange look on his face, and his bottom lip quivered. Then he ran to him, and wrapped him up in his arms, 'Sorry, dad!'

Her father Day Winterhaven hugged the young boy, and held him close. He spoke, tears in his eyes. 'We'll rebuild. You'll see. This is our chance to start again.' He looked up at their mother.

She looked uncertain, then nodded. 'Least the beer's gone now. Maybe a new start for all o' us, eh, old man?'

He laughed, and reaching out grappled Kialessa into the hug as well.

Then they looked at the rubble cooling rapidly in the snow. 'Better see what the gods have left us,' her dad said.

They began sifting through the burnt-out inn, but there was almost nothing. Just a few trinkets were spared the supernatural flames. Mother's pendant from her father, and Dad's shovel and plough, strangely enough. Even stones had burnt in the fire.

They were gathering at the front garden, about to wonder where they would spend the night, when there was a soft jingling of a sleigh coming up the road.

By Dr Joe Ireland

'What do we tell them,' Kiel wondered.

'Noth'n', Mum muttered.

'Hey, Jewel!' Dad protested. 'Still. Um… the fire got in the wine and it all went up in flames before we could do anything about it?'

Kialessa suggested, 'Why don't we just tell them my real dad came by, a murderous arch demon, demanding my life and when we refused him, he set fire to our home?'

'Too much detail, love,' mum said.

'You could say we fought him off?' Kiel suggested.

'More like guilt-ing him into death with the help of a really good-looking angel girl,' Dad muttered.

Mum hit him.

'I think wine related fires are the safest for now,' Dad asserted.

It didn't feel right to Kialessa, but the truth could hurt a lot, sometimes.

The jingling came closer. As the vehicle appeared through the trees Kialessa could see it was a red sleigh, covered with cheerful golden bells, pulled by four large deer led in the front by none other than another student at the college; Natasha the cervitaur, smiling proudly.

The sleigh slowed down in front of the guttered inn, right before the place where the demon had died. Then the stoutest of its three occupants stepped out.

It was King Dunnkan. He stepped down, surveyed the burnt-out abode, and simply stated. 'Well, how'd that happen?'

Kialessa burst into tears and ran to him. She threw herself against his red robe and sobbed like a child, deep cathartic sobs as though every tear in the past season was holding something back, and now it all washed out from her eyes.

She heard the queen alighting the carriage too, and she patted her on the head. Her mother might have said something, but Kialessa could not hear it over her own tears. She wept, deeply from her soul. How she wished she could have stayed at his castle, and never found out who her father was, and what it would cost to stop him!

Finally, she composed herself enough to speak, and to answer his question. 'My father came, my father by birth. And he's the arch demon the Khozmoh Djinn, and he burnt down our whole home because I wouldn't let him kill me,' and she could say no more.

The king hugged her well. 'The arch demon? The Khozmoh?'
She nodded.
He pointed at her dad, a question on his face.

She nodded, 'So did I! But it turns out the Djinn was my real father and he stole me away to his winter fortress and the old storyteller is really the god Winterwillow, and he died trying to protect our family but he married us first oh gosh we don't have a certificate for that either, what will we do!'

'Calm down, calm down. There, there, it will be all right,' the king stood, holding her hand. 'A family? Have you a name then?'

Her father stood up, proud, 'Winterhaven, m'lord. So named of the gods.'

The king laughed. 'Kialessa Winterhaven, what a perfect name! So much better than Tavernskeep, you agree? This is good, very good!'

He looked at his queen, and she smiled. 'We were just on our way to the Greens'holm manor for a mid-winter feast, and I thought to invite you. Perhaps your whole family ought to come along? I am convinced the enchantress will have more than adequate accommodations for you all to weather the winter, what do you say?'

Her mother bowed to the ground, 'A delight, me lord! A delight, most honoured king.'

He waved her fawning aside and led the way on. 'Come, let us get to the manor immediately. Hold to your story, Kialessa Winterhaven. I would hear it all from the beginning once we arrive. Let us make haste! Natasha, my good young woman, are you up for a little sprint!'

　　　　　　By Dr Joe Ireland

'Gladly,' she replied.

'Go in haste, but take the corners carefully!' the third passenger demanded. It was Grudon, the royal steward.

Natasha glared at him, 'I know my craft, Steward!' and with that, she drew in the powers of nature around her. Glistening lights touched their paws and hooves. Then the entire sleigh began to lift up above the ground.

'Well, I guess everything actually did work out, in the end,' Dad said.

Kialessa looked at him as they climbed up onto the sleigh, not sure if he was kidding or not. It had hurt; a lot.

'Tell me you're not taking credit for this, father,' Kiel said, his voice flat and face unimpressed.

'Well, no,' Dad agreed, clutching the side of the open sleigh as it levitated higher into the air, 'but you know, I said it would work out. Sometimes bad things happen for a good reason.'

'Tell that to our inn,' Mum said.

'Hrmph,' Dad replied, looking over at the charred heap of rubble. 'You'll see.'

Natasha grinned, 'Hold on!' and with a, 'Yeup!' they surged forwards.

Running with mystical haste, they made their way to the mansion in under an hour, flying above the treetops. Kialessa and Kiel squealed with delight, while her mother and father clutched each other and looked quite pale in the far seat. Dad took a peek over the side, but it was too noisy to talk. With her permission the queen snuggled Kialessa and Kiel in her robes from the wild, driving breeze.

When they arrived the king left no time for greetings. He pushed her forward by the shoulders. He sat them in the main room, a dozen soldiers holding everyone back with undrawn swords, including her own family.

The Greens'holm manor was magically warmed even in the depths of winter. Everyone was there, Darrix and his entire family, his tall father and beautiful mother, with his older brother and sister and each of their families.

Piex was there with his father, his scholar mother somewhere in Sanmer'el this time of year. Amusingly Posk was there; somehow Piex had gotten a message to him. Allastassia stood with her whole family, including her six aunties who didn't say much, because it was winter and they were effectually trees. Several other nobles and diplomats where there as well, most of whom Kialessa had never met before.

And, of course, the king's four closest protectors – the axe-heavy captain of the king's guard, the lord knight protector, Bon Sure'e. The high priestess of the Eternal in Lenmer'el, the dwarf Jacinthia Stonehall. There was the gentle eleven Sagemaster Cour De'Feur, and the ever-suspicious part fey councillor to the king, bearer of the rod of Lenmer'el, the high steward, Lord Grudon.

The king waved aside all greetings, as though hers was the most pressing matter in the whole entire kingdom. People crowded in.

He held her hands. Then, in front of them all and without any further hesitation said, 'Now, Dame Kialessa Winterhaven, I want you to tell me everything that happened to you this winter. Leave nothing out. Grudon, take notes. You too De'Feur. Tell us all.'

She took a shuddering breath in, and told them. Everything. All of it. She told them about the heart-breaking abduction and how she found out she was not her father's daughter. She told them about the dozens of strange and frightened, yet noble tae'anaryl of the fortress, and how they all dealt with their reality in very different ways. She told them about the misshapen child who learnt to use her gift to become whatever she wanted, and about the self-harming wizard who stopped at nothing to get home to her mother. She told them about her brave, broad winged brother who'd protected her, and saved her life more times than she had realised. About the noble young woman, though she did not tell them her name or powers, who granted her sanctuary and fought by her side. Of the frightened fey tae'anaryn who had only just begun to embrace her powers, and of the hurting terranoid girl

 By Dr Joe Ireland

who'd given her life just on the chance that her enemy might live.

They were silent, and listened with devoted attention. It made the story easier to tell. Only the king and Lord Grudon interrupted her once or twice, asking just a few questions for clarification.

She told them about Ik'skuretza, and what he looked like, and how he loved to chat. She told them about the shadow realm battle, and how the chosen of Ik'skuretza had built a device they had to use to destroy the Dark Trap. She told them about how he had loved, and how much Flameheart had loved him too.

And she told them about the Khozmoh Djinn. About his lies, and his false promises. About how he loved to make them fight, and how he finally lost his power to kill once he'd stolen empathy from one of his favourite children, and how it had become his undoing. How old father Winterwillow had joined them as a family, and then given his life to protect them.

And how the Khozmoh Djinn had finally abandoned his quest for stolen life, and had died rather than steal once more.

'May his soul find rest,' Lady Jacinthia uttered.

Not all agreed.

'So, Tyran Noblax. I would have never guessed it,' the king admitted.

Grudon looked like he'd always suspected it, Bon Sure'e looked deeply disappointed. Cour De'Feur was difficult to read, but seemed to be lost in thought at the matter, and Jacinthia uttered prayers for this sinner's soul.

And that reminded Kialessa of something very important. 'My King, my Queen. There may be up to thirty of my brothers and sisters still trying to flee that fortress, and no one to care for them. Can you help them, will you offer them sanctuary?'

The king looked to agree immediately, but Grudon the steward spoke, 'And the treasury, and the chapel, they are unguarded?'

'I did not say unguarded, but un-cared for… great treasures, yes, but children too… watch out for Rawhawk, he is a dream weaver and air taint.'

That created a stir in the room. The king spoke something his personal bodyguards appeared to have already realised, 'Lords, get to that fortress! Claim all in the name of the king of Lenmer'el immediately!'

'Yes, my liege,' the steward nodded, giving orders, 'call up the elite, have them be ready in an hour, and a hundred men the next day. We four will be leaving immediately!'

'Please,' Kialessa interrupted. 'There are children. They will likely be in the chapel seeking sanctuary. And you will find Parrow and Ipi in the dungeon. You have to bring them out, I promised them!'

'You can come with us tomorrow, once the venue is secured,' the steward promised her right away.

The room shuffled with business. Many petitioners stood to thank, bless, or commiserate with Kialessa and her family. People were pressing coins into her father's hands, soon they became so much Allastassia's mother gave him a great pot to carry them all, till that too overflowed.

With tears in his eyes he approached Kialessa, Kiel at his heals. 'You know what this means! A new inn, by next winter, we will have a brand-new inn, three stories n' all!'

King Dunnkan lent over, 'And I know there are a great number of gnomes in that valley. They would be grateful for the work, and perhaps you can consider putting in a few little rooms, properly suited to their needs?'

'There are gnomes in the valley?' Kialessa interrupted. She was trying to speak her best, but the celebration was very casual.

The king nodded.

'I knew there was gnomes,' her mother confessed.

'I've seen them,' Kiel admitted.

'Never wondered about the wee folk that visited?' her dad asked.

She was amazed, she hadn't even noticed.

'We'll be sure to take better care of the little folk,' her dad promised. 'Thank you, kind king. You are every bit the better man Kialessa swore you are.'

The old king smiled. 'This? This is poor gratitude for a king of such a good and faithful servant. My lady?' he spoke to his wife.

She turned to face him, sitting down beside them all. Her face was young, and round, and kind. Her cheeks were warm, and her hair white, and her smile gentle and welcoming. 'Beloved?' she asked.

'Have we no lands for this family of my greatest subjects?'

'Much!' the queen admitted.

'Perhaps the golden vale, by the summer palace?'

Kialessa's mother gasped audibly.

'The choicest, indeed!' the queen replied.

But Kialessa could not imagine leaving the old inn. A demon had died, yes, but this was where Winterwillow had protected them too. This was the place she knew was her home.

'What is wrong?' he asked.

She looked at him, not sure what to say.

'You like your old valley more?'

She looked at her family. To her surprise they all seemed to agree.

'Them noble types,' her mother muttered.

'Who holds the title on Kialessa's valley?'

The queen grinned, 'Lord Appleson. I am sure I can convince him to part with it all for just a small portion of the golden vale. I will speak to him after the festivities, see what he has to say.'

Kialessa's heart rose with glee. The entire valley? The *entire valley?!*

Kiel and she hugged. The wages on the tax alone would ensure their family was never poor again.

The king smiled at that. 'Yet, I have one more gift. You do not gain land in this kingdom without title…'

He stood up, and drew his golden sword.

The room fell silent in an instant. Kialessa felt very nervous, not knowing what it meant.

'Dame Kialessa, stand before me.'

She stood up. Every eye was on her, and she suddenly felt very self-conscious. She stood before her king.

'Will you kneel?' he asked.

She complied.

He spoke loud enough for all to hear. 'Dame Kialessa. For courage beyond mortal capacity in the face of demonic depravity, for kindness beyond imagining towards those who were trying to be your enemies, for giving council that has broken the yoke of an arch demon upon this land; I knight thee, Baroness Kialessa Winterhaven; mercy hearted, demonbane, wielder of the unicorn's gift. Rise, Maid Kialessa Winterhaven, the Tae'anaryn.'

Everyone applauded.

Tears filled her eyes. Kiel was crying and clapping all at once. Her dad had tears in his eyes, and her mother looked, well… she looked proud of her, for the first time in their lives.

'Ya did good, horns,' her mother smiled.

She smiled back at them, and curtsied to thank her king.

He smiled, calling her and her father in close. Her dad knelt on one knee, and the king didn't seem to mind. 'And I have a little request to make of you, Maid Winterhaven. Next year I am called with the elite of the kingdom to the council of kings, held every four years at the capital of the Great Kingdom at Emerel. Usually we would simply teleport in with the wizard, but I'm feeling so very adventurous this next year, and I will be travelling at the head of the entire company via the Bounteous Shallowsea, on my personal sailing ship "Imagination's Dawn". It will be a terribly dangerous voyage, fraught with challenge and adventure. And I would like very much for you to come along. You've proven to be a certain kind of… good luck, I must confess.'

She stared at him, wide eyed. 'On the sea? An adventure?' Then she realised something very important. 'But the assassin is still out there, you know, I met him. He's trying to get to you. If you leave the safety of your castle-'

'Exactly what I was thinking!' The king said with a wink.

She looked at him; it was an impossibly brave thing to do. To risk drawing out the assassin of kings, far from the protection of his castle and keep? It was a daring adventure indeed. His very life would be in danger constantly.

She looked at him sincerely, 'I would be honoured to help protect you on that journey, my king.'

He laughed at her sincerity, 'Thank you, young maid Winterhaven. I knew I could count on you!' And he dragged her into a very grandfatherly hug. 'I know I will be safe with you nearby, and we will finally get to deal with this … terribly impolite intruder on our people's peace! Oh, you'll have to miss out on our college all year. But don't worry; the High King will be expanding his own college for the students who have to attend next year. Finally, a real college, with hundreds of students!'

She was excited and terrified at once. A new college! But more than that, a dangerous voyage on the Bounteous Shallowsea? Would she actually get to meet the mermaids? And the assassin would be near, nearer than he'd been all year. But this time they'd catch him for sure.

It made her heart feel very, very glad.

Winter had returned, and named her as its own. In only one year she'd discovered her father was not her father, been held against her will not once but three times, and almost died more times than she could count. But through it all she felt she'd learned that she was worth more than her circumstances. That she could take her trials and weaknesses, and make them the very strengths which she could rely on. She could find friends in the most unlikely places, and help people who wanted her to hate them. She had seen love bloom in the darkest fortresses, and hope blossom in forgotten dungeons. In a world of magic amazing things were possible, but being able to choose hope, and life, and love, despite any circumstance, were perhaps the greatest powers of all.

By Dr Joe Ireland

Appendix

Points to ponder

This book asks one of the most interesting, compelling, and at times upsetting questions humanity has ever asked; why do bad things happen to good people? Several answers are suggested, can you find them?

- Day Winterhaven's submission: As undesirable as it may be, the event has to happen for a greater good; to protect others, to teach you, or make life safer. Such as pulling a splinter or giving birth; pain sometimes accompanies the most wonderful things. Many Christian philosophers seem to be informed by this belief at times.

- Amber's advice: Nothing is ever innately good or bad, it just is. Worrying and regret will not change what is, but they might stop you from making things better. For example, losing your job might mean a lucky opportunity for someone else, and can mean a better life for you. Under other circumstances, keeping your job is a 'bad' thing. This view is informed by philosophies such as Stoicism in the real world.

- The djinn guardian of the treasury's karma: You deserve it due to your intentions, in this life or past lives. But once again, this is the 'universe' just trying to teach you to devalue impermanent things, and to value greater treasures. Buddhism may suggest such an idea.

- Lossel's resilience: Bad things happen because people are sometimes jerks; live with it. People are trying to hurt and destroy and control you, but you can rise above their intentions. It doesn't mean you need to become a jerk as well. Be stronger, and as she said; leave the world a better place than it found you.

- Flameheart's revenge: Bad things happen in this world, and you need to look after yourself – who cares who you hurt when you are hurting. Can you relate to this sentiment? Is there a time when you have hurt others, especially those close to you such as your family, simply because there are feelings you cannot understand, or cope with?

- Kialessa's sacrifice: The idea is that justice cannot punish you for crimes you have not yet committed. Perhaps sometimes bad things must happen so that evil will be fully revealed, and thus condemned. "… As if they simply needed yet one more reason to condemn the demon who called himself her father." Can you be punished for a crime you haven't yet committed?

- Beomith's logic: Bad things can happen due to pure random chance, no one is to blame – sometimes a bad thing really is not your fault in any way! You might not get a say in what happens to you always, but you can make powerful decisions on how you choose how you react to it. This view may be influenced by atheistic and agnostic philosophies.

- Mak's affirmation: Sometimes bad things happen, and you have to protect yourself, but you can still be good. 'You think that's the first ever time you're going to have to fight for your life, or the last? … You're a good kid, and you don't want to hurt people. It's good, means you still got a heart. I hope you never forget how bad this makes you feel. It means there's still hope for you. It means you can still tell right from wrong, even in a cruel and difficult world.'

- Kialessa's commitment: Because you can learn from it, and become a wiser, stronger, kinder person.

What might your answer be?

By Dr Joe Ireland

By chapter

The storyteller

This old man stops by Kialessa's inn each winter to tell stories. He was originally in book 1, but he does nothing more there than what he does in this chapter, so I moved him here to help focus the story. Do you approve?

So what does he do in this chapter? Who is he, and what is his job? What does he tell Kialessa, and what advice does he give her, disguised as a story?

The Question

Why do you think bad things happen, even to good people?

The festival at winter's dawn

Kialessa does not like the merchant prince Tyran Noblax, can you give any reason why? We use this chapter to review her biggest accomplishments and best friends of the entire last year, though they play no major role in this story. What are some of the great things Kialessa did, and how might she be feeling about herself at this point in her life?

Why does she not want to dance for the king? In a real medieval society her behaviour of running away would be deeply shameful; it might even make her loose her title 'dame'. Should she have obeyed the king? What do you think?

Home

Is any home better than none? What are the good points about Kialessa's home life and what she finds there? What does she hate about her home, and would you hate those kinds of things too? What does she do instead of waiting around and feeling sorry for herself?

How does Kiel react to confirmation that he is a dreamwalker? What does Kialessa do to help Kiel come to terms with his special talents?

The quote from this chapter is from Oliver Wendell Holmes Sr, taken 21

April 2019 from brainyquote.com "Where we love is home - home that our feet may leave, but not our hearts."

Father

"What is it that makes a man our father? Is it by birth? It is by accepting his teachings? Is it simply a title we bestow upon some man? For whom we may grant such a title in honour, or discipleship, or by birth – who in our lives can we truly say has earned such a noble appellation?"

Who is Tyran Noblax, and what does he want?

Brother

The chapter quote here is based on this quote by American actor Ben Schnetzer, "I grew up with an older brother, and the bond between siblings is unlike anything else, and it can be a real journey to accept what that bond is once you both mature into it. Because it's not always what you want. It's not always what you expect. It's not always what you imagined or hoped. But it's one of the most important things in the world."

Who else can this apply to? Perhaps the whole family; as they say, you can pick your friends but you can't pick your family – even so, how important can a family be? Who is Mak, and what is his plan?

Sanctum Brumae

Sometimes we may not have much choice about where we are, or what we must experience. Can we still be positive; finding friends, looking for solutions, and gaining knowledge? Or should we sulk in a corner and wait for someone else to fix our problem? Kialessa might not have wanted to be in the *Sanctum Brumae*, but she was in a magical fortress of rare treasures and hidden knowledge; what opportunities did she have here?

Today's quote is from Earl Nightingale, "Learn to enjoy every moment of your life. Be happy now. Don't wait for something outside of yourself to

By Dr Joe Ireland

make you happy in the future. Think how really precious is the time you have to spend, whether it's at work or with your family. Every moment should be enjoyed and savoured."

Raynah

Who is Raynah? What are her challenges, and what does she want? What talents does she have that can help Kialessa?

Marian Eigerman is credited with the quote, "A loyal sister is worth a thousand friends," but it's unlikely to be a new idea!

Lossel

"Sanctuary" is a claim for the protection of the strong upon the weak, it used to be claimed of knights by those who arrived in certain places and holy sites such as cathedrals, and apparently one can claim it from Lossel – at least once that is.

Why is Lossel willing to help out? Do you think she might have been willing without "losing a bet" or is it just a convenient excuse to help out without looking like "the good girl"? Who is Lossel, and what does she want? What is her plan?

"Blessings that hurt"?! What does that mean?! Can Kialessa find a way to turn this unwanted experience into a good one?

The tour

Daygon takes Kialessa and Mak on a brief tour of the fortress, where they get to see the throne room, meet Shadowmonger, and visit Raynah in the archives. The tour ends in the lowest of the lowest accommodations in the fortress – a site known only as the 'damp cavern'. Why does Tyran offer his newest children no better accommodations? Is this fair?

What does Mak do about it? Why do you think he not wander off and leave Kialessa to her fate, and go and make some newer, more powerful, less scared friends?

Combat training

The scene here displays a combat training is unfair, unbalanced, and more than just a little cruel. What does Kialessa think about it?

Finally she begins to open up and talk to the other children. In my life, I have decided that most people don't hate me, and they don't love me either, I'm just a feature of their environment until I actually interact with them. By not talking, was Kialessa accidentally giving the other children the impression she hated them? By opening up, listening, laughing at their jokes and maybe even telling some of her own stories, was she helping the other children (all in as bad a situation as she was) to realise she did not want to threaten them, but might even be willing to be a friend as well?

Here the Storyteller returns, as if he still has more to say, but he is turned away. Why would he be turning up at this point of the story once more, do you think?

Favours for the wizard

No one wants to be taken advantage of, and sometimes other people; co-workers, bosses, even good friends, will ask us to do something, "as a favour," that is not right for us. We might have more important things to do, or we might genuinely feel they are taking advantage of us. Do we stay silent?

What are some good ways to stand up for yourself without attacking and insulting and shouting at others? How can we let them know we don't think their activity is appropriate for us, and open a discussion on the matter with them?

And how did Raynah deal with a similar situation once the imps took advantage of her?

Chapel

Again, Kialessa is brought along to a venue she would not have chosen to be in on her own. But here she is!

     By Dr Joe Ireland

In this chapter, she makes the very dangerous decision to stand up for her right to pray to any deity she would choose. Daygon is furious, but strangely enough, Shadowmonger stands up for her by reading the words of the deity Annas. After this, Daygon apologises.

Do you think Kialessa did a good job of standing up for herself? She didn't shout, but she didn't shrink into silence either. She was outnumbered and underpowered compared to others in the room; it was an incredibly brave thing to do.

Shadowmonger's brief sermon is a direct quote from the real-world song "Nature Boy" by Nat King Cole, released in 1958. The song was written in 1947 by eden ahbez (who insisted his name is not capitalised).

The Treasury

"There is some good in everyone here!" What kind of good does Kialessa mean? Can you think of anyone who has ever lived that hasn't had some good qualities, even if they used those qualities to do very bad things?

If you could have any treasure your heart desired, what would it be? Something of great wealth, or a long holiday? A magical weapon or unending supply of quality food?

Now what if you could live forever and have every basic need met? What would your treasures be then? A patient heart? Someone to always love? Ability to be creative and have fun? Mastery of a musical instrument perhaps? Friends? Fame? Power? Peace of heart and mind?

Just what *are* the greatest treasures we can find?

Unsupervised

Why does everything fall to chaos as soon as the merchant leaves? Why do you think Daygon does next to nothing to prevent the children from bullying each other, or can he really stop them anyway?

"She will outlive most of you, if she chooses wisely. She has the potential to be an old woman." According to you, what does it mean to grow old? Is it a privilege?

Nightmare

In this chapter, three of her powerful tae'anaryl siblings try to hurt Kialessa. Who stands up for her? How is she able to use love to defeat another boy's hate?

Note this phrase; "They cannot love you the way you need to be loved," can be a terrible curse, yet also deeply emancipating. Who can say they have found anyone who loves them perfectly the way they need to be loved? And yet those deeply in love often feel to ask nothing more of those they adore. This phrase can be used as an excuse to do great evil, to reject those who offer us their "imperfect love." Can you find love in an imperfect world? What does it look like? Does knowing those we love cannot offer us flawless love then free us from having impossible expectations of those we need in our lives?

What happens to Kiel in this chapter, and what does he do? Is Kialessa, now, truly alone?

Revelations

At the lowest point, Kialessa discovered she can sink even lower. Yet even in the darkest dungeon, she still realises she can find light. "Whether your life is supposed to be like this or not is not going to have any bearing whatsoever on what your life now actually is. Being upset is not going to change it." What do you think? Is this statement cruel, or helpful?

In this chapter Kialessa finds Charl. Who is he, what does he want?

Undercrypt

Kialessa's plan – to record everyone's story, and thus hopefully, help them realise their good points and wonderful qualities of resilience. Even so, knowing our lives once had good that we no longer enjoy can be very defeating. But how can telling the stories of the past, even the sad ones, help

By Dr Joe Ireland

us find hope? As someone once said, "You are living proof that you have survived 100% of what life has thrown at you so far. Chances are very good that you can survive this too."

The beginning

Do you think Charl is trying to keep other people away from him? Charl has an amazing talent, but even he is using it to get lots of personal attention – the kind that keep other people nervous around him. What could he do to help others with his talents in ways that do not draw direction attention to himself and his powers? "Having a seer's sight did not always mean he came with a seer's wisdom." It reminds me of a similar phrase, "Just because you know it, doesn't mean you have to say it". In what situations can this be good advice?

Why does Kialessa want to hear everyone's stories, and what does that mean? How can sharing your "story" help you to know yourself better? How does knowing that someone knows your story, that someone can remember you the way you like to be remembered, help you feel connected and welcomed?

The unicorn

Not all questions need to be answered – but what do you think of death? Is it, "another part of the story we all must journey though"? The unicorn was able to face his own death with confidence and acceptance, why do you think this was? What do you hope to achieve before your time is up in this life? How do you intend to live a life so that you are ready when your 'time is up'?

The god of darkness

Here Kialessa meets a very important being on her world, the god of darkness, mysteries, truth, and the dead – Ik'skuretza, though the humans call him Pumos. He seems to want her to know a lot of very important things in a very short time, but may I ask, did you like him? If you had as much power and wisdom as Pumos, with the power to decide who lives and dies on this world, what kind of person would you become?

Ik'skuretza teaches Kialessa about families, and the limits demons have. Do you think this knowledge can help her?

She also learns that the star that announced her own birth split in two, what do you think this might mean?

Ik'skuretza claims that what the gods envy most about mortals such as Kialessa is their ability to change, to not be what they once were. What do you think this means? Change is not always easy, but have you ever thought that the power to choose and to change might be one of your greatest superpowers, one even gods might envy?

The heart of fire

Flameheart is not related to Kialessa or most of the other students of the prison, but as a tae'anaryn she is kept here anyway. What does she tell Kialessa about the fate of all the children of the fortress?

How do you think Flameheart feels about Shadowmonger? What are they planning to do? Does Flameheart love Shadowmonger?

What does Flameheart tell Kialessa to do if she ever escapes the fortress? Do you think this is a good idea, or is she just giving voice to her own feelings of hopelessness and misery? Do you think it's alright to hurt people when you are hurting, and why do people do it?

Indeed, is it possible to *not* hurt others when we are hurting?

Treasures

This chapter talks about many things that we might treasure – wealth, weapons of great power, knowledge. But there are other treasures mentioned here as well – safety, friendship, and having a body. Note the contrast between someone who takes great care to protect their treasures, and those who are rejecting, even harming, treasures which cannot be

By Dr Joe Ireland

replaced.

What plan do Kialessa and her allies come up with at this point?

Of greatest worth

Here we meet a being, the guardian djinn, claiming to be punished for a past life of greed and violence with treasures beyond count that he cannot touch. Is this fair punishment? Does it help him to reconsider his "hunger" and eventually begin to treasure better things, such as freedom from this hunger and peace of heart? What does it take for him to accept this offered treasure? What was preventing him from moving on, on his own?

Arpil begins speaking again in this chapter, presumably, because she has finally found her "treasure" again. She claims she wants to kill her half-brother Ka, is this justified? Is this, even if it is justifiable, a tactical advantage, or a terrible mistake?

Kialessa's story

What did Kialessa do? Was this a betrayal of those who trusted her, or was it wiser – taking care of the bigger picture rather than the next feast?

What courage does it take to stand up for yourself, and for those who you care about?

Sometimes we are offended and ready to fight over a small matter, when a simple correction will do rather than shouting at someone. Do you think Kialessa's actions were called for?

The lone solider

Who do you think the storyteller really is? How can he appear at the height of the fortress in the middle of the day?

What did Kilpoe do that was so brave? Why do you think the demons could not defeat him, as they even seemed reluctant to fight him? What truth can there be in the phrase, "Was there something about a righteous, powerful decision that made even demons afraid?"

What is meant by the phrase, "Because there are things worth saving in this place"? Why is this phrase important in this book? What kinds of treasures do you think the brave solider was referring to?

Kialessa's conspiracy

Determined now to escape, around half the tae'anaryl risk their lives to align themselves with Kialessa's vision of their value and importance. What obstacles stand in their way to escaping, and even if they do, will they be able to stay safe?

The chapter quote, "I cannot change your circumstances until you change what is in your hearts" is actually inspired from the Quran, 13:11. It reminds me of another thought, "Life's lessons repeat, and keep getting harder, until you learn them." What do you think of this? Whose hearts are changed, and whose hearts have not changed, in the fortress?

What does Shadowmonger give Kialessa in this chapter? Giving his last words, do you think Shadowmonger managed to achieve his most important life goals before he died? What is his greatest treasure, and does he get to keep it?

The Dark Trap

After years of hating Arpil, Ka finally destroys her, only to discover it is an empty victory, and one he fears may have cost him his very soul. Is he brave, or foolish? Or a little bit of both? Why does Ka switch allegiance?

With the Dark Trap destroyed all the children of the fortress are free to flee wherever they want – what stops Kialessa and her closest friends?

Retribution

Daygon was one of the Khozmoh Djinn's best and only friends in the past one hundred years, but perhaps that is not the only reason he did not steal his talents and his fate. Perhaps somewhere deep inside the Djinn knew if he took Daygon's fate, he would be open once more to caring about other people, and until he learnt to control that fate, which might take years, he would be vulnerable to compassion, and sympathy?

Is what Daygon did courageous, or was he a coward simply helping a dark demon slay his own children? Did Daygon redeem himself in your eyes by sacrificing himself to save Kialessa? And why her, now?

Home

Kiel finds out he killed two people defending his family. How does he react? He tells Kialessa he still feels terrible about it. What do you think of Mak's words; "… you're a good kid, and you don't want to hurt people. It's good, means you still got a heart. … I hope you never forget how bad this makes you feel. It means there's still hope for you. It means you can still tell right from wrong, even in a cruel and difficult world." Survivor's guilt is a very real and difficult thing, and Kiel is having trouble coming to terms with his ability to change the world, even if that means he has to hurt people. What do you think; did Kiel do the right thing? Is Mak right?

Kialessa finds her mother hiding from her voice, fully expecting her only daughter to be dead now, and rightly blaming herself for her own role in her daughter's abduction. Is Jewel a good person now? Or is she still a bit of good and bad, and just still learning?

Kialessa's father struggles with some very serious alcohol addiction. Both he and her mother tell her that they are not worthy to be called her parents. What do you think? Is parenthood "earned"? Have they lost that right, or is there still something worth being saved, even in a messed up family like this one?

What does it take to make a family? Who is in your family? How important is the promise to love and care for each other – relatives or not? What does it mean to be a family member to your brothers, sisters, parents and relatives?

The dishonoured soldier

Who are the Demoness and Jasmin? What role do they play in the Djinn's life, and in his defeat? What did the demoness want the Djinn to do, and why? Did you notice the tactics she tried to use to motivate him - fear, guilt, hatred and regret? What about Jasmin's tactics; was there forgiveness, and understanding, and love? Notice how neither of them denied who the Khozmoh Djinn was, or what he'd done. But they clearly wanted him to feel the exact *opposite* ways about **himself**.

In this imaginary world, people live on after their physical death as a spirit. Do you think dying would change a person's personality, their goals and their emotions? What if dying, and becoming a spirit, made it harder to change who you were and what you wanted; would it make sense to let bad people live on a little longer so that they had even just a chance of changing for the better?

Who or what defeated the Khozmoh Djinn? Was it Kialessa's tenacity, kindness, and accidentally mirroring Kilpoe's own defining act of courage? Lady Jasmin's gentle council and forgiveness? How about Daygon's brave sacrifice to help a good man remember his lost compassion? Or was it simply the Djinn's own choice?

The King

This chapter's quote is from Michael Josephson's website https://whatwillmatter.com/ taken 6 June 2019, which is; "When bad things happen DON'T MAKE THINGS WORSE by starting to see yourself as a victim, or someone who doesn't deserve better, or someone who deserves what you got. NONE OF THIS IS TRUE! What happens to you says nothing about who you are or what you deserve, but your response says everything about who you will be and whether the experience makes you weaker or stronger." What do you think? Does it make sense to you, can you agree, or is there something more you'd like to say? How will you answer the question, 'Why do bad things happen to good people'?

Have you ever met someone who went on a long journey to a distant place and experienced wonderful things, and yet when they returned, you found them to be essentially the very same person they've always been? I have. It is a great question about how much life can change us; does life and all its challenges simply bring out what has always been the true you? Or are we never the same once life had touched us?

How does life change us?

And what is the meaning of life? Perhaps we can explore that in the next book, "Kialessa and the voyage of Imagination's Dawn."

The Blood Heart

By Cour De'Feur, Loremaster of Lenmer'el.

The blood heart is a fell talisman, a red jasper cabochon set in a hardened brass setting in the shape of an eight-pointed star, resting on a triple weave necklace of fine-spun deep gold. It is believed to be a medicinal device from ancient times once dedicated to healing. It was 'perfected' or 'perverted', depending on whom you ask, to instead rewrite one's own life code and soul fate at the expense of another being's – in short; it allows its bearer to steal magical and divine powers.

The apparent cost is twofold. First, one must continue to steal life from living beings, at least before the previous victims measure of life is fulfilled, or the internal chaos will destroy the bearer of the talisman. This increases exponentially over time, till the death can occur within moments of failing to feast on another being's life force.

By Dr Joe Ireland

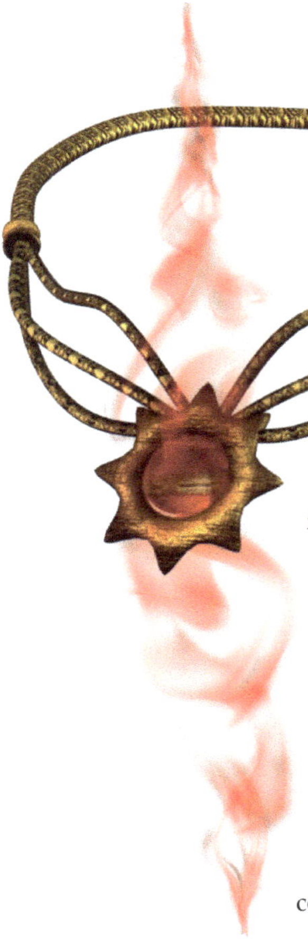

Second, when stealing a being's life, one is also required to take on their life's purpose. Thus, a large part of the Khozmoh Djinn's time was spent on finding out and using the destiny of his victims to further his own vast empire. Even a simple farmer's life, combined with the Djinn's own knowledge and resources, was able produce a spectacularly abundant farm. Naturally, the evil demon hoarded all such and sold the abundance at a premium price, buying out or pruning back any competition that got in his way.

Note, however, that preventing a living soul from completing its life mission is a grievous sin, one of the greatest, and completing said mission on their behalf only serves to alleviate one's own guilt – while it does fulfil the world's need for a specific task or event, it does not allow the victim to grow in the process as the gods have intended.

16 The Blood Heart

By this, there is the assumption that every being born, arguably every being conceived, has a purpose and destiny to fulfil.

Tae'anaryl

By Piex to Sagemaster of Lenmer'el, 314CY.

Venerable Sagemaster, After collating information from several sources, including the recent incursion by maid Kialessa Winterhaven into the *Sanctum Brumae* of the notorious Khozmoh Djinn, and the subsequent confiscation of the venue and its chapel to Pumos by your honoured self and the elite of Lenmer'el, I offer you the following treatise to further enhance our understanding of the tae'anaryl dwelling amongst us. As her life has shown, not all tae'anaryl are given naturally to evil, and it will be advisable to treat them on individual merits, rather than following Lord Tomin's appalling, "slay on sight" policy.

Powers

Tae'anaryl have many forms and powers.

Taint

Various 'taints' grant the tae'anaryl certain affinity with a particular element or inter-planar power. For example, those with fire taint are immune to burning, and are usually able to develop fire-based magic with greater ease and aplomb. Other taints include ice, shadow, lightning, light, or acid. Stranger taints include weapon, evil, goodness, particular emotions, and certain science or historical concepts. Among the *Sanctum* (descendants of angels rather than demons) these were often referred to as a 'blessing' and not 'taint'.

Weaver

More powerful than a taint, a weaver has free access to the mental manipulation of a particular element or interdimensional power. For example, Flameheart was a fire weaver that could create, sustain, manipulate and command all fires nearby as an act of will. Weaving is a form of enchantment that still takes practice and skill. I wish here to note that wizards can effectually mimic the weaver's talent for each and every known element.

     By Dr Joe Ireland

The chosen

This power is held across all races, not just tae'anaryl, and represents an individual's election by a particular deity as special to that god. They may even have a portion of the deity's own soul inside them, making them into what is known as an *avatar*. Chosen appear to have a special relationship with their god; a friendship for want of a better word, and can call on them for favours and wisdom that not even their high priest would dare.

Body type

All tae'anaryl are derived from another race blended with a demon, so there are countless forms of tae'anaryl. It is usually most appropriate to refer to them by *race* followed by the appellation *tae'anaryn*. The first term respects their non-demonic parent, and the second term reminds interlocutors that they are not a full-blooded demon, but a tae'anaryn. While half demon creatures of any race are possible, including posks and drakes for instance, they are referred to as 'half demons', and not 'tae'anaryn'. Only the sentient humanoid races are considered true tae'anaryn, though it may only be a matter of semantics. As most local tae'anaryl are part human, the term 'tae'anaryn' locally refers exclusively to human tae'anaryl.

A tae'anaryn's non-demonic heritage appears to have a very large influence on their form, personality, and powers. For example, human tae'anaryl are highly adaptable, while fey tae'anaryn are often insect-winged and shy. Stone giant tae'anaryl can still be giants made of stone, for instance.

Body forms

Unless noted, all tae'anaryl have forked tongues. Also, unless noted, even if they lack wings or a tail they almost always have the bones and physical structure which might allow for it, further justifying the definition of their beings as a unique race.

Horns

Ram horns – typically associated with wisdom and stubbornness, ram horns are excellent for, well, ramming things.

Antelope horns – long and pointed, these horns are associated with speed and endurance.

Giraffe horns – small yet still quite dangerous, these stout horns invariably grant great height and long limbs.

Kudu horns – a sign of lesser nobility among tae'anaryn, these are often well respected and charismatic individuals.

Bull horns – symbols of power and pre-eminence, often symbolic of great physical strength.

Elk horns – such individuals are usually fiercely independent.

Tails

Most tae'anaryn report their tails 'have a mind of their own', and act more according to their mood their desires, though all can move their tails at will. Perhaps there is some secondary processing occurring along the spine, since the brain is a long way from the tip of the tail, and it cannot react very quickly if it is relying on the mind alone to tell it how to move. All tails assist with balance and climbing to some degree.

Monkey – thin, prehensile tail that can twist back in on itself to form a precision grip. With training, tae'anaryl can hang from their tail or even write with it. A very generalist tail, this often can be augmented with weapons or armour. Kialessa Winterhaven has such a tail.

Roo — similar to a kangaroo's tail, it is like an extra arm. This tail can support their weight in battle, and is used to trip opponents. Mak has such a tail.

Scorpion – a poisonous spine attached to a multi-faceted tail, this tail is rarely exoskeletal and more often snake like. Ipi is one example.

Snake / Rattled – with bone segments, this tail can make a disconcerting rattle in combat. Augmented with enchantments, this can create a powerful fear or warding effect.

Bird / Feathered – this is often broad, like a fan, with wide, extravagant feathers that must be cared for carefully. It provides excellent manoeuvrability in flight, but is not so good for other athletic endeavours.

Hammer / club – these tails have a club or hammer protrusion at the end, and are usually quite strong. While not granting the extra trip or balance of a 'roo tail, they do allow an extra attack. With enchantments and exercise, such bones can penetrate steel shields.

Barbed – these spined tails have sharp barbs that break off leaving the barb inside their adversary. Some are augmented with natural or artificial poisons.

Stub – this tail is too small to be useful, but it is also the most magically versatile, being able to transform into most other kinds with greater ease.

Demon / bladed – quite common, this tail has a sharp, bone spike on the end capable of penetrating most flesh. It also has bony blades in the underside which can enlarge the wound. They are often love-heart shaped, but are still quite dangerous.

Wings

Most tae'anaryn wings are not large or magical enough for flying without some basic enchantments or mechanical help, though they do help with steering in flight, balance, and general athletics. Some can be used as physical defence, and physical attacks. One underappreciated side effect of having wings and tails is that they can often be an unconscious display of the tae'anaryn's emotions and mood.

Bat wings – the standard wing set, while not as useful for flying, does allow for gliding or controlled falls, and often makes excellent secondary weapons. With magical assistance they can be used as shields, and they function as adequate blankets as a covering during sleep.

Bird wings – rare, but still possible. Almost always black, dark blue, or red. They tend to result in excellent flyers, and such wings also make exceptional blankets when cared for almost constantly.

Moth or Butterfly wings – extremely rare, often only the fairy tae'anaryn possess these. They act like magnets for magic, often marking such as magic tainted tae'anaryl.

Magical – Other, rarer wings are noted – fire, lightning, frost, sun, etc., but they are usually conjured and magically formed wings. They require or grant affinity with a particular element. Flameheart, for example, has rods of coal growing from her back that burst into flames when she wants to fly.

Mechanical – rare, but still possible, small wings are sometimes augmented into functioning wing sets using mechanical devices such as steam or crystal power. Some mechanical wing sets are still lying around, disused, in the fortress.

Blood

A tae'anaryn's blood colour is often indicative of the planetary alignment of their personality and physical resonance. As given;

- Red – Mya, the world we dwell on. Resilient and complex.
- Orange – Annas, goddess of love and war. Passionate and romantic.
- Yellow – Serros, the sun. Strong willed and generous (very rare).
- Green – Planas, god of plants. Patent and earthy.
- Light blue – Lumos, the moon. Silent, reliable and scholarly.
- Dark blue – Waglah, goddess of oceans. Thoughtful and educated, yet both dangerous and placid.
- Purple – Pumos, god of truth and the dead. Intuitive, intelligent, yet also cathartic and occasionally morbid.

Other, rarer types have occasionally been noted:
- White – Unknown, Halm? Big picture, creative, but also withdrawn. Natural healers, yet sometimes self-destructive.
- Black – Unknown, Neth? Destructive, yet organised, dedicated, and wise. Highly socially connected, yet also dominating.
- Grey – Unknown, Lallaellaia? Detached, patient, otherworldly. Often have difficulty communicating vast ideas.
- Brown - Unknown, the monster god? Stoic, yet creative. Immovable, yet unpredictable.

Eyes

Unless otherwise noted, all tae'anaryn can see in the dark. A huge variety of eye types are noted, this is but a small sample.

- Human – excellent mid-range colour perception.
- Elven – excellent low light vision, such as for admiring the stars
- Dwarven – discriminate colour in the darkness
- Giant – see through stone
- Gnome – see magical auras
- Fey – clear vision in forested areas
- Merfolk – clear vision underwater
- Blithling – clear vision in obscuring sandstorms
- Caprivald – soul vision and sometimes fate sighted
- Angel – uninhibited by bright, even blinding light
- Demon – able to see in perfect darkness
- Insect – unable to shut their eyes, thus always watching

Skin

Many different skin colours are noted for the tae'anaryl, and often (but by no means always) signifies the creature's taint. In approximated order of frequency of appearance;

- Red – fire taint
- Black – death taint
- Brown – earth taint
- Dark blue – night taint
- Grey – rock taint
- Purple – shadow taint
- Teal – swamp taint
- Pink – untainted
- Light blue – lightning taint
- Orange – light taint
- Green – plant taint
- White – star taint
- Yellow – sun taint
- Silver – emotions taint
- Golden – glory taint

The Tae'anaryn *and the* *Khozmoh Djinn*

By Dr Joe Ireland

By Dr Joe Ireland

Choice, set free

By Dr Joe Ireland

Choice, set free

The Tae'anaryn *and the* *Khozmoh Djinn*

By Dr Joe Ireland

Book 6.5
Kialessa's Midwinter Festival

3 short stories

Available only online as an ebook 2019.

Go to www.DrJoe.id.au

A lot can happen in a week, especially when that week includes the most powerful eclipse of the year, your birthday, and the midwinter festival that heralds the beginning of a new year.

This book also includes vital, **must have** fan service, appendices that explain more about tae'anaryl, creation and use of the items of magical power in Lenmer'el, and the speech given by the enigmatic Eternal at the founding of the golden city.

By Dr Joe Ireland

Book 7

With the death of her blood father behind her, new life and new hope springs forth. Kialessa and the other elite students are taken by their King to the Council of Kings at Emerel. But this means the King must leave the safety of the castle of Lenmer'el, and a dread assassin has been looking for such a chance. Must they sail across the Bounteous Shallowsea and right into the jaws of danger? What new allies and enemies will be forged during this dangerous journey?

Place the date and your personal mark here each time you read this book – libraries included!

Why not share your experiences and thoughts with the fandom! Get a grownup's permission and visit

www.DrJoe.id.au

for fan art, sequels, competitions and more!

 By Dr Joe Ireland